Praise for *Thirty Days in Paris*

'Wow, wow, WOW. Her best and most perfect book yet'
JILL MANSELL

'Captures the romance and magic of Paris perfectly. A blissful escape'
SARAH MORGAN

'A perfect Parisian fantasy every woman will love!'
KATIE FFORDE

'A story of second chances and the most uplifting getaway'
LUCY DIAMOND

'A gloriously escapist read. I absolutely loved it!'
KATE EBERLEN

'A delicious, dreamy, joy of a book'
LIBBY PAGE

'Gorgeously romantic. A lovely slice of Paris life'
JO THOMAS

'I loved this gorgeous, hopeful story of second chances
in the City of Lights!'
LIZ FENWICK

'The perfect weekend read. I was so captivated
I didn't notice I was turning the pages'
FANNY BLAKE

'I was immersed in and inspired by this exquisitely told love story'
HEIDI SWAIN

'Gloriously escapist and filled with joie de vivre'
ALEX BROWN

'Irresistibly romantic and bursting with joie de vivre. I adored it'
PHILLIPA ASHLEY

'A sumptuous, joyfully indulgent treat of a book'
CRESSIDA McLAUGHLIN

'Such wonderful characters and the perfect setting'
CARI ROSEN

Veronica Henry worked as a scriptwriter for *The Archers*, *Heartbeat* and *Holby City*, amongst others, before turning to fiction. She lives by the sea in North Devon. Find out more by following her on Instagram @veronicahenryauthor.

Also by Veronica Henry

The Impulse Purchase
A Wedding at the Beach Hut
A Home from Home
Christmas at the Beach Hut
A Family Recipe
The Forever House
How to Find Love in a Bookshop
High Tide
The Beach Hut Next Door
A Night on the Orient Express
The Long Weekend
The Birthday Party
The Beach Hut
Marriage and Other Games
Love on the Rocks
An Eligible Bachelor
Wild Oats

THE HONEYCOTE NOVELS
A Country Christmas
(*previously published as* Honeycote)
A Country Life
(*previously published as* Making Hay)
A Country Wedding
(*previously published as* Just a Family Affair)

A Day at the Beach Hut (short stories and recipes)
A Sea Change (Quick Read)

Thirty Days in Paris

Veronica Henry

ORION

First published in Great Britain in 2023 by Orion Fiction,
an imprint of The Orion Publishing Group Ltd
Carmelite House, 50 Victoria Embankment,
London EC4Y 0DZ

An Hachette UK company

1 3 5 7 9 10 8 6 4 2

A CIP catalogue record for this book is
available from the British Library.

ISBN (Hardback) 978 1 3987 0313 1
ISBN (eBook) 978 1 3987 0316 2

Typeset at The Spartan Press Ltd,
Lymington, Hants

Printed and bound in Great Britain by Clays Ltd,
Elcograf S.p.A.

MIX
Paper from
responsible sources
FSC® C104740
www.fsc.org

www.orionbooks.co.uk

To my brother Paul
Because we'll always have Paris!

'It is better to forget me. It would be better to forget everything.'
Alain-Fournier, Le Grand Meaulnes

TO LET

Charming 'chambre de bonne' in the 2ème

Situated a stone's throw from the glamorous Rue Saint-Honoré, with its chic boutiques and cafés, this former maid's room is now a bijou apartment equipped with everything you need for your stay in Paris.

Available short or long term.

I

Juliet stood in the middle of the kitchen, overwhelmed by its emptiness. There wasn't a single appliance out on the worktops. There wasn't a cup or a plate in the sink or an empty bottle waiting to go into the recycling box. There wasn't a jar of Marmite or peanut butter cluttering the island; no crumbs or circles of red wine or damp teabags.

It felt almost funereal, with no smell of toast or percolating coffee to soften the edges, just the faint whiff of Cif. Every surface shone, from the granite to the blank blackness of the induction hob. It was pristine, silent, with the perfection of a kitchen catalogue. Just like the picture Juliet had found on Pinterest when they did the extension. A Shaker kitchen painted Mizzle by Farrow and Ball, with vintage knobs Juliet had sourced from a reclamation yard so that it didn't look like every other kitchen extension in Persimmon Road, with their skylights and bi-fold doors out into the garden.

The four of them had practically lived in the kitchen. They would sit there for hours over a platter of nachos, with a raggle-taggle assortment of multigenerational friends and neighbours, debating politics and the issues of the day, as well as more trivial dilemmas. Should Juliet get a tattoo? A unanimous yes. She hadn't. Should Stuart? A unanimous no. He had: a Celtic band around his upper arm, to show off his newly toned bicep. Juliet had to admit it looked good. *He* looked good. Though it was strange. The fitter he had got, the more she'd drawn away from him. This sculpted, streamlined, sinewy version of him felt like a stranger.

Which was one of the reasons they were in this situation. Packing up nearly twenty-five years of life together in order to be apart. Last Saturday, they had thrown a farewell party for all their neighbours and the pair of them had sung along to 'Go Your Own Way' by Fleetwood Mac, seaweed arms waving, pointing at each other. But smiling. It was an amicable separation. There was no animosity between them at all.

They had both agreed it was the right thing to do.

Now, however, there was a lump the size of a squash ball in Juliet's throat as she stared at the door jamb that led into the utility room. Dozens of names and dates written in pencil wormed their way up it. The highest was Nate, at least a head taller than she was, the details inscribed over four years ago. The ritual had started when he was a toddler and had his friends from nursery over for tea and it had ended on a pre-university pizza night when it had become clear they had all stopped growing.

What she wouldn't give to have them here now, wrestling to be measured, Izzy worming her way among them and elbowing them out of the way.

'We can't leave this,' she said, running her fingers over the ghostly names.

4

'Just take a photo,' said Stuart, who seemed to have lost every vestige of sentimentality along with his weight.

Her chin wobbled at the memory of a tiny Izzy stretching herself upwards as high as she could manage while Juliet rested the pencil on the top of her head and carefully drew a line, then wrote in her name and the date. It was more than just a growth chart. It was a diary. A guest book. Proof of the sanctuary this kitchen had provided to an endless stream of youngsters. A reminder of the meals she'd supplied to all and sundry, from turkey dinosaurs (she knew the other mothers judged her for them, but she didn't care) to pasta puttanesca. The advice that had been doled out, the homework agonised over, the birthdays that had been celebrated. But now, Izzy and Nate were both away: Izzy on her gap year, somewhere in South America (terrifying), and Nate in the third year of his four-year business degree, in Copenhagen (not so terrifying).

Juliet flipped open the lid of the toolbox on the kitchen worktop and pulled out a screwdriver.

'Oh no.' Stuart knew her well enough to see where she was going with this.

'They're doing a complete refurb. They're ripping everything out. I heard them when they came to view.' Juliet started trying to prise the door jamb off.

Stuart took the screwdriver out of her hand and put a kindly hand on her shoulder. 'They'll complain to the solicitor.'

'I don't care. This is part of our family history.'

Tears blurred her eyes and she pushed the heels of her hands into her sockets. Stuart looked down at her.

'I'll take it off for you. I'll nip out and get another one from Homebase and stick it on.'

She smiled up at him. He still couldn't bear to see her cry. He still indulged her. And she still felt the overwhelming urge to look after him in return. How were they going to work without each other? Their life together had been a seamless partnership, each one supplying what the other needed without any fuss or debate.

Were they making a terrible mistake?

Or was this separation a sensible, mature, considered decision that gave them both the freedom to do what they wanted with the rest of their lives? A modern decision, and one that had been greeted with curiosity, if not envy, by many of their friends. Couples who had also drifted apart, whose differences became glaringly apparent once the nest became empty, but who tolerated each other because the alternative seemed too brutal.

There'd been no transgression. No infidelity. There weren't even many arguments.

Juliet could track the fault line, though. It started when Stuart signed up for the charity marathon six years ago, press-ganged by some youngster in his office. The furthest Stuart had run before that had been to the off-licence at the end of the road, but something in the challenge had appealed. Perhaps the fact that he had gone from a thirty-two- to a thirty-four-inch waist of late and was mildly appalled by his middle-age spread. Juliet had caught him looking at himself sideways on, his face crumpled with anxiety.

'I've got a paunch,' he'd sighed.

'It's a beer belly,' Juliet had told him. 'The sugar turns to fat. Knock the booze on the head for a bit and you'll be fine.'

She'd written enough articles about weight gain and

miracle diets to know the science. It was, to her mind, pretty simple: eat less, move about more, cut out rubbish. She managed, just about, to hover between a twelve and a fourteen by being mindful about vegetables, avoiding bread and cakes and swimming twice a week. And giving her liver a break every few days. They drank too much. Everyone their age did. Making a decent inroad into a second bottle of wine (between two) on a 'school' night was the norm. It had an effect, on weight, on skin, on temper.

Stuart had let the side down by going over to the dark side and giving up drink completely. The marathon had kicked off an obsession. Parkrun every Saturday. Intense cycle rides every Sunday, whatever the weather; scantily clad, looking like an alien in his shiny Lycra and helmet. And now climbing, his latest passion, the thought of which turned Juliet's insides to ice. What with keeping fit enough to haul his own body weight up a sheer cliff face, and monitoring his heart rate every second of the day, he really didn't have time for anyone or anything else.

They never saw each other. Stuart went to the gym in the evening. Juliet went to private views, restaurant openings and book launches, an extension of her job as a freelance lifestyle journalist and ghostwriter. And when, just over a year ago, they began to talk about selling Persimmon Road – it had shot up in value because of the schools in the area, so it seemed the right time to cash in now that Nate and Izzy had left school – they both wanted something completely different.

Juliet wanted small, period, characterful.

Stuart wanted sleek, spacious, uncluttered.

'We should take half each and do our own thing,'

Stuart had joked, and Juliet had looked at him as they both did the maths. What had begun as a throwaway remark was now a reality. A 'conscious uncoupling' that they now found themselves endlessly apologising for and over-explaining, even though the advantages outweighed the disadvantages: they were still firm friends, but they were going to split the proceeds from the house sale and each buy somewhere that gave them the lifestyle they wanted for the next phase. It felt natural, logical and easy.

It might appear unseemly, to walk away from a twenty-five-year marriage that wasn't actually in ruins, but freedom of choice seemed better than constant compromise. Why should one of them have to live in the other's dream home when they could each have their own? Why should they try to be compatible when they weren't? Juliet had no more desire to go and join Stuart on a cycling weekend than he had to go to the latest play at the National. Wasn't it better for them to do their own thing than feel guilty and have to make excuses all the time?

'It means that when we do see each other, we really look forward to it,' Juliet had explained to her spellbound book club. 'It seems so much better than falling into a spiral of resentment and mutual disinterest. We still really like each other. And we'll always love each other deep down. But we don't want to spend our lives together anymore.'

She hadn't written an article on it yet. After years of doing features on everything from pregnancy cravings to playground politics to perimenopause, she still wasn't sure this experiment was going to work and she didn't feel she could recommend it just yet. Maybe two years in, when the benefits were proven, she would share her template for an amicable midlife separation with the world. She could already imagine the reader comments. Eighty per cent acerbic judginess; twenty per cent 'go for it'.

Stuart had bought a third-floor apartment in a newly built block near the river in Richmond and was putting a water-rower in the spare room, like Kevin Spacey had in *The West Wing*. Juliet had nothing yet. She had looked at over a dozen flats, but none of them was quite right. She didn't know what she wanted – only what she didn't want.

The tyranny of freedom was overwhelming.

2

By ten o'clock, everything was gone. Every last box, whisked away by the removers, to go to either Stuart's flat or Juliet's storage unit on a nearby industrial estate. The house was a shell, not a cobweb or a dust bunny in sight; not a streak on a window or a fingerprint on a mirror.

'Well,' said Stuart, 'I'd better get over to the flat so they put everything in the right place.' He held out his arms. 'Hug.'

She stepped into his embrace yet again, squeezing him tight around his love-handleless middle, trying not to feel rising panic about saying goodbye. To the house. She wasn't too worried about saying goodbye to Stuart. She would be able to see him any time she liked.

'So,' he said. 'Single life starts today.'

'Whatever you do,' she said, 'no Bycra photos on Tinder.'

'Bycra?' He was often puzzled by her buzz words. This particular one was her own invention.

'Bicycle Lycra. No woman wants to see those shorts.

Don't take it personally. It's just a general rule. No Bycra, and no photos with an oversized carp or pints of lager.'

He gave a laugh. 'Fair enough.' He squinted down at her. 'Have you been looking already, then?'

He wasn't jealous. Just curious.

'God, no,' she said. 'It's my job to know these things.'

'Well, when you do start looking,' he said, 'know that you are drop-dread gorgeous and don't let anyone make you feel otherwise.'

She swallowed. She felt mean for the Bycra advice now. It was a good piece of advice, though, as he wouldn't have a clue. Whoever swiped right on Stuart would be lucky. Though she imagined he'd probably meet someone at parkrun. A willowy fitness freak who would make him protein balls and tofu stir-fries. She imagined them giving each other North Face jackets for Christmas and booking worthy, joyless holidays in a two-man tent on a wild and windy moor.

What had happened to the bloke she'd drunk a pitcher of Pimm's with outside a Thameside pub that summer all those years ago? They'd walked back to her flat arm in arm, singing 'Live Forever', weaving along the Hammersmith pavements. He was safe and uncomplicated and funny. Safe, she realised, wasn't as sexy as dangerous, but it was exactly what she had needed after everything that had happened. They'd had barely a cross word. Their relationship had never been passion-fuelled, but it was sustainable. No histrionics, no mug-throwing, no sulking.

For a moment, she panicked about what they were giving up. But, as Stuart kept pointing out, they weren't giving it up. Just reframing it.

'Bye, then,' he said now, giving her a little squeeze on the shoulder.

She watched as he headed out of the door and jumped on his bicycle. She eyed his unfamiliarly narrow bum with a burst of affection, but nothing more. And off he rode, her dear, sweet, now ex-husband, cycling off into his new future with a BMI of 24 and a clear conscience.

As soon as he had disappeared down the road, she ran upstairs to the bathroom. She looked in the mirror and thought of all the versions of herself she'd scrutinised over the years at 42 Persimmon Road. The feisty young journalist. The newlywed bride. The exhausted mum of first one, then another baby. The chair of the PTA. The magazine editor who'd given up a proper job, at forty, to go freelance and write in the attic. The thrower of the best parties on the street because she didn't stress about stuff that didn't matter but made an effort with things that did. Who would host in her trademark dishevelled sexiness, in black leather jeans and a white shirt, half undone and off the shoulder, with bare feet and black cherry toenails, her dark hair in a messy bun. Could she still pull off that look? Or was it time for something more demure and groomed?

Right now, she was not looking her best. Her hair was scraped up into a tight ponytail. The ratty old T-shirt and jogging pants she'd worn to clean the house were heading for the bin. Her skin was grey with grime and the sweat from the exertion had dried on her. She wrinkled her nose, then reached into the bag she'd brought up with her, drawing out a pair of scissors.

She'd watched the YouTube video several times and reckoned it would work. She loosened her scrunchie and tipped her head upside down, then chopped the ends of her ponytail clean away. She stood up and shook out her hair, then grinned at her reflection. There it was, the perfect, just-got-out-of-bed, jaw-length bob. She snipped into the ends to soften the edges, fluffed it up a little and nodded in approval. Once it was washed, she'd be perfect. She reached into the shower and turned on the hot tap.

Half an hour later, she was looking at a new incarnation in the mirror. She wore vintage Levi 501s, a pristine white T-shirt and a tuxedo jacket. She slipped her feet into black ballet flats, then leaned forward to apply liquid eyeliner and her sexiest, reddest YSL lipstick.

She packed the last few things in her bag. A collection of mementoes: a battered A to Z, a faded paperback, a notebook half filled with scribblings. And a vintage Hermès scarf, the slippery silk cool on her fingers, the colours as bright as the day it had been made. She should wear it now, she decided. She tied it the way she'd been taught, spreading it onto her outstretched arm to fold it, then looping it round her neck, tucking in one end and leaving the other loose. It felt like a talisman. A ticket back to the past. She felt a shiver of excitement mixed with uncertainty.

What would she find, in her quest to rediscover herself? A new life? Peace? Contentment? Passion?

She heard her phone ping. Her Uber was here.

She grabbed her luggage and ran down the stairs. She slung on her cross-body bag – purse, phone, passport – and left the house. There was no time to get emotional. The cab was waiting. She couldn't waste precious moments saying farewell to the place that had held her for so long. A clean break was the only solution.

Outside, she opened the door of the car and smiled in at the driver.

'St Pancras?' he asked.

'Yes. Thank you,' she said, sliding into the back seat, dragging her case in after her.

It was only small. If her time on women's magazines had taught her anything, it was how to put together a capsule wardrobe. She could get anything else she needed when she got there.

Paris.

She was going to Paris.

Because Paris was *always* a good idea.

3

Two hours later, Juliet had checked herself through departures at St Pancras and climbed on board the train. She still found it incredible that in another two hours she would find herself right in the middle of the beating heart of the city. The last time she had been there, the Eurostar had been on the horizon, an exciting new possibility that no one could quite believe would really happen. A train all the way to Paris! It had seemed like a dream.

She settled herself in her seat, spreading her hands out on the tabletop. Pale, marbled with the occasional bump of a Roquefort-blue vein, a sprinkling of sun spots, her knuckles like wrinkly knees. She had two stacking rings on the third finger of her right hand, each with a diamond to represent Nathan and Izzy, given to her by Stuart after their births – she never took them off.

Her wedding ring was in a secret compartment in her handbag. She didn't quite feel comfortable abandoning it altogether. She would always be proud of being Mrs Hiscox, whose name had been called out in the doctors' surgery and at parents' evening. For work, she had always used her maiden name. It was useful, having two identities. Mrs Hiscox did the nit checks and had the boiler serviced. Juliet Miller missed the last Tube home and had to get a cab she couldn't afford. Now she would use Juliet Miller full-time. She only needed one identity now.

And here Juliet Miller was, going back to Paris to try to recapture her past, hoping it would kick-start her future. So often over the years, she had thought about going back, but she hadn't wanted to complicate things, not while she was a wife and mum. She hadn't wanted to revisit the memories, good and bad, with her family in tow, because she wasn't sure what her reaction would be. Even now, her tummy flittered at the recollection of both the best and the worst of times.

At twenty, Paris had been her dream. It had changed her. It had shaped her. It had taken a naïve and unsophisticated girl and set her on the path to womanhood. So much of what had happened was wonderful. She had learned things she had never forgotten, found so many passions, discovered a whole new world. She carried all of that with her, still. But she carried the scars too, which was why she'd never gone back.

Until now. She knew Paris was waiting, ready to help her with her next metamorphosis. All of the things she had adored would still be there, to be explored anew, to help her find her new self and the person she wanted to become. Smart, sexy, chic, successful, interesting and interested, adventurous, playful, experimental – she thought of all the words she'd put down to try to manifest this new Juliet. Not that she wasn't already lots of those things, but she needed to recalibrate. Maybe take some risks.

Like many people, Covid had chipped away at her and

ground her down. The strain of having one child away at uni, bewildered and isolated, and another battling the on–off uncertainty of exams, had been enervating. She was used to working from home, but having Stuart there too had clipped her wings rather, and she'd hated having to actually think about lunch rather than idly dipping pitta bread into some ready-made hummus at her desk. And she'd missed trooping into the centre of London a couple of times a week, realised that her social life was a vital part of her identity, and no live screening was going to replace the buzz of queuing for a plastic beaker of wine during the interval. They'd had it lucky, emerging with their health and careers intact, but lockdown had diminished her more than she realised.

Lockdown. Menopause. Empty nest. The end of her marriage. It could have been a deadly cocktail, but Juliet was determined to rise from the ashes. She had no responsibility and no ties. No real money worries, thanks to the sale of the house. No work commitments, thanks to being freelance: for the whole of November, the next thirty days, she wasn't taking on any commissions. No magazine articles, no ghostwriting. She had doubled up her workload the month before to make up for it, typing long into the night to hit deadlines and file features and keep the cash flow buoyant.

Now the only deadline she had was the one she had set herself. After ten years of writing books for other people, she was ready to write her own. And she knew that would be a lot harder. With ghostwriting, she always had source material to give her inspiration and structure and motivation. She would immerse herself in her client's life, whether they were a celebrity or a member of the public with a compelling story, often living with them for a few days while they talked and talked about their experiences, answering her questions, reliving the lives that Juliet would put down into written words to give them a shape.

Some clients were more forthcoming than others. Some were difficult to draw out and she would have to find a way to make them trust her. More often than not, that involved breaking open a bottle of wine or two. Others were impossible to stop: once they had begun their confessions, an endless diatribe would spill out. Then it was up to Juliet to work out what to keep and what to throw out. Which anecdotes provided colour and which provided confusion. And which might end up in a lawsuit! Some of the stories she heard would never be printed; they were unfit for public consumption.

She would take those to her grave, for her greatest weapon was her discretion. The people she wrote for knew she was a consummate professional and that if, after a few glasses of vino, they did let something slip that they regretted later, it would go no further. She never told her friends and family who she was writing for. She never revealed any titbits of gossip or personal details: which famous actress wore no knickers; which celebrity had a secret cocaine habit. Anything they wanted to know, they could read in the books she wrote. More often than not, they were bestsellers. It was strange, seeing something you had poured your heart and soul into on the shelves of a supermarket or bookshop, with someone else's name on the front. Sometimes she had an acknowledgement, sometimes no reference at all. You didn't become a ghostwriter for the pleasure of seeing your name on the cover of a book.

'Doesn't it annoy you, not getting the credit?' people often asked her, but that was the deal. And it had given her a good living, a good life. Money and, more importantly, flexibility; the chance to work from home most of the time, which had been invaluable when the kids were teenagers. Somehow, they had needed her there more as adolescents than when they were small, and she had wanted to keep them close as the perils of puberty had started creeping in. They'd always known she'd be up there in the attic, tapping away at her laptop, not like some of her friends who were still slaves to their jobs, not getting back until gone seven, by which time both they and their offspring were too tired and hungry to enjoy each other's company. Whereas Juliet could break off from her work to make Nate and Izzy a quick cheese toastie or bagel and Marmite when they got in from school, listen to their gossip and complaints, then send them off to do their homework, so that by the time supper came around it was all done and they could relax and laugh.

Now, it was her turn to write her own story. Whether it would be of any interest to anyone other than herself was another thing, but she had spent her whole life wanting to write about what had happened. And even if it ended up in her bottom drawer, it would be a good exercise in seeing what she was capable of. A chance to find her own voice, instead of imitating someone else's. She had a title – *The Ingénue* – for that was what she had been: a naïve young girl navigating a strange city. And a notebook of scribbled memories.

She was giving herself thirty days in Paris to dedicate

herself to her own writing. To immerse herself in the place that had changed her so much, and to give the city a second chance. To put the bad memories behind her, and make some new ones. To walk along the banks of the Seine as the leaves fell, cross every bridge and look down at the glittering water, drink a glass of red wine on every pavement . . . see all the paintings, eat all the food, watch all the people she had missed over the past thirty – thirty! – years.

She reached into her bag to get her laptop, but the paperback she had tucked on top caught her eye and she pulled it out. As she leafed through the pages, the memories seeped back in through her fingertips. She remembered the very moment the book had been handed to her. Her knowledge of how precious it was. Her guilt at never having the chance to give it back . . .

'I remember reading that in sixth form.'

The man's voice made her jump. He was sitting opposite and she blushed, wondering how long he'd been watching her. She'd been so wrapped up in herself, she hadn't noticed him. He was probably five or so years younger than she was, with close-cropped grey hair and a merino polo neck.

'Did you like it?' she asked.

'How could you not?' His right eyebrow twitched in query. 'Le Grand Meaulnes is a classic. The ultimate tale of unrequited love.'

The irony of his observation wasn't wasted on her. She smiled. 'Well, quite.'

'And I always feel it's a warning not to revisit the past.'

Juliet swallowed, looking back down at the book, and didn't reply.

'That looks like an old copy.'

'Mmm hmm.'

'And in French. Impressive. Or are you? French, I mean.'

His eyes flickered over her and it pleased her that he might think she was.

'God, no. But I thought it would help me improve. I haven't spoken French for over thirty years.'

'I must buy another copy. I lost mine years ago. Thank you for the reminder.' He smiled. 'I always think it's the mark of a good bookshop, if they have it in stock.'

'It is.' She smiled back at him, beguiled by his remark. It wasn't what she'd expected, to fall into idle banter about her favourite book with a stranger on a train. She sensed it would be all too easy for them to slide into flirtation. She checked out his left hand and there was no gold or silver band – not that its absence meant anything, as lots of men didn't wear wedding rings. Stuart hadn't.

But although she had carte blanche to embark on anything she liked with whomever she liked, she wasn't ready yet. It would be unseemly, having closed the door gently on her marriage only that morning, to take up with the first person she met. She had written enough about rebound flings to know they had to be handled with caution.

Besides, she had a lot to do before she opened her heart again. With only thirty days to accomplish her mission, there was no time for distraction.

'Excuse me,' she murmured, bending down to pick up her laptop. 'I have some work to do.'

He nodded and picked up his phone to scroll through his messages.

Juliet looked at her watch. She had two hours before they arrived at the Gard du Nord. She could probably write her first chapter, if she got on with it. She had trained herself not to overthink, because the more you thought about what you were about to write, the less inclined you felt to start. It was like getting into an ice-cold swimming pool. You had to take a deep breath and plunge right in.

ADVERT IN *THE LADY* MAGAZINE, OCTOBER 1990

Kind, responsible au pair wanted for a French family with a new arrival in the centre of Paris to help with Charlotte 6, Hugo 4 and baby Arthur. Lovely sunny room and happy household in the *2ème* – we speak a little English between us. Generous allowance and three hours' language classes per week. Immediate start. Three months at least, please.

4

The Ingénue

'Paris.' My mother looked at me as if I'd said Pondicherry. Or Polynesia.

'Yep,' I replied, as breezy as I could manage. I could see panic, suspicion and disapproval in her eyes, combined in one, sharp look. That was Mum. Always looking for the snags. The risk. She liked to keep her world as small and as safe as possible. I could understand that. It made for an easy life. But I didn't have to be the same. This was my first step in making sure I didn't turn into her. Not that I didn't love her. I just didn't want to be her. 'I've got a job as an au pair.'

'A nanny, you mean.' She hated it when I used foreign words. Thought I was getting above myself.

'No. An au pair is different,' I explained. 'It means "equal to". You live as a member of the family. They give you pocket money in return for helping with the children.'

'Oh.' She looked puzzled. 'But why? When you've got a perfectly good job.'

'You know I don't want to work there forever. You

know I want to work in fashion. If I learn some French, and get to know Paris, it would be good for my CV.'

It was all that would be on my CV, given that I'd mucked up my A levels. My first mistake was not staying on at school for sixth form, and going to the college instead, because that's where the cool people went. (Even though I wasn't. Cool, that is.) And the second was thinking I didn't need to revise. (I did.) The upshot being my results were terrible and I couldn't get a university place anywhere decent.

'But you're working in fashion now.'

'No, Mum. I'm working in Ladies' wear, in a frumpy old department store.'

She breathed in through her nose, scrabbling for an argument that would work with me.

'You'll be looked after for life there,' she managed, but that was no enticement for a twenty-year-old. At that age, today was all that mattered.

I shook my head.

'But it's not the life I want. I want to go to London eventually.'

Mum winced and I realised I was going too fast for her. Paris. London. But it can't have come as a surprise. She knew, from the magazines I brought home and drooled over, that I was obsessed with clothes. From the fact that I spent every last penny on cheap copies of the latest outfits in *Vogue*. From the posters up in my bedroom of my idols: Marilyn Monroe, Audrey Hepburn, Debbie Harry, Jackie Kennedy. I pored over their hemlines and heel heights and scoured charity shops for clothing that imitated their style, using my trusty old Singer sewing machine to take in skirts and dresses until I looked the part.

My dream was to work on a fashion magazine, as a journalist, writing about style icons and supermodels and catwalks. I had a long way to go before I got onto the first rung of my fantasy career ladder, but I was determined. The week before, I'd read an article in *Marie Claire* by a girl just like me, who had no qualifications to her name but who had worked her way up and was now a junior editor. It had given me hope.

And then I'd seen the advert for an au pair in *The Lady* while I was wating for a filling at the dentist. There was something in the air, jogging me to do something about my life.

I patted Mum's hand. 'I have to do this.'

Her eyes went a bit swimmy and she looked away. I knew she didn't understand.

Or maybe she did. Maybe she understood only too well and didn't want to come to terms with it. Maybe she was jealous?

Paris was my escape plan. Paris was glamour and adventure and a ticket out. I knew from the article I'd read that if I was going to get out of Worcester for good and come even close to living my dream, I had to have more to offer. I needed polish and to show a bit of initiative. Paris would give me the edge I needed. I would improve my schoolgirl French, absorb some culture and hopefully some of the chic would rub off on me while I was there. I would learn how to wear a scarf just so and get a little *je ne sais quoi*. I would come back soignée, sophisticated and smart and would be just what some glitzy magazine editor needed to help her get through the day. She would spot my potential and I would grab every opportunity and my prospects would soar.

'It's only three months, Mum. I'll be back in the new year.'

Mum nodded, resigned. She had run out of arguments.

I imagined myself walking along the banks of the Seine, chic in a beautiful coat, my hair slightly ruffled from the autumn breeze as the leaves swirled around me, on my way to meet my lover. We would drink red wine in a tiny restaurant, talk about life and love and art, smoke a cigarette or two. I would learn everything there was to know about looking elegant. Irresistible, confident, alluring. A million miles from the parochial shop girl who had screwed up her exams.

Paris was going to save me from myself, and turn me into the person I wanted to be.

Of course I was sick on the ferry over. Of course I was. I sat upright on my chair, one hand on my case to stop it rolling about, the other on my handbag, feeling my stomach churn as the boat pitched from side to side. And the more I tried not to think about it, the worse I felt. The black coffee I'd got out of the vending machine swirled around in the pit of my empty stomach, scouring the lining with its bitterness.

I was riddled with nerves, even though it was only a short trip from Dover to Calais and there wasn't a great deal that could go wrong. But I was worried about making my train connection and kept flipping between looking at my watch and checking the time on my ticket, wishing I'd booked a much later train instead of the morning one. But then it would be dark when I arrived in Paris, and that prospect made my mouth go dry.

This was not the image I'd been aiming for when I'd

got ready to leave. I knew I looked uptight and uncool and it was glaringly obvious I wasn't used to travelling. I wished I looked like the girl opposite me, who was sitting with her feet up on the seat, Discman earphones on, chewing gum, in jeans and a big plaid shirt. I was overdressed in comparison, in my denim pencil skirt and the tweed jacket I'd sewn big gilt buttons onto thinking it would look like Chanel. It did in Worcester, but out here on the open seas it just looked naff. I saw the girl look me up and down and smirk a bit.

I felt the coffee bubbling up again and couldn't bear the thought of being sick in front of her. I dashed as quickly as I could to the toilets, dragging my case with me, not daring to ask her if she would keep an eye on it.

The coffee came straight up as I leaned over the bowl, and I felt instant relief. That's the one good thing about being sick.

It took me ages to open my case and dig out my toothbrush and toothpaste so I could do my teeth before making my way back to my seat.

I sat down again, feeling pale and shaky, and looked at my watch. Only another hour. Normally at this time on a Saturday, I would be in the accessories section of the shop, tidying up the packets of tights, rearranging the scarves and keeping an eye out for anyone who wanted assistance. For a moment, I wished I was back there, safe and sound, wondering what video to get from Blockbuster on my way home. The last movie I'd taken out was *Thelma and Louise*. I needed a bit of their adventurous spirit right now. I tried to look casual and nonchalant. I tried not to worry about whether I was going to make my connection.

By the time I got off the ferry and onto the train to

Paris, I felt giddy with relief. I tried to shut my eyes and go to sleep, but then I worried about missing the stop. I was cold, too. The temperature had dropped and my tweed jacket wasn't very substantial. I had disregarded my mother's pleas to wrap up warm, and now I regretted it. I was still a bit tender inside from the puking, too. I should have got something to eat, to give me a bit of strength, but I was too nervous to leave my seat and my case and go to the buffet bar.

I picked up my book, hoping it would take my mind off it. It was *The Dud Avocado* by Elaine Dundy. I'd found it in the bookshop I frequented on my lunch break, and the title drew me to it, because it was a bit odd. I read the first page and fell head over heels with the heroine, who had dyed her hair pink and was wandering through Paris in an evening dress – in broad daylight. I fell in love with her effervescence.

This was who I wanted to be. A free spirit, in charge of her own future, open to everything life had to offer. It lifted my spirits a little.

Eventually, we hit the outskirts of Paris. It looked forbidding under a dirty yellow sky: a tangle of tower blocks and pylons and the occasional spire of a beautiful church peeping between the concrete. We slid into the Gare du Nord with a wheeze of brakes. I dragged my case off the train and stepped into chaos.

The station was overwhelming. It made Paddington, where I'd been a few times, look sleepy. I couldn't understand a word I was hearing. I wasn't even sure half of it was French. I spotted the Art Nouveau sign for the Métro quite quickly and descended underground, bumping my case on each step and trying not to mind the pushing and

29

shoving as the other passengers charged ahead. I could hear the sound of a violin keening above the hubbub, a wild gypsy jig. I smelled sharp sweat and pungent cigarette smoke and exotic perfume on top of the occasional waft of stale wee. Beautiful women strode past me; hot eyes roamed my body, for what I wasn't sure.

I felt a million miles from home and for a moment I longed to be back in our little terraced house. Dad would be heading to the chip shop later and I imagined the heavy, damp packages being unwrapped with reverence, steam curling.

Stop it, I told myself. This is Paris. This is your dream come true.

I battled my way to the kiosk where I needed to buy a *carnet* of Métro tickets. I'd been to the library to look it all up and memorised my first journey: one stop to the Gare de l'Est, then change to the pink line, then six stops to the Pyramides.

I approached the ticket kiosk, the words I had also memorised repeating themselves in my head. *Un carnet, s'il vous plaît.* Really, there was no margin for error. I couldn't be misunderstood. And I was pleased when the woman behind the glass nodded and picked up a bundle of tickets. I reached into my handbag for my purse.

It was gone.

With a dry mouth, I searched wildly through the contents of my bag: make-up, paperback, notebook, mints, brush, bottle of aspirin. Tears pricked at my eyes as I met the stony gaze of the woman. What was the word for purse? How could I explain?

'*Mon argent . . . il n'est pas là.*'

The woman shrugged, showing only the tiniest flicker

of sympathy, and gave a small wave of her hand to indicate that I should get out of the way for the next customer.

'*La police?*' I knew as soon as the words were out of my mouth I was wasting them. What would the police do? In that moment, I knew this happened all the time. My purse would have been emptied by now, the francs I had ordered from the post office pulled out, counted and pocketed, the purse itself flung into a bin.

What was I going to do? I hadn't a sou on me. I didn't have the language skills to go and tell the police, and they were hardly going to fund my onward journey. They would shrug like the ticket lady. Perhaps even laugh at me.

I had copied out the address of the Beaubois family and slid it behind the clear plastic panel in my purse. Luckily, I had memorised it, though not their phone number. I could look them up in the phone book, somehow, but I had no idea how to make a reverse-charge call or how to explain my predicament to them if I got through. I felt hot with panic and thought I might be sick again on the station floor. I needed to get outside, into the fresh air, away from the crowds, away from the eyes and the hands.

I gulped in the air as I came out into the road: petrol fumes and that sickly cigarette smoke and the smell of onions. I had no choice. I would have to walk. I dug in my bag for the A to Z of Paris I had ordered from the bookshop. I pushed my case up against the wall and sat on it, then took a biro and traced the route over several pages. By measuring the squares, I estimated that it was about two miles.

It was getting dark. I was exhausted and hungry and not a little scared. I gave myself a talking-to. I was here, in

Paris, not so very far away from my destination. I walked that distance every day, from home to work. OK, not with a bloody great suitcase, but I'd manage. It would take me just over an hour, probably, with little stops to rest.

I ignored my throbbing head and my rumbling tummy and put one foot in front of the other, my case banging against my legs as I walked. *Keep going, Juliet,* I told myself.

I distracted myself by trying to figure out the unfamiliar words in the shop windows. *Tabac. Bureau de change. Nettoyage.* I tried to ignore the fact that this was not the Paris I had imagined. The shops were dreary; there was litter in the street; none of the cafés I passed looked welcoming. My heart became as heavy as my suitcase. I remembered the scenes from my favourite film, *Funny Face*, with Audrey Hepburn dancing around all those famous landmarks, arms outstretched, singing 'Bonjour, Paris', her eyes sparkling with excitement. That was how I'd seen myself, not trudging along a lacklustre pavement without a hint of glamour.

As I got nearer, though, the streets became more welcoming. This was more like the Paris of my imagination: the sweeping boulevards with the cobbled streets leading off. The enticing shops and cafés. The smart women and the handsome men. And then, at last, I was on the last page of the journey marked out on my A to Z. It was nearly six o'clock in the evening, and I was considerably later than the Beaubois family would have expected, but I was going to make it.

And then, there I was, on a narrow street, the buildings confronting each other, as if competing to be the most elegant. I searched for the number I'd been given and found a double-height black door with a huge brass handle. Uncertain, I pushed it open and stepped into a paved courtyard. It was slightly eerie, with no sound but the rustle of dead leaves on the trees spaced out in wooden planters, looming like security guards.

I raked the windows looking down on me to try to figure out which might belong to the Beauboises. Some were lit; some blank with blackness. I saw another door, and beside it a row of bells. To my relief, I spotted their name, and pressed the bell next to it.

I waited and waited, not sure how much longer I could stand up. Then the door flew open and a woman stood there with a baby in her arms. She was about my height but thinner than thin, with pale skin and dark eyes that seemed burnt into her face and a wide mouth. I thought she was the most beautiful woman I'd ever seen.

Was this Madame Beaubois?

'*Je suis Juliet,*' I said. '*Je suis l'au pair,*' I added helpfully.

'You are very late.' Both she and the baby stared at me.

'I lost my purse.' I indicated my handbag. 'My money. *Mon argent.*'

I did a mime of someone stealing my purse.

'Oh.' She rolled her eyes in disdain. 'The Gare du Nord. Full of thieves.' She pronounced it 'seeves'. She managed a smile at last. 'I am Corinne. This is Arthur.' She patted the baby on the back, then flapped her hand to usher me inside. '*Entrez. Entrez.* Come in.'

I picked up my case and lugged it into a hallway with a grand stone staircase.

'Leave it there.' She indicated the bottom of the stairs. 'My husband will bring.'

She ran up the stairs and I followed, Arthur still staring

33

owlishly over her shoulder. On the first floor, she headed for a half-open door, calling out, *'Jean Louis! Elle est arrivée!'*

I knew what that meant. 'She has arrived.'

'Ici.' She beckoned me in through a set of ornate double doors.

My mouth dropped open as I walked in. The ceiling was high, with a glittering chandelier in the middle. The floors were gleaming wood, the walls elaborately panelled and the windows along the far side were taller than I was. Two sofas in pale yellow faced each other, and there were gilt armchairs and small glass tables dotted around the room, several bearing vases of flowers. There were huge mirrors and paintings that even I, with no knowledge of art, knew must be valuable.

Corinne was standing in front of a man who, I presumed, was her husband, babbling at him in French, her free hand waving in the air. He was tall, with chestnut hair swept back from his face, and, like his wife, he was very thin. But his eyes were warm and brown and kind, not haunted and burning like hers.

'Juliet,' he said, stepping forward to greet me, and I realised I had never heard my name spoken like that, as if I was someone important. He put his hands on my shoulders and kissed me once on each cheek and they burnt cherry red. 'I am Jean Louis. I am so sorry. Corinne tells me you were robbed at the station. That is terrible. We will replace the money for you.'

'Oh,' I said, surprised.

'It is the least we can do.'

Corinne was looking agitated. 'Jean Louis, we must leave for dinner in half an hour. I must get ready.'

Jean Louis frowned. 'Corinne, we are not going anywhere. Not after what happened. We must look after Juliet. We cannot leave her.'

'I don't mind,' I said, anxious to please, given his generosity.

'No.' Jean Louis was firm.

Corinne frowned. 'I will go on my own,' she said eventually. 'It is too late to cancel.'

She handed Arthur over to Jean Louis, who took him without complaint. As Corinne left the room, he leaned towards me with a smile.

'The people we are having dinner with, I do not like. So, thank you.'

Despite my exhaustion, I giggled.

'Papa?'

I turned, and there in the doorway were two small children. A little girl in a navy-blue jumper and a grey pleated skirt, and a boy in yellow corduroys and a matching polo shirt. Their eyes flickered uncertainly between their father and me. I crouched down to be nearer their height.

'*Bonjour*,' I said to them. '*Je suis Juliet*. You must be Charlotte,' I said, pointing to Hugo. 'And you must be Hugo.' I pointed to Charlotte.

The pair of them giggled.

'*Non!*' cried Hugo. '*Je suis Hugo.*'

I tapped the heel of my hand on my forehead to indicate I was a fool.

'Hugo. Charlotte.' I pointed the right way around this time.

'Say hello, children,' said Jean Louis.

The two of them inched forward. Charlotte put her arms around my neck.

''Ello,' she said, and gave me a kiss on each cheek, just as her father had.

Then Hugo followed. My heart melted as I felt their soft, warm skin on mine, my recent drama forgotten.

Jean Louis pointed to one of the sofas. 'Please, sit. Rest. I will fetch your *valise*.'

Valise. So much more exciting than suitcase. Everything sounded so much more exciting in French.

He left the room, and I sat down, weary and grateful, and the two children scrambled up onto the sofa next to me. They were chattering away to me in French, like two little pigeons cooing. I think they were asking me if I liked cats.

'*J'adore les chats*,' I told them, which seemed to meet with their approval.

Jean Louis appeared in the doorway and smiled at the three of us.

'I will take you to your room,' he said, and gestured to the children to leave me be. They drifted away obediently and I followed him down a corridor.

We passed what must have been the master bedroom, as I could hear the sounds of Corinne getting ready inside, but he said nothing until he reached a door at the end.

'It's small but comfortable,' he said. 'But if you need anything, you must tell me.'

It was at least twice the size of my bedroom at home. The bed was made up with snow-white embroidered sheets, and there was a large wooden wardrobe with a mesh front, as well as a little desk in front of the window. I sighed and Jean Louis looked alarmed.

'It's not good?'

'It's beautiful,' I told him.

36

'You have to share a bathroom with the children. I hope that's OK.'

'Of course!' I had caught sight of the bathroom as we went past. It was palatial. I thought of the queues to our bathroom in the morning. The wobbly loo seat. The pathetic dribble of water that came out of the shower attachment that was either boiling hot or freezing cold. The bangs on the door if you dared to stay in too long.

'I will leave you for a few minutes. Then come to the kitchen. You must be hungry.'

I had almost gone past being hungry, and my stomach still felt raw. But I couldn't refuse his hospitality. He left the room, shutting the door behind him, and I went to lie on the bed for a moment, breathing in the unfamiliar scent of another home. It smelled expensive, of lavender and old wood.

I crept out to the bathroom quietly to use the loo, and wash my hands and face. I looked in the mirror to see what the Beauboises saw: a pale girl with dark shoulder-length hair, sludgy eyes and a gap between her front teeth. An ordinary girl from an ordinary town. All the Beauboises, even the children, looked extraordinary. Arresting looks and an air of confidence and a way of carrying themselves. And their clothes – they fitted them perfectly, hung just so, while by now mine were creased and limp and looked even cheaper than they were.

I was too drained to think about changing or putting on make-up. I went back to my room and pulled a jumper on over the T-shirt I'd had under my jacket, then walked over to the window, opened it and looked out at the street. The houses were pale in the evening light, the roofs gleaming silver beneath the moon, the cobbles black and shiny. I breathed in the Paris night and felt reassured that the morning would bring hope and the trauma of the day would be behind me.

I opened the door and walked back down the corridor to find the kitchen. To my surprise, it was tiny. Smaller than ours at home. Jean Louis was chopping his way through a pile of chives with a knife at an impressive speed. He smiled as I walked in.

'I make you an omelette?'

Omelettes were not my favourite thing. Dry, rubbery egg that tasted of not much. But at this point I would have eaten a chair leg and the air was filled with the nutty scent of melting butter that made my mouth water.

'Lovely,' I said. 'Thank you.'

I watched as he took three eggs and deftly broke them into a bowl with one hand while he swirled the butter around a cast-iron pan with the other. I hovered, wanting to help do something – lay the table, perhaps – but I felt tongue-tied.

And then Corinne whirled in, in a flurry of rapid-fire French. I didn't recognise her as the woman who had come to the door. She wore a sleeveless black shift dress with a plunging back, and high shoes with satin ribbons tied around her ankles. Her hair was in a chignon at the nape of her neck, and there were very large diamonds in her ears. I assumed they were real. She didn't look like the kind of woman who would wear paste. The rings under her eyes had gone and she had on dark red lipstick. I just about gleaned from what she said that the baby was asleep as she took a beribboned box of chocolates out of the fridge.

'*Bon appetit*,' she said to me as she sailed out of the

room, leaving the most incredible scent behind her, like nothing I had ever smelled.

Diamonds. High heels. Intoxicating perfume. Could I ever be like Corinne? I wondered.

I looked at Jean Louis and he gave a smile that gave nothing away.

'Your omelette is ready,' he said. He gestured towards the door. 'The *salle à manger* is this way . . .'

There was a place set for me. Next to it was a plate of salad that looked nothing like the salad we had at home: either a head of lettuce from my grandad's allotment that often hid fat slugs or chopped-up pale green iceberg. These leaves were dark green, some of them red or purple, and glistened with oil. There was a baguette too.

I sat down as Jean Louis placed a plate in front of me. On it was a golden crescent that looked nothing like any omelette I'd ever seen, flecked with the chives he had chopped. He poured me a glass of red wine.

'Enjoy,' he said, as Hugo and Charlotte ran in and sat either side of me.

I felt incredibly self-conscious, but I was ravenous.

'*Merci*,' I said with a shy smile. '*Merci beaucoup*.' And Jean Louis raised his own wine glass to me as he left the room.

The omelette was out of this world. It was soft and creamy and so full of flavour – buttery and salty with the slightest hint of onion from the herbs. I couldn't eat it fast enough, wiping up the remains with slices of crisp baguette. The salad was bitter, but somehow those mysterious leaves were the perfect balance. I drank the wine too. It was dark and strong, but, like the salad, it felt so right. I would never forget that first taste of France. A simple meal, carefully thought out and executed.

By the end of it, I felt like a different person. Not just revived. Enlightened. I sat back with a sigh and the children clapped.

'*Attendez!*' said Charlotte, and she picked up my plate and carried it out to the kitchen. Then she came back with a smaller plate on which was placed a triangle of cheese with a chalky white crust oozing yellow underneath. She put it in front of me triumphantly.

I could smell a slightly cabbage-y pong, and wondered if it had gone off.

'*C'est bon,*' said Charlotte, sensing my reluctance, and Hugo nodded his agreement.

I picked up my knife and cut off a tiny slice, popping it into my mouth while trying to close my nose so I couldn't taste it. But, like the omelette, it was a revelation. It tasted nothing like it smelled. Rich and savoury, it tasted more like mushroom than anything. And once I had swallowed that tiny piece, I wanted more. I devoured it with relish.

When I'd finished, I wasn't sure what to do. I felt awkward being waited on. I picked up my plate and my glass and carried them into the kitchen. As I walked, the wine went straight to my head, and I felt overwhelmed with tiredness. In the kitchen, Jean Louis took one look at me.

'You must go to bed,' he said.

Suddenly, that was all I wanted. I wondered if I was supposed to help with the children, but I didn't think I had the energy. I just wanted to collapse and sleep.

'Thank you. *Merci. Pour le...*' I couldn't think of the word for food or meal. I wasn't sure if it had been dinner, or supper, or what they would call it. '*Omelette*,' I managed finally. '*Delicieux*.'

He smiled and gave a little shrug, as if it was nothing. '*Bonne nuit*,' he said.

And then suddenly I found two little pairs of arms around my legs as the children hugged me. '*Bonne nuit, Juliet*,' they chorused, and I managed to find the energy to laugh and bend down to hug them back.

'*Bonne nuit, mes petits*,' I said, not sure if that was the right thing to call them, but they seemed happy and I guessed that was how I would learn, by trial and error.

In the bedroom, I could hardly keep my eyes open as my clothes dropped to the floor. The sheets were cold and heavy and smooth – I was used to candy-striped brushed nylon, the same sheets I'd had since childhood that always felt a bit sticky and set your teeth on edge. The pillow was one long, hard cushion the whole width of the bed, tucked under the sheet. I thought I would never sleep, it all felt so unfamiliar, but as I snuggled down, the sheets began to feel warm and I sank into the mattress.

The memories of the day replayed themselves: the ferry and the train and the horror of the Métro and the endless walk and my aching arms. And then Corinne, glamorous and a touch intimidating. Gentle, kind Jean Louis, who seemed to be her opposite. And the two little ones, who I had already fallen in love with, and baby Arthur.

I was here, I was safe, I was in a soft warm bed and I was incredibly proud of myself.

5

Juliet was so absorbed in her writing that she didn't notice the banlieues of Paris creeping up. There were more tower blocks, more graffiti than on that first journey, but it was the same grimy, unwelcoming vista that seemed nothing like anyone's vision of arriving in the City of Light. But for true aficionados, this contradiction was part of the appeal: the rough, tough swagger and edginess, the *quartiers chauds* that were a melting pot of races, religions, ideals and philosophies.

She saved her document on her laptop and began to pack away her things, her mind still in the past. Her body was mirroring the fizz of anticipation she had felt all those years ago. She had the same empty stomach and the same surge of adrenaline, only this time she had knowledge and confidence. Nevertheless, she felt protective of the memory of her twenty-year-old self, and was certainly not going to let fifty-something Juliet come to any harm.

'Are you in Paris for long?' Her neighbour startled her with his question. She had been in her own world and had forgotten him.

'A while,' she said, vague but polite.

'If you'd like a drink while you're here, I'm staying in the *4ème*?'

She had to admire his persistence after her initial rebuff. 'I'm married.' Her smile indicated that was the end of the conversation. It wasn't a lie. She and Stuart had decided to leave their marital status for the time being. Neither of them could face the upheaval and the paperwork of divorce just yet, and they had always kept their finances separate. Maybe this would change, in time.

He gave a little shrug. 'This is Paris.'

She laughed, despite herself. 'Thank you, but no.'

He got the message this time, graciously, and stood up to take his coat from the luggage rack overhead. Before he left, he handed her a business card.

'If you change your mind,' he said. 'It can be just a drink.'

She smiled at him, admiring the way he had managed to be persistent without being sleazy. Paul Masters, she read on the card, before tucking it into her bag, where it would join all the receipts and scraps of paper that lived in there.

As Juliet stepped onto the platform, she began to walk, fast and purposeful. There was no way she would be a victim this time. Her cross-body bag was under her jacket. She knew where she was going. She had years of international travel under her belt. She might never have been back to Paris, but she'd visited any number of capital cities. None of them had stolen her heart in quite the same way. Nevertheless, she was wary. She knew there were sharp eyes and light fingers wherever you were in the world.

She made her way through the throng to the taxi rank

and joined the queue. She had made a promise to herself to walk everywhere she could while she was here – Paris was surprisingly small, so most places were accessible on foot and she needed the exercise – but on this first night she was going to treat herself.

The cold night air and the bright lights sharpened her senses and raised her pulse. Any city at night was exciting, but this was something she'd been looking forward to for a long time. She couldn't wait to get under the skin of the Paris she had left behind.

In less than ten minutes, she was in a taxi and soon they were circling the Place du Marché Saint-Honoré, a little square lined with restaurants, their lights twinkling, the pavement terraces still crowded with people eating and drinking outside despite the time of year. Waiters wove in and out of the diners, bringing cocktails, *coupes de champagne*, grilled goat's cheese salad, steak frites... Her mouth watered, but now was not the time to stop.

At the far end of the square, the taxi drove down a quiet street until they arrived at the building housing the apartment she had rented. She punched in the door code, pushed open the door into the hall and summoned the lift. She pulled back the latticed metal gate and stepped inside. It clanged shut. Inside, it was terrifyingly tiny, with only just enough room for her and her suitcase, but she took it up to the fourth floor, then dragged her case up the final flight of stairs to the very top. Another code, and she pushed open the door.

As she flicked on the lights, she gave a gasp of delight.

The entire apartment was only fifteen feet wide, tucked into the eaves of the east side of the top of the building, the left-hand wall a slope that went from the ceiling to the floor. The walls were covered in pale grey paper with a delicate shell motif picked out in silver, so it felt as if you were wrapped up in mother-of-pearl. At the far end was a bed piled high with square pillows and a velvet coverlet. A little dormer window with white shutters looked out over the street, and you could see straight into the houses opposite, with their sash windows and ornate wrought-iron balconies.

In the middle was a small sofa and a coffee table, as well as a console table with a pretty pair of gilt chairs fit for Marie Antoinette. There were paintings in battered frames and several mirrors, their surfaces soft and foxed, reflecting the light from a surprisingly large chandelier with millions of tiny crystal droplets that shimmered and twirled, throwing diamonds of light into the far corners.

At the near end was a miniscule kitchen with just enough work surface for a kettle and a toaster, a two-ring hob, a fridge and a sink. A round table with two chairs sat in front of another dormer window. And off that, a bathroom smaller than the downstairs loo at Persimmon Road.

Juliet sighed. It was perfect. Everything she needed for thirty days in Paris. It was a boudoir and a writer's garret; a potential love nest; a place to rest, recharge and renew.

It was anything she wanted it to be.

Once she'd unpacked, she pulled a string bag from a hook on the kitchen wall and headed down into the twilit streets. Nearby, she found a Carrefour mini-market tucked between the boutiques. She paused to choose some fruit from the display outside: a bunch of dark red grapes and some rosy apples. She watched as a man in a dark blue coat chose some tomatoes, intrigued by the care he took over the task. She couldn't imagine any man in England paying such close attention to the ripeness, the smell, the colour, before finding the perfect specimen. It was a ritual. A necessity. Something he was born to do.

Inside, the narrow aisles were crammed with temptation. She bought a ripe Camembert, a tub of celeriac remoulade, some *jambon de Bayonne*, unsalted Président butter and a baguette. Oh, and a bottle of ice-cold white Burgundy from the fridge. Finally, on impulse, she pulled a bunch of roses from a bucket, blowsy and white with just a hint of pink at the edges.

On her way back, she passed a store that was a mixture between an old apothecary and an antique shop, with everything displayed on gorgeous old tables and shelves. A scented candle was just what she needed for the apartment. She could have spent all evening trying to choose, but eventually she found one that spoke to her and seemed appropriate for her Parisian adventure. Usually, spending that kind of money was for birthdays or Christmas, but she felt as if she deserved it.

Back at the apartment, she unwrapped her purchases, setting out the cheese to come to room temperature, putting the fruit in a bowl on the table. She lit the candle and placed it on the console table, where its flame danced in the mirrors. She trimmed the stems of the roses and put them in a vase next to the candle. She found some Juliette Gréco on her phone and paired it with the mini speaker she had brought with her – the kids had given it to her for her birthday. And then she opened the window and let in the soft night air. Voices from the street below floated upwards as people made their way out to dinner, to a concert, to see friends.

She poured herself a glass of wine, letting the rich, viscous liquid roll over her tongue. She felt the tension of the last few months slide off her shoulders like a discarded fox fur, and realised that now, with her little touches, she felt at home. She would read back over what she had written on the train, perhaps write a little more if the mood took her. Music, wine, candlelight – what more could she ask for to bring out the muse?

6

The Ingénue

I had no idea where I was when I woke the next morning. I could hear the unfamiliar sound of a baby wailing, and high shrill voices. I saw a wardrobe looming at the foot of my bed, and long linen curtains, and my coat on a hook on the back of a door. Puzzled, I sat up. As yesterday's memories filtered through into my brain, I could smell coffee – dark, smoky, delicious. It was enough to get me up.

In the kitchen, Corinne was hacking at a baguette, dressed in a black silk dressing gown. She almost looked as if she was sleepwalking, and the rings under her eyes were even darker than when I had first seen her. The baby was slumped in a bouncy chair on the floor, cawing away to himself.

'Hugo! Charlotte!' Corinne croaked, her voice gruff, and her eyes flicked over me. She gave a curt nod, grabbed a coffee pot off the stove that was about to boil over and swore as she burnt her hand. Suddenly, the whole room was in chaos. Corinne howled with the pain, Charlotte and Hugo ran in and Arthur began to cry.

'You must run it under water,' I told Corinne and she

looked at me blankly. I pointed to the sink, ran over and turned on the cold tap, pointing to her hand. '*L'eau froid.*' I nodded encouragement, wondering how a woman of her age with children didn't know simple first aid.

She just stood there. I picked up Arthur to comfort him.

'*Eau froid*,' I repeated. Hugo and Charlotte were jumping up and down, only adding to the drama. I tapped each of them on the shoulder and pointed to the baguette. '*Mangez*,' I told them, but they were too concerned about their mother to obey. She was staring at the red mark on her hand. I thought perhaps she was in shock.

And then Jean Louis walked in, wearing a short navy-blue dressing gown and velvet slippers, his hair rumpled, his eyes bleary, and the noise re-erupted. Corinne's voice rose higher than the children's and Arthur doubled his wails. Jean Louis looked at the running tap and guided his wife towards it, holding her hand under the stream of water while she protested.

'It's OK,' I said to the children, hoping they understood me. I put a finger to my lips to indicate they should be quiet, then pointed again at the baguette. '*Petit déjeuner. Mangez.*'

I was rubbing Arthur's back and eventually he slumped onto my shoulder. I found it quite comforting, having him snuggle into me like a little koala, because I was finding it all very strange, being plunged into this family drama miles away from home when I hadn't even woken up properly yet.

Hugo and Charlotte took a plate each and some bread. Corinne was quiet now, staring at her wound as the cool water ran over it. I saw Jean Louis shut his eyes for a moment and breathe out. Then he opened them and looked at me and gave a nod of gratitude. I smiled, feeling confident that I had done my best in a situation that had been heading out of control.

'*Café?*' he asked me, heading for the culprit that was the coffee pot.

I normally had a cup of strong tea with two sugars. Something told me that I wasn't going to get a cuppa here, though, and I'd have to change my ways. When in Paris . . .

I nodded. '*Merci.*'

I braced myself for something strong and heart-pounding. I watched as he heated some milk, poured a little coffee from the pot into it, then served it up into three blue bowls. The two little ones took one each, and the third was for me. We carried the bowls and plates into the dining room, me with Arthur still clinging on gamely, and I watched the children dip their bread into the milky coffee. I sat down and sipped mine, and it was delicious, not strong at all.

From the dining room, we could hear Jean Louis and Corinne having a heated discussion. The children didn't seem worried by the raised voices, so I supposed it was normal. Anyway, Arthur was making them laugh by reaching out for bits of bread which they fed to him. Soon I was covered in crumbs, but I didn't mind. I sat him on the table, holding him under his arms, and he burbled away happily. They were so sweet, the three of them, Charlotte and Hugo in matching chambray pyjamas with red trim and Arthur in a white Babygro dotted with pale brown rabbits.

Eventually, Jean Louis came in. He looked strained,

but he smiled. He spoke to the children, then explained to me that Corinne was going back to bed.

'We will go for lunch,' he said. 'I'm so sorry, I will need some help. I wanted you to have the day to recover from the journey, but . . .' He held up his hands in mock despair.

'I'm fine,' I told him. 'It's no problem.'

'If you can help the children get dressed,' he said, 'I can manage this one, I think.'

He took Arthur from me, holding his son up in the air, and the baby chortled with laughter, paddling his legs as Jean Louis beamed up at him, his face suffused with love.

I took the children and helped them choose their clothes for the day. Their bedrooms were immaculate: Charlotte's room was pale yellow and Hugo's pale green, and they both had white beds and chests of drawers and gingham curtains in the same colour as their walls. I couldn't believe the amount of clothes they had – piles and piles of crisply ironed shirts and blouses, neatly folded jumpers, snow-white underwear and rolled-up socks, all colour-coded. Winter coats were hung on a rail, and underneath were shoes for every occasion.

Afterwards, I rummaged through my suitcase trying to decide what to wear for lunch. In the end, I wore a black Lycra dress, black tights and black suede boots, thinking all one colour might be chic. But I didn't look chic, I thought glumly as I peered into the mirror on the inside of the wardrobe. I looked a little bit plump and a bit pale. Not interesting pale, like Corinne, just peaky. Even my pearls looked wrong: the big gobstopper ones I'd saved up for and been so proud of. I was hoping they would make my skin look creamy and luminous, which was what pearls were supposed to do, but they didn't, because they were fake.

We gathered in the hall, Arthur tucked into his pushchair, Charlotte and Hugo buckling up their shoes. I had put on my tweed jacket again, conscious that it was unravelling in a way that Coco Chanel would never have allowed. Jean Louis swung on a camel overcoat that settled on him as if his tailor had just stepped away from applying the finishing touch.

'*Allons-y.*' He smiled, allowing me through the door first while he followed with the pushchair.

My A to Z hadn't told a single lie. Paris was just as it should be, everything was just where it should be, and everything was so close. Within five minutes, we were walking over the pale ground in the Tuileries, the park that ran from the Louvre to the Place de la Concorde. It looked so familiar that I expected Audrey Hepburn to run into shot at any moment, clutching a bunch of balloons, but I tried to keep on top of my excitement and look casual, as if I wandered through these gardens with monotonous regularity. For Charlotte and Hugo, this was their local park, and they jumped onto the low wall of the circular pond to run around it.

'We have to wait,' said Jean Louis, rolling his eyes fondly. 'For them to go all the way round.'

And then we were crossing the Pont Royal, and I knew what that meant. St-Germain-des-Prés. Writers, philosophers, actresses, chanteuses. We stopped halfway across and I looked up the river. The sun had dragged itself out of bed and shone a trifle reluctantly, not really able to dredge up much heat, but obliging us by making the water sparkle. I could see so much of the city I'd dreamed of, all its beauty laid out in front of me. I shivered.

'You are cold?' Jean Louis was concerned. 'We are not far.'

I couldn't tell him it was excitement, the emotion of it all. The pinch-me disbelief that here I was, that I had escaped, that I was heading for lunch where all those icons I'd read about had eaten and drunk and quarrelled and fallen in love and worked out the meaning of life.

The boulevards of St Germain were wider and busier than I had imagined, and I thought that Charlotte and Hugo must be getting tired – any English child worth their salt would have been whining by now – but eventually we turned off and finally arrived at a restaurant on the corner of two cobbled streets. Its double doors were dark red and clad in brass, and between each of its long, tall windows was a panel declaring 'VINS BISTRO CAFÉ RESTAURANT PÂTISSERIE LIQUEURS' in art deco writing.

Jean Louis lifted Arthur out of his pushchair, snapped it shut and opened the door. We followed him in. Immediately, I was enveloped in a fug of smoke, garlic, hot butter, vanilla, burnt sugar and coffee. Crowded booths lined the mirrored walls, and a battalion of waiters were debating menus and opening bottles with reverence. The largest waiter of all, his stomach swathed in a snow-white apron, came forward to Jean Louis and kissed him on each cheek before hustling us to an empty table, conjuring up a high chair out of thin air and giving me a nod of welcome.

Paper menus were passed to us, and I looked at a bald list, recognising a few of the words, some of which filled me with dismay. *Rognons*, I was pretty sure, was kidney;

veau was veal and there was no way I was eating that. I was searching for something familiar when Jean Louis took the menu out of my hand.

'We will have the *poulet rôti*,' he said. 'Don't worry – no frog legs or snails for you today. Not yet.'

He was teasing me, but kindly, and I felt relieved that I didn't have to risk being faced with a plate of something I couldn't stomach.

I sat back and relaxed, looking around at all the other customers, eyeing the plates of food being carried to the tables, listening to the laughter and snippets of the language I was trying to acclimatise to, congratulating myself when I picked out a word or phrase I recognised. Before I knew it, another waiter had appeared with two flutes, one for me and one for Jean Louis.

'Kir royale,' he announced, and as I sipped at the pinky-golden bubbles, I was filled with a glow of happiness. This was everything I had dreamed of and more when I'd caught sight of that advert.

While we waited for our lunch, we kept up a lopsided conversation in my bad French and Jean Louis' perfect English. When I described something to him, he would explain the key words to Charlotte and Hugo, who would repeat them back, and in turn they would give me the French. I told them that my father was a train driver.

'Train driver!' said Jean Louis. 'Every little boy's dream, eh?' He ruffled Hugo's hair. 'And your mother?'

Mum worked part-time as a cashier at a building society. I had no idea what the French for building society was, or even if they had them, so I told a white lie and said she worked in a bank.

'*Et vous?*' I asked him, emboldened by the Kir royale.

'*Je suis agent immobilier*,' he said. 'Estate agent?'

I nodded politely. Estate agents in England did not have a good reputation. They were either posh in tweed suits, or dodgy in shiny suits, and either way they were sure to rip you off and tell you lies. Jean Louis didn't seem to fit in either category.

'It's my family business. My father began the company. We have offices here and in the South of France, where my parents live. I am in charge in Paris.'

'And Corinne? Does she work?' I was curious about his wife.

'Corinne has a business doing interiors for our clients. But she has been off for a while.' He inclined his head towards Arthur with a smile of explanation. 'She starts back to work tomorrow.'

Jean Louis took another sip of his drink and cleared his throat before leaning towards me. He didn't want his children to hear what he had to say next.

'She has found it hard, being a mother of three,' he confided. 'I am not so sure about her going back to work yet. But she is determined.' He pointed at me. 'Which is why we need some help.'

'That's what I'm here for.' I beamed at him, happy to be useful.

'It was my idea to have an au pair. She was not so happy with the idea. But I hope she will soon get used to you.'

That probably explained Corinne's lack of warmth towards me. I could see why you might not want a stranger in your home, especially with a new baby. I thought I could probably win her round, by being helpful and keeping out of her way.

Before I could say anything, the waiter approached the

table with a whole roasted chicken. It was laid reverentially in front of us and carved with precision and an extremely deadly knife. With it was a tower of thin, crispy chips and a pile of deep-green watercress. A bottle of red wine was opened too. I loved the theatre of it all; the attention and the anticipation.

If you'd said to me lunch was going to be chicken and chips, I wouldn't have got excited. But two bites in and I was enraptured. Hot, crisp skin. Melting white meat that held a trace of smoke from the fire it had been cooked over. Salty *frites*. I couldn't eat it fast enough but tried to be delicate and not eat like a total savage. I'd never tasted anything like it.

I watched Charlotte and Hugo dig in with gusto, their napkins tucked into their collars. Even Arthur was angelic, as Jean Louis fed him little mouthfuls of creamed spinach the chef had sent for him.

When the chicken had been devoured, Jean Louis ordered a whole *tarte Tatin*. It arrived at the table, the upturned apple halves glistening with golden caramel, and the waiter cut it carefully into slices, plating up some for us and taking the rest away to be put into a box.

'It's Corinne's favourite,' Jean Louis explained, and I thought how lucky she was, to have a husband who thought to bring home her favourite dessert.

By the time we had finished the tart, I felt a bit woozy. The rich food, the wine, the heat in the restaurant, the concentration of trying to understand and speak French, yesterday's travelling... my eyelids were almost too heavy to keep open. Jean Louis noticed and laughed.

'You are like Arthur when he needs to sleep. We must get you both home.'

*

When we got back to the house, Corinne was up and dressed and seemed very composed, in jeans and a polo neck, her hair smoothed into a ponytail and her arms outstretched for Arthur. She seemed a different person as she sat the baby on her knee and listened to the children telling her what they'd had for lunch. She stroked Arthur's cheek with the back of her hand and he leaned his head against hers, staring at me as if I was a perfect stranger and he hadn't been eating *crème fraîche* from my spoon less than an hour ago.

'You can go to your room, if you like,' she said to me with a smile.

I understood I was being dismissed, like a parlourmaid, but I didn't mind. The food and the wine were tugging at my eyelids. I curled up on my bed, intending to have a little snooze.

I didn't wake until the next morning.

7

Juliet lifted her arms over her head and stretched out her shoulders. Darkness had crept in while she'd been writing, throwing pale grey shadows into the corners of the room. She'd paused only to snap on the lamp beside her desk so she could carry on. She loved it when that happened: when you got so absorbed in your work that time passed without you noticing. As a writer, you could never tell if the words were going to come easily or if they were going to be elusive and difficult to pin down, but today it had felt effortless. She'd written twice as much as she'd set as her target.

Now, she needed fresh air, and to stretch her legs. She pulled on her Skechers and headed out into the chill November night. She knew exactly where she was heading. It was less than a kilometre away. She knew the route like the back of her hand, for she'd taken the children to the Tuileries often enough, so it was a question of making her way back up towards the Opéra.

Whether she was right to go back was another question, but she wanted to see if her memory was accurate, or if there was some detail she was missing. Write about what you know, they said. But did she still know it or had her mind played tricks?

The street hadn't changed an iota. It had a hushed air of quiet privilege and exclusivity that made you wonder who was lucky enough to live here. The stone was creamy and unblemished; the greenery on the balconies manicured; the paintwork gleamed. Not a single brick or windowpane seemed different.

She felt herself drawn towards the huge black door, as imposing now as it had been the night she'd arrived. What if she'd never stepped inside that courtyard? What route would her life have taken if she'd never seen the advert, never entered the Beaubois household?

And what if she stepped inside it now? She touched the handle for a moment, the metal so cold on her fingers, it felt like an electric shock. She could push it open and go in search of her past. Would they still be there? Would her ghost still be there, standing at the window, looking out at the same moon that was hanging overhead?

Emotions had memories just like muscles, she thought. It was more than just nostalgia. She was almost reliving every moment, her heart skittering and her pulse racing. She could feel the nerves she had felt that first night, her stomach raw and churning. And the turmoil of walking out for the very last time, hearing the door clang shut behind her. But she could also remember the times she had bounced through it, ready to embark on some new adventure, or pushed it open without a care in the world, a bag of croissants in her hand.

How had it all gone so wrong? Which tiny moment was the catalyst? What could she have done differently?

It all became too much. The feelings. The questions.

Confronting her past in real life was so much more visceral than putting it on the page, and she felt vulnerable. She turned on her heel, hunching herself under her jacket, and walked away, angry with herself. Why had she come here? It was not as if she'd had any intention of causing a scene. It wasn't her style.

Juliet had never been confrontational. She wondered now if that was a good thing. Was lack of confrontation just cowardice? Did not standing up for yourself mean being a doormat? Or was not rocking the boat a sign of strength? Writing had always been her way of dealing with uncomfortable things: a diary, a letter, an article. And now a book.

Thirty-something years on, she was using words to make sense of her past so she could make sense of her future. But how far should she go? After all, you could tell lies as you wrote, edit out the bits that reflected badly on you, rebalancing things to create a narrative you felt comfortable with. She had to be honest with herself, she realised. She couldn't skirt around the things she didn't feel proud of. There was no point in an airbrushed reconstruction.

She turned left at the bottom of the street and quickened her step in her hurry to get away. The air temperature had dropped and the wind needled into her. Suddenly, Paris didn't feel so welcoming. She was all alone in a strange city, without anyone to go back to. No husband; no children; no friends. None of the people she cared about were giving a second thought to her tonight. They were all getting on with their own lives. She had thought she could manage getting on with hers. She had thought she was tough and independent and resourceful and resilient. But, right now, she felt small and unloved.

She'd been putting a brave face on it all. She'd been fooling everyone, even herself. The bright voice she had used to her friends, to justify her and Stuart's decision, had been a façade. The description of all the exciting plans she had was a mirage, a fantasy she had conjured up to paper over her fear. She had used Paris as a distraction, painting a picture of an exciting new chapter in her life, making herself an object of envy, whereas, really, she was to be pitied.

She shivered, but it wasn't the wind. It was the chill of realising the bleakness of her situation. A foolish woman who had agreed to throw away her marriage because her husband seemed to love his new bicycle more than he loved her? She hadn't paid him enough attention. If she had been a good wife, if she had been worth keeping, she should have taken an interest, shouldn't she?

Panic was pooling in her stomach. She'd burnt her bridges. The house was gone. All she had was money in the bank – admittedly quite a lot, more than she ever thought she would have at her disposal – but what good was that when there was no one to make plans *with*?

She stopped at a red pedestrian light and looked around. She had no idea where she was. The street names were unfamiliar. She didn't recognise the buildings, or remember passing them. Somehow, she must have taken a wrong turn. She pulled out her phone and pressed Google Maps, but just as the grid of streets began to fill the screen, it went black. Her phone was dead.

It was her own fault. She was useless at keeping her phone charged. It drove everyone mad: Stuart, the kids.

But she wasn't as obsessed with her phone as they were, so she didn't notice when the battery was low. But suddenly she realised just how much she relied on it, even though she thought she didn't. How was she going to find out where she was?

She carried on to the end of the road and found herself in a wide, noisy street full of jostling crowds, garish shops and noisy traffic. Car horns, loud music, laughing and shouting, the smell of fried onions and cheap oil. Crowds of youngsters in bright puffer jackets and ostentatious trainers trailed plumes of vape and sometimes something more exotic.

She wanted to find a map and get her bearings without looking too obvious. She sensed she looked out of place, a fish out of water. Exactly like a middle-aged English mum who'd got herself lost, not some streetwise Parisienne. She'd thought she was so cool, remembering her way without a map. But her mind was blank and she had lost all sense of direction. She felt as if there were eyes upon her, weighing her up.

She drew her coat around her and tried to look casual. If she'd still smoked, she'd have lit a cigarette, playing for time, but she and Stuart had given up long ago. No one she knew smoked anymore, which, by and large, was a good thing – until you needed a prop and to look as if you didn't give a shit when actually you were bricking it.

She told herself to think. Visualise her internal map of Paris, work out where she had gone wrong. She must be in Les Halles, near the Forum des Halles, the old food market once known as the belly of Paris. It was a harmless enough area, with its huge chain stores and fast food, a magnet for the young who'd come in from the suburbs. If she kept her wits about her, she would come to no harm. She needed to head south, towards the river, and then loop round along the Seine until she was back in the Rue Saint-Honoré. But she felt as if she'd been blindfolded in a game of Grandmother's Footsteps and turned around until she was dizzy and disorientated.

Just walk, she told herself. Paris was small. She would find her way out of the neighbourhood in five minutes. If she ended up in the Marais, the wrong direction, then she'd have a longer walk home, but at least she would know where she was. She put her shoulders back and walked on, dodging the gaggles of oblivious teens, chiding herself for her schoolgirl error in letting her phone die.

A wave of homesickness enveloped her as she trudged through the crowds. She would give anything to be back at Persimmon Road right now, pouring a glass of the Argentinian Malbec their wine merchant neighbour had recommended, grappling with the ingredients of some recipe in last week's *Guardian*. They always got the Saturday papers and circled what they were going to watch or download on their Kindles or cook the next weekend. Juliet's resolution the year before last had been to rustle up something new every Saturday night, and she had done quite well, only occasionally falling back on the old favourites she could make in her sleep, and had become quite cavalier with miso and harissa and pomegranate molasses.

But in the last year Stuart had eschewed their Saturday-night wine indulgence and wanted 'clean' food. He favoured a plant-based diet. Juliet was all for vegetables – she loved them – but she knew he didn't mean a tian of aubergine and courgette soaked in olive oil, rich with garlic and parsley, oozing mozzarella and topped with breadcrumbs. Plant-based in his new world meant joyless. Tofu, kale, chard, quinoa, bean sprouts, alfalfa – everything measured in macronutrients, or was it micronutrients?

As she turned a corner and saw the Rue de Rivoli in front of her, she felt a wave of relief. She was back on familiar ground. She felt her confidence returning, and quickened her pace. And she realised, as she walked, that it was old Stuart she was missing. Old Stuart she was in mourning for. The one with the slightly too-long hair and the squidgy tummy; the one who would top up your glass without asking and blast out Pearl Jam after a few too many. She'd love that Stuart here with her now. They'd have devoured steak tartare and *frites* in a buzzy brasserie somewhere, stopped for digestifs on the way home, maybe wandered back along the river, her arm hooked in his.

New Stuart would be on Strava, looking at the best runs. She imagined him limbering up in their apartment, pulling on his Saucony trainers, and felt a pang of regret that somehow they had lost the camaraderie that had bonded them from the day they met. They'd been part-ners in crime rather than passionate lovers. Friends with benefits who had gone on to make a life together because, somehow, it was easy and it worked.

And now they were friends without the benefits . . .

Just before the street that led to her apartment, she passed a hotel so discreet and chic it made you want to run away with a secret lover on the spot. Set on a corner, the façade was cream, with perfectly symmetrical sash windows and a door flanked by classical pillars. A few yards down the side street was another door, and above it hung an intricate panel depicting a golden shell, surrounded by bunches of grapes and a garland of leaves.

Before she knew it, she was making her way inside and found herself in a tiny bar. A barman in a snow-white shirt mixed Martinis for a couple sitting in the furthest corner, their fingers entwined as they murmured to each other and laughed, their faces lit by candlelight.

Juliet slid onto a velvet stool at the bar. She might be on her own, but it didn't matter. She was an independent woman on a mission to rediscover herself, and she wanted a cocktail mixed for her in a glass so cold it burnt. The barman gave her a little nod to indicate he would be with her as soon as he could.

She picked up the cocktail menu and absorbed her surroundings. The bar was decorated in black and gold, which could have been harsh, but clever lighting, luxurious fabrics and the softest carpet made it mellow. She wanted to stay there for ever, wrapped in its promise. As she ordered a Sidecar, she felt a flash of triumph. She was here, being looked after, indulging herself. She didn't need anyone else to make the most of Paris.

She knew instinctively that if she was to make the best of her new life, she had to be self-sufficient. To fall in love with *herself*. To be happy in your own company was a skill not everyone had. Ordering a drink in a bar and drinking it without feeling self-conscious was a rite of passage. She'd ordered drinks by herself in bars before, but usually somewhere she knew, and usually while waiting for a friend. This time, she was somewhere unfamiliar and there was little to no chance of someone she knew sauntering in. But she was surprised to find it felt OK.

It helped, of course, that the barman was charming and served her as if she had been a regular for years.

'You are on holiday?' he asked, as he delivered her drink with a flourish.

'I'm here to work,' she replied. 'I'm renting an apartment for thirty days. To write a book.'

'That's so cool.' His eyes lit up. People were always intrigued by writers. 'What's your book about?'

'*Une femme d'un certain âge,*' she replied with a twinkle. 'Who rediscovers herself in Paris.'

She was surprised by her description. Was that what she was working towards?

'Oh,' he said. 'So you're here for research? Let me know if I can help.'

He was flirting with her. His eyes were teasing. Was he daring her? She smiled, enjoying the frisson, but also the knowledge that she had no intention of picking up on his subtext. He was, after all, trained to make people feel special.

She raised her glass to him with a smile. 'I will. Thank you.'

'You must come in here whenever you need to. I will look after you.' He set a little dish of olives at her elbow. 'A writer needs a good bar. Like Hemingway, eh?'

The drink was ice-cold but burnt hot inside her, the traces of Cointreau lingering on her lips. She felt her earlier anxiety melt away. She didn't feel a shred of self-consciousness or any need to explain why she was here alone. She was a woman enjoying her own company, and it felt wonderful. She sipped at her drink and watched as the other customers came and went. Friends greeted each other, cashmere coats sliding onto the backs of the chairs, butter-soft handbags placed on the floor, the air filled with mingled perfumes.

Her drink finished, she set it back on the bar. The barman smiled and said '*Bonne soirée, madame. À bientôt*' with such warmth, she decided he was right. This was where she would come when she felt wobbly, or lonely, or even just because, for an aperitif or a digestif or a pick-me-up. It would become her special place, just as The Ritz was for Hemingway. She imagined a line in a magazine feature: '*This was where the author Juliet Miller would come for her habitual Sidecar. She was a familiar figure in the evenings, alone but never aloof, the epitome of a sophisticated woman . . .*'

The fantasy might be ridiculous, but it had buoyed her up. She laughed as she made her way back up to her apartment in the lift, and headed straight for her laptop without hesitation. Biting the bullet was the only way to make her dream come true.

8

The Ingénue

Monday morning was a baptism of fire. I overslept, knocked unconscious by the travel and the food and the wine the day before, and was woken by a ferocious knocking on my door. I leapt out of bed and pulled on jeans and a sweatshirt and rushed into the kitchen to find Corinne prancing about quite unashamed in a black mesh bra and tights, trying to feed Arthur.

'*Desolée, desolée*,' I panted, mortified I'd screwed up on day one. This was her first morning back at work. She was bound to be feeling under pressure. She thrust Arthur into my arms.

'*Merci*,' she said, indicating her scant outfit with a wry grimace. 'I must get ready.'

The children seemed to have lost their sweetness of the day before. They were tired and scratchy and reluctant to co-operate.

'*Vous n'aimez pas l'ècole?*' I asked them, wondering if they weren't keen on school, and they both shook their heads.

I held up my fingers to show them how many hours before they would be home again.

'*Huit heures,*' I tried to reassure them, but they weren't consoled and I couldn't blame them because, actually, eight hours was a long time.

It was difficult, managing all three of them. I rubbed the banana off Arthur's dear little face just as Charlotte spilled milky coffee on her pinafore dress. I was dabbing at the coffee stain with one hand, getting very flustered, when Jean Louis eventually appeared, looking immaculate in a blue suit. He ruffled the older children on the head, kissed Arthur and slid out of the door without a backward glance. Houses to sell, money to make, I supposed.

By eight, Charlotte and Hugo were ready, by some miracle, with their teeth cleaned, hair brushed and coats and shoes on. I knew it was a fifteen-minute walk to their school, so I was anxious to leave, but there was still no sign of Corinne, who was in charge of taking Arthur to his nursery.

Eventually she emerged. She looked as dressed up as she had on Saturday night, in a short black skirt and tight black jacket with large diamanté buttons and very high boots. I felt drab and unkempt in comparison.

'Wow,' I couldn't help saying. She gave me the ghost of a smile and took Arthur as we all headed down the stairs in a tangle of school bags, baby bags, handbags, suffocating in a cloud of Corinne's perfume.

Chaos hit as soon as we all got out into the street. Corinne was about to head off in one direction when Hugo suddenly threw his arms around his mother's legs and wouldn't let go. Charlotte joined in, the two of them howling. Gone were the sweet charming moppets of the weekend. I suspected it was an act, at least in Charlotte's case. I could see her looking for my reaction out of the corner of her eye.

Corinne froze in panic, not sure what to do, for there were too many passers-by for her to be able to remonstrate with her unruly offspring. She tried pushing them off with the arm that wasn't holding Arthur. I was rooted to the spot. Should I drag them off her?

Then Arthur joined in the cacophony. People were starting to look. I turned to Corinne, to ask her what to do, and to my horror, I saw there were tears streaming down her face too. Although I was intimidated by her, I felt a wave of pity. The poor woman was just trying to go to work.

'*Pauvre Maman*,' I declared, and stepped forward to take Corinne in my arms to console her. '*Pauvre Maman*.' I patted her on the back. I could feel Corinne tense, clearly not used to spontaneous embraces or sympathy.

Hugo and Charlotte both looked up, startled. The faces were free of tears, little beasts, but they looked shocked at the sight of their mother's. I knelt down, taking a hand each.

'*Maman* must go to work,' I said firmly. 'And we must go to school. *Courage, mes enfants. Courage.*' I raised my fist in a gesture of solidarity, dredging up as much encouraging French as I could remember.

Miraculously, they peeled themselves away from Corinne, and by now Arthur had stopped crying too.

'*Au revoir, Maman. À bientôt!*' I sang, and my charges repeated my refrain.

Corinne stood rooted to the spot, still in shock. '*Mon maquillage?*' she asked. Her make-up was her only concern, it seemed.

'*Ça va,*' I said, though it was a little bit streaky, but that was her daytime look anyway, the slightly grungy bed hair and the smudgy eyes.

'*Merci,*' she said. '*Merci...*'

She looked broken, and I wondered if perhaps she was more vulnerable than she appeared. Instinctively, I patted her on the arm. She flinched, drew in a deep breath, flashed me a glimmer of gratitude and stalked off down the pavement. I watched her go, striding along like a model on a catwalk on her spindly heels, Arthur peering over her shoulder with his owl eyes. Then I turned on my heel and began to skip.

'*Vite, vite!*' I called to the children.

The distraction technique worked. Hugo and Charlotte began to skip after me, immersed in giggles. By the end of the street, I was out of breath and had to slow to a walk, but it had done the trick. We were on our way to school.

It wasn't even half past eight and I was already exhausted.

Somehow, I managed to get through the first two days. As a shy person, it was torture navigating my way around an unfamiliar household, a strange neighbourhood and a different language. Every encounter took all of my courage, from handing the children over at the school gate to following the shopping list provided by Corinne, scouring the shelves for mysterious ingredients and hoping I had got the right item and the right amount. Then came the task of working out what to do with it. The children ate proper grown-up food. There was no sign of chicken nuggets or oven chips. Everything was made from scratch, except the beautiful cakes and pastries I was allowed to buy for dessert. I was used to my mum cooking for me, and my kitchen skills were not advanced. For the first few days, I relied on rotisserie chicken and the grated carrot with raisins the kids seemed to snack on – there wasn't a packet of pickled onion Monster Munch to be seen. But I was keen to learn, because my palate was adapting quickly. Eating in France was a joy.

When Wednesday arrived, I was to have the afternoon to myself, as the children only had a half-day and Corinne was picking them up. I was signed up for language classes, and my stomach lurched at the thought of walking into a classroom environment with a bunch of strangers. Another challenge. But it was going to be the quickest way to meet people of my own age, so I screwed up my courage, put on some make-up and headed for the language school. It couldn't possibly be harder than trying to order cheese at the counter in the supermarket, when the man had looked at me blankly until I resorted to pointing and demonstrating how much I needed by making a wedge shape with my fingers.

If I was going to survive in Paris, I needed to make myself understood.

9

Juliet was woken the next morning by a bell, plaintive and plangent, striking eight o'clock. The sound was both melancholy and reassuring. Time is on your side, it seemed to tell her. Whatever happens, the hours will still pass. It's up to you what you do with them.

Watching the sun rise over the rooftops opposite, Juliet sat in the shaft of light as it filled her with an energy she hadn't felt for a long time. She lay there, revelling in her freedom for a moment.

How had this happened? How had she gone from reading bags and packed lunches and dentist appointments, sports days and carol concerts and prize giving, that torturous whirl of maternal responsibility, to being able to do exactly as she pleased, seemingly overnight?

Of course, it hadn't happened overnight. It had happened gradually: the practical tasks had got fewer as the children got older and were able to look after themselves (in theory – she was still nagging Izzy and picking up after her right until the day she left), but the emotional responsibility was still huge. She had lived every moment of Izzy's exam anxiety last summer, helping her with a complex revision timetable, making sure she got enough sleep and ate properly. Then the agony of waiting for results: she had been awake most of the night, running over Izzy's options, depending on her grades. Of course, Izzy had aced every one, and now she was off on an adventure.

My work here is done, Juliet had thought with a wry smile, although she knew that, of course, it wasn't, that mothering did not stop at eighteen at all. There would be periods of not being needed, like now, but she knew the kids would always turn to her in a crisis, and crises there would be. You were just on hold.

But for now her life was her own. Time spooled out in front of her in reams, unpunctuated by appointments and commitments and deadlines, so she could no longer complain that she didn't have any. She'd written so many features about carving out 'me' time, the importance of putting yourself first in order to keep everyone else afloat, that suddenly having every minute of every day free to do whatever she liked was a little overwhelming. It was second nature to check her diary, and the to-do lists she made, for all the tiresome necessities that went with running a house and the lives contained within it. Stuart had been pretty hands-on as a husband and dad, for which she was grateful, but she was aware that what she was experiencing was a luxury, and it was her duty to make the most of it.

Her regime, she decided, was going to be to write as much as she could in the morning, when she was her sharpest. Once she had hit a reasonable word count, the rest of the day would be hers to do whatever she liked. She knew she would have to be strict with herself, for it would be all too easy to procrastinate. The writer's worst enemy, procrastination, second only to being distracted by the internet – and, of course, one could fuel the other. She had decided not to hook up her laptop to the apartment's Wi-Fi, for then she couldn't wander online under the pretence of doing some research. She didn't need to do any, after all. It was her story, in her head, and everything else she needed to know was waiting for her outside.

But first, she had resolved to go for a run each morning. She was well aware, despite her mistrust of Stuart's obsession, that her own fitness was not all it could be. Sitting was the new smoking, potentially as dangerous to your health as a twenty-a-day habit. To start the day with a gentle jog would hopefully go some way towards offsetting what was fondly known as 'writer's arse'. She pulled on her gym kit and trainers and headed out into the pearl-grey morning.

She knew there was a circuit of about one mile around the Tuileries – a distance she thought she could manage and that was, most important of all at this point in her regime, flat. She ran down the terraced steps into the manicured perfection of the gardens and headed for the path between the horse chestnuts, keeping a slow and steady pace, enjoying the sharp, bright November air, the bareness of the branches overhead, the satisfying crunch of the pale-yellow surface beneath her feet. At the far end, she slowed to a brisk walk and found herself in front of Rodin's *The Kiss*. Her eyes travelled slowly over the marble figures, and for a moment she was taken back in time to the memory of exploring another body, all the passion and the intensity. She felt her throat tighten with longing. She would probably never feel that wonder again.

She left the park and headed back along the colonnades

of the Rue de Rivoli, where the shops were starting to open, with their glittery shiny souvenirs of Paris: key rings and snow globes and fridge magnets. She turned back onto the Rue Saint-Honoré, and smiled as she passed the high-end boutiques that sat oh-so-casually alongside cafés and bars, chocolate shops and florists. The contents of the windows made her mouth water, and she found herself swooning over the cut of an outsized bouclé coat, the swoop of a tulle skirt, the tobacco-brown suede of a pair of ankle boots.

She promised herself that if she worked hard, she would treat herself to something each day. It might be something small: a tiny box of chocolates or a magazine. Or it might be something from the list she had written, of classic items she wanted to invest in: a trench coat, a white shirt, a signature perfume. She had set aside some money from the house sale to give herself a makeover so she could embark on her new life as a single woman. And where better to create a new identity than Paris?

There were other things on the list too. Places to go. Monet's *Water Lilies*. Saint Laurent's atelier. Maybe Versailles.

And people to see. Perhaps.

She had been right to come here. You couldn't hide from something, somewhere, someone you had fallen in love with, for the rest of your life, just because things had gone wrong.

For a moment, she let her imagination wander, re-calling the faces of the past, but now was not the time. She found a patisserie and went in, eyeing up the tarts and cakes and pastries lined up in the cabinet – chocolate and strawberry and lemon, all perfectly glazed and iced.

After her run, she felt justified in leaving with a plump *pain au raisin* in a brown paper bag.

As she walked back to her apartment, she felt elated. Was this the runner's high Stuart had been banging on about? No, she decided. Her lightness of heart was all about freedom and possibility and her own potential. The joy of stumbling across a masterpiece on her morning run. As she bounded in through the entrance door and pressed the button to summon the lift, she was beaming from ear to ear.

As the lift clanked down and ground to a halt, she stood to one side to let the occupant out. It was a young woman in her early thirties, dressed in an elegant yellow coat.

'*Bonjour*,' sang Juliet.

'Hey,' said the girl with a smile. 'How are you doing?'

Juliet made a face, laughing. 'Is it that obvious?'

'Oh no, sorry. It's just our landlord told us there was an English lady moving in.'

'Just for a month. I'm Juliet.'

The girl held out her hand. 'Melissa. I live with Bernard, right next door.'

'It's nice to meet you. And I'm guessing you're not French either?'

'I'm from Boston. But Bernard is Parisian.' She pronounced it Pareezhan. 'I've lived here five years now. So what are you doing here?'

Juliet was slightly taken aback by her blunt questioning. 'Well,' she said, 'I'm on a bit of a life break. Revisiting my lost youth. Trying to find myself.'

'*À la recherche du temps perdu?*'

'Kind of. And I'm writing a book while I'm here. Trying to, anyway.'

'Oh. What kind of a book?'

'Good question. Right now it's exactly a memoir/coming-of-age mash-up, but I'm waiting to see where it will take me.'

'I've always wanted to write a book,' Melissa laughed. 'A kind of Parisian Miss Marple, head-to-toe in Chanel, with a little miniature dachshund as a sidekick. Maybe you can inspire me to get started?'

Juliet smiled. If she'd had a pound for everyone who said that, she'd be in head-to-toe Chanel herself, but she didn't say anything.

'So what brought you to Paris?' she asked instead.

'I came here as a student and never left. Fell in love with the guy in the apartment upstairs from me.' Melissa's eyes sparkled. 'Now I run tours. All kinds of tours. Food tours. Literary tours. Art tours. Any kind of tours you want.' She made a face. 'Even *Emily in Paris* tours.'

Juliet laughed. 'Sounds fun.'

'Oh, it is. Come join one. Free, I mean. Check out my website.' She dug in her bag and gave Juliet a card. 'I'd better run or I'll be late for the grand cheese tour. Weirdly, it's my most popular. Who knew? We'll catch up soon?'

With a wave, she disappeared out of the front door.

Juliet smiled as she got into the lift. She had hardly been here twelve hours and already she was collecting people: a stranger on a train, a charming barman and now a friendly neighbour. That was the great thing about being on your own: you fell into conversation in a way you didn't when you were with someone. It opened your mind.

Back inside, she made a coffee, put her *pain au raisin* on a plate and settled herself at the desk in front of the window. She read through what she had written the day before, resisting the urge to spend time making changes – if she did that, she would be fiddling forever. Forwards was always the key.

But something was playing on her mind. It was all very well meeting new people, but she couldn't fool herself that what she really wanted was to rekindle the friendship that had meant more to her than any other. Perhaps because of the age she had been – wide-eyed, young, impressionable. Perhaps because of the way it had ended. Abruptly.

She had never found anyone to fill that particular hole in her life.

She reached into her laptop bag for her research folder. As a features writer, it was important to see what her competitors were up to, see what the trends were, and she would religiously go through all the monthly magazines and cut out anything of interest. She leafed through the most recent sheaf and found the page she was looking for.

It was a double-page spread of 'Cool Things to do on a Winter Weekend in Paris' from a Sunday supplement. In among the inevitable pictures of pastel macarons, bijoux boutique hotels and padlocks on the Pont Neuf was a photo of a woman in black jeans and a black apron, standing with her arms crossed underneath a sign which read: *She Cried Champagne*.

Juliet read the article again:

Franco-American Nathalie du Chêne moved from New York to Paris when she was nineteen and never left. She was working in retail when she realised what she really wanted to do was run her own bar. And so *She Cried Champagne* was born. Tucked into a backstreet in the hip Sentier district, it serves a hand-picked selection of dazzling wines and, of course, champagne, as well as cheese, charcuterie and small plates. The name of the bar was inspired by a song composed by Carla Bley, and there is cool jazz playing that will make you feel as if you are in a film.

Juliet's heart had turned over as soon as she saw it. Of *course* that was what Nathalie was doing. She was born to be a hostess, born to draw people into a world she had created so they could enjoy themselves. She felt a burst of pride, then envy. Her friend looked no different, still with her trademark bright red bob and the mischievous eyes and the plum lipstick she had always worn. She could feel the confidence radiating off her photograph. Nathalie had always had enough balls for all of them.

She felt a thrill at the possibility of seeing her again. They had kept in touch sporadically over the years. Juliet had been the more assiduous: regular Christmas and birthday cards. There would be radio silence from Nathalie for years, then a lengthy letter filled with apologies and capital letters and exclamation marks and silly drawings. The last one had been some years ago, but then Juliet had also become lax. The last time she had been minded to make contact, there had been little to say that could possibly be of interest. She had hesitated before filling in Nathalie's name on the blank Christmas card, then just signed her name with a big kiss, knowing then that she wouldn't send one the next year.

Now, the thought of Nathalie filled her with yearning.

The unique energy that she had, making you do things you thought you wouldn't dare, like dying your hair a crazy colour.

Or talking to the beautiful boy you secretly admired from afar.

And the spirit of Nathalie was the reason she was here. When Juliet had seen the article, it had given her the push she needed to book her little apartment. Even from a distance, even thirty years later, Nathalie was able to inspire her. You didn't meet people like that every day.

You didn't, unless you were a fool, let them go.

10

The Ingénue

I set off for the language school that afternoon, one street back from the Quai de l'Hôtel de Ville, by the river. It was swarming with students, mostly American, and it was a relief to hear English being spoken. My brain was exhausted from constant translation. I found my name on a list and made my way to the shabby, draughty classroom on the first floor.

It was weird, being back in a learning environment. I'd hated school, the hierarchy and the competition, and was always the last to put my hand up, which meant I was often picked on by the teacher.

The other students all seemed to know each other already, and my mouth was dry with nerves. Especially as no English was to be spoken for the next three hours.

To make matters worse, we were made to stand up and introduce ourselves. In French. I braced myself for humiliation.

'*Je m'appelle Juliet,*' I stammered. '*Je suis de Worcester en Angleterre. Je suis au pair pour une famille à Paris.*' I scrabbled about for something interesting to say about myself that might make some of the others want to know me. I'd tell them I wanted to work for a magazine. '*Je veux travailler pour un magasin...*' I stopped, remembering that *magasin* meant shop, not magazine, and couldn't remember the word for magazine. '*Non. Pour un journal. Non, un magazine...*'

Of course! Magazine was '*magazine*'.

'*Un magazine de quoi?*' asked the tutor, a thin, bespectacled woman with a sour face who did nothing to make me feel confident.

'*Un magazine de mode*,' I said, and she looked me up and down as if to say I really needed to make more effort if I was going to work in fashion.

I sat through six more introductions, not feeling as if any of the students would be my partner in Parisian crime. And then a girl my age sauntered to the front. She had a heart-shaped face, a bright red bob and wore a very short skirt with cowboy boots.

She gave the class a dazzling smile and her luminous eyes dazzled us.

'*Je m'appelle Nathalie*,' she said. '*Je suis de New York. Mon père est français et j'habite ici avec ma tante. Elle est très chic.*' She did a little shimmy à la Marilyn Monroe to illustrate her aunt's glamour, and her armful of bracelets clanked. '*J'adore Paris. J'adore les Gauloises et le pastis et les garçons.*' The teacher scowled at this. '*Je veux être...*' She held out her arms and gave a Gallic shrug with a mischievous grin. '*Quelqu'un.* I want to be someone.'

She spoke with utter self-belief. I imagined her with her aunt in a chic apartment, all cocktail cabinets and potted palms. She was everything I was not. Go-getting. Certain. Ambitious. In a flash, I knew that if I wanted to live my dream, I had to be more like her. No one in the class had paid any attention to anyone else's introduction, but everyone was gazing at Nathalie, rapt.

I wanted her as my friend.

If I was going to get through the next few months, I needed an ally. I suspected there was nothing much about me that would appeal to her, except maybe the fact that I was English. But as I watched her throughout the rest of the lesson, I decided she was worth the risk of rejection. She was smart, quick, funny, bold – but not unkind. She never made a joke at someone else's expense, only her own.

At four o'clock, everybody pushed back their chair and stood up ready to go. I could see she was making for the door. I stepped out in front of her.

'Oh God, sorry. I wasn't looking where I was going.' I was gushing. It was excruciating.

'It's OK.' She went to move past me.

'Hey.' I reached out and put a hand on her arm. She looked up, surprised. 'Do you want to get a coffee?'

She stared at me. I blushed.

'It's just... it's so great to speak English. My brain is mush.'

'Coffee?' she said. 'No. I don't want to get a coffee.'

'Oh. That's OK. Fine.' I felt crushed by her bluntness. This was the rejection I had feared. 'Sorry.'

Then her face broke into a smile. 'I don't want a coffee. I want wine.' She pointed at me. 'I know the cutest bar. Let's go.'

She swept through the doorway and I followed, smitten.

II

Nathalie du Chêne. Bold, funny, loyal. The memory of her lingered as long as the heady scent of vanilla she had trailed. If she shut her eyes, Juliet could smell it now, sweet and intoxicating. Traces of it would linger on her own skin if they spent the evening together, for Nathalie kept you close by her side, arms linked.

By six o'clock, having spent the day writing about her friend, Juliet had convinced herself to reach out. What did she have to lose? She could handle rejection, but if her memory of Nathalie was accurate, she was pretty sure she would be delighted to see Juliet. There was nothing wrong with popping in to the bar for a drink on the off chance that her old friend might be there. Satisfied she had made the right decision, Juliet opened the suitcase she hadn't properly unpacked yet.

What should she wear, to appear as if she hadn't tried too hard, but also look as if she hadn't let herself go? By her photograph, Nathalie seemed as if she had achieved the impossible: maintaining her own identity but moving with the times. She looked super cool but recognisably herself.

Juliet knew she had stopped making an effort with her appearance over the past few years. Working from home meant she didn't try to keep up with fashion like she had when she'd gone to an office every day. Jeans, Converse and sweatshirts were her uniform. In some ways, it was liberating, not to be a slave to hemlines and heels, but just setting foot in Paris gave her an urge to present herself better.

Until she had the chance to go shopping and work her way through her wish list, she would have to make do with what she already had. Of late, she had barely bothered to change if she was going out, unless it was something very dressy. But here; she needed to look pulled together, in the most 'I haven't bothered at all' way.

She pulled her favourite black velvet jeans from her suitcase and put them on with a black polo neck – there were some who said you shouldn't wear black over a certain age, but Juliet didn't subscribe to that philosophy – then tied the Hermès scarf in a loose knot. The silk hung just so, reminding her of the day she had bought it.

She slipped on her blazer, ruffled up her hair, put on her red lipstick and smiled at herself in the mirror. Why had she stopped bothering? Because she hadn't seen the point. Because no one was looking at her anyway. She'd lost her confidence and it seemed easier to make yourself invisible.

Maybe it was no great surprise Stuart had invested so much in his own appearance? Perhaps he'd been horrified by her decline? Had it been her fault, the split? She tutted, realising that yet again she was being too hard on herself. Another habit that came with middle age. She'd never criticised herself in her thirties or forties. It was as if, when you reached a certain age, all those teenage insecurities came flooding back and magnified. That would have to stop. She put her hands on her hips, à la Victoria Beckham, and gave a sultry pout, then laughed.

She looked OK, she thought. She wondered if Nathalie would recognise her as the shy English girl who had hung on her every word. Over the years, she had mused that the loss of her friendship with Nathalie was the biggest price she had paid for what had happened. She'd never had the courage to go back and visit, and it was going to take a bit of nerve now, to see if she could get that friendship back. Thirty years was a long time not to have seen someone, and Nathalie would have packed more into that time than most. She would have made more friends than most people would have had hot dinners. Maybe she didn't need some random pen-pal from her dim and distant past popping up to say hello?

But Juliet's urge to see her friend was stronger than her fear of rejection. She wanted to revel in Nathalie's success. Perhaps some of it would rub off on her? The emotion of the past few months had caught up with her – the decision to separate, the house sale, Izzy leaving for South America, saying goodbye to Stuart – and she needed a shot in the arm. An accomplice. Maybe even a sounding board.

She knew there was another reason too. Maybe Nathalie would know – no, that wasn't fair, to use her for intel. She should have the bloody nerve to do her own dirty work. Her own digging. She'd been pretending all this time she wasn't going to look for him, but just the possibility that they were in the same city, breathing the same air, was starting to bring back memories, triggered by the statue early that morning. Perhaps that was why she felt a little high? Was she being drawn back in?

She steadied herself for a moment. She had to protect herself. She didn't have to revisit the bad bits. She could control this journey if she kept her head screwed on. Going to the Beauboises' house last night had been foolish, but she could easily relegate them to the past. Setting the record straight with the people she had cared for, however . . . That wouldn't do any harm.

She stood for a moment by her laptop, a pulse fluttering at her throat. Of course, she hadn't been able to stick to her resolve not to connect to the Wi-Fi in the apartment – how on earth was she going to keep on top of her emails otherwise? She hated poking out replies with her forefinger on her phone. She'd never mastered the two-thumb technique the kids used, firing off replies in milliseconds.

She called up her search engine. Her fingers hovered over the keyboard, hesitating. The moment she typed his name into the image search, she was crossing a boundary. For if he appeared, what would she do? What was she hoping for? Was she making herself vulnerable – again?

She could handle it, she told herself. She was so much older and wiser than she had been at the time. She was a grown woman. And the need to satisfy her curiosity was greater than her caution. A surge of courage flew to her fingertips as she typed his name.

Olivier Godard.

The Ingénue

Nathalie led me through the winding narrow streets north of the language school.

'This is the Marais. It's the cool place to be. It's not chichi or up itself. It's got an edge to it.'

The *quartier* certainly felt more mysterious, with its mismatched medieval shopfronts that seemed to lean in on each other, not like the rigidly upright Haussmann buildings in most of Paris. I felt as if I was being led into another world, possibly a dangerous one, but I'd have followed Nathalie to the ends of the earth at this point. She stopped eventually, outside a small bar painted dark green, with bicycles lined up outside, wedged between a patisserie and a jeweller.

Nathalie marched in as if she owned the place, and I trailed behind her, somewhat apologetically. I didn't feel as if I belonged somewhere like this. The bar was dark, atmospheric, smoky and full of people who looked as if they had torn themselves away from writing or painting a masterpiece. Nathalie began to greet them, which took a while, with the requisite two kisses on each cheek, and as she introduced me, I had to go through the ritual too.

I tried my best not to feel awkward, but no one batted an eyelid at kissing this stranger from England.

'How do you know these people?' I asked as she sat down at a table.

'Just from around,' she said airily.

She ordered a bottle of wine without asking me what I wanted. I baulked.

'A whole bottle? In the afternoon?'

'Why not?'

'I can't go back half drunk!'

'It's fine – this is France. People expect you to have had a drink. It would be weirder if you hadn't.'

Nathalie happily poured us each a hefty slug and then raised her glass to me.

'Cheers, classmate. Now, I want to know everything about you.'

'Honestly, there's nothing much to tell. I'm really boring.'

She was looking at me with narrowed eyes. 'Tell me about the family you're with.'

'Well, they seem very nice.'

She laughed. 'You're so polite. So English. Come on. Spill.'

'Well, the dad is very charming. Very handsome. Very nice clothes.'

'Very French. What about his wife?'

I made a face. 'She's stunning. But I'm a bit scared of her.'

'Don't be.' Nathalie pointed at me. 'She needs you more than you need her.'

'I don't think she wants me there at all. I think it was her husband's idea to get an au pair.'

'She's very lucky. To have her very own Mary Poppins. What what?' She put on a faux-English accent.

I laughed. 'Yes. But without the magic bag or the talking umbrella.' I sighed. 'The children are adorable, though. I didn't think I'd know what to do with kids, but they're really sweet. And they seem to like me.'

It was strange, how they'd attached themselves to me already. Maybe I was a novelty. Maybe they knew I'd let them get away with things their parents wouldn't. I knew I was a soft touch.

'Well, that's because you're adorable yourself,' Nathalie told me, and I glowed at the compliment. 'I would have loved a nanny like you.' She slouched back in her chair with a sigh. 'I was just stuck in front of the TV all day.'

'That's normal, isn't it? My aunt sticks my cousins in front of the telly from six o'clock in the morning.'

'Yeah. But I bet they're not left on their own, right?'

'No. Of course not.' I was shocked at the thought. 'Were you?'

Nathalie nodded. 'My mum wasn't interested in me. She was ... is ... an alcoholic. My father refuses to believe it. Which is why I'm here and I'm never going back.'

There was a bleakness in her expression that scared me. Part of me wanted to dig deeper, but I didn't really know what to say. I didn't yet have the knack of interrogation. I couldn't bring myself to ask deeply personal questions – not in those days. I was scared of what might come out.

'Oh. Gosh,' I managed instead. 'I'm really sorry.'

'Hey. Don't be. What's the problem? I get to spend the rest of my life in Paris with my amazing aunt. Who seems to like having me around, unlike my actual family.' She grabbed the bottle and topped up our glasses and I sensed the difficult part of the conversation was over. 'I'll take you to her store. She sells second-hand designer clothes. You'll freak when you see them.'

The rest of the afternoon passed in a blur as we demolished the wine, watching the ebb and flow of the clientele. Every single person who came in looked as if they had a story to tell. They looked so different from the people I was used to. Just the assertive way a man would swirl the wine in his glass, or how a woman would light her cigarette from a stranger. I feasted my eyes on them, picking up their characteristics, noting the ones I would adopt in my attempt to become more cosmopolitan.

We were three quarters of the way down our bottle when the door opened and a boy about our age sauntered in. He was wearing a pale-yellow scarf tucked into his overcoat and the sight of it made my heart thump. Sometimes it's just the tiniest thing that starts an obsession. I could imagine it between my fingers, as soft as a feather: it was the colour of ducklings and I wondered if someone had chosen it for him, then tortured myself wondering who.

He unwound it and draped it on the back of a chair, then pulled a paperback from his coat pocket and sat down to read, pausing only to look up at the waiter with a smile and order something. I had never seen anything like him. Shaggy tousled blond hair, cheekbones to die for, and a mouth that was made for... well, the very thought made me melt. He was running his thumb over his bottom lip as he read, and I imagined its warmth. I gulped some wine and caught Nathalie's eye. She was laughing at me.

'Who is that?'

'That's Olivier. Olivier!' She called over to him, and he looked up.

For a moment, his expression didn't change, then his gaze fell on me. I could barely breathe. He stared at me intently for a good five seconds. I couldn't look away.

'Don't get too excited,' murmured Nathalie as he stood up to walk over. 'There's a massive queue.'

'I'll bet.'

'And he's a total heartbreaker. I have wiped up a lot of tears.'

That didn't matter, because I wouldn't have a hope. But even if I wasn't in the running, I smiled to think I was in a city where someone like Olivier could just walk in and sit at the next table. I had never seen anyone like him in Worcester. Not even close. The cafés I went to had spotty youths or fat middle-aged men wiping up their egg and bacon with fried bread. Otherwise, I went to pubs, where the men drank beer as fast as they could.

'Hey, Nathalie.' He pulled out the other chair at our table and sat down. 'Hi,' he said to me, and laid the book he'd been reading on the table. I glanced at the title. *Le Grand Meaulnes*. I didn't know what that meant, but he had seemed lost in the pages.

'Olivier, this is Juliet,' said Nathalie. 'She's at my language school.'

'Hello,' I said, Julie Andrews-prim.

I took in his soft sweater, his long legs in black jeans, the battered baseball boots. He was still looking at me, and I blushed.

'The brightness of those cheeks would shame those stars,' he said. It sounded impossibly sexy in French.

'Are you drunk?' Nathalie asked him.

93

'It's Shakespeare,' I said. *'Romeo and Juliet.'*

Nathalie rolled her eyes. 'Show-off.'

'Doesn't everyone quote Shakespeare to you?' Olivier asked me.

'Not really,' I laughed. 'No one I know knows any. Even though I live near Stratford-upon-Avon.'

'You do?' This seemed to pique his interest.

Nathalie was looking backwards and forwards between us.

I felt awkward, being the centre of attention. 'It's about twenty miles away.'

'Wow.' Olivier had a dreamy look in his eye. 'So, what's your favourite Shakespeare?'

I floundered for a moment. I could answer this question. I'd done plenty of it at school. 'I guess *Macbeth* for drama,' I stumbled. *'A Midsummer Night's Dream* for comedy. But for love – it does have to be *Romeo and Juliet.'*

'Of course.' Olivier nodded, thoughtful. 'But *King Lear.* That is the greatest.' He circled his thumb and forefinger to confirm his opinion.

'I've seen it,' I said, excited. 'At the theatre in Stratford.'

It wasn't quite true. We'd been shown a film of the performance, in English Lit. But I was desperate to impress him, and I was fairly sure he couldn't disprove my claim.

He shook his head in amazement. 'You are so lucky.'

I felt as if we were in a bubble. As if everyone else in the bar had melted into the background, their voices a distant buzz.

'I don't want to break up the Shakespeare Appreciation Society,' said Nathalie. 'But this bottle's empty. Are we going to get another?'

'I will get it.' Olivier stood up and sauntered over to the bar. I gazed after him.

'Oh my God,' breathed Nathalie. 'I've never seen that before. An actual real-life *coup de foudre*.'

13

Juliet's screen was filling with dozens of pictures, for Olivier Godard wasn't that unusual a name.

She searched hungrily for his face, dismissing each one: too gaunt, too old, too young, too dark, too grizzled. She had to look closely, for a person could change a lot in thirty years. Hair loss, weight gain – there were many things that could alter someone's appearance beyond recognition, but his features were embedded so deeply in her memory, she would recognise him.

And then, after she had nearly given up, there he was. Older, but possibly even more alluring for it, wearing his age beautifully. Shorter hair, a few laughter lines, wisdom in his eyes where once there had been the defiance of youth, which, if you knew him, was obviously to cover up his shyness. He was at a table, his right hand curled around a glass, giving a wry half-smile to the camera.

Juliet took in a sharp breath. She could almost smell him, across the years. She imagined his Ralph Lauren mingled with her Dewberry from the Body Shop. Their scents had summed them up, his so sophisticated for the time – she imagined his Parisian *maman* wrapping it up for him for Christmas – hers so mainstream and high street and naïve.

Nowadays, she wore exclusive boutique perfumes with ridiculous names bought from Liberty. Scent was one of her indulgences. It didn't require you to be a particular size, but it always made you feel dressed up and she had a dressing table cluttered with bottles. *Had* had. Most of them had been jettisoned during the pre-move declutter. She reminded herself that was on her list, a new scent for her new incarnation.

She turned her attention back to Olivier's photo. Her indecision hung in the air. Should she dig further, and try to track him down? Try to find out if he was on Facebook or LinkedIn? Most people her age with a child or a job were on one or the other. Or she could see if there were any articles mentioning him – perhaps some infamous lawsuit, if he'd ended up following in his father's footsteps?

Slowly, deliberately, holding her breath, she swapped the search from Images to All.

There were links to any number of Olivier Godards. An economist. A thermal engineer. Several young ones on Facebook. One who had written a book on climate change.

And then – there it was. An article in a French magazine.

'*Olivier Godard – propriétaire de la Librairie des Rêves*,' read the headline.

The owner of The Bookshop of Dreams.

And underneath, a photo of him, her Olivier, leaning against a brick wall with a pile of books in his arms, one leg crossed in front of the other. He was in jeans and a linen jacket, a checked scarf tied in a knot around his neck, and wearing a pair of tortoiseshell glasses. And she felt that same feeling he'd always aroused in her. That peculiar warmth that was both comforting and unsettling. The pulse in her neck was suddenly replicated somewhere else, deep down inside, and she started with pleasure. She hadn't felt that for a long time.

She swallowed as she translated the words under the photo.

After twenty years' as a copyright lawyer, Olivier Godard realised his dream and opened a bookshop in the 10ème, *turning his back on the corporate world. 'I was tired of court cases, and after being in court myself after my divorce –* Juliet's eyes widened – *I wanted to try something new. I haven't had a moment's regret.*

He had made his dream come true. It might have taken half a lifetime, but he had pursued the thing he wanted more than anything else. She was taken back, to the memory of a boy in a bookshop, his eyes shining. And now that boy was a man—

Suddenly, she clicked on the x in the corner of the screen and his photo disappeared. This was too much, too soon. The article was a few years old, yet already it had told her more than she could hope for. But there was still too much in the way. Her guilt and shame and regret felt like an insurmountable obstacle. She was still carrying it with her, and even though it seemed as if Olivier might be in reach, he wasn't, not really. What she had done had made certain of that.

She shut the lid of her laptop, chiding herself for opening Pandora's box. Why prise the lid open now, after so long? She supposed it was because she was back in Paris, indulging in reminiscence, nostalgic for a time when she'd been filled with the thrill of it all, the excitement and the exhilaration of feeling slightly out of control, swept along by new people and new experiences. But maybe this was her last chance to relive those thrills? Jump-start her heart into feeling something more? Something primal and wanton.

She bit her lip, suddenly feeling guilty that perhaps she was betraying Stuart with this urge. She would never discount him as second best. He had been a wonderful husband. She wasn't betraying him. It had been a mutual decision to part, so whatever she craved now, she was entitled to, just as he was entitled to *his* heart's desire.

She chewed on her thumbnail, pacing around the little flat. She was jumping ahead, that was certain. Before she did anything else, she needed to connect with Nathalie. In some ways, she needed friendship more than anything, to give her ballast. Friends were more important than anything in life, for they were what held you together when everything else fell apart.

Juliet left the apartment and ran down the stairs, too excited to wait for the lift, then headed out into the street. She loved Paris at this time, as everyone got ready for the evening ahead. A sense of expectation hung in the air in a way it never did in London, as people stopped by their favourite *épicerie* or *pâtisserie* or *boucherie* to buy something to eat, or picked up a bottle of wine wrapped in tissue paper, or called in to their local bar for an aperitif. Bicycles sped past, groups of runners pounded along the pavement, a gaggle bearing yoga mats headed for an evening class. Conversation spilled out in clouds of white breath. Even the air felt different here. It caressed your cheek, full of promise. London air chivvied and nipped at you and threatened rain.

As she crossed the wide Avenue de l'Opéra, Juliet felt quite at home. She'd regained her confidence since last night's mishap. A lot had changed, of course, but the familiar blue street signs, the cobbles, the awnings outside the bars and cafés and restaurants, set the stage for a new performance. It would be a different cast and a few new props, that was all. It was like unearthing an old dress, or an old coat, and slipping it on, and finding it still fitted you, just so.

She crossed the Place des Victoires, the statue of Louis XIV astride his rearing horse gleaming in the lamplight, and headed up towards the Sentier, the old clothing district. There were still shopfronts crowded with bolts of fabric, but now they were jostling with interior design stores and artisanal cafés. It was gentrification at its best, where old sat alongside new and both flourished from the juxtaposition. She turned into the street she was heading for and searched for the building she had seen in the magazine.

There it was. A flat, rather austere stone front with black metal windows and doors, and above them in blood-red paint were the words: She Cried Champagne. It was a slightly forbidding edifice, but inside the light was low and welcoming. Juliet peered in and could see a black-and-white-tiled floor, wooden tables in burnished oak and red enamel lights hanging from a high ceiling. There were just a few people inside, but Juliet knew that in the next hour or so there would be no chance of a table, or a seat at the bar that ran along the back. She pushed open the door and stepped inside.

The warm, yeasty scent of fresh bread, strong cheese and charcuterie hit her straight away. Along one wall were ranks of open-fronted wooden cubes filled with wine bottles. Behind the bar, a huge mirror had a menu painted on it in white italics: *Croque monsieur au Comté et jambon de pays. Sardines. Saucisson. Brillat Savarin.* In the background, a piano plinked and a girl sang of new love and long nights.

It had a rough glamour that oozed sophistication. Everything, from the thick white china to the chunky glasses and sharp wooden-handled knives, had been chosen to suit the mood: unpretentious, utilitarian, but somehow just right. Who wouldn't want to sit here with their lover, starting with a Campari, the medicinal sweetness giving you a gentle buzz?

A girl in the same long black apron Nathalie wore in the photograph approached her.

'*Bonne soirée, madame.*'

'*Bonne soirée. Je cherche Nathalie? Elle est ici?*' Juliet said, suddenly awkward.

'What is your name, please?' the girl asked in English.

Juliet felt a flicker of disappointment that, despite her best efforts to speak French, it was being ignored. '*Je m'appelle Juliet,*' she replied, not giving in.

The girl nodded and walked away to a door at the back which presumably led to the kitchen. Juliet's heart was thudding as she waited. She tucked her hair behind her ears and tried to catch her reflection in the mirror to check it. Was her makeshift bob holding up, or did it look as if she'd hacked it off with the kitchen scissors?

And then Nathalie was there, walking towards her, her arms crossed just as they were in the photograph. Just as Juliet remembered her, that gesture of semi-defiance, semi-self-protection.

'Nathalie.' Juliet felt a wave of something that could only be love, it was so strong and sweet. She stepped forward with a smile.

'Avez-vous une réservation?'

Juliet stopped in her tracks. 'No,' she replied. 'But I know the owner. I thought she might swing me a table.'

There was one more agonising moment while Nathalie stared at her, then she couldn't maintain her act any longer. She began to laugh.

'Juliet goddam Miller. What the fuck?' She grabbed her and hugged her. 'You didn't think to warn me? You could have messaged me. There's this thing called Facebook, for keeping in touch with old friends.' She punched her on the arm in chastisement. 'I hate surprises.'

'I used to send you messages all the time,' said Juliet. 'You never picked them up.'

'Oh shit.' Nathalie looked shamefaced. 'I'm terrible at getting back to people. I know I am.'

They stood for a moment, the two of them, hugging each other, breathing each other in, feeling the familiarity of each other's warmth, feeling their friendship flicker into life again. Juliet could feel Nathalie's energy, her muscles coiled, ready to spring like a tiger, always in fight-or-flight mode.

Juliet had more friends than she knew what to do with, collected over the years. Friends for different moods: friends for drinking, friends for shopping, friends for mulling over the meaning of life. Friends she adored; friends she sometimes wanted to kill but who somehow redeemed themselves in the nick of time. But none of them had opened her eyes to a new world and a new way of being like Nathalie had.

'It's so good to see you,' she breathed.

Nathalie slid out of her embrace. Emotion was always on her terms. If she hadn't initiated it, she found it claustrophobic. She went behind the bar to the wine fridge, pulling out a bottle of white wine slick with condensation, then took a piece of chalky white cheese from a cabinet to put on a plate and headed over to the nearest table.

'You're honoured to get this.' Juliet watched as she opened the bottle deftly. 'I was saving it for a special occasion.'

She poured an inch into a glass, swirled it around and inhaled deeply, then took a mouthful. She rolled it around her tongue, then nodded in approval and filled Juliet's glass before topping up her own.

Juliet looked around the little bar. It was still early, but she could imagine it full of chatter and laughter, heated debates, whispered compliments, shared secrets, promises, farewells... It held the two of them, the dimmed light making their skin glow, the air filled with the tang of freshly lit candles.

'This place is wonderful,' Juliet said. 'It's like you, come to life.'

Nathalie shone with pride. 'It's the thing I'm most proud of in the world. But it's incredibly hard work. And you can't just walk away. It's a bit like having a child.'

There was a momentary flicker of something in her eyes, but Juliet didn't press her. Not yet. There was time for the hard stuff to come out. She wasn't ready to share either.

Instead, they clinked glasses, and drank. Juliet could tell immediately she was drinking something more interesting than anything they usually had in the fridge at Persimmon Road. The wine was rich with a smoky edge, filling her mouth with a burst of flavour.

'Try this,' said Nathalie, picking up a knife to cut into the cheese. 'It's Pelarton – a goat's cheese from the Languedoc.'

Juliet ate hungrily, realising she hadn't had anything much to eat that day since her pastry. The cheese was fudgy and nutty and she savoured it appreciatively – it was perfectly ripe, and the wine they were drinking set it off to perfection. Somehow everything tasted better in Paris.

'So. Where do we begin?' asked Nathalie. 'I mean, what are you even doing here?'

'To cut a long story short, I've just separated from my husband. So I've booked an apartment for the whole of November. I've given myself thirty days in Paris to "rediscover" myself.' She put quote marks around the word *rediscover* with her fingers.

'Well,' said Nathalie, 'you've come to the right place. Though I'm sorry about your separation.'

'Oh, it's fine,' Juliet assured her. 'We just grew apart. We still love each other, blah, blah, blah, but we have nothing in common anymore. We decided to separate and "find" ourselves.' Another set of quote marks around *find*. 'Oh, I'm making it sound so corny and self-indulgent. But, honestly, we are still the best of friends. It was all amicable.'

Nathalie raised an eyebrow. 'Is there such a thing as amicable? Really?'

'Actually, yes. I'd still trust Stuart with my life. There's no one I'd trust more in the world.'

This was true. Stuart played with the straightest bat. He was disarmingly honest and never tried to fiddle anything. He disapproved of people who massaged insurance claims, or put things through on company expenses that were clearly for personal use. He wasn't preachy, he simply felt life was easier if you played by the rules. Even if you didn't agree with the people making them up.

Nathalie's eyes widened. 'Wow. I don't know if I could give up someone like that.'

Juliet sighed. 'I don't mean this in a weird way, but we became like brother and sister. We love each other dearly, but . . .' She shrugged, embarrassed, but also feeling protective of Stuart.

'You don't wanna jump him anymore?'

Juliet laughed, remembering how great Nathalie was at getting to the point. 'Exactly. I know it seems a very superficial reason to end a marriage. But I guess we both felt there was something else out there, and if we didn't change things, we'd never know.'

'That's really brave.'

'I suppose so.' She held up her glass. 'Anyway. Here I am. With Paris at my feet. Thirty days to find a new me.'

'And a new man?' Nathalie's eyes twinkled.

'Oh God. I don't think so. That's the funny thing. I'm not all that interested. I expect Stuart will find someone straight away. Men always do.' She still wasn't sure how she was going to feel about that.

'Where's he going to find someone better than you?'

'At the climbing wall. Or on a marathon. He's become

a fitness freak. And I just can't get enthusiastic about running or cycling or any of it.'

'No.' Nathalie looked unimpressed as she cut another piece of cheese. 'So tell me what else you've been doing. I remember you were working on a magazine. I remember you sending me a cutting of your first article.'

Juliet looked down at the table, stroking the worn wood. 'Oh my God, that was years ago. "How to shop for vintage clothes". It was your aunt who inspired me.'

'I know. I showed it to her. She wondered where you'd gone. I told her what you said – a family crisis.' Nathalie looked at her over the rim of her glass. 'Is that really what happened?'

Juliet knew she was displaying the classic signs of lying. Touching her face. Avoiding eye contact by looking at the crumbs of cheese on her plate. 'Crisis, certainly.'

'You can tell me. You know I'm unshockable.'

'I don't know if I'm ready yet.' Juliet looked up. 'It's hard. Remembering. And I don't want it to spoil my time here. It's weird. It's as if I need to revisit everything to work through it. But...' She felt tears gather in her eyes.

'Hey.' Nathalie put a hand on hers. 'It doesn't matter anymore. It's wonderful to see you. Let's draw a line and start again.'

'I will tell you, eventually.' Juliet drew in a shaky breath. 'It's been a bit emotional, that's all. Leaving Stuart. Being back in Paris. Finding you.'

'I get it.' Nathalie nodded. 'I have a lot of questions but...' She shrugged.

Juliet smiled, grateful that she wasn't persisting. Old Nathalie would have been on her like a dog with a bone, but she guessed everyone grew up and learned when to drop a subject. And she was grateful that she hadn't mentioned Olivier. There was plenty of time to open that door, if she wanted.

'So, do you still work on a magazine?' Nathalie asked.

'I'm freelance now. I write lifestyle features for anyone who'll have me. And for the past ten years I've been a ghostwriter – mostly for reality stars and influencers and celebrities. And manuals – decluttering, manifesting, parenting teenagers – that kind of thing.'

'Seriously? That's awesome. Would I have read any of them?'

Juliet got out her phone. 'It's easier if I show you.' She had an album of screenshots of the covers of the books she had ghosted. She scrolled through them, and Nathalie gasped in admiration at some of the names she had been behind.

'No way! I love that actress. Was she nice to you? Or was she a total diva?'

They spent the next ten minutes gossiping and sharing anecdotes. Nathalie told her about all the stars and celebrities who had been in She Cried Champagne, for it was a favourite haunt for those in the know.

It was as if the years had rolled away as they laughed and speculated and finished each other's sentences.

'Do you remember those introductions we did at the language school?' Nathalie sat back in her chair, wistful. 'We were so green and naïve, but here we are. Wise and successful and completely amazing. To us, I say!' She clinked her glass against Juliet's.

'I'm so glad I came here,' said Juliet softly. 'I nearly didn't.'

'I'd have killed you if you hadn't. Thirty days? I'm going

to get you right back on track. We are going to have such fun.'

All the fun she had never got to have in the end, thought Juliet.

Nathalie was looking around the bar, which was starting to fill up. 'Listen, I'd better get back to work. We're down a waiter tonight so I need to be hands-on.'

'Oh God, I'm sorry I distracted you.'

'It's fine. I'm the boss.' Nathalie turned the bottle upside down and put it back in the ice bucket. 'Hey, let's meet for lunch tomorrow. It's easier to take time off then.'

'I would love that.'

Nathalie pulled out her phone. 'Let's trade numbers. I'll WhatsApp you where to meet. It won't be early – I have to go to the market first.'

'That's fine by me.' She could do some more work, Juliet thought. She hadn't told Nathalie about her book yet. There'd be time over lunch.

Nathalie hooked an arm around her neck. 'Welcome back, old friend.'

It was so nice, thought Juliet, to have the warmth of friendship. One of her reasons for coming to Paris was so she wouldn't be under the microscope of her friends at home, asking if she was OK, if she'd found somewhere to live, someone to date. They would over-analyse her progress, possibly with an element of self-interest, in case what had happened to her happened to them. She knew how much they all cared, but she wanted some time on her own to figure out who she was and what she wanted. Getting Nathalie back was the perfect substitute. Someone who knew her, but no one else in her life, so she could behave as she wished without being the subject of speculation, or any of it getting back to Stuart as idle gossip. It made her feel safer, secure, more confident. Thank goodness she'd had the courage to come back, she thought, as she slipped out of the bar and into the night's embrace.

Back at the apartment, Juliet looked at her watch. She might have had half a bottle of wine, but she felt wide awake, the memories buzzing in her brain. She knew from experience that it was important to seize the moment and write while the images were vivid, for they might fade into obscurity and become blurred if she waited. So she made herself a strong black coffee and sat down at her desk.

14

The Ingénue

'You can borrow whatever you want.' Nathalie's aunt waved her hand around the racks of clothing in her tiny emporium.

I felt completely overwhelmed. It was heaven. Reams of as-new clothing, beautifully laundered and pressed, at a fraction of the price they must have cost.

'Are you sure?'

'Yes. Just look after them. They've already been worn, so what does it matter?'

Gigi was as chic as Corinne, but not nearly as terrifying. She had a kindness and warmth that made me understand why Nathalie adored her so much. She'd found her niche here in Paris and was an underground success. Those in the know flocked here for last season's cast-offs. It was smart and I felt nothing but admiration as I searched through the hangers. Silk and suede and lace; chiffon and bouclé and merino slipped through my fingers. There were shoes and boots too, and a couple of belts, and several scarves. I felt giddy with it all as I recognised some of the labels – Agnès B, Chloé, Lanvin. I lifted up a fine sweater and felt a thrill as I wondered what I would look like, what I would become, in these clothes.

'Try this.' Nathalie handed me a black leather skirt.

'Do you think?'

'Yes!' said Nathalie, in that tone of voice I'd come to recognise, the one that urged you to take chances.

I shimmied into it, amazed that it fitted. I did up the zip, then pulled on a lace shirt to go with it. I slipped into a pair of high-heeled ankle boots and gasped: I looked a stone lighter, for the clothes were fitted and tailored, designed to flatter. The leather and lace clung to me and I felt a confidence I'd never experienced before. I couldn't believe the power a simple change of clothing had given me. It frightened me a little bit. What would this new Juliet be capable of? I wondered, as I turned to the side and admired my sleek new look.

For a moment, Olivier's face flittered into my head. What would he think if he saw me? I couldn't stop thinking about him. We had talked for ages that afternoon, Nathalie barely getting a word in, until I realised I had to get back to help with bedtime. He'd told us about a gig he was going to at the weekend, in Pigalle. My stomach had been in curlicues since, knowing I might see him.

'Try this.' Gigi walked over with a scarf and looped it round my neck, foulard-style.

I put up my hand to touch it and felt the sticky slither of silk. I could see the name in one corner.

'Hermès?'

'Every girl should have one,' Gigi told me.

It hung there, around my neck, and transformed my outfit from obvious to subtle. I felt incredibly grown-up and sophisticated. A step closer to the person I dreamed of being.

'I want to buy this,' I said, knowing it would transform everything else I had. I looked at the price tag. It was still astronomical.

'Give me a few francs a week,' said Gigi. 'It doesn't matter how long it takes.'

I didn't know how I would ever repay her generosity.

I was babysitting for the Beauboises that evening when I heard the front door bang just before ten o'clock. I rushed out into the hall and down the corridor, alarmed, but it was them.

'You're back early.' I smiled at them, then realised Corinne looked tear-stained and Jean Louis a little strained. 'The children were as good as gold. I haven't heard a sound.'

Corinne managed a smile. Her eyes were red, and there were black circles under them. '*Merci.*' She turned to Jean Louis. '*Je me couche. Bonne nuit.*'

He went to kiss her on the cheek, but she jerked her head away and walked off towards their bedroom. Jean Louis let out a long sigh.

'Is everything OK?' I asked.

'Yes,' he said. 'She needs to sleep. We should not have gone out. But...' He shrugged, as if to say there was no arguing with Corinne.

I could see the last thing he wanted to do was follow her to the bedroom.

'Would you like something to drink?' I asked him.

He looked grateful. '*Un petit café, peut-être. Merci.*'

We walked towards the kitchen together. I could feel

the tension in the house since their return, and it unsettled me. I wasn't sure if my presence added to it, or defused it. Or perhaps even caused it – it must be hard having a stranger in your home. You couldn't really be yourself or relax properly, though I tried to be unobtrusive.

I had noticed that Corinne's mood depended on how tired she was and how much chaos there was in the house. She had a short fuse when she was under pressure. She wasn't one of those serene types who glided through the day. It was like living on eggshells, for you never quite knew which Corinne you were going to get. I had learned, though, to ride out her moods, that she didn't mean to be snappy, that she apologised quickly once she realised how her mood was affecting everyone. In some ways, she was more difficult to handle than the children. I sometimes felt it was Corinne who needed looking after, not them.

As I fiddled with the coffee maker that I still hadn't quite mastered, Jean Louis produced a bottle of brandy. I'd been meaning to head off back to my room, but when I handed him his coffee, he nodded his head towards the drawing room in invitation. I felt it would be rude to refuse, and he looked as if he needed company, and he was easy to talk to – I felt quite comfortable trying to speak French to him and was eager to get in some practice. He never made me feel an idiot if I got it wrong, just corrected me in a kind way.

He put on just a couple of lamps so the room felt cosy and poured us each a glass of brandy. I took mine from him, tentative, as I wasn't used to slugging a nightcap so close to bedtime. He sank into one sofa with a sigh of what sounded like relief, tipped his head back and shut his eyes, as if the evening had been a terrible ordeal.

I sat on the sofa opposite him and took a sip: a mouth-ful of fire that tasted like burnt apples.

'Oh!' I spluttered in surprise. 'Oh.'

'*C'est Calvados.*' He didn't open his eyes, but he was smiling as he took a sip himself. 'From my grandparents' farm in Normandie.'

'*C'est delicieux.*' I took another sip, imagining an orchard somewhere in the depths of the French country-side, the trees swinging with rosy apples.

'We go there, with the children, for holidays. My heart is there. I hope to live there one day...' He drifted off.

I took another sip of the drink and curled my feet up under me, sinking back into the plump sofa cushions. My limbs were languid, and I felt a gentle thrumming in my blood. It was my heartbeat, I realised. I should say goodnight, go to bed, but I felt pinned to the sofa, almost as if I'd been drugged.

Eventually, Jean Louis opened his eyes and leaned forward. 'Thank you, for being so kind. To the children.'

'They're lovely.'

'They are. But Corinne... she finds that they can be mischievous.'

'They're very well-behaved,' I defended them. 'Mostly.'

A judicious finger wag usually stopped the big two in their tracks if they were being naughty. They wanted to behave, but the arrival of Arthur had turned their world upside down somewhat, and they were always pushing, looking for attention from their mum. Unfortunately, they got the wrong sort when they played up, and often everyone ended up in tears.

'Still, it is not easy for her.' Jean Louis paused for a moment, choosing his words, not wanting to be disloyal, perhaps. 'Corinne has always been a career woman. She's very talented.' He waved his hand around the room. 'This is all her.'

The room really was like something out of a magazine. Nothing matched, yet everything went together. I couldn't imagine having the courage to mix the things she had: a yellow sofa with black-and-white-striped silk cushions; modern art next to old-fashioned oil paintings; huge flower arrangements in oriental vases. If I'd done it, it would just look a mess.

'She's really good.'

'Yes. But interior design is hard and the clients are demanding. I don't think she is ready to go back to work.'

'But if she wants to . . . ?'

'Yes, I know.' He looked troubled, though. 'I don't want her to risk her reputation. It is a fickle business. Word gets around.'

I hadn't thought of that. I could only imagine the cut-throat competitiveness of the Parisian interior design scene.

'I guess you need to be tough.'

'You do. And Corinne is very vulnerable, though she won't admit it. Arthur was a difficult birth. The first few months were very hard. He did not sleep.'

'He does now.' Arthur had settled down for me tonight without a murmur, all squidgy and warm in his little romper suit.

'Yes. Now. But she is still very tired. I am worried.' He paused. 'Would you keep an eye on her for me? If something troubles you . . .'

'Of course.'

I was touched by his concern. But he was right to be

worried. Corinne was on edge a lot of the time: she was jumpy, and her clothes might be immaculate, but her nails were bitten to the quick. She didn't eat much, just drank a lot of black coffee and smoked a lot of cigarettes.

'Thank you. Now we have you, maybe it will all be OK.' He raised his glass to me. 'You have changed our lives.'

I squirmed a bit, overwhelmed, not used to being appreciated. We didn't really do compliments in my family.

'I love being here,' I told him. 'I love Paris. I love the children and your home.'

'If there is anything wrong ever, please say.' His eyes were burning pretty intensely. I could see flecks of copper in them, glinting in the lamplight. 'I'd do anything to keep you.'

'Everything's fine,' I assured him. 'I'm very happy. *Très, très heureuse.*'

My words were heartfelt. In just a few days, I had experienced more than I ever had in Worcester. I was speaking French, not quite like a native, but I was making myself understood. Every morsel of food was out of this world, from the morning croissant to the last nibble of cheese. I'd got clothes that made me feel like I'd stepped out of French *Vogue*. And tomorrow I was going out with Nathalie. My stomach flipped at the possibilities that might bring.

I would stay here forever if I could.

15

Juliet was jolted out of her sleep by her phone ringing the next morning. She peered at the screen: Stuart. Immediately, she thought something must have happened to one of the children, so she grabbed it. It was a knee-jerk reaction, from over twenty years of mothering, to assume a crisis. 'Hello?'

'Hey.' His voice was relaxed, so she fell back on the pillows, relieved. After so many years together, she could tell straight away if something was wrong or not. 'Just thought I'd see how things are going in gay Paree?'

She flipped her phone onto speaker so she could look at the time. Eight-thirty. Damn. She was going to miss her morning run because she wanted to go to the market early. She couldn't admit that to Stuart, she thought, smiling. He would crow if he thought she was getting into running. But there was a big difference between looking after yourself and becoming obsessed.

'Oh, that's nice. Um ... good.' Her voice sounded husky with sleep.

'Have I woken you up?' He knew her so well.

She cleared her throat, feeling guilty at being caught

out. Then realised she had no reason to feel guilty, or lie about the fact she was still in bed. 'Yes. I pulled a *nuit blanche*.'

'Eh?'

'French for an all-nighter. Well, nearly an all-nighter. I got to bed at three o'clock.'

'Blimey!'

She laughed. 'Don't worry. I wasn't out on the town. I was writing. How are you?'

'Yeah, good. It's a bit weird. I've unpacked all my stuff but it doesn't feel like home yet.'

'It'll take a while, I guess.' Privately, Juliet didn't think the flat he'd chosen would ever feel homely. It was too sleek, all shiny surfaces and everything hidden away behind soft-close doors. She yearned for crooked walls and wonky floors.

'I set up the rower. It arrived yesterday.'

'Oh.'

'It's an amazing bit of kit. I've just rowed across Lake Zurich. Virtually, obviously.'

'Wow.'

'Hang on two secs.' She heard the whine of his Nutribullet and imagined the green sludge he'd be whizzing up for his breakfast. 'Sorry. So what are you up to today?'

'I need to go to the market. Then I'm going to see if I can manoeuvre myself into the bath. It's about the size of a recycling box.' She laughed. 'Classic Paris apartment sanitation facilities.'

'Great.' There was a small pause. 'Well, I just thought I'd make sure you were OK.'

'I'm all gravy.'

This time, they laughed together. It was one of Nathan's sayings, which they adopted when they were pretending to be down with the kids. Then they stopped laughing and there was an awkward silence.

'Ju...'

'Yes?' For a moment, she thought he was going to say he missed her.

'Do you know what the Netflix password is?'

She gave a sigh of relief. She wasn't sure if she'd have been able to return the sentiment. She realised she'd been so busy, she'd barely thought about him.

'I'll text it to you.'

'Thanks. I want to catch up on the new series of *Ozark*.'

He'd taken their big telly. She didn't mind. It had been almost seamless, the division of who got what. There was hardly anything they had fought over. That kind of said it all.

'I'd better get going,' Juliet said, 'or the market will be shutting.'

'Sure. Maybe we could do a Zoom with the kids sometime?'

'Definitely. If we can get everyone together in the same time zone.' Was there an edge to her voice? She didn't mean there to be.

There was a small pause.

'I think it's important. For them,' said Stuart.

'Of course it is. I'll be there, whenever you can organise it.'

'OK. I'll WhatsApp them on the family group chat.'

She felt a flicker of guilt that she hadn't been on it much lately. Should she be sending them daily reports of what she'd been up to? Probably not. It was funny how being in another country helped you unpeel yourself. In England, at Persimmon Road, she used to send messages each morning, bright and breezy with a subtext of anxiety, for she needed constant reassurance they were OK. They'd only replied occasionally. She was used to being kept in the loop on a need-to-know basis.

It had taken Paris to blot up that anxiety. To give her something else to think about other than fretting over her children's whereabouts and well-being. Of course they were OK. She would hear soon enough if they weren't. That was how it worked, when they left home. She'd written about it, how to sever the umbilical cord and give them their freedom. It had been a million times more difficult than anything that had happened when they were small. Teething and toddler tantrums; SATs and sleepovers – it had all been a breeze in comparison to letting go and allowing them to make their own mistakes. Loss of control was so alien. But you had to do it.

The pay-off was your own freedom. The worry never left you, of course, but the trick was not to worry until there was something to worry about. They'd be doing all sorts of things that would give her sleepless nights if she knew, she was sure.

She thought of her own mother, and what she'd have felt if she had known what twenty-year-old Juliet had got up to. She wouldn't have slept a wink.

'Right. I'll leave you to it, then.' Stuart broke her reverie. 'Speak soon.'

'Speak soon,' Juliet echoed.

He sounded very happy, she thought as she hung up. He was obviously relishing singledom. Or was there a hot date on the horizon? It was possible, in this day and age, to fix yourself up almost immediately should you feel like it. She wasn't quite sure how she felt, about Stuart hitting the dating scene. She wouldn't be jealous, but it would be strange.

She had asked him, when they'd first discussed their possible separation, if there was someone else.

'Because I'd much rather know,' she had told him. 'And I wouldn't blame you if there was. I know I haven't been very . . .' What was the right word? 'Attentive' seemed horribly euphemistic. 'You know. It's not exactly *Fifty Shades of Grey* in the bedroom these days. It's not your fault, by the way. Or anything to do with you. It's me.'

'Don't apologise.' He had looked upset on her behalf. 'I know you're finding it difficult. Please don't blame yourself. And I promise there's no one else,' he'd assured her. 'But I'm worried that one day there might be. And I don't ever want to hurt you. I don't ever want to betray you.'

She'd admired his honesty. She'd appreciated the fact that he hadn't made her feel bad for her lack of enthusiasm where sex was concerned. She'd spoken to him about the menopause; about how negative she felt about herself, and about how it was normal for women of her age to go through this. She'd done loads of research for features she'd written, and she wanted him to understand the effect the change in hormones was having on her so he wouldn't take it personally.

She'd been braced for it for years before it arrived, in all its sweaty, mood-swinging, waist-thickening glory. She felt like an imposter in her own skin, dreary and sluggish where once she had been vibrant. The nights were the worst: she lay, overheated, teeth gritted with raging insomnia as the hours dragged by. In the end, she had gone into the spare room to try to get a night's sleep, unable to bear the heat of Stuart's body next to her, let alone the sound of his stertorous breathing that wasn't quite snoring.

And that was how they'd come to have separate rooms.

'Oh God,' her friends would say. 'What bliss.'

Somehow, they had all forgotten the intimacy they'd once craved, sleeping tangled up in their partners; those days when you were almost as one, unable to get close enough. With middle age, distance was the holy grail.

And separate rooms had led to separate lives. Had she subconsciously pushed Stuart to their decision? Could she have done something to prevent it? She could have forced herself to pretend to be enthusiastic. Kitted herself out in some new knickerage and engaged him in a bit of adventurous role play. But she had felt self-conscious about gaining weight when he was losing so much, and wouldn't have felt confident strutting about in black satin Coco de Mer wielding a spanking paddle. Not that she was enormous, but she'd always been able to wear what she wanted and now, with that extra half a stone mostly settling around her middle, she felt her choice was restricted, and she was much more comfortable covering up and not drawing attention to herself. Once, a few weeks' calorie counting and a couple of swims a week at the local pool would have seen off those unwanted pounds, but she needed the comfort of carbs and couldn't be bothered to put more exercise into her diary. She didn't *care* enough about herself to take control. She knew full well this was symptomatic of the menopause, and hoped that one day she might get her mojo back.

Strangely, now she was in Paris, the city of the thin, she felt liberated, and much more willing to dress up, albeit it for herself. And there seemed to be a point to self-care and exercise. As if somewhere between St Pancras and the Gare du Nord, she had stepped back into her old self and rediscovered a lightness of heart. Had the weight of her marriage been that inhibiting? Had Stuart been burdened by it too, the strain of operating as a twosome?

As their nest emptied, marriage felt cumbersome, riddled with compromise, from what they had for supper to what they watched on telly – in the end, they had bought two: the big screen for Stuart's sport and a little one for Juliet's occasional box-set binges. You could never truly be yourself, always bowing to the other's desires or feeling guilty because you'd won the toss to eat the wild mushrooms with pappardelle rather than risotto. They were tenants in common: in the past couple of years, they had felt like lodgers, passing like ships in the night, nodding at each other by the fridge or bumping into each other outside the bathroom.

Now, they could both do exactly as they pleased. And Juliet was determined to lean into it. She lay there for a few more moments, dozing. She could sense the sunlight on the other side of the grey linen curtains but didn't quite have the energy to get up and open them yet. Her dreams, once she had finally climbed into bed, had been torrid. Olivier's presence had been there on the edge of it all, and she could still feel him there now she was awake, so real that she had thought she might see him standing next to the bed when she opened her eyes again.

He wasn't, of course.

She threw back the covers and jumped out of bed. She

needed to go shopping. The little supermarket round the corner was convenient, but she wanted to stock up on real food, and that meant the market in the Place de la Bastille, which took place on a Thursday. She pulled on jeans and a sweater and grabbed her basket, heading out into the street.

She was a little later than she'd intended to be, so she plucked up the courage to take one of the bicycles available for anyone to use. She'd downloaded the app and unlocked a bike with the barcode. Paris was full of cyclists nowadays. She'd seen women dressed in skirts and high heels pedalling off to work with not a hair out of place; men in pristine suits and shining brogues with their briefcases strapped behind them. You needed a little bit of nerve and to stay alert, but it seemed the most practical way to get around if you were in a hurry.

It took a few minutes for her to get accustomed to riding a bike again, but before long she was sailing happily along the Rue de Rivoli and had soon arrived in the Place de la Bastille. She docked her bike, feeling very pleased with herself, then wandered amidst the stalls sprawling up the middle of the Boulevard Richard Lenoir, feasting her eyes on the extravagant displays, resisting the urge to buy everything. She was here for four weeks. She would have enough time to work her way through all the temptations.

She stopped in front of a tomato stall, marvelling at the shapes and sizes and colours, from deep purple to blood-red to citrine-yellow. Next door, lettuces were piled up, from pointed and pale green to frizzy mop heads in incarnadine red, and next to them were radishes, plumply pink and white.

The neighbouring cheese stall lured her with its scent

of stable floor. Tiny milk-white goat's cheese sat next to slabs of golden Comté and wedges of marbled Roquefort – there must have been fifty, a hundred, to choose from, their names and prices displayed in curly black writing. A flower stall was crammed with bunches of winter blooms wrapped in brown paper and tied with string. The salty brine of the sea drifted over from an oyster stall. A tower of freshly baked boules was gradually shrinking and she snapped one up before they all disappeared.

There were queues everywhere, each customer talking earnestly to the stallholder about their purchase, taking a sample from a proffered knife before committing. Tasting and choosing was a serious business, and no one got impatient, no matter how in-depth the conversation between shopper and seller.

After making her way down one side of the market and up the other, Juliet decided on a rotisserie chicken, spatch-cocked and roasted in harissa until the skin turned red-gold. With that went salad things, some *saucisson sec*, a slab of duck *rillette*. With care, this haul should last her a few days for lunch and dinner, supplemented by daily bread. She also bought fat lemons, a packet of butter studded with salt crystals from the Camargue and some coffee beans.

And then she hovered in front of the rows of pastries, each a work of art. *Un plaisir coupable* – a guilty pleasure – to have as a reward when she had finished two more chapters. *Tarte aux pommes, mille-feuilles, religieuses, èclairs, babas au rhum, Mont Blancs*, a coffee-soaked *opéra*... In the end, she chose a praline-stuffed *Paris-Brest*, and a bag of madeleines to dip into her coffee.

Her bulging basket was heavy as she made her way

back, and she decided not to risk her luck putting it on the back of a bicycle. Instead, she meandered home through the Marais. The little streets were thick with tourists and Parisiennes alike, heading for the bustling cafés and restaurants offering bagels and falafel and spicy kebabs.

She passed the little café where she and Nathalie had hung out. Where she had met Olivier for the first time. It hadn't changed a bit. If she stepped towards the door and breathed in, it even smelled the same, minus the cigarette smoke. She could see the table they used to commandeer. For a moment, she was tempted to go in and have a coffee, telling herself it was research so she could get everything right – the colour of the paint, the etchings on the glass. But she didn't have time now. Nathalie had messaged Juliet to meet her at a restaurant called Pink Mama up in the *9ème*, so she had to get back, contort herself into the bath and get dressed up. She would come back later in the week to try on unsuitable shoes, and exotic perfume, and buy something from *Mariage Frères*, the tea merchants, with its tantalising display of tins inscribed with exotic names.

An hour later, she was bathed, coiffed and had put on the one little black dress she'd brought with her. With her flat black boots, it didn't look too formal, but she felt as if she was making an effort. Once she'd put her blazer over it with the sleeves pushed up, and knotted her trusty scarf at her throat, she felt confident.

On her way out, she met Melissa again in the foyer, and told her where she was going.

'Pink Mama's amazing. It's an Instagram dream,'

Melissa told her. 'It's perfect for a girls' lunch. You'll love it.'

'I'm meeting my oldest friend. We haven't seen each other for over thirty years.'

Melissa looked astonished. 'Thirty years?'

Juliet realised Melissa probably wasn't even thirty herself. 'It feels like five minutes.'

'You'll have a lot to catch up on. Hey, listen, if you're free tomorrow evening, why don't you come for a drink? We're having a few people round.'

'That would be lovely.' Juliet was delighted by the invitation.

'It's nice to have someone next door who's here for a while. Usually, people stay for a week at the most.'

'That's very kind of you. Can I bring anything?'

'Oh no. Just yourself.' Melissa looked pleased too. 'Around seven?'

'I'll see you then.'

Wedged into the point where two streets converged, Pink Mama was, as its name suggested, spectacularly pink, with lush greenery spilling out of the windowsills and down the facade. Inside, a mismatched display of pictures and mirrors and plants were crammed onto the walls and floors in a blowsy and unashamed show of maximalism. Juliet loved it on sight for its lack of restraint and joie de vivre.

She wished more than anything that Izzy was here with her. It was just the sort of place she would love. As soon as she was back from South America, they would come here, to Paris. Izzy was a committed tourist and loved a souvenir – Juliet could already imagine her buying an

Eiffel Tower key ring and a striped Breton top and a beret and begging to take a river trip along the Seine.

In that moment, Juliet suddenly missed her daughter's energy and her wide-eyed love of everything life had to offer. When she was flagging, Izzy always lifted her spirits with her glass-half-full attitude. Juliet was pretty optimistic, but Izzy made everyone else look like Eeyore. This place was like her daughter come to life: youthful and exuberant, it brought a smile to everyone's face as they walked in.

She made her way to the top floor, where the walls and roof were entirely made of glass, ivy-clad lanterns swinging from the rafters. Nathalie waved at her, a bottle of rosé already open. She jumped up, chic in a white tweed jacket and very wide palazzo pants, the glamorous antithesis of her working self.

'You do not want to know what I had to do to get a table here,' she laughed.

'I love it,' said Juliet. 'It's the prettiest restaurant I've ever been in. And look at you!' She touched the white camellia on her lapel. '*Très Coco Chanel.*'

'It's my rebellion against always wearing black in the bar.'

Juliet made a face, indicating her own outfit. 'I need your top shopping tips. I've got a whole bucket list of stuff I want. I threw out nearly all my wardrobe when we emptied the house. I want to start again.'

'You don't need to ask twice. Think of me as your personal shopping queen.'

'Does your aunt still have her shop?' Gigi must be old by now. Eighty perhaps?

Nathalie sighed. 'I'm afraid Gigi passed away a few

years ago. She was the reason I was able to open the bar. She left everything to me.'

Juliet touched her arm. 'I'm so sorry.'

'She meant the world to me. But she would be so proud of what I have done. The song I named it after – she had that at her funeral. She was so into her jazz. Still going to festivals six months before she passed.'

The two of them sat down. Juliet had a full view of the sun-drenched room, with its wooden floor and the view out over the street, and the turquoise bar at the end.

Nathalie filled her glass and proposed a toast.

'To renewed friendships. I have a feeling we are going to be very good for each other. And I think you've come back into my life for a reason.'

'Oh?'

Nathalie made a tentative face. 'I've got a proposition. Stop me right away if I'm being presumptuous – there is nothing more annoying than someone who thinks they have a great idea when actually it's terrible – but . . .' She trailed off, suddenly uncertain.

'Go on.'

'It's something I've been thinking about for a while. And a few people have suggested it. I haven't done anything about it because I wouldn't have a clue where to start. Which is where you come in.'

Juliet reached out and put her hand over Nathalie's. 'I think I know what you're going to say.' She smiled. 'A book. You want to write a book.'

Nathalie blinked. 'How did you know?'

'When I left yesterday, I started thinking what a great story She Cried Champagne would make. I was going to suggest it to you. And now you've told me about Gigi too, I'm even more convinced.'

'Oh my God. It's meant to be, right?'

'Maybe it's synchro-destiny? Maybe, when I saw you in that magazine, something made me get back in touch for a reason?'

'Synchro-destiny, fate, luck – I don't care what it was. I'm just so thrilled you think it's a good idea.'

'I do. But tell me your vision. How *you* see the book. What makes it special? What makes it stand out?'

Juliet was asking the questions she always asked her clients, for she knew if they couldn't answer them, it would be hard to find the magic.

Nathalie took a gulp of wine and looked around the room for a moment before starting to speak.

'I see it like a diary and a recipe book and a wine guide and a love letter to Paris. Very intimate and revealing and raw – all the tears that went into She Cried Champagne, like Gigi dying, but also the laughter. And the people. All their stories. My staff and my customers and the people I buy from. All the mistakes I made and the arguments I had and how I nearly walked away ten million times but something drove me to carry on.' Nathalie was nearly in tears, overwhelmed by the emotion. 'It was so tough, but if I inspire one other person to live their dream, it will be worth it. And if not, they can have a little bit of my dream in their own home. They can make my grilled crottin, or my crème brûlée, and pretend they are there with me. I want great photographs but great words too. I want to make people cry. I want them to feel everything I felt. My frustration, my fear, my terror. But also my joy. I want them to feel my joy.'

She sat back, exhausted.

Juliet nodded.

'I can see it. Even better, I can feel it.' She put her fist to her stomach. 'There aren't many projects I can feel in my gut. And I wouldn't do it if I didn't get that tingle of excitement. I would love to help you. I think it would almost write itself. Although . . .' She held up a finger. 'A book like this is complicated. It's a competitive market. There's a lot of technical skill that goes into making it balanced. There's a lot to think about.'

'I don't doubt it,' said Nathalie. 'It's always the simple things that need the most care. I know that better than anyone. There's nothing to hide behind.'

'Exactly. But we can put together a proposal. Write as much of it as we can.'

'I have a photographer I'd love to use. One of my wait-resses. Her work is very stylish but playful. She embraces imperfection – makes something a little rough around the edges look more appetising.'

'I'm all for that,' said Juliet. 'Perfection is so intimidating.' She held out her hand for Nathalie to shake. 'I'm here until the end of the month. Let's see what we can do.'

'What about your fee? I'm not expecting a favour. I want to be businesslike.'

'This would be a passion project for me. Something I really believe in. I think you've got it all in there. I'd just guide you.'

Nathalie looked doubtful. 'OK. But while you're here, you can eat at the bar any time you like. On me.'

Juliet sat back with a smile. 'Fair exchange is no robbery.'

She was genuinely excited. She hadn't mentioned her own book to Nathalie. Not yet. She knew Nathalie would worry she was taking away from her time. But Juliet was used to juggling. She could manage them both.

The waitress arrived with their starters – plump balls of creamy burrata with olive oil and basil – and they tore into them with groans of delight. For the rest of the meal, they just chatted lightly, enjoying each other's company, remembering what it was they loved about each other and why they made each other laugh. They took a selfie in front of their towering lobster linguine for two and sent it to Izzy.

'I can't wait for you to meet her. You'll love her.' Juliet imagined the three of them in Paris. 'You'd love Nate too, he's a sweetheart, but he's not going to want to go to *Angelique*'s for hot chocolate or try on shoes.'

'Send her to work for me,' suggested Nathalie. 'She'd have a ball.'

'I might hold you to that,' said Juliet.

As their coffee arrived, Nathalie tapped her spoon on the edge of her cup.

'OK, so I've had several glasses of wine and so have you. It's time to talk about the elephant in the room.' She looked into Juliet's eyes.

Juliet swallowed. 'You mean Olivier.'

'Was it something he did? Is that why you left?'

'Oh my God, no.'

'Because he thought it was. He thought he'd done something terrible, and that you'd run away. From him.'

'Absolutely not,' said Juliet fiercely. 'Olivier Godard was the best thing that ever happened to me. He changed my life.'

16

The Ingénue

'*Defense de cracher*' read the sign.

    I wrinkled my brow, wondering what '*cracher*' meant.

'No spitting,' Nathalie translated, seeing my puzzlement. 'In case you're tempted.'

I laughed. 'I'll try to resist.'

I could feel myself breaking into a sweat. It was freezing outside, but down here in the Métro it was smoky and steamy. After what had happened only the week before at the Gare du Nord, I was nervous. We were heading to Montmartre and I would have much preferred to walk. But Nathalie was having none of it.

'Just be bold, stare back at people, and keep your bag under your jacket,' she instructed me as she held my hand and we ran down into the unknown at the Place de la Concorde, leaving daylight behind.

Nathalie had been in Paris less than six months but she seemed to belong here. Even though she knew little more French than I did, she was far more confident about spitting out expletives or requests. '*Excusez-moi*,' she would say, with a baleful glare, if someone was in her way. I was not yet so bold, endlessly muttering '*pardon*' and scuttling about like a demented beetle trying not to bump into anyone.

At the platform, a train was waiting. Nathalie pushed me into a carriage, and we were thrust into the middle of a Saturday-afternoon crush. There was no choice but to be pressed up to whoever was next to you. Gradually, I began to let the half-inch of milky pastis we'd thrown back work its magic. After three stops, I started to relax, swaying in time with the train as it thundered through the belly of Paris to Abbesses, to the Sacré Coeur, where our evening was to begin.

I grinned at Nathalie. We were dressed up to the nines. I had the leather skirt and lace shirt on, and had borrowed Nathalie's plum lipstick, as well as lots of black eyeliner. Nathalie had on a very short plaid dress, her cowboy boots and a fur-lined denim jacket. I gazed at our reflections in the train window, mesmerised. Despite my nerves, I had never felt so free, so liberated, so full of anticipation. A Saturday night out in Worcester wouldn't give anyone butterflies. There was an inevitability to it that was soul-destroying. Had I still been at home I'd probably have been in the pub, searching the pallid crowds in vain for a potential soulmate. The night would end in disappointment and a kebab.

Here, in Paris, anything could happen.

'Your whistle-stop tour starts here,' said Nathalie, as we burst out onto the street and headed for the wide steps that led up to the basilica. We raced each other up, panting and laughing as our breath came in white bursts, then stood against the stone balustrade looking out at the city of light, the sugar-crystal domes of the Sacré Coeur behind us. As the sun set, there were streaks of orange and purple along the skyline, a multicoloured backdrop to the hundreds and thousands of Parisian rooftops.

'Look,' whispered Nathalie, pointing, and as I followed her eyeline, I could see the Eiffel Tower in the distance, looming over the city as if safeguarding it. I caught my breath and felt tears in my eyes.

Nathalie nudged me with her elbow. 'You're crying.'

'I am not.' I laughed through my tears.

'You know what? I cried when I first saw it too. It's just so goddamn... Paris.'

She was right. It was overwhelmingly Paris, and I loved it. The night air was teasing my hair and filling my lungs with a cold sharpness, my veins sang with pastis and joy and before me were spread a million opportunities, twinkling underneath the silver sky.

Nathalie tugged at my arm. 'Come on. We'll go to the Place du Têtre. Just don't catch anyone's eye, unless you want to be ripped off. If you want your picture painted, I'll negotiate.'

Minutes later, we were in a packed cobbled square. It was lined with dozens of restaurants, and the smell of *frites* and *crèpes* tempted hungry tourists to take a seat under a canopy and order something to eat, perhaps with a *chocolat chaud* or a *verre du vin*. Amidst the bare plane trees in the middle were dozens of artists and their easels, surrounded by examples of their work. They were wrapped up in heavy coats and scarves and fingerless gloves, men and women, some aloof, some keen to engage in conversation, most of them smoking while they waited for a willing victim to have their likeness captured. I could feel the history in the air, the ghosts of all those bygone artists who had struggled to make a living. The camaraderie, the drunkenness, the affairs, the passion: their legacy was still in the faces of their successors. Some had achieved fame, and that gave the generations that followed in their footsteps hope.

'Come on.' Nathalie grabbed my hand and pulled me through the crowds. I'd soon learned that she wasn't one for lingering. She led me to a little restaurant, the tables outside covered in gingham, red to match the canopy, the windows above framed by white shutters. The light from the windows spread gold onto the cobbles.

We ate *crêpes* with ham and cheese. Mine seemed to melt on my tongue, salty and savoury and not big enough – the walking had sharpened my appetite – so afterwards we ordered sweet ones with caramelised apple and whipped cream. It reminded me of the Calvados I'd drunk with Jean Louis the night before. I wondered if I should talk to Nathalie about the Beauboises, but it seemed indiscreet, even though I was a little worried about Corinne and not sure how to handle her.

By now, Nathalie had finished her *crêpe* and was signalling to the waiter for the bill. I was flagging somewhat – the travelling, the walking and the food were making me weary, but I had a feeling this was only the beginning of the evening and there would be no escape. I was also learning that keeping up with Nathalie was a challenge.

'OK,' she said, jumping up as she slapped some franc notes onto the table on top of the bill. I scrabbled for my purse, but she waved me away. 'We're done with the tourism. Now we're going to see the real Paris. *Allons-y!*'

*

Pigalle was something else. Like nowhere I'd ever been, sheltered little mouse that I was. Nathalie, of course, had been brought up in New York, so the bright lights were nothing to her. I was dazzled. I'd never known anywhere so frenetic, so buzzy and bright and noisy. I held on to Nathalie's arm as we wound our way down the Boulevard de Clichy, blinded by the neon flash of 'XXX' outside the cinemas.

I was terrified but elated. It was so blatantly and unashamedly wicked. Everyone was bold and beautiful. I'd never seen clothes so tight or short; I'd never seen so much skin on a cold night, or so much lipstick, or so much smiling. The traffic, the music spilling out of the shopfronts, the laughter made my head spin. I gasped as I caught sight of the outrageous clothing for sale in a shop window: straps and PVC and studs and six-inch heels.

Nathalie was laughing her head off at the expression on my face.

'Welcome to the red-light district, honey. Haven't you seen anywhere like this before?'

'No, I have not,' I said, sounding prim.

'They don't have sex shops in Worcester?'

'Not that I know of.' My throat felt tight. I wasn't sure how safe we were in an area like this. Yet there was something thrilling about being on the edge of danger. It was seedy and sleazy, but there was something joyful about it. Nobody cared what anyone thought, which was, I realised, the exact opposite of where I came from, where everyone worried what everyone else thought all the time. I shut the image of my mother's disapproving face out of my mind. I could only imagine how horrified she would be to see me here: exactly the kind of place she had feared I might end up the moment I mentioned Paris.

And it made me even more self-conscious about how inexperienced I was. I'd had one serious boyfriend, Anthony. Sex with him had not been the thing I'd hoped it would be. Not horrible but non-eventful – in that I never got anywhere near a state of abandonment. And then there'd been Hux – Mark Huxtable – who was probably the reason I'd flunked my A levels. He had taken me at a party one cold winter night, in a spare bedroom, warm mouth and cold hands everywhere, and had shown me what the fuss was all about. And then never spoke to me again.

Would Olivier be the same? Was I setting myself up for humiliation? Was I a fool to think that because he'd seemed to find me fascinating he'd be pleased to see me tonight? Or would he blank me, like Hux?

Just as I'd got used to the Métro, I got used to the brashness of Pigalle. Occasionally, a man would look at us with interest, but Nathalie would give him such a hostile glare that he soon moved on. You had to have attitude to survive in this city, I was realising, and that I didn't have. I was too meek and submissive. Too quick to apologise; too eager to please. But if I was going to survive, I'd have to pretend. I held my head up higher, pushed back my shoulders, put a haughty expression on my face and lengthened my stride. It seemed to work.

'Wait up,' said Nathalie, as I charged on ahead. We hooked arms, people stepping aside to let us past and looking at us to see who we were, for we walked as if we owned the street, smiles wide, eyes bright, powered by our youth.

Eventually, Nathalie led us off down a side street, then another, scanning the signs over the doorways. Here, there were takeaways and tanning salons; grubby little bookshops selling dubious magazines. Litter scuttered along the gutter; men bent down to talk to the inmates of cars dawdling on the kerbside. I didn't want to know what they were discussing. I felt more vulnerable here than in the bustle of the boulevard, for there were too many shadows. But, eventually, Nathalie's eyes lit up.

'Here we are.'

As soon as the door was open, I could feel the music reach out and grab me, pulling us down a set of wooden stairs, the red walls covered in ripped and torn posters. We were catapulted into a room full of people transfixed by a band. There were almost as many people on stage as there were in the audience: I counted at least twelve, all in a circle around a girl with black hair piled high on top of her head, with a tight-fitting emerald-green dress and huge gold hoops in her ears. She sang in a husky voice, her eyes shut, her smile wide, the music that accompanied her going from gentle seduction to wild abandonment as she shimmied and glided among the musicians. There were drums and trumpets and saxophones and the thrum of a double bass. It should have been a cacophony, but it was hypnotic and beguiling and joyful all at once.

The song built to a crescendo and came to an explosive finish, followed by ecstatic applause as they left the stage for an interval. Nathalie was heading for the bar, and as I followed, I saw her bounce up to someone, and my heart skipped a beat.

There he was. In a white shirt with the cuffs unbuttoned, and black jeans. Nathalie beckoned me over. My mouth was dry with nerves. I had no idea what to say to him, even though he was smiling over at me.

I went to hold out my hand, English to the core, but he ignored it, leaning forward and kissing me on each cheek. Beside me, Nathalie's eyes were gleaming as she nodded in approval.

'*Bon soir. Ça va?*' I sounded so gauche, and laughed to cover up my awkwardness. '*Le band – c'est . . . fantastique.*'

'*Oui, c'est mon groupe préféré. Ils sont incroyables.*' He stopped as he saw the panic in my eyes. 'My favourite band. I see them every week. They play all over Paris.'

I felt a flood of relief, that he didn't seem to mind speaking English. It was hard enough with all the noise. Even though the band weren't playing, the background music was loud and everyone was talking and laughing, so I was already straining to hear what he was saying. He was pointing to us both.

'*Quelque chose à boire?*' He indicated drinking from a bottle with his hand.

'*Oui! Merci!*' Nathalie accepted on our behalf. '*Deux bières.*'

She handed him a crumpled note and he sauntered off to the bar obligingly.

'Oh my God. He's totally fallen for you!' Nathalie crowed. 'The way he looks at you!'

'I don't get it.' I didn't. What did he find so fascinating?

Nathalie frowned. 'You really need to work on your confidence.'

She was not wrong. I had never been confident. I had never admitted it to anyone, but failing to get into university had secretly been a relief. I was amazed I'd actually had the courage to make it as far as Paris, but alarm bells had gone off inside me over the summer. I knew I had to take action if I didn't want to go down the path my mother had plotted for me: marry a nice local boy with a useful trade and get a house down the road. If I'd entered into my third year of small-town life, I'd have never got out.

'You're so pretty,' said Nathalie. 'And you're smart and funny in a very quiet and English way. Like – the total opposite of me. He would never look at me.'

I felt a burst of pride. I'd come a long way. Literally – for here I was, in a sweaty nightclub in Pigalle, eyeing up the boy of my dreams.

When Olivier came back with the drinks, I took a bottle of beer from him, raised it in a toast and drank deep.

A ripple of applause broke out as the band made their way back out of the wings.

'Come on,' Olivier said. 'We'll go to the front.'

He put a hand on my shoulder to guide me towards the stage, pushing through the crowd. I turned back to check if Nathalie was following, but she raised her hand with a smile, then disappeared into the throng. She'd be fine. Nathalie was not the kind of person to be freaked out by being alone at a gig.

We stood one behind each other, me and Olivier, close but not quite touching. My head was filled with the scent of him, and I could feel the heat from his body behind me, only inches away. The singer was at the microphone, her eyes shut, swaying suggestively from side to side, singing the introduction softly, whispered words of seduction. Every one of my senses was highly charged, yet at the same time I was more relaxed than I'd ever been, because this felt like the moment I'd been waiting for all of my life.

I resisted the urge to lean myself against him. He was only slight, but his chest seemed like a safe place to me, and the longing made my throat ache. I took a swig of beer to calm myself, not sure what was happening to me. I wasn't given to urges, but perhaps Paris was unlocking something in me.

The crowds were beginning to jostle as the tempo of the music increased and became wilder and wilder. Someone lurched into me, and straight away Olivier reached out a protective arm and curled it round me, pulling me into him without taking his eyes off the stage. We stood still amidst the melee, feeling each other breathe. I felt like a bottle of shaken champagne, bubbles flying around my veins, ready to explode at any moment, wondering if he could feel my pounding heartbeat. How could I feel so strongly about someone I had only just met?

Coup de foudre, I remembered Nathalie saying. Until now, I hadn't believed in love at first sight– or, at least, hadn't believed *I* would experience it and for someone else to feel the same. Nathalie had seen it between me and Olivier, the mysterious chemistry that connects two people who have no previous knowledge of each other. And she was so thrilled for me. I couldn't believe that someone could be so kind and selfless. The girls I knew in Worcester would have fought me tooth and claw for him.

On stage, wild trumpets competed with each other, urged on by a ferocious drumbeat and a thunderous bassline, the singer's voice keening above it all. Olivier took my hand and twirled me round so we could join in the dancing. We were in perfect time, moving to the beat, not taking our eyes away from each other, our feet tapping out the rhythm. Nothing showy, no fancy moves, just our own secret routine that to an outsider would have seemed perfectly rehearsed.

As the band reached a climax and the show came to an end to ecstatic applause, we stopped and looked at each other, smiling, each a little shy suddenly.

Nathalie bounded up and broke the moment, dishevelled and sweaty. She'd definitely had a few more drinks since I'd last seen her.

'Hey, guys,' she said. 'There's a bunch of us going on to another club. You coming?'

I hesitated, unsure.

'I think,' said Olivier, 'maybe we will have a quiet drink. Just us.'

'Cool,' said Nathalie, her eyes bright with glee.

'Will you be OK?' I asked, suddenly anxious. It would be irresponsible to let my friend head out into the night alone with a bunch of strangers.

'Hey, I'll be fine. I can look after myself, I promise.' She reached in and gave me a hug, whispering in my ear, 'He is beautiful. You're beautiful together. Have fun.'

Olivier and I fetched our coats and came out into the cold night air, hand in hand. We set off down the street, and I panicked for a moment that I didn't really know where I was. If something went wrong, how would I find my way back? Did I have the courage to go on the Métro on my own, late at night? I swallowed down my panic, not wanting to divulge my doubts.

'I know a good bar on the Rue des Martyrs,' he said. 'We can have a drink, then I'll walk you back.'

I looked at him, uncertain.

'Don't worry. I'm not a crazy person. And Nathalie told me she will kill me if anything happens to you.'

I burst out laughing. 'She means that,' I told him.

He smiled ruefully. 'I know.'

And off we went, back into the mayhem of Pigalle, where he took my arm and steered me firmly through the chaos until the streets became calmer. My feet were starting to rub in the unfamiliar boots, but I didn't want to complain. We were walking very close to each other, and at some point our fingers became entwined. I asked him about himself, what he was doing in Paris, his hopes and dreams, and he told me he was studying Law at the university.

'I have to follow my father. I would like to study literature, but there is a job waiting for me.'

'Did your parents force you?'

He shrugged. 'I have no choice. It is how it is for me.'

His world was so far away from mine. A world of privilege and wealth. His mother was a dancer – she had given up ballet and was running her own dance school. I imagined her, beautiful, elegant, and I felt sad when I thought about my mum. Small and round and dumpy. I told myself I must not feel ashamed. My parents were good and kind and loved me and that was all that mattered.

We had arrived at the bar that he knew. It was noisy and smoky in the front, but he led me through to a little table at the back and ordered us a glass of wine each. For over an hour, we talked, and I told him about my dream, to work on magazines, to be a journalist, and I was a bit embarrassed when I explained I didn't do well enough in my exams to get into university.

He gave another dismissive shrug, that shrug I was starting to get used to when French people didn't agree with what you were saying.

'It will make you a more interesting person,' he said. 'You will not think like everyone else.'

'Do you think so?' I hadn't thought about it like that. I'd felt a failure.

'You will learn from real people. What to think, what to say, what to read.'

I remembered, when I first saw him, how he had been deep inside a book.

'That book you were reading in the bar. What was it?'

'Ah,' he said. '*Le Grand Meaulnes*. Alain-Fournier. It is the best book in the world. I read it twice a year.' He put a fist to his chest. 'It makes me feel. It makes me hope. For love.' He reached inside his coat and pulled it out of an inside pocket. 'You can borrow it.'

'Are you sure?'

I turned it over, opening the cover, seeing the inscription written to him from someone called Delphine.

'It's in French, I'll never get through it.'

He frowned. 'But you must read it. Everyone must read it.'

'I'll try. Thank you. I promise I'll give it back.'

'Don't lose it,' he said. 'It was a present from my godmother.'

I tucked it into my handbag. I would guard it with my life.

'What is your favourite book?' he asked, and I thought my answer probably mattered a great deal.

'*Wuthering Heights*. Emily Brontë.'

'*Wuthering Heights*,' he said, nodding, and I tried

not to laugh at his pronunciation. *Wuzzering Ites.* I was impressed he had heard of it. I couldn't have named a nineteenth-century French novelist if my life depended on it. I had some homework to do. I was wasting my life on fashion magazines when I should be delving into literature and improving my mind. So I could impress beautiful, clever Olivier, who was looking at me as if I had the answer to everything.

What did he see in me?

Maybe me being English was as exotic to him as him being French was to me?

Maybe he was taken in by my designer clothing?

Or maybe it was simple chemistry? We certainly couldn't tear our eyes away from each other, and took every opportunity to brush fingers or touch each other on the arm. There was an undercurrent of something more to come thrumming between us. It was thrilling. Like nothing I had ever felt before.

The bar was starting to close. It was gone midnight by now. We finished our drinks reluctantly and stepped out into the oyster-grey of a Paris night. I shivered in the persistent breeze that seemed to follow us around every corner. He took the yellow scarf from around his neck and wrapped it around mine, tying it in the kind of knot I would never be able to manage. I stood stock-still under a lamp post, gazing up at him, thrilled by his chivalry, his kindness, his gentle touch. He held onto the ends of the scarf for a moment, then used them to pull me closer to him.

To be kissed for the first time in the lamplight, under a watchful moon, in the middle of Paris, is a wonderful thing.

17

Juliet looked at Nathalie as she remembered that night, that very first kiss. How much should she tell her? She wasn't sure she was quite ready yet to disclose the past. She was still trying to make sense of it herself, and she hadn't reached the turning point in her story yet. The moment she'd regretted every night of her life since.

Maybe telling Nathalie what she'd discovered today would put her off the scent. She got out her phone and found the link to the article. Yet again, her pulse quickened as she saw Olivier's image on her screen. He felt so near, and yet so out of reach.

'I found this, just before I came out. What do you think?'

Nathalie's eyes raked through the words. 'Oh my God. I had no idea. We lost touch, just after he got married. I don't think his wife cared much for me. She was very buttoned up.'

'Did you meet her?'

'She was American too. Very Ivy League. Very conscious of status. She one hundred per cent married him because of his parents.' She tapped Olivier's image on the screen. 'You need to get in touch.'

'He'll have met someone else by now,' Juliet said. 'I mean, look at him.'

'But maybe not.'

'He won't want to see me.'

'You're kidding? I had to pick up the pieces when you disappeared. He was bereft. Night after night, I had to listen to him wondering what he'd done wrong. He was broken, Juliet.'

'I'm sure he's got over it by now.'

'But maybe the magic would still be there.'

'He'll have some stunning millennial girlfriend. He won't be interested in me.'

Nathalie sat back in her chair and crossed her arms, scowling. 'I didn't have you down as a coward. I'm disappointed.'

'I'm not a coward. I'm just realistic. It's better to leave the past where it is.'

'Well, I'll go and find him, then. Tell him you're here. Then he can decide if he wants to get in touch.'

'No!' Juliet panicked at the thought; she knew Nathalie wasn't joking. That she would make it her mission. The only way to stop that juggernaut was to agree. 'OK. I'll think about it.'

'Just call into the shop and say hello. Casually.' Nathalie laughed. 'Buy a book. Then take it from there. You'll know, straight away.'

The idea that she could walk into his bookshop and he might be there was overwhelming.

'I can't!'

Nathalie gave an impatient huff. 'What have you got to lose?'

'My dignity?' She couldn't bear the possibility of a look of horror on his face.

Nathalie gave her a stern stare. 'Don't be a pussy.'

'I need to think about it. And figure out, you know, the right outfit.'

'No, no, no – if you think about it, you'll never do it. And you look perfect. Trust me, you won't find anything better. Just muss your hair up a little.' Nathalie reached out and tousled her bob. 'Touch up your lipstick, then kiss the back of your hand to tone it down. Maybe one more button undone? Work it, baby.'

It was as if they were twenty again, Nathalie directing her, urging her on.

Juliet felt a pulse start up inside her she hadn't felt for a long time. It spread a ripple of warmth into the very core of her; a secret thrill. Images of bare skin on bare skin flashed into her mind. She pressed her legs together in an attempt to be chaste, but her thoughts wandered to places they hadn't been for a long time.

'Are you OK?' asked Nathalie. 'Do you want some water?'

'I'm fine,' said Juliet, trying not to laugh. 'Shall we get the bill?'

She needed to be alone with her thoughts, and the newfound discovery that Olivier was not so very far away. Of course she was going to go and find him, but she needed to go at her own pace, not Nathalie's bull-in-a-china-shop full-speed-ahead gallop.

*

In the bathroom, she looked at herself in the mirror and tried to see herself through Olivier's eyes. Would he recognise her, after all this time? Would he forgive her, for what she had done? She got out her red lipstick and applied it, a little hesitant, then did as Nathalie had directed and kissed the back of her hand. She stared at the imprint on her skin for a moment, then washed her hands.

If she didn't go now, she never would.

She ran down the stairs of the restaurant and began to walk towards the 10th. Would it feel the same? The chemistry between them? That syrupy, narcotic pull she had never felt with anyone else? She was going to find out, at last. The moment she had dreamed of so many times was about to become a reality.

18

The Ingénue

Can there be anything more intense, more perfect than being plunged into a Parisian love affair?

It's as if the city sets couples up for her own amusement, matching the people she feels are right for each other, making sure they stumble across one another, somehow, somewhere, in her cobbled streets, and then sets them loose to gaze at each other, to hold hands, to share long, lingering kisses that are the envy of anyone passing. Players on her stage, against a magical backdrop.

Olivier and I parted outside the Beauboises' house at two o'clock that morning.

'Can we meet tomorrow?' he asked, sparing me the agony of wondering all night if he would want to see me again.

'*Oui*,' I said, without hesitating, forgetting to play it cool. I didn't see the point. I wasn't going to pretend.

'I can show you more of Paris.' He looked down at my boots. 'You have more comfortable shoes?'

I laughed. 'I do.' I had almost forgotten how much my feet were hurting.

'*Je t'attends au Pont des Arts, à midi.*' He had pulled

me back into his arms and was whispering in my ear. I thought I might melt with the joy of it. I didn't want to let him go, but we couldn't stand here all night.

'*Pont des Arts, à midi*,' I nodded. '*À demain.*'

'Night night,' he said, and his accent made my heart melt.

I twisted the huge iron handle on the door, pushed it open and slipped inside. I felt so different from the girl who had stepped outside into the street this afternoon. How could twelve hours bring about such a change? I floated across the flagstones and opened the door to the apartment block, kicked off my boots as soon as I got inside and crept up the stairs.

I let myself in as quietly as I could, not wanting to wake anyone and also conscious it was much later than I'd thought I would stay out. I didn't want them to judge me if they noticed what time I'd got in. I hung my coat on the peg in the hall and I realised I was still wearing Olivier's yellow scarf. I took it off and pressed it to my face, my head spinning as the smell brought his presence back to me. I slept with it all night.

On Sunday, I stood on the Pont des Arts at midday, not sure on which side of the wooden bridge we were supposed to be meeting. It was one of those incredibly bright autumn days, when the sky seems unnaturally blue, and everything stands out against it with a sharp clarity. The Seine was showing off, her surface glittering, proud to be wending her way through the middle of this glorious city, showing off her bridges and the splendours on her banks. I was right in front of the Louvre, and in the distance, like a lucky charm, I could see the Eiffel Tower again, as if it was reassuring me that, yes, I really was in Paris.

Dozens of people were walking backwards and forwards over the bridge from the Left to the Right Bank, embroiled in their Sundayness. Perhaps they were going to see family, or friends, or, like me, a new love, but wherever they were going and whoever they were seeing, there was an aimless purposefulness in the air that comes with the weekend, the joy of doing something for yourself, the luxury of not having a deadline, being free from the tyranny of work.

On the wide banks, I saw artists setting up their easels and it reminded me of the Place du Têtre the night before. Everywhere in Paris made me want to paint or sing or write and I felt a surge of energy that must have been inspiration. How did I capture that feeling and do something with it? How could I share my experience of this incredible city? I wanted to stretch out my arms and dance across the bridge, revelling in the joy I felt.

But as the minutes passed, and I realised I'd been standing alone on the bridge for more than fifteen minutes, I began to feel anxious. What if Olivier had woken up this morning and cringed when he remembered last night, realising he'd made a massive mistake? Or what if he was the kind of guy who picked girls up for fun, then dropped them? Or, the worst scenario of all, what if some girl from his past had turned up at his apartment this morning with a warm *pain au chocolat* and an even warmer embrace? All thoughts of meeting me would have disappeared from—

At last, I saw a figure coming towards me at great speed. I laughed as I realised that Olivier was rollerblading, the distance between us getting smaller and smaller until he arrived in front of me with an impressive twirl, arms outstretched.

'I'm sorry to be late. I could not get in the shower – my flatmates...' He gave one of his dismissive shrugs. Then his face lit up with a smile, and he pointed at his feet. 'So I had to put my skates on.'

He fell about laughing and I laughed with him, impressed by his command of English.

'You're crazy,' I told him, my heart swelling with even more adoration. He was such a mixture, of supercool and silly. He looked so intense some of the time, yet didn't take himself seriously. 'Are you going to keep those on?'

'No!' He sat down on the bridge and began to take his skates off, pulling a pair of trainers out of a rucksack on his back. 'This is my secret way of getting quickly around the city.'

As he sat there tying his laces, I looped his yellow scarf round his neck, secretly hoping he would tell me to keep it, but he didn't. Instead, he tied it in an impossibly chic knot, then jumped up. 'Let's go.'

I followed after him. 'Where are we going?'

'To the best experience in Paris.'

'Which is?'

'Père-Lachaise.'

He looked triumphant as he said it, but I shook my head.

'*La cimetière?* The cemetery?'

I stopped in my tracks, dismayed. 'A cemetery?'

'Trust me. It is where all the important people are buried. It is a... *pèlerinage*? I don't know how you say...'

'Pilgrimage?'

'*Oui. C'est ça.* Oscar Wilde, Chopin, Edith Piaf. Jim Morrison.'

'Let's go, then. Seems like the perfect way to spend an afternoon.' I laughed, realising that I was never going to get the expected with Olivier.

We set off along the banks of the Seine, walking hand in hand underneath the bare trees until in front of us was the Île de la Cité, and Notre-Dame in all her magnificence. I gasped, and Olivier looked proud.

'*Elle est belle, Notre-Dame, non?*'

I nodded, feeling a bit overwhelmed by it all. I put it down to the very late night, but how could I be here, in Paris, hand in hand with a boy who was beyond my wildest dreams, feeling as far as possible from the drab little shopgirl who had arrived here the week before? The buildings on the island glowed in the sunshine. I blinked back tears, just as I had the night before with Nathalie, wondering why on earth this place was having such a profound effect on me.

Olivier peered at me, concerned. 'Why are you crying?'

I shook my head, laughing to chase the tears away. 'It's nothing. It's beautiful, that's all.'

He picked up my hand and nodded his head. 'Come on. We have a long walk. We will never get there if you stop and cry at everything beautiful.'

Part of me longed to go inside Notre-Dame, but Olivier seemed set on his plan and so I brushed away my tears and we set off again along the river, then up past the Marais to the Place de la Bastille. Then it was a long walk up through the *11ème* until we finally arrived at the cemetery gates. And within them, lining the cobbled pathways, was a tangle of the most elaborate memorials I'd ever seen. Miniature temples, grand mausoleums, obelisks, crucifixes, white marble angels, lifelike statues, intricate carvings, ornate grilles, everything crammed together with no rhyme or reason. Moss softened the hardest surfaces; there were epitaphs in gold letters as long as a chapter of a book; bronze had turned to verdigris.

'Wow,' was all I could manage, and Olivier grinned as if to say 'I told you so'. We meandered along the paths, and he pointed out the graves of Balzac, Proust, Géricault, Molière ... I didn't know much about any of them, but I resolved to find out more. There was Chopin, whose heart was cut out after he died and sent back to Poland, for his greatest fear was being buried alive. We saw the tomb of Piaf, the little sparrow whose songs touched so many hearts, covered in roses. Rossini. Modigliani. And Oscar Wilde. His memorial was starkly modern, a very angular angel, its wings streaming out behind.

'When he died, he was a pauper, but his friends bought him this plot and had this made for him.' Olivier looked solemn. 'The only thing he was guilty of was love.'

It brought a lump to my throat, knowing the writer had been hounded out of England and found his final resting place here. I hoped he'd found peace.

Jim Morrison's tomb was much less elaborate than most of the others in the cemetery but smothered in gifts left by people who wanted to show their respect to their idol: red roses, candles, bottles, cigarettes, incense sticks, photos, drawings and declarations of love. There was one single glass of champagne, recently poured, and it seemed poignant. A toast for an idol who couldn't respond.

On our way out, we saw Heloise and Abelard. I didn't know their story, but Olivier told me the tragic details.

'He was her teacher, and they fell in love. She had his baby, and he sent her away to be safe. But her uncle was enraged and sent his henchmen to cut off his...' Olivier pointed towards his trousers. I winced. 'She ended up in a nunnery, and he became a monk, and they wrote love letters to each other until they died. And here, they are together, at last.'

I gazed down at the two marble figures, side by side with their hands pressed together in prayer.

'It is a terrible thing, to be parted so cruelly,' Olivier murmured, and I shivered as a cold chill crept around my heart. Perhaps it was the melancholy of Père-Lachaise, all those stories of lost love and tragic endings, but I suddenly felt a terrible sense of dread. What if I never saw Olivier again after this? What if that was it, my one brief chance of happiness, and something happened to tear us apart, like Heloise and Abelard?

'Hey.' He looked down at me, concerned. 'You're cold. I'm sorry. I should not have brought you all the way here. We will go somewhere more cheerful. Somewhere you will love. Come here.'

He put his arm around me and held me close as we left the cemetery and headed for the Mètro.

An hour later, we stood in front of a bookshop tucked into a little street on the Left Bank. It was ancient and crooked, painted yellow and green.

'Shakespeare and Company?' I read the words over the door.

'It is perfect for you, no?' Olivier smiled as he led me inside.

It was a dream come true. Room upon room stacked high with every book imaginable, from an ancient battered paperback to a weighty tome. It had a chaotic order to it, combined with the feeling that if you stayed long enough and searched hard enough, you would find the perfect book for you, wherever you were in your life. It was bohemian and scruffy and eclectic, filled with the spirit of all the writers who had spent time there, searching for inspiration. Hemingway, Anaïs Nin, Scott Fitzgerald, James Joyce – the list of literary stars who'd made this their temporary home was dazzling.

I always had a tingling feeling when I went into a bookshop, but here the urge to put pen to paper, to share my thoughts and feelings in words, even if no one ever read them, became overwhelming. We spent more than an hour amidst the shelves, wandering up and down the precarious wooden staircases, running our fingers along the spines.

'I come here every weekend,' Olivier told me. 'It is the place I feel at home. More than my own home. It speaks to my heart.' He patted his chest.

'I can see why,' I said. I'd never been anywhere so sure of itself. It was magical.

I finally managed to choose what to buy. A copy of *The Hunchback of Notre-Dame*, for you could see its spires from the second-floor window, and an illustrated hardback of *The Little Prince*, which I would share with the children. They might not understand the story, but the pictures were charming and would capture their imagination: the little blond prince in his flying jacket, standing next to his friend the fox. It was all I could afford for now, but I promised myself I would be back, to try something new every time I came.

'When I come here,' said Olivier, 'I just want to live among books for the rest of my life.'

'So why can't you?'

He shrugged. 'I must work for my father. That is my future. But at least I can come here at weekends.'

We stopped in a tiny café on the way back. By now, the light was fading, and I was starting to feel the coldness of November creep its way inside me. It was gloomy with dark wood walls and peeling lino on the floor, and the waiter's apron looked grubby. I didn't like to object, as we took a small, rickety table and Olivier ordered for us without even looking at the menu.

Two earthenware bowls of onion soup arrived within minutes and all my doubts evaporated with the steam rolling off the deep, brown liquid. It was incredibly rich, with strands of onion that dissolved into sweetness in my mouth, and chunks of bread smothered in melted cheese that left strings of molten goo. Within moments, I was warm again. I sighed with contentment as I put my spoon back in my empty bowl.

Olivier pulled out a paper bag from inside his jacket and laid it on the table.

'This is for you,' he said.

What book had he chosen for me? I opened the bag, intrigued, and pulled out a yellow notebook. I looked at him.

'It is for you, to start to write. You can't just talk of writing.'

He was right. I had spent too long *thinking* about writing, I realised now. Words were no use to me in my head. I had to find the courage to pin them down.

'It's the best present anyone's ever given me,' I told him.

'I don't think so,' he laughed. 'But I hope it will give you courage. Writing is how we make sense of the world.'

I flicked through the blank pages, imagining them filled with my thoughts and dreams and desires; my memories. This notebook was a talisman. My turning point. 'Thank you,' I breathed, feeling tears pricking behind my eyelids, a little overwhelmed that someone understood me so well. Both my ambition and my fear. My yearning and my reluctance.

Olivier looked at his Swatch, his face falling. 'I have to go,' he said. 'Sunday night I eat with my parents, every week.'

Although his parents lived on the outskirts of Paris, he shared a flat near the university with fellow students, but he seemed to go home a lot.

'OK,' I said, swallowing my disappointment.

We left the café. It was dark now, and we huddled together as we walked back down towards the river. The lamps on the pavement sprang into light, the windows glowed golden and the air was thick with the smell of cooking as chefs began to prepare for their evening service. By the river, we sat on a bench as Olivier put his skates back on. He was going to be late for his family, so he needed the speed. He was worried about me walking back, but I felt familiar with the route now, in this city that was becoming my home.

'I will see you soon,' he said, his hands on my shoulders, and he leaned in to kiss me. He lips were full and soft on mine, and I could hardly bear to let him go. 'I have lectures all week, but meet me for dinner on Friday.'

'Of course.' I memorised the instructions he gave me.

How was I going to wait five whole days before I saw him again?

'*À bientôt*,' he said, and skated off.

I watched him glide away, to a home and a family I didn't know, my sweet, crazy, romantic, sexy French boy. He was the first thing in my life that mattered, that was for me and me alone, and as I stood on the riverbank, the *bateaux mouches* gliding past on the silver water, I relived every moment of the day we'd spent together.

I would relive it every day for the rest of my life.

19

Juliet hadn't been to the *10ème* before, for it hadn't been the fashion when she was last in Paris, but now the Canal St Martin was one of the coolest places to hang out. It forged its way through the trees, deep green, its banks lined with bars, cafés and restaurants, the nearby streets full of vintage clothes shops and record stores. It had a slightly bohemian feel, with its bursts of graffiti, and she fell under its spell straight away. The light was starting to fade, so she hurried on, crossing over a green metal bridge to the far side, searching for the frontage of the shop.

There it was. Nestled between a *papeterie* and a tiny delicatessen. As she approached, she slowed down. Until this moment, finding Olivier had been a fantasy. She had the power to turn it into reality, but would she have the courage?

She approached the shop cautiously from the other side of the road. The front was floor-to-ceiling glass, and on it in white lettering were the names of thousands of authors. Juliet took a deep breath and crossed the road, then stood as close as she could to the window, but she couldn't make out anyone inside through the lettering without putting her face flat against the glass. She could either walk away or she could push open the door and walk inside.

In the end, Nathalie's insistent voice as they left the restaurant helped her decide: 'You guys were both convinced you were the love of each other's lives. You have to see if that's still true.'

Juliet didn't see how it could be. They'd been so young. Yet no one had ever made her feel the way Olivier had. Did you only get that the first time you fell hard and fast? That magical heat, the rush in your veins, that feeling of coming home? Was she even capable of having those feelings again, at her age? Nothing much held magic anymore, she had noticed as middle age crept in. No birthday butterflies, no pre-holiday excitement, no tingle as Christmas approached.

Though Paris, she had to admit, had woken something in her. She'd felt a rush when she arrived, had been wide-eyed as she began to explore the city anew. She had felt more pleasure since she'd got here than she had done for a long time: pleasure in small things, like a tiny *tarte* brought back to her apartment in a cardboard box, but also the huge joy of finding she could be independent, be *herself*, without the eternal guilt of being a wife and mother. Life was on her terms here in a way it could never be in London, and the promise the city held thrilled her as she thought of the possibilities.

Everyone comes to Paris to become someone else; someone new.

She took a deep breath, pushed open the door and stepped inside. Everything was painted white – the brick walls, the high ceiling, the wooden floorboards – but for the shelves, which were matt black. Above them were signs in typewriter script marking out each category: *la philosophie*, *l'architecture*, *les romans*. There was a copper counter with half a dozen high stools, an Italian coffee machine and a glass dome containing a pile of golden madeleines.

She loved it. It was a million miles from Shakespeare and Company, with its crooked walls and books piled precariously on every surface and dust motes twirling in the sunlight. But it still gave her that overwhelming sense of wonder for what she might find among the shelves; a tingling in her fingertips as she touched each spine.

It was perfectly named, she thought, for this was a dream come true. A place for booklovers to hang out, to be inspired, to share recommendations. On a chalkboard was a list of upcoming events with authors. She imagined the room filled with buzz and chatter, a rush to have books signed, perhaps the chance to have a conversation with a writer whose work you had admired for years.

She felt a burst of pride for Olivier for having the bravery to turn his back on what was expected of him, to walk away from the family tradition and achieve his ambition. It must have taken a lot of courage.

And then she stopped in her tracks, for there he was. Perched on a stool at a wooden desk at the back of the store. He was lost in the pages of whatever he was reading, just as he had been that very first day in the café. His hair was a little duller than the blond of his youth, but it fell over his forehead in just the same way. She could see the angle of his cheekbone, the line of his jaw, the fullness of his mouth. As she watched, he ran his thumb over his bottom lip just as he always had when he was concentrating. She felt a pool of sweetness in her stomach and her pulse double, triple. He looked so familiar, and any doubts she'd had left her as she walked towards him, putting her hand in her bag to pull out the book she had put in there earlier that morning, intending to start to read it again.

'*Excusez moi – avez vous une copie de ce roman?*' she asked. 'I must give this one back to the owner.'

She pushed the battered copy of *Le Grand Meaulnes* across the desk towards him. He looked at the book, put out his hand to touch it, almost reverently, then looked up at her.

She couldn't read the expression in his eyes. Maybe he was waiting for a reaction from her? Now she was closer, she could see the smile lines at the side of his mouth, the soft grey hairs hidden among the blonde ones, the face she had carried with her through the years.

She reached out her hand so their fingers nearly touched on the cover of the book. 'I only borrowed it,' she said.

'For thirty years?' he said. His voice was deeper than she remembered. The voice of a man, not a boy. The side of his mouth lifted a centimetre and she knew it wouldn't take much to turn it into a smile.

Around them, the browsers carried on their business, but they might as well not have been there. Unspoken questions looped backwards and forwards between them, like a current along an invisible telephone line. She tucked her hair behind her ears, suddenly nervous, as he looked her up and down more closely, taking in her neck, her collarbone, her décolleté. Eventually, his face broke into a full smile.

'Hello, Juliet,' he said.

She remembered the way he said her name, caressing

the J and lingering over the t, almost giving it an extra syllable.

'Olivier.' She could only manage a whisper.

All she wanted was for him to stand up, come around from behind the desk and take her in his arms. But that was for movies, not for the middle of the afternoon in a busy shop.

Then, to her surprise, he did stand up, beckoning to her to follow. 'Come with me.'

He headed to a shelf marked '*Classiques*'. He ran his finger along it until he found what he wanted, pulled it out and held it out to her. A brand-new copy of *Le Grand Meaulnes*.

She reached into her bag for her purse, but he frowned.

'No,' he said. 'It is a present. To say thank you for bringing the other one back.'

'I'm sorry I kept it for so long.'

'I thought I would never see it again.'

Her tongue felt heavy in her mouth; she couldn't speak. Should she walk away now? Save them both from awkwardness? What on earth had she been thinking? That bottle of rosé had a lot to answer for, making her imagine some sort of passionate reunion as he pushed her up against a bookshelf and kissed her.

'Or you.'

She started as he spoke. 'What?'

'I thought I would never see you again.'

She put her hand on her throat, feeling the words stuck inside.

'It's the first time I've been back, to Paris,' she managed eventually. 'Since I left. And I wanted to return the book. I know how much it meant to you.'

He nodded. Was he angry? Or just . . . not particularly interested? Glad to have his book back but eager to get shot of her, eager to avoid any embarrassment? What was he thinking?

'When I was young, I would dream of this,' he was saying. 'You appearing out of the blue. Eventually, I gave up dreaming . . .'

'I'm sorry,' she said. She was still trying to figure it out, whose fault it had been, how culpable she was, what she could have done differently. That was why she was writing her story. She was getting closer to the moment everything had gone wrong. She was hoping it would give her clarity. Perspective.

'Listen,' he said. 'We can't talk here. Let's go somewhere. Do you have time? Give me a moment to tell my staff.'

Five minutes later, they were making their way along the canal, the atmosphere changing as it began to dress slowly for night. The street lamps were coming on, reflected in the water, and the windows started to glow amber and tortoiseshell. As they walked, Olivier chatted about the area, how much he loved its spirit and energy, how it had regenerated itself into something vibrant and exciting, but she knew it was just a distraction technique, that the moment of reckoning was getting nearer, that she would, at some point, have to come clean.

But the more she thought about what had happened, the less she wanted to reveal the truth.

20

The Ingénue

The following Saturday, I walked with Corinne and the children to the Rue Montorgueil to buy food for the weekend. It was a market street in the next arrondissement filled with butchers and bakers and florists and fishmongers. Everyone had their own favourite vendors and their own routine, queuing patiently with their baskets and trolleys between the stacks of wooden boxes piled on the cobbles. I read the signs: *pains et olives, coiffeur, vin* – anything and everything you could possibly want was here.

Corinne was in a good mood. She made a point of telling me the words for all the things she was buying, and then made me have a go. She was encouraging, and I found myself warming to her. When she was relaxed, she had a generous spirit, and she was funny, because she was so rude about people and what they were wearing. She would nudge me in the ribs and point in disbelief.

'*Oh, la vache – les chaussures!*' she would say, pointing to a towering pair of peep-toed platforms on a woman of a certain age. '*Jamais avec une jupe si courte.*'

And I would laugh along. Fancy wearing shoes like that with such a short skirt!

At the pharmacy, she made me buy a red lipstick, a colour I had thought I couldn't wear, but she chose one which flattered me. I hadn't realised there were so many kinds of red. I looked totally different, my mouth now the focal point in my face, whereas I'd always focused on my eyes. Under her direction, I was getting more confident. It was like having a big sister.

We returned to the flat in time for lunch, chattering away, and I could immediately see how happy Jean Louis was that we were getting on, and that Corinne seemed relaxed. We all had lunch together – three kinds of cheese that we had bought, and *carottes râpées* – and Arthur did his funny face again and we laughed until our sides hurt.

'*Arrête! Arthur! Ça suffit!*' pleaded Corinne, wiping tears from her cheeks.

I got up to clear the plates away and Jean Louis touched me on the arm, giving me a smile of appreciation, which I knew was more for boosting Corinne's mood than my waitress service. The atmosphere in the house was as frothy as whipped cream and my heart felt full of the joy and anticipation you get on a spring day, when the sun kisses your face for the first time since winter.

When I went to my bedroom to figure out what to wear that evening for my dinner with Olivier, Corinne knocked on my door and put her head around it. '*Je peux vous aider choisir?*'

I had told her I had a date, and she seemed excited by the prospect. I was grateful for her offer, for I was unsure quite what look to go for. Part of me knew Olivier wouldn't care what I wore, but getting ready for a date is a particular torture you have to put yourself through.

We ended up choosing the lace shirt with black trousers, my Hermès scarf wound tight around my throat. Corinne surveyed me.

'*Attends*,' she said, leaving the room and coming back with a pair of scissors. She pointed to my hair. '*Je peux?*'

I was slightly alarmed. She seemed to want to cut it. My hair was long and dark and straight, all the same length, and I have to say it was one thing that never let me down: it was shiny and behaved itself and I could always rely on it. But Corinne seemed to have a vision, and for some reason I trusted her judgement.

'*Oui*,' I agreed.

She pulled strands of my hair forward and began to cut. Five minutes later, I had a fringe. I stared in the mirror, unable to believe the difference it made. It framed my face perfectly. I looked sophisticated and mysterious. And, with the red lipstick, undeniably chic.

'*Pas mal*,' Corinne said with typical understatement, nodding, then she steered me out to the living room for Jean Louis' approval. '*Pas mal, eh?*'

He looked at me. It was almost as if he didn't recognise me. I felt awkward, as if he didn't approve, but then he smiled.

'*Fantastique!*' he said finally. '*Comme Jane Birkin, non?*'

I shook my head. I hadn't a clue who Jane Birkin was, but Corinne flipped open a coffee-table book and showed me a photo of a young woman with a fringe and long dark hair and a gap between her teeth, like mine. She looked far more glamorous than me, but if they wanted to make that comparison, it gave me even more confidence.

'*Merci*,' I said to them both, beaming, then reached out to Corinne. '*Merci*.'

This time, she let me hug her, though she flinched slightly as I put my arms round her. She wasn't great at physical contact. But I was on cloud nine. I was confident about how I looked for the first time in my life. I was excited about my dinner with Olivier. And I was helping to make this a happy house. I was so proud that I'd had the courage to come here. Life really was about taking risks.

As I was starting to realise was the norm in this house, the atmosphere changed for no apparent reason. Clouds gathered and chased away the sunshine we had all basked in over lunch. I had no idea what set Corinne off, but I knew by now that it didn't take much. She could be as happy as anything, then something would unsettle her, and a blackness would descend. She either became sullen and moody, filling the house and everyone in it with tension, or would fly into one of her tantrums. It was hard to know which was worse. The moods carried on for longer, with everyone waiting for an explosion that sometimes didn't come. The explosions were shocking: she could rant without taking breath for at least five minutes, and there were often tears too. I wasn't sure how to handle it, for I came from a household that didn't indulge in emotional outbursts, but I noticed how desperate Jean Louis was to reassure her, soothing her as if she was one of his children, trying his best to calm her.

Usually, I couldn't understand half of what she was shouting about. Tonight, I understood very clearly. As I came into the kitchen to see what the commotion was, she was pointing at Arthur, shouting at Jean Louis that it was him who had wanted another baby, not her.

Jean Louis went white. Corinne began to sob. I think she had even shocked herself, and she was heading into hysteria, possibly as a distraction from the awful thing she had said.

'Charlotte. Hugo.' I scooped up Arthur, held out my hands and took the three of them off into Hugo's room, even though I wasn't supposed to be working. It was only just before seven. I could afford a little time – I wasn't meeting Olivier until eight.

I picked up one of the Babar books. The stories about the little elephant and his family had quickly become my favourite, and as I read his next adventure to them with Arthur on my lap, I wondered if he had been named after Babar's cousin. I loved the children's names too – Pom, Flora, Alexander and Isabelle. I tucked them away for future reference.

I couldn't think about what Corinne had just said. I was glad Arthur was far too young to understand, and I hoped that the others were too. They were both sitting very close to me. In the other room, I could hear Jean Louis, his tone reassuring as he dealt with Corinne, and eventually I heard them walk down the corridor to their bedroom. I kept looking at my watch. I couldn't leave the little ones until they were settled, or until Jean Louis came back.

'Let's give Arthur his bath,' I said to Charlotte and Hugo, and they leapt at the suggestion. All they wanted was calm and normality.

We all squished into the bathroom, lined up by the side of the bath while Arthur sat like a little king gazing at us benevolently through steam that smelt of honeysuckle. They piled his bath bubbles on top of his head, and soon there were peals of laughter from all three of them, which lifted my heart. I hoped Corinne could hear them. I hoped it lifted her heart too. I was very worried about her. I didn't think she could help her behaviour. There was something wrong. She wasn't a bad person. I'd seen the good side of her. But something was bringing out the worst in her.

I dried Arthur and tucked him into his night things, and the three of us put him to bed, Charlotte carefully winding up the musical mobile which played '*Au Clair de la Lune*'. The slightly wobbly plink of the notes always seemed to soothe him. We said goodnight and crept out of his room, just as Jean Louis came out of the master bedroom. He held out his arms and Hugo and Charlotte ran to his side.

'*Maman* was very tired. She is going to sleep now,' he told them, and they seemed reassured. He looked at me. 'Thank you so much,' he said. 'I think this week has been tough. She needs to rest.'

I hesitated. I was unsure about leaving them all, but Jean Louis pointed to the door.

'Go. Or you'll be late. We'll be fine.'

I didn't need telling twice.

I glided through the streets on my way to the restaurant. My clothes made me walk taller; my lipstick made me smile wider; my hair made me feel wanton and alluring. I pictured Olivier's face, his eyes widening in surprise as he saw me. Every time I thought of our next kiss, my heart buckled.

As for the thought of what might come at the end of the evening... I fantasised about him leading me back to his apartment, then running his hands through my hair, down my neck and over my shoulders as he slowly undressed me.

I couldn't control the heat inside me. No one had ever made me feel like he did. Hux had unravelled me, but there had been something dark in the way he'd made me feel. With Olivier, there was a purity to my lust. I revelled in it. My blood ran around my body like sweet dark wine. Occasionally, a passer-by would catch my eye and smile at the joy spilling out of me. I wanted everyone to feel like this. Electric. Radiant. As I passed the statue of Louis XIV in the Place des Victoires, I felt as powerful and invincible as he must have done.

I turned down the Rue des Petit-Champs, only moments away now, my heart thumping. I counted the restaurants on the left, following Olivier's instructions – one, two, then came to a halt outside the third. It didn't look much, with its faded awning and missing letters and the tattered wicker chairs in the glassed-in terrace, but I remembered the scruffy place Olivier had taken me to after our visit to Shakespeare and Company and how wonderful that had been. He was the kind of person who knew the best-kept secrets, the hidden treasures, and he wasn't one to hide behind showy displays of extravagance. He was more confident and sophisticated than that. I knew he came from a wealthy background, but he showed it by his behaviour rather than any material display. That casual confidence came from privilege, something I didn't have much experience of.

It was five to eight. I wondered if I should linger outside for a few minutes, as I felt self-conscious about going in on my own, but there was a chill wind tearing up the street, so I braced myself to walk inside. It was full of dark wood tables with red velvet lampshades, the matching carpet worn and threadbare. I peered into the gloom to see if I could spot Olivier anywhere, but there were just a few couples scattered around the room.

A grumpy-looking *maître d'* arrived and I managed to explain, in halting French, that I was waiting for my dining companion. He muttered something unintelligible and beckoned me to follow him, placing me at a table near the back. I sat down and he growled something else I didn't understand, so I just smiled and said, '*Vin rouge, s'il vous plaît,*' hoping he'd asked what I wanted to drink.

It was bang on eight o'clock.

Five minutes later, the *maître d'* returned with a large glass of red wine and plonked it in front of me. I drank gratefully, as my nerves were gathering, now I was sitting down, trying not to look at my watch too often. He had been late last time we met, I reminded myself. Maybe punctuality wasn't his thing.

I drank my wine very quickly and as soon as my glass was empty, the *maître d'* swiped it away and brought me another. By half past eight, I felt a bit drunk and agitated, a horrible combination. Several more people had arrived during this time, and I tried not to look at the door whenever it opened, but every time it wasn't Olivier, my heart fell a little further.

By a quarter to nine, I knew he wasn't coming. I summoned the *maître d'* and tried to explain, and asked for the bill for my wine, but he waved his hand to tell me it was on the house. I was equally touched and humiliated by his kindness as I left my seat and headed for the door, my cheeks burning with Médoc and embarrassment, wondering if people were nudging each other as I left.

Outside, it was pouring, with determined and cruel rain, the kind that mocked you for forgetting an umbrella and being too vain to have a suitable coat. Before I had got to the Place des Victoires, I was soaked. By the time I got back to the Beauboises', I was shivering. As I walked in, Jean Louis came out of the kitchen at the sound of the door shutting, not expecting me back so soon. He looked at me in dismay, a sodden mess, mascara running down my cheeks, my previous ebullience washed away somewhere in the gutters of the *2ème*.

'*Il vous a posé un lapin?*' he asked. I didn't understand the idiom. 'He stood you up?'

I gave the shrug I had seen so many times. '*J'ai attendu quarante cinq minutes...*'

He gave a snort. 'That is Paris boys for you. There is always someone better.' He saw me flinch and patted me on the shoulder. 'Not better than you. Just better in his head. He is a fool.'

I managed a smile. I was shivering hard by now, from the rain and the distress and the humiliation.

'Go take a bath,' said Jean Louis. 'I will cook for you.'

'No, no, you don't have to do that. I'll just go to bed.'

'I am cooking for myself. So a little extra is no problem. Fifteen minutes.'

He smiled at me. All I wanted to do was to hide under the covers and cry myself to sleep, but Jean Louis was being so kind. Even though the last thing I wanted was food, I couldn't refuse. And I figured that after Corinne's display earlier, maybe he could use some company. So I thanked him and headed to the bathroom, filling up the tub and peeling off my wet clothes.

I lay in the bath for fifteen minutes. Gradually, the heat of the water warmed my skin and then my bones, and I stopped shivering. But nothing would warm the chill in my heart. I couldn't stop wondering where Olivier was, or what had been more enticing than an evening with me. I had misjudged him. I'd thought he was caring and considerate, but it seemed he put himself first without giving a moment's thought to me or how I might feel at being stood up. I supposed it was better for me to find out now, at the beginning, than to invest too much time in a relationship. It was crushing, though. The hollowness inside me was the complete opposite of the delicious warmth I'd felt earlier. My heart was a hard lump that was barely beating at all. I was hardly able to drag myself out of the water and dry myself with a towel.

I wanted to crawl into bed. Black velvet sleep would bring me respite. But Jean Louis was cooking for me, and it would be rude to refuse, and I had to admit that part of my hollow feeling was hunger, for I'd had nothing since lunchtime. So I pulled on some jeans, and my favourite fleecy sweatshirt with Snoopy on the front and a pair of thick socks. I combed my damp hair and didn't bother putting on any make-up. I couldn't bear to look at myself in the mirror.

All I wanted was to be on the sofa in Mum and Dad's sitting room, waiting for Dad to get back from the chip shop. I longed for the vinegar-scented steam, and the awful trashy telly we watched: *Noel's House Party* and

Blind Date and *Stars in their Eyes*. I hadn't felt homesick until now. It had all been too exciting, and I'd been proud of myself for being independent, but now I'd have given anything to be transported back to Worcester.

But that wasn't an option, so I ventured into the kitchen. Jean Louis was clattering about, an apron on over his chambray shirt and jeans. The kitchen smelt of hot butter and garlic and frying chicken. He poured me a glass of pale gold wine.

'Viognier,' he told me, and I tasted peaches and apricots and sunshine. It lifted my spirits a little and took the edge off the ache in my chest.

'*Je peux vous aider?*' I asked, wanting to help, but he shook his head as he ran his knife expertly through a pile of mushrooms and tossed them in the pan, then threw several handfuls of spinach into a pan of water.

'Maybe the table?' he said, and so I laid it carefully. Everything they had was heavy with quality but soft with use, the bone-handled cutlery worn from years of being held, the linen of the napkins falling into gentle folds. Everything I touched, I wanted, from the etched wine glasses to the marble pot of salt. It wasn't fair to compare it with home. My parents were simple, ordinary, hard-working and down to earth, not wealthy Parisians who'd had generations of grandeur and luxury handed down to them. And, I reminded myself, it was Corinne's job to make everything look covetable.

After a second glass of wine, the trauma of the evening began to fade a little. Besides, Jean Louis was being so kind, I couldn't be churlish and sulk. And the food was as good as anything in a restaurant: plump, golden chicken breasts, the mushrooms mixed with a spoonful of *crème fraîche*, with a little spinach on the side.

'The *crème fraîche* is from a farm near my parents,' Jean Louis told me with pride.

I was starting to understand the French way of cooking. It was attention rather than fuss that made the difference: attention to where the food had come from, attention to what went with what, a certain simplicity – in England this meal would have come with a mound of potato and piles of vegetables – and precision timing. Nothing was left in a pan longer than necessary – though if it did need time, that was OK too. Each ingredient was treated with reverence and given its own place on the plate.

'I hope I can cook like you one day,' I told him, my knife cutting through the chicken as if it was a pat of butter.

'I learned from my *grandmère*. We spent each summer on the farm, and each night one of us would be her sous-chef. She made sure we all knew how to cook *boeuf bourguignon, coq au vin, cassoulet . . .*' He kissed his thumb and forefinger, then grinned. 'She told us it was the best way to get a wife.'

I imagined him as a little boy, standing on a chair watching his grandmother add carrots and onions to a giant pot on a big old range cooker and letting him stir it with a spoon.

'She did a great job,' I said.

He shrugged. 'You must eat three times a day. So you might as well eat well.'

I marvelled that he was so slim. But I'd also noticed that the French didn't stuff themselves with seconds and thirds like we did in England. They had everything so right. How to cook, how to dress. How to love.

I tried not to think about it. The wine was helping. I noticed the bottle of Viognier was nearly empty and realised Jean Louis had been filling my glass and I'd been glugging away. And I felt surprisingly happy. It had anaesthetised me.

The chicken devoured, Jean Louis produced two little bowls of chocolate mousse, which we ate with tiny spoons, and with it he poured me a glass of Sauternes, sticky and luscious.

'It's the best meal I've ever had,' I sighed, as I put my spoon back in the empty bowl.

'The mousse, that is the best trick I learned. For seduction.' He winked, then realised what he had said. 'I'm sorry. I don't mean ... It was a joke. A bad joke. I hope you don't think ...'

He was mortified, thinking I might think he was trying to seduce me. I just laughed.

'Don't be silly,' I said. 'I wouldn't think that in a million years.'

He looked at me, and I laughed again, and took another sip of Sauternes. Its syrup was making its way into my veins and my head felt a little swimmy. I went to clear the table, but Jean Louis stopped me.

'*Non.* It can wait. We can sit for a while in the *salon*. Finish our drink.' He raised his glass. 'And I want to say thank you. For being part of our family. I know it is not always easy, but you have made our lives so much better.'

'Thank you. The children are very easy to love.'

'They are. And Corinne – I know she appreciates you too. She does not mean to be ...'

He shrugged. He was finding it impossible, to put his feelings about his wife into words. It must have been hard for him, when she flipped like that. He was so kind and patient with her.

I flopped onto one of the sofas in the living room, sinking into the cushion and curling my bare feet under me, while Jean Louis pointed a remote control across the room and Sting started crooning 'Moon Over Bourbon Street'. The slight huskiness of his voice made me shiver.

Jean Louis held out his hand. '*Tu veux danser?*'

I froze for a moment. First, because he had called me '*tu*' not '*vous*' for the first time, a sign of familiarity. And second, because I wanted to jump up and join him but it seemed wrong.

'*Samedi soir*, it's for dancing, no?' he reassured me.

He was moving to the beat, clicking his fingers. The music was infectious, and if he thought it was OK, then maybe I was overthinking it. So I got up and began to dance too.

I was the sort of drunk where you thought you *were* the music, that it was part of you, my limbs doing exactly what I told them. I was smiling to myself, singing along – it was an album we'd played over and over at school, swooning over Sting's good looks, and it brought back good memories.

Then Jean Louis was in front of me and we were dancing together. Sting had moved on to 'If You Love Somebody Set Them Free', and the tempo was a good bit faster and we were singing along, laughing, doing silly finger pointing and pouting. Then suddenly he took my hands and twirled me around and somehow I ended up in his arms.

I should have stepped away, smiling, without making a fuss, and gone to sit back down, but I liked the feeling of being in his embrace. We were only dancing, after all. His hands were only light upon me. There was no groping. It was all quite above board. Just the two of us, enjoying moving to the music. Messing about on a Saturday night. So I relaxed.

The hi-fi flipped to a track I didn't know. There was a swirling organ – it reminded me of my dad's favourite song, 'A Whiter Shade of Pale' – but then a man and a woman began to sing, declaring their love for each other in breathless French.

'This is her,' said Jean Louis. 'Jane Birkin. The little English girl who stole Serge Gainsbourg's heart.'

We stood, barely moving, as their voices became more intense. Their lust was palpable, and I blushed to hear what sounded like them making love, on record. I'd never heard anything like it before. It was thrilling. I felt as if I was right inside the song. Inside their passion.

Jean Louis was singing along. I shouldn't have, but I moved closer to him, suddenly wanting his attention. He looked at me in surprise and I could see those copper flecks in his eyes. He deserved to be loved, not treated badly, I thought. I deserved to be loved too, not abandoned.

One kiss, I thought, would make us feel better. I leaned in and brushed my lips on his, fleetingly. Then stopped.

I could taste Sauternes. I could sense danger. I put a hand to my mouth.

'I'm sorry. I shouldn't have done that,' I said.

'No,' he replied, but he didn't move. He looked

overwhelmed. Almost shocked. As if he was in pain. For a moment, I thought he was going to cry.

I was mortified. What had come over me? There was a pounding noise in my ears, the rush that too much wine gives you, the rush that makes you lose all sense.

Then he put his hand up to stroke my hair. Everything tingled, inside and out. I shut my eyes, revelling in the feeling, craving more, ignoring the warning at the back of my mind that told me this was a step too far. No one would know. We were just two people looking for distraction from our troubles. Solace.

This time, he kissed me. All I could think was how differently he kissed from Olivier. Firmer, stronger, hungrier. I put my hands in his hair. I pushed up against him, feeling his hardness, and I knew he would give me the feeling I'd dreamed of for so long. I was already halfway there, melting inside. He was kissing my neck. I could barely stand. I heard him moan, and I felt powerful in that moment. I felt as if I was made of molten gold.

Then suddenly he stopped. He put his hands to his head and walked out of the room. I stood there, my heart still racing, the blood pounding around my body. The music had stopped and, suddenly, there was a chill in the air. The wine that had tasted so sweet had a bitter aftertaste. I started to feel a little sick. Not because of what I had drunk. But because of what I had done.

21

Juliet and Olivier walked, each of them with their hands in their pockets, braced against the damp as a pale mist rolled along the canal and enveloped them. Unspoken words hung heavy between them, but somehow Juliet felt as if the companionship they had once shared was still there. The complicity of former lovers, forged in intimacy. Curiosity and dread and anticipation curdled in her stomach. Was it pure vanity that had driven her to seek him out? The urge to be told he hadn't stopped thinking about her?

One thing was certain: whatever it was that had drawn her to him in the first place was still there. Every time she glanced sideways at him, she felt the same jolt, the same longing. Whether he felt the same was hard to tell, but he could easily have rebuffed her.

He pointed to a small café on a corner, and they ducked inside, revelling in the warmth and the rich scent of roasting coffee. They took a pair of seats at a zinc counter, and she watched him as he ordered two espressos. He placed his elbows on the counter, steepled his hands and rested his chin on his knuckles, gazing at her with a directness that she remembered as if it was yesterday. Did she have mannerisms he remembered too? She tucked her hair behind her ears, aware this was her default reaction when she felt nervous.

'So,' he said, 'what took you so long to come back?'

'I've just separated from my husband,' Juliet explained. 'My children are abroad. I work for myself. So I decided to spend some time in Paris to ... rediscover myself.'

She gave a self-deprecating smile, realising how self-indulgent it sounded, but he didn't seem to find it pretentious.

'I'm sorry. About your husband.'

'It's OK. It's fine. We agreed it was for the best. There's no ill feeling. We're still very good friends.'

He lifted one eyebrow very slightly. 'You are lucky.'

'I know.' Juliet smiled. She touched his arm. 'And I'm writing a book, while I'm here. I've given myself thirty days to write as much as I can.'

'It's taken you this long?' His smile was teasing.

'No. I've written lots of other books. I'm a ghostwriter.'

He frowned. 'A ghostwriter?'

'I don't know how to say it in French.' Juliet realised she should have worked that out earlier. 'I'm paid to write books for other people. Celebrities, usually.'

'Ah.' He nodded his understanding.

'But this book is my story.'

He held her gaze. Oh God, she thought, remembering the little notebook he had given her. How often she had thought of his encouragement.

'And what is your story, Juliet?'

Was there an edge to his voice? She felt her chest tighten.

185

He leaned forward. 'I was devastated,' he said. 'I was waiting at the cinema for you. And you never arrived. And I never saw you again. Nathalie did not know what had happened. I went to the house, but they wouldn't say where you had gone. I wanted to call the police, but my parents didn't want me to. I think they were worried there might be trouble, and they didn't want me involved.' He put his hands up to his head, running them through his hair. She wanted to do the same.

'I'm not sure,' she said, 'if I'm ready to tell you what happened yet.'

'Really? After thirty years? How long do you need?'

'I'm still trying to figure things out.' Suddenly, she sensed danger. Telling the truth, even after all this time, would have implications for other people. She had to be careful. She had been impulsive, finding him, before she'd got everything straight in her head first. Like many stories that revolve around love – unrequited love, betrayal, infidelity – it wasn't always easy to see who was right and who was wrong. The blame could shift depending on the perspective. Or the narrator. Sometimes, everyone was in the wrong. For love could make you a little bit mad. And no one knew that better than the French. Here they understood a *crime passionnel* – a crime of passion.

But would Olivier understand? Or would he judge her? She still wasn't sure of the part she had played in her own downfall.

'Then why did you come to find me?'

It was a fair question.

'I don't know. I had lunch with Nathalie. There was wine. I wanted to see you...'

She went to reach her hands out to touch his, but pulled them back just in time.

'Nathalie.' His face brightened at the mention of her name. 'We lost touch. She was a good friend to me. When you disappeared, I was a mess. She helped me a lot. She always said one day you would come back.' He gave a wry smile. 'Kind of a little late, though.'

'Oh.' Disappointment dug a sharp little knife into her ribs.

Olivier just looked at her. 'It is a shame. We were so in love. When you left, I dreamed of you every night. For years.'

Juliet stirred some sugar into her espresso while she found the courage to ask the next question.

'But you found someone, in the end?'

'I did,' he said with a sigh. 'Emma, my wife, came from New York to work at my father's company. She fell in love with France. With Paris. With me, apparently.' Juliet detected a trace of bitterness in his voice. 'We got married here – all her family came. It was perfect.' He gave a shrug. 'We got a beautiful apartment in the Fifth. We had good friends, great dinners, weekends on the Côte d'Azur. We had two children. Charles and Emily.' He smiled. 'The names work well for both French and English. I thought all was well. For ten years, it was good. Every other *Noël* we went to her parents in Boston. Then, one day, when Emily was ten and Charles was twelve' – he snapped his fingers – 'she told me it was over and she was going home. She wanted a divorce. And she was taking the children with her.'

'Oh my God. Oh, Olivier. That's terrible. How could she do that?'

He shrugged. 'I don't know, but she did. And what could I do? I worked for my father. I couldn't go to the States and live there if we were no longer married. It was impossible.'

He paused, finding it very painful. He took a gulp of coffee, and Juliet saw the glitter of tears in his eyes even now.

'Three months later, they were gone. I go to visit twice a year. There is FaceTime, but I don't feel like their father. She has married someone else. He takes them to the pool, to sport, wherever.' His expression was bleak.

'I don't know what to say, Olivier. That was so cruel. How could any woman do that to her kids?'

'Emma always knew what she wanted and how to get it. It is a good trait in a lawyer but not a wife.'

'Is that why you left your job?'

'*Oui*. I had a *dépression nerveuse*. I could not work in law anymore. My mind was...' He indicated all over the place. 'I had some money from my *grandmère*. I left my father's company and decided to open the shop. My comfort was always books. I surrounded myself with them. It was a good decision, I think.'

'It's a wonderful shop.'

He smiled. 'And next year, Charles is coming to Paris to do law. He's going to live with my parents. It's his decision, and I am so proud. I will have my son in the same city as me. And maybe Emily will do the same.'

Juliet reached out and touched his hand. 'I'm so pleased it's worked out. But I'm so sorry.'

'It has been very difficult. But I'm OK.' His smile was a bit twisted. 'I work hard in the shop, to make it the best bookshop in Paris. It keeps me sane.'

Juliet felt uncomfortable asking what she was about to ask, but she needed to know. She tried to sound casual. 'There's no one else, then?'

He looked at her with a wry smile. 'Sometimes I have a date. Dinner. But no more. Usually.' Juliet imagined the occasional sultry, slinky temptation that he gave in to. Was he lying? Was there a different woman in his bed every weekend? 'I don't want to make anyone a promise. Or for them to make me any. Promises are only there to be broken.'

'That's awful. To think like that.'

He stared at her. She shrank back a little at the look in his eyes.

'It took me a long time,' he said, 'to trust, after you vanished. Emma was the first woman I put my faith in. And what she did was worse. The worst.'

Juliet couldn't help her gaze wander towards the wedding ring on his left hand. He saw her looking. He held it up.

'It's the easiest way to keep people away.'

Ouch, thought Juliet. That was a pretty clear statement. He was not interested.

'I'm so sorry,' said Juliet. 'That what I did made it so hard for you. I thought you would forget me by the new year. I thought you would find someone like that.' She clicked her fingers.

He looked down at the table. Then back up at her. She could see there was pain in his eyes. How much had been caused by her, and how much by his wife, she couldn't be sure, but sorrow, and guilt, held the words back in her throat. What more could she say, except sorry?

Then he blinked, and smiled, and the pain dissipated,

replaced by the gentle sparkle she remembered so well, the soft grey of his gaze that had always made her feel warm when it settled on her.

'So, what else are you doing with your thirty days in Paris? You're not just writing in your attic?'

'I'm going to do all the things I didn't get to do when I was here. All the sights. The art. All the shopping, because I feel like being frivolous. And food. I'm basically going to eat Paris.' She laughed.

He nodded his approval. 'You know, I have a confession.'

'What?'

'I have never been to the Eiffel Tower.'

'You haven't?'

'Are you shocked?'

She thought about it. 'Well, I haven't been to the Tower of London. So maybe it's not so strange. But I think you should. I mean, the Eiffel *Tower*? It's iconic.' She paused. 'We should go.'

Her tone was light, but there was meaning underneath what she said. A challenge. An invitation. How would it land with him?

He sat back in his chair, gazing at her thoughtfully. She folded her hands, finding her racing pulse with her thumb.

'You know the best way to see Paris?' he asked.

'On rollerblades?'

He laughed. 'My rollerblading days are behind me. No – on a bike.'

'I know. I took a bike this morning, to the market. I was so proud of myself.'

'Notre-Dame, Tour Eiffel, Champs-Élysées.' He listed the sights. 'We can do it all in one afternoon.'

'Are you offering to be my guide?'

She was flirting. Was she pushing too hard?

'Sure. Why not?' He pulled out his phone, flipped through his calendar.

'You don't have to work at the shop?'

'The staff love it when I'm not there. They're always telling me to take a day off. But I never have a reason.'

'Oh.' She bit her lip to stop herself from smiling too widely. She liked being a reason.

'How about tomorrow?' He grinned. 'How do you say it? Strike while the iron is hot.'

22

The Ingénue

I woke the next morning with the taste of Sauternes and bitter guilt on my tongue. I kept my eyes shut, hoping to fall back into unconsciousness so I didn't have to face the memory of the night before, my stomach curdling with rich food and remorse.

If I had thought Olivier standing me up felt bad, nothing was worse than knowing what I felt now was entirely my fault. I tried to burrow deep under the covers, but the guilt followed, needling at me. My watch had stopped, so I couldn't tell what the time was. I could see it was light outside, but grey November never gave much away: it could have been dawn or dusk. I strained my ears to try to hear the children. Nothing yet.

I was a fool. I had betrayed Corinne, and the children, and let myself down. All of the excuses I had given myself for what had happened with Jean Louis faded away in the frigid, frosty daylight. Sunday morning had no truck with the misdemeanours of Saturday night and did nothing to reassure or absolve me. On the contrary, it lay the blame firmly at my door.

I crept out of my room to use the bathroom and brush

my teeth, splashing water onto my face, trying to wash away the memory of his lips on mine. In the mirror, my unfamiliar fringe framed my face, white and waxen, my eyes ringed with charcoal smudges of yesterday's mascara. I could hear someone in the kitchen so I shot back into my room and shut the door.

I sat on the bed. How was I going to get out of this awful situation? I would have to run away. I would wait for them all to go out – hopefully they would be going somewhere for lunch today. I would pack everything up and make my way to the Gare du Nord as soon as they were gone, get a train to the ferry, catch the next crossing, whenever that would be. And head home to normality and safety. I was out of my depth here, in a world I didn't know how to navigate, giving away my heart and my self-respect, behaving like a fool.

I felt comforted by my plan. Perhaps it was cowardly not to face up to my transgression, but I couldn't see any other option. I could leave a note, explaining I was homesick. They would soon find another girl to pick up where I left off. Their memory of me would fade like a photograph left in the sun, bleached to nothing.

I wouldn't have to face Jean Louis. And I wouldn't have to live in fear of bumping into Olivier. The humiliation of him having to apologise or explain why he'd stood me up, or even simply ignoring me, didn't bear thinking about. I was sad I wouldn't see Nathalie before I went, for she had been a wonderful friend, but I couldn't begin to articulate to her any of what had happened. I didn't want her to know the truth of who I was. What I was. I knew she would have no sympathy, after what her own father had done, and I couldn't bear the thought of her judging me. Or bringing our friendship to an end.

I began, as surreptitiously as I could, to fold all my clothes and put them in a pile on the bed so as soon as the house was quiet I could get my suitcase out and pack. I was halfway through when there was a knock on the door. I flipped my bedsheets over the clothes and stood up, my face red with guilt.

The door opened and Corinne put her head round.

'Can I come in?' she said.

'Of course,' I replied. What else could I say?

She was in pyjamas, grey satin with white piping. Even her nightclothes were chic, especially compared to the pale pink nightie with Minnie Mouse on the front I was wearing under my dressing gown. She looked better than she had last night, her eyes brighter. She looked younger too. When she was uptight, the tension in her face made her look much older. The pill must have made her sleep well and untangled all those ageing frown lines.

She sat on the bed and crossed her legs, as if she was a friend who had come for a sleepover, ready for gossip. I was standing there, awkward, with no idea what to say, tightening the belt on my dressing gown for something to do.

'I have to say sorry,' she began. 'For last night. I was . . . so tired. I sometimes don't know what I am saying.'

'That's OK.'

'You are so kind. With the children.' She pulled her sleeves over her hands, hugging herself. 'I don't know what we would do without you.'

My mind was racing, trying to figure out what to say, and how to react. 'Thank you.'

'I hope…' She looked around the room and her eyes fell on my passport on the dressing table. She frowned, then pulled back the sheets to reveal my folded clothes. 'You are leaving.' Her voice was flat.

I sighed. 'I miss home. I'm sorry.'

'Please don't go.' Her eyes were beseeching. 'We need you. I need you. The children… they would be…' She put a fist to her chest to indicate heartbreak. 'What can I do?' She jumped to her feet. 'I can give you more money.'

'No! It's not that.' I was on the verge of tears now, horrified by the trap I'd laid myself. Disgusted by my behaviour.

'Then what?' She sighed. 'We are horrible. I know I am horrible.'

'No. No, no, no. I miss my parents. That's all.' I wasn't going to be so treacherous as to let her think it was her fault.

She nodded, her eyes filled with sympathy. She put her hands together, as if praying. 'Please don't leave. Please give us a chance to show we can make you happy.'

This was awful. I wanted to run from the room, out of the apartment, out into the street, and never come back. My mouth was dry, my head was throbbing and I was breaking out into a cold sweat.

'I think I need to rest.' I put my hands on my stomach. '*J'ai mal à…*' I gave a wince to indicate my discomfort. It was a cop-out, but to blame period pains seemed the easiest way to get rid of her.

'Aaaah.' She nodded, as if that explained everything. 'Everything is bad when you have the pain. Tomorrow you will feel better.'

'*Oui.*' It seemed easiest to agree. I just wanted to be left alone, to think.

In the background, I heard the sound of the children racing down the corridor, and then Jean Louis' voice. I tried not to react, knowing Corinne was looking at me. Then she gasped, making me jump. Had I blushed? Could she see guilt in my eyes?

'Your rendezvous? It was good?'

She obviously hadn't spoken to Jean Louis yet. He would have told her I'd been stood up.

I shook my head and shrugged. '*Il n'était pas là.*' He wasn't there.

'*Putain!*' She looked outraged on my behalf and I almost laughed. I knew that was the worst word you could call someone. She patted me on the arm. 'There will be another one. A good one.'

I gave a half-nod, a half-shrug.

'You want breakfast? *Un petit café?*'

My stomach churned at the thought. I felt sick with the subterfuge. I wanted to sleep, and wake up uncomplicated.

'*Non, merci.*' I patted my stomach again and pointed to the bed. '*Je vais dormir.*'

She nodded. It was the perfect excuse, one any woman could understand.

'*Dormez bien,*' she said. 'We will be quiet like mice.' She put a finger to her lips, smiling.

As soon as she left the room, I crawled under the covers. I was trapped, in a nightmare of my own making. Wherever my mind turned, I felt filled with despair. Olivier had abandoned me, and I still hadn't had time to go over why. What had happened to make him change his mind? Was it me? Or a better offer? Or a terrible accident? My heart lurched – that hadn't occurred to me the night before. I suddenly imagined him in a crumpled heap on his rollerblades, his earphones still in, having skated out in front of an oncoming car.

As for Jean Louis, what was I to do? I was trapped here for now, and whatever I did next, I would have to face him. What had happened last night had seemed impossible to resist at the time, in our heady haze of sweet wine and moonlight and music. We each had wounds. Today, what we'd done appalled me and I began to shiver with the shock of the memory. Thankfully, eventually, sleep came to rescue me, and I fell into a deep dark hole while my mind sifted through the evening, trying to make sense of it all.

23

The irony of going cycling with Olivier when she would have done anything to avoid cycling with Stuart was not wasted on Juliet. But after trying it out the day before, it seemed logical to use a bike to tour a beautiful city, stopping off en route to admire the landmarks and maybe get a coffee or lunch. Stuart's idea of fun on a bike was to be head down and pedal as fast as you could, covering forty or fifty kilometres. And he wouldn't have given the time of day to the bikes dotted around Paris for public use. They were far too utilitarian and slow. Stuart's last bike had cost an eye-watering amount of money. Juliet hadn't resented his purchase, for she knew how much joy it brought him. She just didn't quite understand the thrill he got, or the endless amounts of equipment he seemed to get a kick out of buying to enhance his experience.

As she waited at the Vélib' Métropole nearest to her apartment, where they had agreed to meet, she felt a squiggle of excitement. There were five bicycles left in the rack, and she hoped Olivier would be here before they were all taken. She tried to look cool, thanking God for her sunglasses as she raked her eyes up and down the

Rue de Rivoli, searching for his tousled mop amidst the tourists who were already thundering towards the Louvre.

And then she felt two hands on her shoulders, and jumped. She turned, and there he was, holding up his Vélib' card.

'Hey,' he said. 'Our whistle-stop tour of Paris starts here. *Ça va?*'

He swiped the card over the first bicycle in the rack and pulled it out, pushing it towards her.

'*Oui. Ça va,*' she replied, holding on to the handlebars.

'So,' he said. 'We'll cycle up along the Right Bank, over Pont Alexandre and then head for the tower along the river. Does that sound good?'

'It sounds perfect.' She looked at him, admiring his figure in faded jeans and a waterproof blouson jacket that should have looked terrible but somehow looked the height of cool. She was in her running gear, and thanked God she'd invested in some new leggings from Sweaty Betty during lockdown. It wasn't her ideal fantasy-date outfit, but at least her sweatshirt covered her bum.

Suddenly they were off, swooshing along the Rue de Rivoli. She rode carefully, keeping one eye on the traffic and the other on Olivier. A pale blue sky emerged as the clouds drifted away obligingly to present the perfect November day: a little sun, a little breeze, a little chill in the air. She felt a smile spread across her face. She was cycling through Paris with Olivier. How on earth had this dream come true so easily? Was it a reward for all the angst? Would she wake up suddenly and find herself in an empty bed?

Eventually, they headed over the stunningly baroque Pont Alexandre, flanked by gilded winged horses and studded with cherubs and nymphs. Juliet smiled, revelling in its exuberance, this film-star of a bridge, feeling as if she herself was being tracked by a camera. She imagined the stage directions:

Juliet flies across the bridge on her bicycle, a wide smile on her face as she tries to keep up with her lover...

At the foot of the Eiffel Tower, they returned their bikes to another rack and headed towards the tourist trap that nevertheless spelled Paris and shouted its name louder than any other landmark. They rode up in the lift inside the belly of the great iron tower, then stood side by side on the viewing platform looking out over Paris: the deep green of the Seine, the trees along it tinged with autumnal orange, the white of the buildings sparkling in the sun, cars beetling along the Champs-Élysées. It reminded Juliet why she was here, why she had embarked on this adventure, and how this time she wasn't going to let anyone take this away from her.

As she stared up at the metal girders crisscrossing over her head, she thought how much her dad would have loved seeing this magnificent feat of engineering and felt a pang. He had passed away five years before, just two years after her mum, and for a moment she missed them both fiercely. She put a hand up to wipe away a tear.

'Hey,' said Olivier. 'It's not supposed to make you cry.'

'I was thinking about my parents,' she explained. 'I miss them both so much...'

He patted her arm. She didn't need to explain.

'It's weird,' she said. 'This time of life. It seems to be all about endings. Losing people. Making changes. Life not being what you expected. Trying to figure out how to live the rest of it.'

Olivier looked at her, concerned. 'You are very philosophical. Perhaps you have been in Paris too long already.'

'Don't you feel the same?' she asked.

He didn't reply straight away. He looked out over the city as if Paris would give him the answer they were after then looked at Juliet.

'It is up to us,' he said. 'To make new beginnings.'

She wiped away another tear, nodding, trying not to read too much into what he was saying. 'Yes,' she whispered, wondering if he felt as close to her as she felt to him, as if they could rewind and go back, to the time when they had meant the world to each other, when every second together had been pure joy.

For a moment, she thought he might lean in to kiss her. It was the perfect opportunity, high up above the city, for him to take her in his arms. She stopped breathing, waiting, hoping, too scared to make the first move.

Then he turned away to look back out at the view and the moment was gone.

24

The Ingénue

I spent all day between blissful sleep and wretched wakefulness, until five o'clock came around. The Beauboises needed me on a Sunday night more than any other night, for it marked the change between downtime and routine, and it was my job to make sure everything was ready for the week ahead and to get the children into bed early. It wasn't in me to let Corinne down as I knew she found this time of day the hardest, so I got out of bed and headed to the bathroom.

During the endless hours of self-flagellation, I had come to the conclusion that running away was not the answer. I would not let what had happened shatter my dreams. One thing I did know: I was still in love with Paris. I didn't want to leave. I still had so much to discover. I had begun to feel confident in this beautiful city, to speak her language, to adapt to her ways. Fleeing back to Worcester was the coward's way: if I did that, I would revert back to my old self, any dream of being chic and sophisticated evaporating.

And I didn't want to leave Nathalie. She was the first person I had met in my life who made me the best version of myself. With a friend like her, I could do anything. I knew that she would be there to help me cope with losing Olivier, that she would help me deal with the crushing disappointment I was feeling and give me hope. She would shore me up and rebuild my confidence.

I was going to stay, for now.

I felt nervous about facing Jean Louis, though. I couldn't be sure what his reaction to me would be. I decided I would be my usual self and pretend nothing had happened. I would keep out of his way as much as I could to avoid any awkwardness and make sure I was never alone with him. I couldn't think of another way of handling it. With any luck, he would do the same. I felt ashamed of what I – we – had done, but I knew I couldn't undo it. I wasn't going to blame anything or anyone but myself, but I had learned a lesson: self-pity and Sauternes were a deadly combination.

Charlotte and Hugo came running to me when I walked into the kitchen.

'Juliet! Juliet!' they cried, tugging at me.

Corinne smiled over at us. 'I never get such a greeting.'

I smiled, awkward, for it was true. They never seemed to clamour for her attention the way they did for mine. I guessed it was because I was a novelty.

'Go and wash your hands,' I told them, and I began to make *jambon-beurre* for their tea.

Corinne looked at me appraisingly.

'You look much better.' She nodded her approval. 'You slept most of the day?'

'Yes. Thank you. I feel fine now.'

'And you are more happy?'

I wasn't sure I'd ever be happy again. 'I guess.' I busied myself washing some tomatoes.

'Bravo,' said Corinne. 'You do not need a bad French boy. They will never make you content.'

'*C'est vrai*,' I agreed.

I looked up to see Jean Louis standing in the doorway.

'*Bonne soirée, Juliet.*' His smile was tentative.

'*Bonne soirée.*' I smiled back at him, not missing a beat as I turned away to cut more bread.

Thankfully, Charlotte and Hugo rushed back in at that point and sat down at the tiny kitchen table. I sat down to eat with the children. I couldn't face eating with Corinne and Jean Louis tonight. From now on, I would keep my distance and be professional. Au pair might technically mean being an equal, but I needed to be one step away and not consider myself on a par with them.

I hoped Jean Louis felt the same and would keep out of my way, and eventually we could just pretend it had never happened. But he stayed in the kitchen until Corinne decided to go and give Arthur his bath. I was tipping out little pots of Petits Filous onto the children's plates, ready to be sprinkled with sugar. He was pouring himself a glass of wine. He held up the bottle to me.

'*Un verre?*'

I shook my head. I couldn't face wine. I didn't trust what it did to me.

He waited until Charlotte and Hugo were eating their fromage frais, then came to stand near me. I felt myself redden with panic. My hands were shaking as I brushed away the breadcrumbs. He spoke in a low voice so the children couldn't hear. In English, so they couldn't understand – they were picking up more and more from me, but not enough to comprehend an adult conversation.

'Juliet. I must apologise to you.'

I plunged my hands into the hot water in the sink, keeping my head down. I couldn't look at him.

'I behaved very badly,' he went on.

'It was my fault,' I stuttered. 'I'm sorry.'

'*Non*.' His tone was forceful. The children looked up in alarm. 'It's OK,' he said to them. '*Finissez!*' He pointed at their plates with a smile, then turned back to me. 'I have no excuse,' he said, sotto voce. 'For a moment, I was mad. Too much wine maybe, but that is no excuse. Please forgive me.'

I looked up, managing to meet his gaze. He looked mortified.

'I don't know what I was thinking,' I said.

'You must not blame yourself.' He frowned. 'Please forgive me and please pretend that nothing happened. All that matters is that you are happy here.'

I set the plates I was washing carefully on the draining board. I wasn't sure what to say. I wasn't sure he should take the blame, for it was me who had stepped over the line, but for the time being it seemed the easiest way out of the predicament.

'You will stay, won't you?' His tone was urgent.

'Of course.'

He shut his eyes for a moment, clearly overwhelmed with the relief.

'It will never happen again,' he said. 'I promise. And thank you. The children love you so much. And Corinne too . . .'

'Corinne?'

'She sees you like a daughter.'

I was surprised. I didn't think she viewed me as much more than an extra pair of hands. Yes, she had moments of kindness, and she'd definitely been trying to win me round earlier today, but I didn't think she cared that much. Nevertheless, I felt sick at what I'd done. What effect would it have on her, if she knew how I'd thrown myself at her husband? Imagine if she had walked in and seen our little display? I felt queasy again.

I pulled the plug out of the sink and watched the water start to drain.

'OK. Let's pretend nothing happened,' I said to him with a bright smile, sounding more Mary Poppins than ever.

He nodded. 'Thank you.' I had never heard so much gratitude in someone's voice.

As I started to dry the dishes, I felt calmer, the torture I'd been putting myself through fading. We were both grown-up enough to put what had happened behind us. What a relief, I thought, shuddering to think how things could have ended had we not kept our heads.

We'd put everything behind us and all would be well.

The next morning, I had dropped Hugo and Charlotte at school. I was going to go back to the house and tidy the kitchen, then distract myself by heading to one of the big art galleries. I had loved art at school and had always wanted to see Monet's lilies. I was determined to educate myself first-hand and get some culture. Not be the sort of person who only knew great works of art from the postcards stuck on their bedroom wall.

I was about to push on the door into the courtyard when someone came up behind me and put a hand on my shoulder.

'Juliet.'

I jumped. A residue of guilt still clung to me and I was braced for confrontation. I turned and looked straight into the stricken face of Olivier. He looked terrible, as if he hadn't slept.

'I'm sorry,' he said. 'I had to come and find you. I couldn't just let it go. I need to understand. Why?'

I stared at him. 'Why?'

He put his hands up. 'Where were you?'

'Where were *you*?' I asked. 'I waited. Until nearly nine o'clock.'

'What?' He looked confused. 'But I waited too.'

I frowned. Was he pretending he hadn't stood me up? Had he woken up this morning and decided what he'd done was a bit cruel? Had his alternative arrangement not been to his satisfaction? I wasn't going to be second best.

'I sat at the table for nearly an hour,' I told him.

He shook his head. 'But you were not there.'

'I was! Third restaurant on the left.'

'Yes.'

'Rue des Petits-Champs.'

He tapped his hand against his forehead. 'Rue Croix des-Petits-Champs. *Croix. C'est la prochaine rue, après* Rue des-Petits-Champs.'

'Oh my God.'

I had taken the wrong street off the Place des Victoires. I had seen 'Petits-Champs' and forgotten the crucial extra word. And this meant Olivier hadn't stood me up at all.

He had been waiting for me, in another restaurant, thinking I was the one who'd bailed.

'Olivier, *je suis desolée*. I'm so sorry.'

We both laughed, a little shakily, as we realised we had been sitting streets apart, both thinking the worst.

'I would never do that to you,' I said.

The next moment we were in each other's arms, kissing with a fevered relief, overjoyed to have worked out the misunderstanding. I thought I would faint from happiness. I breathed him in, the trace of his cologne mixed with the scent of his anxiety. He ran his fingers through my hair, tweaking my fringe.

'*Qu'est-ce que c'est?*'

'My new fringe.'

'Fringe.' He tasted the new word as he brushed it away from my eyes. 'I like it.'

For a moment, I had a flashback of the last time someone had stroked my hair. I must have tensed, for Olivier asked if I was OK.

'Yes. Yes, of course.' My stomach roiled at the thought of him knowing what I'd done afterwards. He mustn't ever find out. I pictured myself lunging for Jean Louis, dishevelled and unsteady. The father of my little charges. The husband of the woman I was supposed to be helping, the woman I could see was suffering. My confidence in our reunion drained away. He wouldn't want to be with me if he knew.

'When can I see you?' he was asking.

It would be OK, I thought. Jean Louis and I had our pact. Olivier need never know. I knew I would never make a mistake like that again. I had to learn to trust him, have faith in us. We worked out we could meet for lunch the next day, near his university by the Panthéon. I had free time in between dropping off the children and picking them up, as long as I shopped for their food ready for their evening meal.

We shared one last embrace and I floated back in through the courtyard on a cocktail of emotions. Joy at having Olivier back in my life, but also horror that not trusting him had led to such insane behaviour. My chest tightened with anxiety at the memory of standing in the moonlight, swaying to the music, feeling crushed by Olivier's rejection and bolstered by apple brandy, letting Jean Louis' attention heal my hurt. It had been reckless. I vowed I would never speak to anyone about it. Certainly not Nathalie, and definitely not Olivier. I was ashamed of what I'd done.

Later on, my chores complete, I walked as fast as I could until I reached the river. I stood on the bank, watching the *bouquinistes* setting out their stalls – the books, the prints, the postcards, all the souvenirs people lugged home to remind them of what they had left behind. The city that promised so much. The city of romantic dreams. The city where to fall in love was inescapable, even if it was just with Paris herself.

I loved her so much. I had jeopardised everything with my foolishness, but I'd had a lucky escape. I began to breathe more easily.

Everything was going to be all right.

25

After they'd come down from the tower, they cycled back along the Left Bank. Juliet's legs were starting to feel like jelly. She wasn't used to this much exercise. She looked ahead at Olivier. He was sticking his legs out, freewheeling, playing the fool, and she remembered this side of him, the mischievous silly boy, and her heart pounded a little faster. He had always been able to make her laugh.

They crossed over to the Île de la Cité, the island in the middle of the Seine, and headed for Notre-Dame, looking up at the towering cranes. Juliet had watched the television in horror as the flames took hold that night: it had seemed impossible to believe it was happening, but here was the evidence, right in front of them. The site was surrounded by hoardings and on them were photographs of the fire and the damage it had caused, and the plans for renovating everything using the very best master crafts-men. It was sobering, but there was hope. Notre-Dame would rise again from the ashes.

They cycled over the tiny bridge that led from the Île

de la Cité to the Île Saint-Louis and pulled up outside Berthillon.

'Ice cream?' said Juliet. 'It's the middle of winter.'

'Just wait,' he told her, as they racked up their bicycles.

Ten minutes later, Juliet was looking down at a ball of luxurious vanilla ice cream in a porcelain mug, drowning in hot chocolate and slathered in praline cream.

'This is the ultimate in decadence,' she said happily.

'Simple pleasures.' Olivier gave her a slow smile and held her gaze just a second too long. She blushed and picked up her spoon. She felt as if there was a ball of melting ice cream deep inside her, spreading its sweetness through her veins.

'Thank you,' she said. 'For a fantastic day.'

'It's my pleasure. And now I can say I have seen the Eiffel Tower.'

Silence settled itself upon them as they scooped up the last of their affogatos. Juliet felt nervous. The next few minutes would dictate their future. She summoned up her courage.

'I'm having drinks with my neighbours tonight. Would you like to come? They said I could bring a friend.'

He paused before replying, thinking it over.

'Thank you,' he said, and for a moment her heart leapt with expectation. 'But I have stuff to do. There's always a payback when you take a day off.'

'No problem.'

She understood. She really did. He had any number of reasons not to turn back the clock. Not least that she had hurt him. And hadn't yet explained the past to him. And the wedding ring he had been wearing spoke volumes.

For him it must still represent the love he felt for his wife. Maybe he was living in hope?

But the main reason was, no doubt, that he was wary of getting hurt again. They might think they were tough at their age, but they were as soft as anything underneath their shells. They were vulnerable. Unlikely to bounce back. Just as they had more physical aches and pains, so they had more emotional ones too. Bruises lingered. Sores were there to be prodded and poked at. He was wise to be cautious.

That didn't make her any less disappointed.

They left the bicycles on the Île Saint-Louis and walked over the Pont Marie onto the Right Bank. The sun was low in the sky, the plane trees on the banks of the river casting long dark shadows on the water.

'I go this way,' said Olivier, pointing to the east. 'You will be OK? Your legs still work?'

She needed to know if she would see him again, but she couldn't show it.

'Oh, I'm fine. I can always get an Uber if I flake out.'

'Have a good evening.' He was suddenly stiff and formal.

'And you.'

Was that it? Would they not see each other again? She couldn't find the words to ask. Had today just been an act of chivalry on his part? Had it meant nothing? There'd been moments when she'd felt a warmth between them flicker into life, but somehow he had always backed away at the final moment.

'You're here for a while, right? Message me if you are at a loose end.'

He smiled, put his hand up in a farewell gesture and walked away.

She had no idea what to think. *Message me if you are at a loose end?* It was the kind of thing you said to a business associate who had rocked up in your city. Or a very old friend you weren't that bothered about seeing again. He was just being polite.

The sun slipped behind the horizon, taking any vestige of warmth with it. The lamps along the Seine glowed in defiance. The river turned to pewter. Headlights gleamed, pointing the way through a rush of evening traffic. Everyone stepped up a pace, eager to get home before the rain fell, for you could smell it in the air.

It began before Juliet had walked two hundred yards. Fat drops that started slowly, then gathered pace, until they were falling so fast that everything smudged into a symphony of gold and grey. If she stopped to get a cab, she would get even wetter. She hurried on, head down, pulling her cagoule out of her rucksack, struggling into it far too late, for she was already soaked to the skin.

At last, she reached the apartment. She shivered as she headed up in the lift. The last thing she felt like was going to drinks with a room full of strangers. She felt deflated. All the shine of a wonderful day had faded to nothing, swallowed up by her insecurity. Melissa wouldn't miss her. Her friends would all be young and vibrant and beautiful. They didn't need her there reminding them they would reach middle age one day and have the light inside them dimmed.

Inside the apartment, she gave herself a talking-to. A shower, fresh clothes, make-up – she would feel a different person in less than half an hour if she put her mind to it. Melissa had been so kind to invite her, and she was in Paris to step out of her comfort zone, not sulk on the sofa scrolling through her phone and bemoaning her lost youth. Self-pity was probably the least attractive characteristic. She was the only person who could snap herself out of it – and she had the perfect opportunity.

At just past seven o'clock, she knocked on Melissa's door with a bottle of champagne from the *cave* down the road, wrapped in white tissue.

'Oh my God, I'm so pleased you came. There are so many people dying to meet you.'

'There are?'

'Everyone wants to meet a real live writer.' Melissa drew her inside.

The apartment was twice the size of hers, bright white with colourful works of art and the kind of modern furniture that looked deeply uncomfortable but was designed to make you sit there forever. There were more than a dozen guests milling around, mostly in what looked like very expensive jeans; the women in silk shirts and high heels; the men in cashmere sweaters or beautifully cut jackets. For a moment, Juliet felt daunted. Not only did she know nobody but she didn't speak the language very well.

Then a man descended upon her with a tray. 'You must be Juliet,' he greeted her. 'I'm Bernard. Kir royale?'

She couldn't think of a nicer way to give herself some Dutch courage.

'*Merci.*' She smiled, taking a glass.

'Melissa tells me you're a writer,' he said. 'Everyone is so excited to meet you.'

'Oh, it's not that exciting. I just sit at a desk all day.'

'Oh, but it is,' he said, charming her. 'Come with me.'

Within ten minutes, she was embroiled in conversation with Eloise, who ran a cookery school nearby.

'We have one space left in our class tomorrow,' Eloise told her. 'I'll trade it for a write-up on our blog.'

'You have a deal,' said Juliet, delighted.

'We're doing *hors d'oeuvres*.' Eloise beamed. 'For *apéro dînatoire*. Everyone is crazy for it these days. Drinks with a table of canapés, for everyone to help themselves.'

It would make a great feature, thought Juliet. She would be able to pitch that as soon as she got home, in time for Christmas. The class started at nine, so she would have to be up early, but it was exactly what she needed. A sense of purpose to replace the slightly desolate hole inside her. She raised her glass in a little toast to herself.

She was home by nine-thirty, talked out and a little tipsy, but not so drunk she'd plummet back into gloom. She opened the window and leaned out, staring up at the stars, sifting through her day, the myriad emotions. She couldn't help wondering what Olivier was doing. Thank God she hadn't drunk enough to pick up her phone and send him a gushy text of thanks.

She did, however, send a text to Nathalie. She would still be at the bar, but she would be dying to know how the day went.

Amazing day with Olivier. Cycled all around Paris and went up the Eiffel Tower. But home alone. I think that ship has sailed. But good to put it to bed. Xx

She looked at her laptop, waiting patiently on her desk. Could she find the energy to plough on with her story tonight? She was getting to the most important part, and maybe once she'd written it all down she could find the courage to let him read it. She had always found written words easier to share than spoken ones.

She had a strong suspicion that it was the past that was keeping her and Olivier apart. It wasn't surprising he was wary, after what she had done. But if she could explain why she'd left, perhaps he would find a way to trust her again? The thought spurred her on. She changed into her pyjamas, poured herself a glass of water so she wouldn't feel dehydrated in the morning, and began to type.

At midnight, she climbed into bed. She checked her phone. There was a text from Nathalie.

As we say in NY, the show's not over till the fat lady sings.

26

The Ingénue

Everyone should fall in love in Paris at least once in their lifetime.

We fell hard and fast in that city, Olivier and I. It was a strange combination of feeling as if we had known each other for ever, yet wanting to uncover all the little details about each other as quickly as we could. We shared everything we loved, pulling each other into our opposite worlds. I introduced him to The Cure and baked beans on toast – I'd found a source of Heinz in one of the supermarkets. In return, he gave me Les Négresses Vertes and Anne Pigalle and Carambars and Camus and I worried I was getting the better deal. But then I was in his country, so he was able to share more with me.

I couldn't imagine him in Worcester. What would I show him there? A river and a racecourse and a cathedral. Parisian life seemed so sophisticated and exotic by comparison, and he was so insouciant about it, moving seamlessly between going busking with his mates in the Métro and attending a prestigious ballet gala with his parents: I saw the photos of them, glamorous in evening dress, his mother a tiny doll, his father suave and handsome.

And there was chemistry. We couldn't get close enough, taking every chance we could to kiss, on street corners, on bridges, in dark alleyways and shop doorways, lost in each other. I'd had a poster on my bedroom wall at home, *Le Baiser de l'Hôtel de Ville*, by Robert Doisneau, of a young man kissing a young woman as the rest of Paris walked by, and it used to make my throat ache with longing, wondering what it would be like to feel that depth of passion. And now I knew that fierceness mixed with tenderness; the moment when desire takes over and nothing else matters.

It was another week before we slept together. We went to the cinema to see *Les Amants du Pont-Neuf* with Juliette Binoche, and although it was in *version d'origine*, I was swept up in the intensity of the love story, crying my eyes out at the seeming impossibility of a happy ending between the two vagabonds, then sobbing with joy at the final twist as they set off into the future together, the most unlikely lovers. It was the most raw and passionate and exciting film I'd ever seen.

Afterwards, Olivier led me by the hand back to his apartment. As we kissed in the confines of the tiny elevator, I knew what was coming next. We didn't speak as we headed straight for his bed and it felt effortless and natural, so unlike my previous experiences, as he took me for the first time and we glided into synchronicity, riding into an explosion of fireworks that never seemed to end. Afterwards, I stared at the ceiling, dazed with wonder, laughing and crying until he kissed my tears away and we did it again to prove it was real.

The best thing of all was that he had given me the courage to start writing. I filled page after page in the

218

notebook he had given me with my observations about life as an au pair in Paris. I was trying to find my voice, trying to hit a tone, trying to write things I could include in my portfolio that might attract the attention of a magazine editor. 'How Not to Get Fat on French Food'. 'How to Look Chic on a Shoestring'. 'The Power of Red Lipstick'. Gradually, I grew in confidence and began to see stories everywhere, honing my journalistic eye. Though I didn't want to think about that next phase of my life. That would involve decisions I wasn't ready to make.

Olivier would read through everything I had written and tell me what he liked and what he didn't. What could be more funny. What could be more emotional. I was impressed with his insight. He had an innate understanding of what was important in writing: to leave the reader feeling something. Yet again I questioned the wisdom of him doing law. It seemed so dry, so driven by facts and rules and laws, so black and white.

'Maybe it won't be forever,' he told me. 'But I would be letting my family down, if I don't follow my father.'

I was impressed with his sense of duty, but I felt sad for him that it didn't speak to his heart. I knew how much he loved books, and reading – his room was piled high with paperbacks. He couldn't pass the *bouquinistes* without buying something to add to his collection. But he seemed resigned to his fate, so there was nothing I could do or say.

I didn't neglect Nathalie in all of this. I'd always disliked girls who dropped their friends when they fell in love. I had plenty of time to see her during the day, when Olivier was at lectures. My usual routine was to tidy the children's rooms and make their beds, put on a wash, then go into the kitchen to make a shopping list. Then I'd head out to meet Nathalie for a coffee at the café at the end of the street, sitting outside if it was sunny, reading a few pages of *Le Grand Meaulnes* while I waited for her. It was a slow process, and I needed my mini *Collins Gem French Dictionary* for more than half the words.

She would bounce up, always late, always full of some crazy story, always looking amazing, wearing things I would never dare to. She relished every detail of my love affair with Olivier, living it vicariously, for she shied away from relationships, blaming her father's infidelity. She had casual flings, but she didn't seem to want to get close to anyone.

'Not all men are like your dad,' I told her.

'Yes, but I don't know how to figure out which ones are and which ones aren't. So it's easier not to get involved.'

I found it sad that she was so scarred by her dad's behaviour, but it was the main reason I didn't divulge what had happened between me and Jean Louis. She was vituperative about the secretary her dad had run off with, and I didn't want to be the object of her disapproval. She was terrifying when she was scathing, and anyway, I had berated myself enough.

I did share my worries about Corinne with her, though. I still could never tell what mood she was going to be in.

'Honey, all Parisian women are difficult. You won't find one who's easy to work for.'

'There's something more, though,' I protested. 'It's not just that she's difficult. I think she might be ill.'

'Maybe she has PND?'

'PND?' Nathalie was full of acronyms I didn't understand.

'Postnatal depression.'

'Oh, you mean like baby blues?' I remembered my mum bandying the words around when my aunt had my youngest cousin and didn't seem to be coping very well.

Nathalie nodded. 'It can drive totally normal women nuts. I think my mum had it, after my brother was born. That was when she started drinking. Like, really drinking.'

I could see her getting agitated. She hated talking about her family. As far as Nathalie was concerned, her life had started the day she landed at Charles de Gaulle and Gigi was waiting at the arrivals gate to greet her. So we dropped the subject.

December arrived, and with it the excitement of Christmas around the corner. I was staying in Paris, because it was too expensive to travel, and although it would be strange, being away from home, I was looking forward to it.

Corinne seemed full of festive spirit and began to decorate the apartment. The decorations were opulent: strings of glass baubles and huge bunches of dark red roses and swathes of ivy, and a massive tree that took two men to drag up the stairs.

'What would the children like for Christmas?' she asked me one afternoon, her pencil poised over a list.

'Oh, Charlotte wants roller skates, more than anything,' I told her. She would gaze at other children skating in the Tuileries, her eyes round with want.

'*Bonne idée!*' Corinne looked delighted with this suggestion and wrote it down. 'And for Hugo too?'

'No. Hugo wants a kite.'

'*Un cerf volant!*' She seemed to think I was a genius,

and, for a few minutes, we felt quite close, laughing together, almost like sisters.

She was complicated, I decided. She seemed like two different people – or maybe more. There was the scary businesswoman – all spindly heels and dark nails. There was relaxed Corinne: the warm, loving mother and wife and thoughtful boss. And then there was the vulnerable, needy one who would appear out of nowhere, who would descend into a total wreck at the drop of a hat. I hadn't seen that version for a while and thought maybe she was gone for good. I even thought it might be because of me that she was on the mend. Somehow, I'd forgotten the roller coaster, how her mood would plummet for no reason, out of the blue.

One day, when I got back from shopping, I found her catatonic in the bath, an empty wine glass on the side. She'd left her bathroom door wide open. I rushed in, plunging my hands in the water to pull her out. She was freezing.

'Have you taken something?' I asked her, panicking, thinking she might have overdosed on the sleeping pills I knew she took.

Her lips were blue, but she shook her head. I wrapped a big towel around her, then led her into her bedroom.

'You must get dry, and warm. I'll make you a hot drink.'

I ran to the kitchen. My hands were shaking as I made her a hot chocolate. There was something really wrong with her. I thought about my conversation with Nathalie. But Arthur was nine months, nearly. Not a newborn. I wondered if she'd been like this before he was born. Should I ask her? Or maybe I should ask Jean Louis, in private.

I found her under the bedclothes, still shivering. She

hadn't dressed, and her skin was covered in goose bumps and a horrible shade of mauve. I put the hot chocolate on the table next to her and sat down on the bed, cautious. I patted her.

'Corinne. I am very worried for you. I think you need a doctor.'

'*Non.*'

'But you are so unhappy sometimes.' I was trying to be as tactful as I could.

She stared straight at me, and there was something in her eyes that made me feel uncomfortable. '*Oui.*'

I tried to smile, but I felt at that moment as if she knew exactly what had happened between me and Jean Louis. But she couldn't have. She'd been fast asleep that night, with a sleeping pill. And surely if she'd seen us, she wouldn't have let it go. She would have confronted us. I told myself I was being paranoid.

I swallowed. 'Is there something the matter?'

She shut her eyes. Her lids were like blue marble. '*C'est trop difficile.*'

I wondered what she found so difficult. She was doing what she wanted, they had plenty of money, as far as I could see, and as well as my help, there was a housekeeper twice a week.

'*Je téléphone Jean Louis?*'

Her eyes opened. '*Non,*' she said. 'Please don't.'

Maybe she had a friend she could talk to? I didn't feel as if I could be her confidante.

'*Je peux téléphoner une amie?*'

She shook her head. '*Je veux dormir.*'

She wanted to sleep. I understood that urge. To sleep was to escape from your troubles.

I did my best to make sure she was warm and comfortable. I offered to bring her some soup, but she refused that too. I left the bedroom feeling unsettled.

I decided to phone Jean Louis. He had given me his office number, when he had asked me a while ago to keep an eye on her. As soon as I spoke to him, he said he would come home.

I waited, in the kitchen, until I heard him come in. I crept out to the hall and put a finger to my lips.

'She is sleeping,' I said, and he nodded. We crept back into the kitchen and I told him how I had found her earlier. He looked distressed.

'I just don't know what to do,' he told me.

'I wonder, maybe, do you think she has postnatal depression?' I had looked it up in French. '*Dépression postnatale?*'

He shrugged. 'I don't know.'

'I think she should go to her doctor. I think she needs help.'

I saw there were tears in Jean Louis' eyes.

'I want her back,' he said. 'I don't know where she has gone.'

I reached out and touched his hand, spreading my fingers over his and squeezing. It was very different from the last time I had touched him. This time, I was trying to reassure him. To give him some comfort. He squeezed my hand back, holding it tightly, and I could see it was all he could do not to break down.

And then I looked up and saw Corinne in the doorway. She was staring at us with a blank expression on her face. Almost catatonic, like she'd been in the bath.

I pulled my hand away and Jean Louis jumped to his feet.

'Corinne.' He walked over and took her in his arms. I could see her staring over his shoulder. Not at me. Not at anything.

About a week later, I was getting ready to meet Nathalie to go shopping and send some presents back home. I thought maybe a scarf for my mum and some gloves for my dad. They were the sort of people who only bought things when they needed them, but I wanted to get them something really nice. Paris had taught me that beautiful things were never a waste of money, for they would last. We were going to the big department store, *Au Bon Printemps*, and were planning to splurge on ourselves too. The language school was having a party, and there would be other impromptu celebrations, so new outfits were needed. I felt happy and festive and excited.

I was grabbing my coat from the hook by the front door when Jean Louis appeared.

'Juliet. I have something for you.'

'Oh.'

'An early Christmas present.'

'You don't have to give me a present.'

'I want you to have these, as a thank-you. A keepsake.'

A keepsake? I looked at him doubtfully. I felt awkward as I took the little box from him. It was old, made from thin shiny red leather with the jeweller's name embossed in gold on the top. *Cartier.*

I gasped as soon as I opened the lid. There, inside, was the most stunning pair of earrings I had ever seen. I had no great experience of real jewels, but I knew just by looking that these were real: two teardrop-shaped sapphires surrounded by a cluster of diamonds. I had no idea what they were worth, but holding them in my hand made me panic.

'I can't take these.' I held them out to him.

He put his hands behind his back. 'They are yours. That's the end of it.'

I stared at them.

'They belonged to my grandmother. She told me to give them to someone special.'

'You should give them to Corinne.'

He shook his head. 'They're not her style. She wouldn't appreciate them. She has enough already.'

'But when would I wear them?' I was stammering. 'I'm not a diamond kind of person.'

'Oh, but you are,' said Jean Louis. 'Every woman is.'

I tried to think. 'Charlotte,' I said. 'Save them for Charlotte.'

'I have decided.' There was firmness in his voice. 'They are yours. Forever. To remember us.'

Us? I swallowed. What did he mean?

'The family,' he clarified, seeing the look on my face. 'It's the only way I can thank you, for what you have done.'

I had looked after Corinne for three days after I found her in the bath. She'd slept and slept, and I'd made soup and *coq au vin* and omelettes, under Jean Louis' instruction and to his grandmother's recipes, while he sat by her bed. And afterwards, she seemed a little better. Perhaps she was just exhausted, taking on too much work and trying to be perfect.

At the back of my mind, though, something felt a

little off. I couldn't help thinking that this was his way of rewarding me for keeping quiet about what had happened between us. I didn't need to be rewarded. Not when I'd been complicit. Somehow taking the earrings meant admitting what had happened, and keeping the memory of it alive, when all I wanted to do was forget. But I decided that the easiest thing for now was to play along. Protest would end in an argument. I would find a way to give them back, eventually.

'Thank you. They're beautiful.' They were dazzling. So dazzling I couldn't ever imagine wearing them.

'Don't lose them,' he said. 'If you lose them, it will bring you bad luck.'

'Of course I won't.'

I stuffed them into my pocket. The sharp edges of the box dug into my thigh. Whatever I did with them, the earrings were going to make me feel uncomfortable.

I rushed to meet Nathalie in the restaurant at *Printemps*, underneath the stained-glass cupola that threw shards of blue and red light onto our faces. I'd been so excited about our shopping trip, and the shop was so glamorous. All the Christmas lights and the glitter and the smell of a hundred perfumes and the gorgeous clothes: black velvet and red silk and diamanté. But I felt a bit sick. I'd taken the earring box out of my pocket and put it into my handbag, and I was tempted to show them to her and ask what I should do. But I couldn't do that without telling her the whole story. Instead, we ordered *crêpes suzettes* and talked about all the parties we were going to and eventually I felt my anxiety melt away. I resolved to hide the earrings in my drawer and forget about them.

Nothing was going to spoil my first Christmas in Paris.

27

The next morning, Juliet joined a dozen students seated around the stainless-steel island of the cookery school. She sat at the far end by the window that overlooked the Seine, observing them all with a writer's eye, working out what they were doing here, in Paris, learning to make canapés. Like her, most of them were women of a certain age, but there were a couple of men too, and a trio of what were probably hens.

Eloise stood at the head of the island, in crisp chef's whites, running them through the order of the morning. All the equipment they needed was laid out in front of them, along with the ingredients.

'We have a lot to get through, so you'll have to focus. But by the end of the morning, you'll be able to cater your own drinks party and wow your guests with your skills.' She twinkled. 'This is all made from scratch, except the pastry, so they'll be super impressed. I'll give you the recipes to take away, but remember: organisation and preparation is the key. You can't get halfway through and think, shoot, I forgot the Parmesan.'

Juliet laughed along with everyone else. That was so

her. She wasn't a bad cook, but she knew she was a dis-
organised one. Always running out of self-raising flour
and replacing it with plain, or substituting muscovado
for demerara sugar.

'So here's our menu. We'll start with the *gougères* –
basically choux pastry with cheese. Then the Roquefort
tartlets. Mini savoury madeleines you will fall in love with
– if you want to buy a madeleine tin to take home, may
I point you in the direction of E. Dehillerin, where Julia
Child used to get her cookware.'

There was a collective sigh of longing. Juliet made a
note to visit – another great feature idea, for who didn't
love a bit of kitchen porn? She sat back and let Eloise's
words wash over her. She had forgotten how much she
loved learning. Loved watching someone who knew what
they were doing. Loved to be inspired to push herself into
something new. She needed to do more of that.

As the class began to gather their ingredients and watch
Eloise demonstrate the rigours of choux pastry – theo-
retically simple, but there were tricks to getting it just
right – she felt herself beginning to relax. It was great to
be working under someone else's instruction, instead of
having to be self-motivated. Cooking together was soothing. It had a rhythm to it and a camaraderie. They were
all scared to make mistakes, yet they all knew it didn't
matter. It was canapés, not brain surgery. And Eloise
was a great teacher. Quick to correct mistakes, and very
disciplined – safety was paramount, and hygiene – but
she made everything look easy and was very encouraging.
The kitchen skills of the students ranged from clueless to
semi-professional, but no one showed off. They were all
in it together to have fun.

At the end of the first hour, the air was filled with the scent of baking and buttery fried onions which were going to become a compôte to serve on the side. As they broke for coffee, Juliet chatted to the women beside her, two friends from York who were here as a fiftieth birthday treat to themselves. She liked them immediately. They were her kind of women: smart and funny and warm.

When they found out Juliet and Stuart had separated amicably, they were agog.

'Oh my goodness,' sighed Sarah. 'You're so lucky. I love Philip dearly, but he drives me insane. He's obsessed with bloody golf. We never see each other. He won't even have noticed I'm not there. Not until he needs clean underwear.'

'Quite,' said Lisa. 'We often say we should all swap houses. Men in one, and us girls in the other. They could visit us from time to time.'

'Not for *that*, though,' laughed Sarah. 'I'm all done with bedroom antics.' She gave a little shudder. 'Is it great, not to be, you know, *bothered*? By your husband, I mean?'

Juliet wasn't sure how to answer. It felt disloyal to Stuart.

'I'm just getting used to my freedom,' she said. 'And there are things I miss. I'm still very fond of him.'

As she said it, she realised she was. She was nearly at the end of her first week in Paris, and so much had happened that she hadn't had much time to think about him, but suddenly it hit her. These women would be going back home at the end of the week to their husbands, but she wouldn't be. Ever again. A wave of something like homesickness hit her. The women were looking at her with wide-eyed envy, but suddenly she envied *them*. The note-swapping of what had gone on over the weekend, the little rituals of home, the way the tasks were shared out – Stuart would always put her passport back in the safe whenever they got home, in case of burglary. She was going to be responsible for her passport now for the rest of her life. She was perfectly capable of it, but that wasn't the point. It was that unspoken looking-after she was going to miss. The thought that someone cared about you enough to do those little things automatically.

'Are you OK?' said Eloise, coming by to inspect their efforts.

'I'm fine,' replied Juliet. 'This is such fun. Don't worry, I'm taking notes.'

'No problem,' said Eloise. 'I just thought you looked at a loss.'

Maybe I am at a loss, thought Juliet. *Maybe I've been in denial ever since I got here, chasing around after forgotten dreams and lost love. Trying to live out some fantasy. Maybe I need to get my shit together.*

She needed somewhere to live, and a life plan, and some structure. She might have money in the bank, but she wasn't old or rich enough to stop working, not for at least another ten years. What was she thinking, drifting around Paris buying *pains au raisin* and pretending to be a proper writer?

'*Oeufs mimosas*,' said Eloise, plonking a pan full of freshly boiled quail eggs in front of them. 'Would you peel those for me, please?'

By lunchtime, the island was filled with plates full of their accomplishments, and Eloise served them all a glass of *crémant de Loire* while they devoured their handiwork.

'Why don't you come to my apartment for a drink

before you go home?' Juliet asked Sarah and Lisa on impulse. 'I can practise my canapé skills on you.'

'We won't want to leave, though.'

'You'll give us ideas.'

They looked at each other. 'Thirty days in Paris,' said Lisa. 'Can you imagine?'

'We could do it,' said Sarah. 'What's stopping us?'

Juliet laughed, and they arranged to come over on Monday night, and she gave them her address. Was she going to start a trend? Was Paris going to be inundated with flocks of women coming to reinvent themselves?

When the class ended, she went back via E. Dehillerin and wandered the aisles in amazement. It was like stepping back in time, the shelves crammed with every utensil you could possibly imagine, and several things she had no idea what to do with. The copperware was the most lusted after – gleaming golden saucepans, pots and moulds lined the wall – but there were more workaday items too, like chopping blocks, whisks, rolling pins.

She had to buy a madeleine pan, and a couple of wooden spoons, too, to christen the kitchen in wherever she was going to end up. She felt like a tourist asking the assistant for her paltry items, but at least she tried to speak French and was pleased to make herself understood. Delighted with her wares, she headed back home.

When she got to the apartment, her misgivings of earlier faded. She turned on the lamps, lit her scented candle, put on some music and felt a sense of peace settle over her. She started to write a list of what she would need for when Lisa and Sarah came to visit. Then she thought – why not have a few more people? Do *apéro dînatoire* with the things she'd learned? She could ask Melissa and

Bernard, and Nathalie, of course – the bar was shut on a Monday night, so she would be free, hopefully.

And Olivier. She couldn't pretend this wasn't an excuse to reach out to him again.

She sat down at her laptop. There was one more chapter to write. She would have to share it with him if they had any chance of a future together, whether as friends or something more.

28

The Ingénue

A few days later, I came back from my language class to change before heading out to the cinema with Olivier. We were going to see the new Doors movie with Val Kilmer at a little cinema near his apartment. It was the perfect evening for me, for I knew I would have him all to myself, in the dark, for two hours, and I wouldn't be too late home. Sometimes it was tiring, going out with his friends, and I would struggle to get up the next day. I had already popped Arthur into bed, and the two big ones were having some quiet time in their rooms before going to sleep.

Corinne rapped on my door. 'I need to speak with you.'

Her face was so serious, I immediately thought there was something wrong with one of the children. '*Les enfants?*'

Irritation flickered across her face. 'They are fine. Follow me, please.'

There was something horribly formal about her tone as she headed towards the drawing room. My heart thumped. Whatever she wanted to talk about, it was not good news. What could have happened?

Jean Louis was sitting on the far sofa going through some paperwork with a glass of wine, which he often did before dinner. He looked up as we came in, surprised.

'*Qu'est-ce que c'est?*'

'We have a little problem,' Corinne told him, and he frowned.

'What is it?' I asked, wondering if one of the children had said something to worry her – but I couldn't think what I could have done.

Then Corinne held something up in her thumb and forefinger.

A red box. A small red leather box with Cartier written on it.

I looked at her. I was not going to speak first. This felt like a trap and I was wary of incriminating myself.

'I found this in your bedroom. In a drawer.' She raised her eyebrows at me.

I should have hidden it somewhere better. I should have left it in my handbag. But I had been scared of being robbed, so I'd tucked it in with my underwear.

I frowned. 'I don't understand. Why were you looking through my things?'

Corinne's face was hewn from stone, her eyes boring into me. 'You know what's inside, don't you?'

I gave a non-committal shrug. I was playing for time. Looking for clues.

She snapped open the box and the earrings flashed their brilliance at me. Jean Louis cleared his throat nervously and crossed his arms. I looked over at him. His face creased in a combination of apology and pleading.

Don't give me away, his eyes said.

I couldn't tell her he'd given them to me. It was too

suspicious. I had known all along that the gift was more than just a thank-you for supporting the family. It was more meaningful than that, and Corinne would know, if I told the truth, that we were hiding something.

'I am so sad,' said Corinne, gazing at the jewels. 'I did not take you for a thief.' *Seef.* I remembered her saying the word on the first night, with the same disdain. 'These earrings are worth a fortune. But I guess you know that.'

'I don't know anything about them.' I thought denial was the best tactic.

'So why were they in your knicker drawer?' *Kneecker.* She spat the word out like a cherry stone.

Jean Louis cleared his throat. 'Perhaps one of the children put them there by mistake?'

It was his only attempt to come to my defence. And now he couldn't tell her the truth. That the earrings had been a gift to me.

'Why would they do that?' asked Corinne.

Jean Louis shrugged. He wouldn't look at me. The air in the room was thick with tension and the pollen from the bouquet of lilies on the console table. I could feel it coating my throat, the tiny particles blocking my airwaves and stopping me breathing.

In the background, I could hear the children laughing. I could tell her the truth. But if I did, I would be smashing up their family. I couldn't be responsible for ruining their marriage, and the children's lives.

If I hadn't been able to see the very spot where Jean Louis and I had been standing in the moonlight that night, I might have brought him down with me. But what would be the point? Besides, if I hadn't encouraged him, hadn't twisted my fingers in his hair when he kissed me, tipped my head back while he pressed his mouth to my neck, run my fingers under his shirt to feel his warm skin, then none of it would have happened. It was my fault. I had started something I couldn't – shouldn't – finish, and it had run away with me. And this was my lesson.

'I don't know,' I said eventually, deciding that to play dumb was the best option.

Corinne gave a bark of laughter. '*OK.* You can have it that way. I don't need a confession. I have the evidence.' She snapped the little box shut again and I blinked as the light from the diamonds disappeared. 'I have booked a driver to take you to the ferry.'

'What?' She couldn't be serious.

Jean Louis jumped to his feet. 'Corinne – we should talk about this. Maybe—'

'Maybe what?' She gazed at him levelly. 'We do not want a thief in our house. Looking after our children.'

There was nothing he could say. He looked at me for a moment, but I wouldn't meet his eye. Corinne would know, in an instant, that we were complicit.

'The driver has instructions to make sure you get on board the next boat back to England,' she told me.

'No!' I shook my head, appalled.

'If you don't, I will call the police. They will take this very seriously.' She held up the little box. 'Do you know how valuable these are?'

I put my hand on my chest. I could feel my heart crashing about inside. What would the police do? Would I be arrested? Probably. The earrings must be worth thousands. My throat tightened even further as I realised I was trapped. There was nothing I could do to get myself out of this situation without unleashing something even more terrible.

I took the risk and turned to look at Jean Louis.

'Please?' I said, hoping it looked as if I was appealing to him for support.

Couldn't he think of someone else to blame? Couldn't he pretend it was a joke? Or a test he had set me to see how honest I was? Surely he wasn't going to see me sent home? Or arrested? I was amazed that he trusted me not to give him away. He must have nerves of steel.

He met my gaze and spread his hands.

'There is no choice,' he said, his voice low.

I sank back down into the sofa and put my face in my hands. I didn't want to leave Paris. I loved my life here. And I was passionately in love with Olivier.

Corinne stood up. 'You must go and pack. The driver will be here in an hour. Please stay in your room until then.'

'Can I say goodbye to the children?'

She gave me a withering look.

'I will go and put them to bed,' said Jean Louis.

I watched as he left the room, making his escape. What a coward. He didn't even have the courage to apologise to me in private. Or to say thank you.

Corinne and I faced each other for a moment.

'I'm very sorry. You were a great support. But what you have done is unforgiveable. I'm sure you understand.'

I couldn't be sure if she meant the earrings or if she was alluding to Jean Louis.

She lifted her hand and pointed towards the door, indicating that I should leave.

I went to my room and pulled out my suitcase. I felt

numb. I thought about running out of the door while they were with the children, but Corinne would send the police after me. Besides, where would I go? How would I explain things to Nathalie or Olivier without telling them the truth about what I had done? It was my own stupid fault, for crossing a line that should never have been crossed. My sins had caught up with me. I deserved what I had got.

I began to shiver as I packed, the shock of what was happening impacting on my body. The whole situation made my head spin. Although I could see why she wouldn't want a thief under her roof, I was outraged that she had searched my room. What had made her suspicious? How had she known to look for something? Or was it something she did as a matter of course?

It didn't really matter why now. She had found the earrings and that was that. And the truth behind my supposed theft was a worse crime. I deserved my punishment.

When I'd finished packing, Corinne led me out of the flat with my suitcase. Jean Louis was reading the children a story and I hesitated on the threshold, longing to give them one last hug. But she pushed me through the door and herded me down the stairs, through the courtyard and out into the street. There was a car waiting outside, the driver smoking a slim cigar. He barely looked up as Corinne opened the back door and motioned me inside. She spoke fast to him, and handed him an envelope of money, then turned to me.

'He has the money for your ticket. He will not leave until you are on the boat.'

I didn't look at her, or reply. This was my last chance to tell her the truth. But even if I did, it wouldn't let me off the hook. Even if it had, I couldn't have done it to Hugo, Charlotte and Arthur, who adored Jean Louis. I had to sacrifice myself to save their marriage, and for the children.

So this was goodbye. To Paris, to adventure, to my dream and to the beautiful boy I had grown to love.

As the car drew away down the street that I had started to think of as home, tears began to trickle down my cheeks. I hadn't wanted the Beauboises to see me cry, but the reality hit me as I realised I would never run down the pavement knowing that in a few minutes I would be in Olivier's arms, my mouth on his in a lingering kiss, our fingers entwined.

The driver didn't say a word, just fixed his eyes on the road ahead. He drove with quiet determination through the streets, and I felt everything slipping away behind me: the Eiffel Tower, the Sacré Coeur, the bridges over the Left and Right Banks I'd come to know so well. There would be no more melting *croque monsieur* to devour when hunger hit, no more dumpy glasses of *citron pressé* to make my tongue tingle, no more bottles of cheap red wine that made your teeth purple if you drank too much. I wouldn't need all those words I'd learned that fell from my mouth so easily now: *Oh la vache! Chouette! J'ai la pêche!* I wasn't fluent, but I felt much more comfortable speaking French than I had done. I didn't need to think so hard when I spoke it.

As we hit the autoroute that led to Calais, I fell into a troubled doze. When we stopped at the *aire* for a break, I didn't even have the spirit to think about doing a runner while the driver was in the toilet. I could have hidden somewhere, then hitched a lift to . . . where? Instead, I used the phone to call my parents. It was ten o'clock in England, nearly time for them to go to bed.

Thank goodness my dad answered. I imagined my mum on high alert, knowing that whoever was calling would be the bearer of bad news at this time of night, watching Dad's face for his reaction to measure the extent of the calamity.

'Dad,' I said, my voice small. 'I'm coming home.'

'All right, love,' he said, with the calm that made him good at his job.

'I'm getting the night ferry.'

'Do you want me to come and pick you up?'

Normally, I'd have said no. It was an awfully long way for him to drive. But my longing for the comfort of family was bigger than my conscience.

'Yes, please.' My voice was choked with tears.

I felt the driver's hand on my shoulder. I turned to gesticulate I would be two minutes and he nodded. For a moment, I saw a flicker of compassion on his face. I didn't know how much he knew, only that he'd probably been paid enough not to sympathise with my plight.

'I'll be there,' said my dad. My kind, dependable, wonderful dad. I imagined him in his tracksuit trousers and corduroy slippers, flapping a hand at my mum, who would be hopping up and down in anguish, longing to put her two pence in.

Five minutes later, we were back on the road.

At Calais, the driver bought me a ticket, slipped it inside my passport and led me to the queue of foot passengers. I was shivering: the sea air was so much colder than the city air, filled with salt and an invasive damp that worked its way through my coat. He stood with me

241

until I reached the head of the queue and handed over my ticket, gave me a nod of farewell as I reached the entrance to the gangplank, then disappeared off into the night, his mission completed.

I spent the first part of the journey on the deck in the freezing cold, gripping the handrail, staring down into the black water. I must have been crying, for at one point a woman put an arm around my shoulder, led me inside to the canteen and bought me a watery cocoa.

'No man is worth your tears,' she told me as we sat at a plastic table, the boat pitching and rolling. I put my head in my arms, exhausted, and she patted my back for a few moments. When I looked up, she was gone and my hot chocolate was cold, covered in a slimy skin. I threw it in the bin and huddled up on one of the passenger chairs, remembering the journey over and my excitement, my anticipation, my nerves. Now, I was filled with despair and a cold dread.

At Dover, I saw my dad on the other side of the barrier, in his grey Saturday jumper with the zipped neck. I buried myself in his arms, smelling the familiar scent of washing powder and shaving foam and him.

'It's all right, love,' he told me.

It wasn't, and it never would be. But I was going home.

29

It was two o'clock in the morning before Juliet finished writing. She felt drained with the effort, but it was done. She reread her words, trying to be objective. Even now, she could still feel the pain of her betrayal, the bewilderment, the sense of loss... Of course, in comparison to some situations it was hardly traumatic, just a series of events involving human beings who were fallible, who had made mistakes, but she had definitely been the one who had paid the highest price. At the time, she had thought she deserved it, but now, she wasn't so sure. She felt a surge of anger at the injustice as she closed her laptop.

Olivier and Nathalie had paid for those mistakes too, and she owed them both an explanation. She was gratified at how generous they had both been, welcoming her back into their lives without judgement, and part of her was anxious that once they knew the truth, they might not be so forgiving. But at her age, she knew honesty and transparency were invaluable and crucial. She had to be courageous.

She fell into bed, and slept surprisingly soundly before waking later than usual. Outside, she could hear the bells from the church in the next street. It was Sunday morning. She could lie in until noon if she wanted. But she wasn't in the mood for indolence. She was on a mission. She had plans.

She looked out of the window and saw Melissa coming back from a run. She jumped out of bed and stepped out of her apartment into the corridor just as Melissa came out of the lift.

'Excuse my pyjamas,' she said. 'But two things. Would you guys come for a drink tomorrow night? And do you have a printer I could borrow?'

'Yes, on both counts.' Melissa smiled at her. 'All my friends loved you, by the way. You're like a role model. A total badass living the dream.'

Juliet laughed. 'It won't always be like this. I'll be back to reality in less than a month. In the meantime, I'm making the most of it.'

Melissa high-fived her. 'I'll go tell Bernard he's on printer duty. I'd only end up throwing it out of the window.'

By ten o'clock, Juliet had a neat stack of printed paper sitting on her desk. Her story so far. She ran her hands over it, wondering if what she was about to do was the right thing as she put it in a large brown envelope.

Then she picked up a postcard which had been in with her mementos. It was a little grubby, from being shoved away in a drawer for so long. On the front was a vintage picture of the Eiffel Tower covered in glitter – there were only a few specks still on it – that she remembered finding in a dusty little tourist shop. On the back, it was addressed to Olivier, and she had written a quote from

Le Grand Meaulnes: '*It is better to forget me. It would be better to forget everything.*'

There was a stamp in the corner, an English stamp, but it had never been sent.

She swallowed down the lump in her throat as she tore a page from the notebook he had given her. She'd been using the empty pages to write notes while she was here.

This is my story, she wrote. *I hope it will help you understand why I left. I took this postcard to the postbox so many times, but I never had the courage to send it to you. xx. PS I am having some people for drinks tomorrow night if you would like to come.*

She wrapped the note around the postcard and tucked them both in with the manuscript, then sealed the envelope and wrote Olivier's name on the front. Then she added PRIVATE AND CONFIDENTIAL in the top left-hand corner.

She showered and dressed, then put the envelope in her bag, grabbed a bicycle from the rack down the street and cycled off towards the tenth. The traffic on Sundays was much quieter, so she took the scenic route, gliding through the Place Vendôme, the huge square with its golden obelisk, surrounded by shops with elegant facades and marbled walkways; shops she would never go in but could dream about. Then she headed north-east, towards the canal, wondering if he would be there, if she was doing the right thing, and what on earth she hoped to get out of it. 'Message me if you're at a loose end,' he'd said. Not turn up and dump a full confession on the table. But Juliet knew in her heart that until she *did* get the past out there, she wasn't going to move forward.

On the way, she cycled past a boulangerie painted in

pale blue and gold with Art Nouveau panels. There was a long queue outside. She'd read about *Du Pain et des Idées* and its cult following, so she stopped and joined the queue. She was thinking about pitching a feature about the best bakeries in Paris and their specialities, smiling to herself as she remembered how much she loved her job – what was there not to like about this kind of painstaking research? Besides, she was starving.

It was worth the wait, the inside spectacular, with gilded mirrors and a hand-painted ceiling and dark wooden counters crammed with irresistible baked goods. She had already decided to succumb to one of their famous *escargots* – a pastry swirl stuffed with chocolate and bright green pistachio cream. As she devoured every last flaky crumb, she decided it had been worth the trip even if her mission came to nothing. She took a few photographs on her phone and scribbled down a few notes as an aide-memoire.

The canal was quiet and still, the last of the night mist rolling off the water. It still felt as if everyone was sleeping off the night before, just a few shops and cafés opening up with a yawn. She hesitated outside the bookshop for a few moments. Maybe the past was best left where it was? She knew she only felt that because she felt shame, and knew that she would be judged, but she had to find the courage to admit her transgression. She couldn't hide it forever, and live in its shadow. She pushed open the door and walked in.

She sensed straight away he wasn't there. She would have been able to feel his presence.

'Olivier will be in later today,' an earnest assistant behind the counter told her. 'You are welcome to wait.'

Juliet felt a stab of disappointment, but she couldn't face the thought of waiting. 'Could I leave something for him?'

'Of course.'

She handed the envelope over. 'Please make sure he gets it. It's very important.'

'I'll give it to him as soon as he gets here.'

Juliet watched as the assistant placed it behind the counter, suddenly anxious about leaving it. Then she reasoned that even if it fell into the wrong hands, it didn't much matter. The story only had relevance to very few people. No one else would care about what had happened to a twenty-year-old girl, thirty years ago.

She left the shop, wondering what on earth she could do to take her mind off the agonising wait. She wouldn't be able to relax until she had heard from Olivier. Monet's *Water Lilies*. She reminded herself she had vowed to see them, and she loved to spend a peaceful Sunday wandering around an art gallery. She couldn't remember the last time she had, for Stuart wasn't really an art aficionado: old paintings bored him, and modern art made him apoplectic with fury. Juliet loved both; loved the warm tingling feeling you got when a painting really spoke to you.

She climbed back on her bike and set off towards the Tuileries, depositing her bike and walking through the bare trees until she reached the Musée de l'Orangerie and joined yet another queue.

She stood in the middle of the circular room that housed Monet's collection, surrounded by the most beautiful artwork she had ever seen. *Les Nymphéas*. *Water Lilies*. The huge panels followed the curve of the walls, one evoking sunrise and the other dusk. The softness of the colours, the splashes of brightness, the trailing weeping willows, the total immersion into the watery world Monet had created, his passion, made calm settle upon her.

She felt overwhelmed by the presence of such genius. The scale and the certainty. The ambition. This was what she was here for. To be moved, and to feel awe, and to be inspired. You couldn't be truly creative unless you immersed yourself in other people's work, even if it wasn't aligned with what you were doing yourself. And these paintings moved her deeply.

For a moment, she wished Olivier was here, so she could share the paintings with him, talk about their meaning and their purpose. Olivier had often cried when he experienced something that moved him: a film, a book, a record. She remembered him listening to the Cocteau Twins for the first time, tears streaming down his face, and her kissing them away. They'd been hot and salty on her lips.

At the thought of him, she took her phone out of her bag to see if there was a text. And there was. She stood, in the middle of the gallery, the lilies wrapped around her resplendent in green and gold, and read his words.

I would love to come for drinks. I will read your story tonight. O

She stared at the painting in front of her, her feelings reflected back in the colours of the brushstrokes. Deep dark green was the uncertainty she felt; bright yellow was the excitement at the thought of Olivier coming to her apartment. Blue as black as night was the darkness of the memories she was sharing with him. She turned slowly on the spot, following the canvasses around.

There was no beginning and no end, just a circle of eternity, and she wasn't sure of the way out.

30

By next morning, there was no word from Olivier.
Juliet couldn't pretend that she hadn't spent all night imagining him wherever he lived, leafing through the pages. She tried to picture his face as he read. Would there be sympathy or horror spread across his features? How would he feel about her now? Or maybe he hadn't read it. Maybe he'd got home from work and flopped, tossing the envelope onto a coffee table and putting on the television?

She told herself there was no point in trying to second-guess his reaction, or be a slave to the phone all day. She messaged Nathalie instead, checking she was still OK to come over for drinks. She definitely needed moral support.

Of course! I can't wait to see Olivier again. The
Three Musketeers!

Juliet had told her he'd said he was coming, but not what she'd done that morning. She needed to tell Nathalie the story face to face. Or maybe she should already have told her? Juliet sighed. It was a delicate situation, and sometimes she felt that whatever she did, it would be wrong and someone would get hurt. On the other hand, they were all grown-up now, and maybe she was overthinking it and it was water under the bridge to both Nathalie and Olivier? Maybe she was alone in worrying about the past?

To distract herself, she went out to buy wine from the nearby *cave* on the Rue Saint-Honoré, and managed to have a halting conversation with the assistant about the best vintage to serve, then lugged it back and stored the bottles in the fridge. Then she made two batches of savoury madeleines with her new tin in the tiny oven in her kitchen. She scoured the cupboards for glasses – they were mismatched, but it didn't matter; it was a look – and pulled out dishes and chopping boards and trays to serve the food on.

Then she headed for *Plisson*, the incredibly chic foodstore on the Place du Marché Saint-Honoré. With its snow-white walls and pale wooden floor, it was filled with every delicacy you could possibly wish for, beautifully packaged and stored in ranks of pristine refrigerators. In the centre of the store, wooden vegetable boxes were piled high with fresh produce. She bought a selection of *saucisson* and some cheeses and some very expensive biscuits, as well as little cornichons, then added rocket and radishes and cherry tomatoes.

It was still only two o'clock. Too early to lay everything out. She couldn't sit here alone with her thoughts, checking her phone every two minutes.

Now all she needed was something to wear. Something fitting for her first occasion as a hostess in Paris. She knew exactly where she would get something and headed straight for the glass frontage of Zadig and Voltaire in the Marais. Normally, she wouldn't have the courage to darken its door, but she felt empowered by her new life, and inspired by the style of the women she saw in the streets every day. She had lost her way of late, hiding under big jumpers and baggy shirts, never wearing anything that invited attention, but she was determined to get her fashion mojo back. She would never have the daring of her twenties and thirties, but she could still make a statement.

Undaunted, she flipped through the racks of dresses, knowing she would find the right one. And there it was, a dark green satin shirt dress, its colour reminding her of the Monets, with very long sleeves, a plunging neckline and a knot at the waist which meant the fabric draped flatteringly and fell to just above the knee. The clever tailoring gave a softness to its military feel.

'*Je peux essayer?*' she asked the assistant, who showed her to a changing room.

She stared in disbelief at the woman she saw in the mirror. How could the right dress do that, turn you into who you wanted to be? She looked sophisticated, edgy, sexy, yet also comfortable. It felt as if it had been made for her. The perfect outfit to feel strong but not overpowering.

She took it to the counter to pay. She hesitated for a moment before handing over her card: was she overinvesting? Was the dress too much for what was just supposed to be a casual drinks party? Of course, a little voice in her head reminded her that the dress was for Olivier, but she managed to ignore it. In the end, Juliet decided she deserved to dress up and feel good, so she handed over her card.

The assistant wrapped the dress in tissue and put it into a sleek carrier bag, passing it over to Juliet with a wink.

'You will have a good time in this dress,' she said. It felt like an omen.

On the way back, she stopped at Frederic Malle to choose herself a perfume, overwhelmed by the array of squat, round bottles with their black lids, the names so tantalising, the scents so intoxicating. She thought about who she was, and who she wanted to become. She wanted to keep the things she liked about herself, but mix in her fantasy ego: someone more sensual and daring and impulsive.

In the end, she chose French Lover: spicy, powdery, musky and warm on her skin. It gave her the confidence to take on an air of allure; a movie-star magnetism. It was like a talisman. She pressed her wrist to her nose and breathed it in.

She strode back through the streets, delighted with her purchases. Even if it was only for a short time, she was a chic, sophisticated Parisian woman, independent, glamorous, in charge of her future.

And then, as she came towards the end of a small cobbled street, she saw something that made her stop in her tracks. A sign in the French windows behind a wrought-iron balcony. *À vendre* – for sale. And underneath, the name of the *immobilier*:

Jean Louis Beaubois.

She had known she might come up against his name at some point, and she'd tried to prepare herself for it, but seeing it, so bold and brazen and *smug*, almost, made something boil up inside her. A mixture of panic and anger and the bewilderment she had felt at the time, a bewilderment that had made her feel powerless. She'd thought the fact that she was now a grown woman with years of life experience would have made her a touch more blasé, that she might even have laughed it off, but she stood there, staring, a lump in her throat and tears in her eyes, remembering her twenty-year-old self huddled up in her coat, tears streaming down her face, staring into the icy depths of the Channel, her fingers white on the handrail as her world collapsed around her.

She hurried on, swapping her bags from one hand to the other, eager to leave behind what she had seen before she had any foolish ideas about taking down the number. She felt exposed, as if layers of skin and bone had been peeled away to reveal her bruised and battered heart. She'd spent years carefully wrapping it, protecting it from further harm, but the damage was still there. Her earlier confidence evaporated. Would she never be able to escape from what she'd done?

It was dark by the time she got back to the apartment. She had just over an hour before everyone arrived. It meant she couldn't brood over what had happened, but had to throw herself into the preparations, leaving just enough time to get changed and put some make-up on.

By six o'clock, everything was perfect. The *saucisson* and the cheese were laid out, the madeleines piled high, the radishes and cornichons and tomatoes in bowls. The glasses were polished and the bottles were chilling. She folded up a white linen cloth to wrap around them while pouring.

She slipped into the new dress, pleased that it hadn't

done that awful trick of not looking nearly as good now she had got it home. If anything, it looked better, especially once she had put on her make-up and fluffed up her hair. As she stared at herself in the mirror, she thought that if she caught sight of herself, at a book launch or a private view, she would want to know who she was.

The last thing she did was to put Melody Gardot on the speaker. She tried not to think about the two tickets she'd bought to see her in two days' time. She loved Melody's music, the laid-back smoky jazz, her sexy, sultry voice, the romantic lyrics, and, seeing that she was performing in Paris, had decided to treat herself. Who the other ticket was for, she couldn't yet be sure.

The doorbell buzzed. Juliet realised it was going to be down to her to do everything – from answering the door to opening wine to introductions – and she had a moment of panic. Stuart had always been brilliant at parties. Endlessly amiable and patient, happy to be bossed about, content to do the less glamorous chores while Juliet sparkled. In that moment, she wished he was there, to get the wine out of the fridge while she answered the door. But he wasn't.

Melissa and Bernard were the first to arrive, and Bernard very sweetly offered to be in charge of drinks.

'It is very difficult, when there is just one of you,' he told her, undoing the wire cage on the first bottle. 'It is better that you speak to your guests.'

Juliet was charmed by his understanding.

'Where did you find him?' Juliet asked Melissa, who laughed.

'He has very few faults,' she told her. 'I'm keeping him, for sure.'

The bell rang again. To steady her nerves, Juliet took a sip from the glass Bernard had handed her. She was going to be on high alert every time it rang, wondering if it would be him.

It was Nathalie, behind an extravagant bunch of red roses. She threw off her coat to reveal an electric-blue jumpsuit more suited to Studio 54. Juliet felt a burst of fondness for her ebullient, eccentric friend. How had she survived thirty years without her?

'This is as cute as!' Nathalie exclaimed, looking around the apartment, then she introduced herself to Melissa and Bernard. 'Hi. I'm Nathalie. Did Juliet tell you how far we go back? Over thirty years. I'm not even kidding.'

Of course, she and Melissa started swapping notes, both being American. Juliet found a vase for the roses, then took the warmed madeleines out of the oven and the apartment filled with the scent of rosemary.

Melody Gardot sang about the rain outside.

The bell rang again. It was Lisa and Sarah, brimming over with excitement, bearing champagne and a box of pale green macarons.

'We did the macaron class today, with Eloise,' said Sarah. 'Oh my God, look at this. How are you ever going to drag yourself back to England?'

'It's gorgeous,' sighed Lisa. 'We thought our Airbnb was nice, but this is next level. The mirrors! The chandelier! I'd never dare put a chandelier in a space like this.'

Juliet felt as proud as if it was all her own. She passed around the madeleines, turned the music up a little as the chatter got louder, tried not to look at her watch.

'Stop looking at your watch,' murmured Nathalie. 'He'll be here when he's here.'

Juliet didn't tell her that Olivier might well have changed his mind after reading the manuscript. There would be time afterwards. Her heart felt heavy, though. If he wasn't here by now, nearly eight o'clock, he probably wasn't coming. She tried to console herself that she had an apartment full of wonderful friends, old and new, and they were all having a great time, if the chatter and laughter were anything to go by. She should go and enjoy their company. She was the hostess. She couldn't lurk in the kitchen nursing her disappointment.

She poured herself another glass of fizz and went to mingle.

Half an hour later, when they were on the fourth bottle and the pile of madeleines had vanished, she heard a text come through on her phone. She tried to ignore it for a few minutes, for once she had read it, she would know the truth. Eventually, she couldn't bear the suspense.

'Excuse me,' she said, and slipped away to pick up the phone from her desk.

I won't make it. I have to Zoom with the kids.
Desolé. O.

Whether it was the truth or a lie, she couldn't argue with the excuse. Children always came first. And no matter how much she tried, she couldn't read any more into it. Couldn't figure out if he'd read her story and decided to keep away, or if—

Of course he'd read it. And now he knew the truth, he didn't want anything to do with her. He was angry. Rightfully so. But what else could she have done? The truth was better than lies.

257

She turned away, back to her guests, determined not to punish herself a moment longer. In the background, Melody Gardot sang about her foolish heart.

By half past nine, all the guests except Nathalie had drifted away.

'That was so fun,' said Nathalie. 'I think that's the first party I've been to for years. I never have time. I'm always working . . .' She trailed off as she saw Juliet's face. 'Oh shit, babe. I'm sorry he didn't turn up. But you can't spend your life waiting for a man. You know that, right?'

'I know,' said Juliet. 'But I think it's my fault.'

'I thought you had a great day together? If he's not here, maybe he has other issues? What did his text say?'

'He had to Zoom his kids.'

'Well, there you go.'

'His wife took his kids back to America.'

'Bitch.' Nathalie scowled. 'That might explain why he doesn't want to rush into anything.'

'I think,' said Juliet, 'it's because I gave him the opening chapters of my book to read.'

'What book?'

'I've been writing a book while I've been here. My own book.'

'You didn't tell me you were writing a book!'

'I know. Because I was excited about what we're going to do together and I didn't want mine getting in the way. It's called *The Ingénue*. It's about what happened. Why I left.'

'So he gets to read it and I don't?' Nathalie put her hands on her hips, indignant.

'Don't be angry. I'll just tell you instead.'

Nathalie grabbed the last half-bottle of crémant. 'OK,' she said, topping them both up. 'I've got all night. Shoot.'

'It was the night I got the wrong restaurant,' began Juliet. 'That's when it all went wrong. When I muddled up the street names, and thought Olivier had stood me up...'

'I'm so sorry.' Nathalie's eyes were filled with tears as Juliet came to the end of her story. 'I never imagined that was what had happened in a million years. How do people get like that? So selfish that they are prepared to ruin someone else's life? You were a baby, for God's sake. You took the bullet for that guy.'

'Listen, I was complicit—'

'Oh, shush. You had a drunken kiss. In a moment of vulnerability. He was totally working you. When you woke up the next day, you knew it was wrong and you didn't carry on. Do *not* blame yourself.'

Juliet sighed. 'But I threw myself at him.'

'Listen. I know those kinds of men. They are my dad. They have a sneaky way of sending out signals, and somehow, the woman always ends up blaming herself. Trust me, you would not have thrown yourself at him if he hadn't been giving you the come-on. It's very subtle, and it works particularly well on young girls.'

Nathalie was scathing. Juliet considered what she was saying, and for the first time in her life she began to see that she might be right. Jean Louis had fed her, he had plied her with wine, he had put on music and invited her to dance. She had been played. Something, thank goodness, had made Jean Louis see sense that night just in time. The fear of being caught? Probably, given his eventual cowardice.

'What I can't figure out,' she said, 'is if Corinne knew I didn't take the earrings. If she knew full well Jean Louis gave them to me, then threw me under the bus.'

'Either way, she's a manipulative piece of work and he's a slimeball. You should go find them and call them out.'

'They must be well into their sixties by now. There's no point.'

'That's no age! They'll still be swanning about Paris, using people and throwing them away.'

Juliet sighed. She didn't think it had been as calculated as Nathalie made out. It had been a perfect storm, of vulnerability and naïveté and confusion.

'It was tough. They had three little children. And looking back, I'm sure she had postnatal depression. Don't you remember us talking about it? Nobody really knew much about it in those days. Certainly not men. It probably made Corinne completely paranoid and irrational.'

'And his excuse?'

Juliet sighed. 'I think *he* was struggling. To keep the family together. He didn't understand what was going on with her. She was very tricky. And he was probably desperate for a bit of affection.'

Nathalie rolled her eyes. 'You are such a good, sweet person. I can't believe you're excusing him.'

'I know. But it's one thing I've learned from writing people's stories. Things aren't always black and white. There isn't always a bad guy. Sometimes there are two bad guys. Or no bad guy, just an impossible situation. Or a mistake. People make mistakes and behave badly. But behaving badly doesn't make you evil. And hopefully you learn and don't do it again.'

She stopped, slightly taken aback by her own diatribe. She'd never vocalised what she felt about what had happened to anyone.

'I do get that,' said Nathalie. 'I've made more than my fair share of mistakes and done things I'm not proud of. But he should have had the balls to save you.'

'I know.' Juliet suddenly felt drained by it all.

Since she had seen the estate agent sign with Jean Louis' name on it, she couldn't get out of her mind how he had betrayed her loyalty. How he had turned her life upside down, snatched away her first chance of happiness, destroying her confidence and her self-belief and her belief in other people.

Now she was here, thirty years older and wiser and with nothing to lose, could she let him get away with it?

'He is still in the city. I saw his name in an apartment window this afternoon. Do you think I should go and find him? Confront him about what he did?'

Nathalie's eyes glittered like a mirror ball.

'I'm sure my *andouillettes* would be all the better for a pair of his testicles,' she said.

Juliet snorted with laughter. Although they were both making light of it, she didn't want to be in the shadow of what had happened a moment longer. Even now, it was impacting on her, as she awaited Olivier's verdict. It was time to take control of the situation. For the first time in thirty years, she wanted the voice she had never been given.

'I'll bring them to you,' she said. 'On a silver platter.'

31

The first thought Juliet had when she woke the next morning was that she still hadn't heard from Olivier. Maybe she never would? She certainly wasn't going to hound him by texting him. That would be embarrassing for both of them. She still wondered if his excuse had been genuine, or if it had been the kindest way for him to step away from her. After all, she had hurt him before, so why would he want to risk being hurt again? And she thought he probably still loved his wife. There was profound sadness in his voice when he spoke of her. Juliet didn't know why you would still be in love with someone who had been so cruel, but that was the strange thing about love. It wasn't always logical.

The second thing she thought was that today was the day she might finally get some closure on the past. The prospect of confronting Jean Louis at last filled her belly with fire. After talking to Nathalie, she saw everything so much more clearly. If only she'd had the chance to talk to her friend at the time. Nathalie would have given her ballast and made her fight. But every escape route had been closed off, by making her feel culpable. Was it too late to stand up for herself now and make herself heard? Was there any point?

She had to do it, for young Juliet. For the foolish creature she had been. But, also, for the relationships that had been smashed up as a consequence. Her first love. Her deep friendship with Nathalie. She had lost the two people who had been so instrumental in her becoming the person she had dreamed of being.

It had taken a long time to rebuild herself and get herself back on track. She picked up the notebook that was on the bedside table, flicking through the jottings she had made that winter: the memory of that first lunch, the crispness of the chicken and the melting *tarte Tatin*, the visit to Père-Lachaise and the ghosts of the past, a review of *Les Amants du Pont-Neuf*, a description of Paris as the city prepared for Christmas. Naïve ramblings, some of it, but in the end, they had been the saving of her.

She'd written them up and used them as her portfolio to get a job as assistant to the redoubtable Maggie Lansdown, editor of *Front Door*, a magazine aimed at middle-class, middle-aged ladies like her. Maggie had a ferocious memory, could write a thousand-word feature in less than an hour and had her first gin and tonic at midday on the dot. Juliet had done everything Maggie didn't want to do, from writing book reviews to recipes to answers on the problem page. The pay was dreadful, but she got digs in a sprawling house in Hammersmith full of Sloany girls her age who were much more fun and much kinder than she would have imagined, generous with their clothes and the contents of the fridge and who had an extraordinary ability to party all night and still get up for work. That had been the start of her recovery.

She put the notebook back on her desk. In some ways, she thought, her story was only just beginning.

It was easy to track down Jean Louis' office. It was near the Palais Royal, so business was obviously good. To calm her nerves, Juliet took some time to wander through the gracious courtyard and peer in through the windows of the shops in the *galeries*: all out of her league, like those in the Place Vendôme, but there was never any harm in looking. She gazed at the frocks in Didier Ludot: at Balenciaga and Courrèges and Chanel, marvelling at the handiwork and attention to detail, the tiny buttonholes, the beading, the handmade lace, the luxurious fabrics and immaculate tailoring. She had always loved vintage clothing, but this store was one step beyond: a place that spoke of film stars and princesses and first ladies and a lifestyle most people would never be a part of. The love affairs, the assignations, the broken hearts. Perhaps this suit had been worn to the reading of a will that had changed lives; maybe that dress had been worn to break off an engagement; another to the funeral of a secret lover. An idea took seed in her mind. If these clothes could speak, she thought, perhaps she could be the one to tell their story?

She stopped for a moment to gather her thoughts, and listened to a cellist playing Bach's *Suite Number One*. As the music floated towards her, she felt her emotions stirred with each mournful note. It was as if he was playing in memory of the girl she had once been. Perhaps, after what she was about to do, she would be able to leave that girl behind and concentrate on herself. Paris had so much to offer. She had been here a week already and had done so many things that chimed with who she was, as if the city was coaxing the real Juliet out of hiding. Not that she had been stifled, exactly, but sometimes motherhood and responsibility and work commitments smothered you, and of course lockdown and the anxiety of Covid had eaten away at everyone. She knew how lucky she was to have this chance of – what, exactly? A kind of renaissance. She had to make the most of it, and that meant shutting the door on the Beaubois household once and for all. The shadow it cast was far too long.

She made her way over to the office, his name emblazoned in gold over the door. The office was smart, on a corner, the entrance flanked with potted olive trees. The photographs of the apartments for sale made her mouth water. Floor-to-ceiling windows, the light flooding onto the gleaming parquet floors, wood-panelled walls, high ceilings, terraces and balconies, cobbled courtyards – the cream of Parisian real estate. The prices were steep, many of them well over a million. Juliet imagined the kind of people who might be able to look in this window without daydreaming, who could actually choose the one which ticked their boxes, make an appointment to view and a few weeks later have the key to their home. The kind of people who might buy a vintage dress at Didier Ludot, she supposed.

But amidst the grandeur were a few smaller apartments that she could actually afford, including the one she had stumbled across in that tiny cobbled street just between the *3ème* and the *2ème*. It was tiny, of course, but perfect, with its second-floor balcony and open-plan living space, with everything you might need on the doorstep. There was a boulangerie a few steps away, a little café with a burnt-orange awning and umbrellas on the pavement – Juliet could almost smell the coffee and croissants in the air – and a hip cocktail bar behind a black door with standing room only. What more did a woman of a certain age need? A table by the window for a laptop, a bed with a decent mattress, a rail for a capsule wardrobe...

She still couldn't get used to the idea that she had money in an account that could take her life in a completely new direction. Her fair share of a house they had bought when the area was run-down and no sane person wanted to live there. A house that had been riddled with damp and rotten window frames and a kitchen that cried out for a tetanus injection. Between them, she and Stuart had poured money and time and love into the four walls. And now, they had reaped the benefits of their foresight and hard work.

As she gazed at the real estate on offer, she began to have the tingling feeling that came from seeing somewhere you could imagine living. There was no reason why she couldn't live in Paris – thanks to her passport courtesy of an Irish grandmother. What was stopping her?

She had given herself thirty days to accomplish her mission. After that, she had planned to head back to England to find herself somewhere to live, to pitch some features in the run-up to Christmas, and perhaps find the courage to submit what she had written so far to a publisher for consideration. Although she knew that, to be taken seriously, she had to finish the book, and she still didn't know how it was going to end.

And then there was Christmas itself – the challenge of establishing some new traditions to fit their new way

266

of living. After years of Christmas-card lists and stocking fillers and filling the freezer, she still wasn't sure how that was going to work.

She was so swept up in her thoughts, she almost didn't notice Jean Louis come out of the office. His coat was pale caramel with a velvet collar. His chestnut hair was streaked with grey, still thick, swept back from his brow. She was close enough to smell him: a drift of something exclusive, expensive, subtle. He turned, sooner than she expected, and she realised she was blocking his way.

'*Pardon*,' she said. His eyes flickered over her and he gave her a smile of acknowledgement, a little nod of appreciation at her good manners, but nothing more. No flicker of recognition. She could reach out an arm to touch him. Declare herself. But this wasn't a confrontation she wanted in the street. Instead, she brushed past him and pushed open the door to his office.

'*Bonjour*,' sang a perfectly made-up assistant in a sleek grey trouser suit. '*Je peux vous aider?*'

'You have a little apartment for sale, between the Third and the Second.' Juliet pointed towards the picture in the window.

'*Ah, oui.*' The woman smiled. 'It is very desirable.'

'I'd like to see it, please.'

'*Bien sûr.*' She sat down behind a computer and began to type, bringing up the details. 'When are you free?'

'As soon as possible.'

'How about tomorrow morning?'

At the thought of this becoming a reality, Juliet felt her mouth go dry and her heart pound. She had got this. She was in control. She wasn't going to be afraid.

'*Parfait.*'

267

A door opened and a woman came out with a sheaf of papers.

'*Excusez moi,*' she said to Juliet, barely registering her, and went to put the papers on the table next to the assistant, rattling off instructions in that familiar voice.

Corinne. In a chocolate-brown sweater dress and high suede boots, confident, soignée, as chic as she ever had been. Juliet stood patiently until they had finished their conversation, then Corinne swept away back into the office and shut the door. Like Jean Louis, she hadn't recognised Juliet. Of course she hadn't. She hadn't given her any attention at all.

The assistant smiled up at her. '*Dix heures? Demain?* Ten o'clock tomorrow morning.

'Perfect. Thank you.'

She breathed in as the assistant wrote the appointment down on a card and handed it to her with a smile.

'Monsieur Beaubois will see you there.'

Juliet called in to She Cried Champagne for lunch, and to tell Nathalie she had made an appointment.

'Do you want me to come with you?' Nathalie asked, bringing her a glass of white Bordeaux and a slab of terrine studded with apricots and pistachios. 'I totally will.'

For a moment, Juliet was tempted to have her friend's back-up. Jean Louis wouldn't stand a chance with Nathalie in tow. Juliet almost laughed at the thought – Nathalie wouldn't pull her punches. But this was her battle. She had to have the courage to face him by herself.

'That's fine. But I'll be OK.'

'Call me straight after.'

'Of course!'

'In fact, come over to my apartment. It's my morning at home doing admin.'

'Yes,' said Juliet. 'We need to get started on the book.'

Nathalie hesitated. 'Are you sure? I mean, you have your own to worry about.'

'Of course I'm sure. That's why I didn't tell you about it.'

'I have so many ideas, but they're all whirling around my head. I need you to help me focus.'

'That is exactly my job,' Juliet said, smiling.

The thought of harnessing Nathalie's energy and channelling it onto the page filled her with excitement. And that was what she was good at: capturing the spirit of a person and finding a way to share it with readers. Establishing order from the chaos.

When she got back to her apartment later that afternoon, she sat down and began an email to a publisher she'd worked with before on a couple of celebrity food books. She loved Molly's energy and thought she would fall in love with Nathalie. She was young and ambitious and confident enough to take risks. It was worth a try.

Dear Molly,

I'm writing to you from Paris, the City of Lights. A glorious month all to myself, drifting among the pavement cafés, devouring hot chocolate and sinful cocktails and growing plump on cheese and *pains au raisin*. And I've fallen across an old friend, Nathalie du Chêne, who has a little bar *'bistronomique'* called She Cried Champagne. I know, right – don't you just want to go there already?

Anyway, her story is really inspiring, *and* the food she serves is out of this world but super simple. Imagine the most divine grilled goat's cheese drizzled with truffle honey and served with bitter leaves. I expect you know where this is going . . . Her story would make such a great book, with recipes, of course, and I wanted to share the idea with you first as we have done so many successful projects together and you know how I work. I'm attaching a link to her website, and would love to talk to you more, if it tantalises you.

Bisous, as they say here!

Juliet x

It might come to nothing, she thought, as she pressed send. But if she had learned anything in life it was to be bold, to play to your strengths and to use your contacts.

She checked her phone for the millionth time to see if Olivier had made contact, but there was nothing. She had to come to terms with not hearing from him again. At least she had been honest. At least she hadn't lured him back under false pretences. She felt wistful, thinking back to the day they had spent together, and what might have been.

She decided to go for a run. It might clear her head and make her feel less melancholy. She smiled at herself – was she going to come back from this trip a committed jogger? Not that she had been very committed, but the very fact that a run appealed was surprising. Maybe Stuart had been right all along about this fitness lark? She wondered how he was getting along, and decided to send a text.

Hey. You'd be proud of me. Putting on my trainers
to go for a run along the Seine. How are things
going? Xx

She was just about to head out of the door when her
phone rang. It was Stuart.

'Hey.'

'Don't forget to warm up and stretch.'

She felt a squiggle of pleasure at the sound of his voice.
It was teasing, not hectoring.

'I won't.' He had a point. She had been forgetting to
stretch.

'I need your advice.'

'Of course.'

'I've got a date tonight.' He sounded a bit sheepish.

She stopped in her tracks on the way to the door. 'Oh!'

'I've been set up by someone at work. I don't really
want to go.'

'So who's the lucky lady?' Juliet cringed even as she
said it.

'She's an A and E consultant.'

'Wow.'

'I'm not sure I'm going to live up to her expectations.'

'Of course you are!' Juliet felt a surge of indignant
loyalty.

'Anyway, I'm committed now, so I need to know what
to wear.'

'You know the answer. Jeans and a nice shirt. The
striped Paul Smith. Or the flowery one I got you for your
birthday.'

She could picture him in it. He'd been very unsure

about flowers at first, but she'd assured him that nothing was more irresistible than a man in a flowery shirt.

'I was thinking of getting something new. Maybe plain white.'

Perhaps he didn't want to go on a date wearing a shirt his ex-wife had given him.

'White works. You'll look great whatever.'

'I think I'll go to Westfield.'

Westfield? Once upon a time, she wouldn't have been able to drag him there in a million years. 'If you need advice just send me photos from the changing room.'

'Thanks.'

'And have fun.'

'Mmmm.' He sounded less than enthralled.

When she hung up, she felt odd. Not jealous exactly. Perhaps a little panicky that she'd made a mistake? Or maybe she felt protective? Stuart was such a darling and she wasn't sure he was tough enough for the dating scene. Women could be brutal about their expectations and she didn't want some uppity A and E consultant crushing him because he didn't tick all her boxes.

But she couldn't worry about him. He was a grown-up, and she had her own issues to sort out. *Not my circus, not my monkeys,* she told herself. But when she was bombarded by a slew of photos of him in a changing room, she spent a long time considering the options before texting him back.

The blue. By a country mile. Smokin'! xx

32

The next morning, Juliet woke with a lump of dread in her stomach. It wasn't too late to cancel. Or she could just not turn up. But then Nathalie texted her a string of emojis – biceps and flames and thumbs up and hearts – and she felt a renewed determination. She dressed in a black-and-white silk shirt and her velvet jeans, hoping she looked like the kind of person who could buy a studio apartment on a grey November morning in Paris.

She decided she would walk rather than cycle. She was proud not to have taken the Métro once since she'd been here. She had read somewhere that your activity level over the course of the day was more important than an intense workout if you wanted to keep on top of your weight, and it looked as if that was true. Despite her indulgence on the food front, she had lost a bit of her middle-age spread from all the cycling and walking.

She set off, walking past the café that had become her favourite, tempted for a moment to abandon her mission and head inside for an almond croissant. She watched the street cleaners emptying the bins and washing the pavements, the *papas* in immaculate suits walking their children to school, the delivery vans unloading fruit and veg. A young man sat in a doorway, engrossed in a paperback book, and she felt a momentary pang. A young girl smoked a cigarette and argued with a man in unnecessarily large sunglasses. An ancient woman shuffled along the pavement with a minute dog clad in a tartan coat. Morning in Paris. It made her ridiculously happy.

Maybe this was where she belonged?

She arrived at the bottom of the street and looked up it, to the battered cars parked along the pavement, the occasional splash of graffiti that gave it a tiny bit of edge. The silver of the roofs, the dormer windows, the black wrought iron of the balconies: it was so unmistakably Paris. Could she feel at home here? she wondered.

She thought she already did.

The front door of the building was propped ajar. She went inside and climbed the stairs to the first floor. The door of the apartment was open too. She could sense Jean Louis as soon as she stepped inside, the cologne she had smelled on him when they had passed in the street making her stomach flip slightly with anticipation. Not fear, for she had rehearsed her every movement and had given Nathalie the address of where she was going just in case. Her boots rang out on the parquet as she walked into the main room.

He was standing by the window, admiring the view he would use as the primary selling point. He turned with a charming smile. 'Madame Hiscox?'

She had used her married name.

'*Bonjour, Jean Louis,*' she replied, and he frowned. Clients would not normally call him by his first name.

He examined her for a moment. She probably was very

different from the girl he had once known. Older, wiser, her hair shorter, undoubtedly more curvaceous. And a little more glossy. Certainly more confident.

'It's Juliet,' she prompted him. 'Juliet Miller?'

He still didn't click, unless he was a better actor than he had been.

'Your *au pair*. You must remember.' This was a statement not a question.

'Juliet.' He managed a smile. She could see him desperately trying to assess the situation and work out what the hell she was doing here. '*Quelle coincidence.*'

He spoke French, presumably to gain the upper hand.

'No. It's not a coincidence.' For a moment, she relished the power of seeing him panic.

'You're here to view the apartment?'

'I'm here to see you.'

He tried to take in what she was saying. He frowned. 'I must ask you to leave. This is a private home. I have a viewing—'

'Yes, yes, I know. The viewing is with me.'

'I see.' He understood now, that he had been trapped.

'You can show me around while we speak. It looks very nice.' She took in the shuttered windows that looked out onto the street, the herringbone floor, the mid-morning light turning the wood a buttery yellow. The bleached beams. The minute kitchen in reclaimed wood.

He gawped at her, with no idea what to say.

Suddenly, all she felt for him was pity, not fear. 'I want you to know that what you did to me was very, very wrong, Jean Louis.' Using his name made her feel powerful. She would never have called him that before. 'I don't mean the kiss. It was just a moment, and we both knew it was wrong. It was what you did afterwards.'

'Juliet.' He ran his hands through his hair, still plentiful and luxuriant. 'Do you not think I know?'

'I don't know. Do you?'

'I was out of my mind. I was so terrified. Not of Corinne, but of what was happening to her. I knew . . . if she knew . . . about us—'

'I know why you did it.' Juliet's tone was sharp. 'But you could have found a way. I would never have betrayed you. I would never have told her what happened between us.'

'I know. You protected me even though I didn't deserve it. You were so much better than me. So much stronger.'

He'd gambled on her loyalty. He had known she was honourable. And he'd used her integrity to save himself. All the rage she had been bottling up for thirty years came bubbling up to the surface.

'You ruined my life. You took away everything that meant something. I lost my friends, my job, the love of my life, my future, my confidence . . .' She must not cry. 'You sat there, next to Corinne, knowing you could have saved me.'

She would not cry, even though she felt as if she was on that sofa, the two Beauboises staring at her, about to sentence her. She remembered how helpless she had felt, even though she was innocent. She locked eyes with Jean Louis, staring at him, remembering how he had avoided looking at her. She wasn't going to let him get away with it now.

She took in a deep breath and drew herself up. 'But I was OK, because there are good people in the world.

Good people who protected me and built me up again and restored my faith. And now I'm strong enough to come back and look you in the face and tell you what a coward you were.'

His fists were in a ball and his jaw was clenched and, for a moment, she felt afraid he might turn on her. But, to her surprise, he crumpled in front of her eyes.

'I know,' he said. 'I tried to forget what I had done to you. I told myself you were young and smart and beautiful and you would be OK. But when Charlotte grew up into a young woman, it hit me. I would have killed any man who did that to her.' He shut his eyes, pressing his fingers over his lids as if to blindfold himself from the memories. 'What do you want from me?' he asked finally.

'I don't *want* anything,' she replied. 'I've said everything I need to. I can't change the past. But I needed to lay some ghosts so I can have the future I want. It's taken me this long to come back to Paris, to the city I fell in love with, because I couldn't bear the memories.'

'I am truly sorry.' He looked up. 'I thought of you often. I would have sent you money, but—'

'Money?' Juliet shook her head. 'Money would have made no difference.'

There was silence for a moment. They stood, heads bowed as if in prayer, letting the wrongdoings of the past settle. Eventually, Juliet looked up.

'I saw Corinne,' she said. 'In your office.'

He nodded. 'It was thanks to you,' he said. 'That she got better. After you left, I made her go to the doctor. She was very ill, and it was you who saw that. You brought her back to me, the woman I loved.' He sighed. 'Still love.'

He looked at her. 'Tell me – what happened to you. You seem happy. Strong. You look beautiful . . .'

Juliet held her head a little higher and put her shoulders back. She felt a gentle calm descend as something deep inside her unknotted itself. She was surprised to find that she was glad that Jean Louis and Corinne were still together, for it made what had happened worth it. If their marriage had crumbled, it would all have been for nothing.

She didn't want to tell Jean Louis about her life. She didn't want him any closer than he was now. All that mattered was that she didn't have to live in the shadow of what had happened, the guilt mixed with regret and anger and despair, hating herself for her weakness, both of them for what they had done, and then not having the courage to defend herself. She had faced up to him, and suddenly, he was nothing.

She looked at her watch. 'I only have half an hour. Would you show me the apartment?'

Her voice was crisp. It was clear this was now business. He understood the segue. That conversation was over.

'Of course. This is a very special apartment – we don't get them like this very often, in such a good location. It has been restored to the best specification. The underfloor heating, the recessed lighting, all the internet and wireless speakers.'

He had switched, seamlessly, from deep emotion to business mode. Juliet could only imagine his relief, that she hadn't been bent on some hideous revenge, *Fatal Attraction*-style. It had never been about revenge. It had been about her self-respect.

As they moved through the apartment, Juliet had to

admire how cleverly it had been done. All the mod cons hidden behind the period features. She imagined Corinne directing the renovation, demanding perfection. Would it be completely insane, to buy a flat here? After all, she felt more at home here than she had in London for a long time. Paris inspired her. It made her want to cook, eat, write, dance, love, laugh . . .

There was nothing wrong with looking.

33

Nathalie greeted her with strong coffee and a plum and almond cake she was recipe testing for the bar. She cut a huge slice and served it to Juliet with a spoonful of *crème fraîche* as she described her confrontation with Jean Louis.

'It's funny. It felt a bit like that scene in the *Wizard of Oz*, when Dorothy pulls back the curtain and finds the little old man there. As soon as I confronted him, it stopped mattering. All the bad feelings melted away.'

They were sitting at the dining table by the French window in Nathalie's apartment. Nathalie's décor was re-strained decadence: a leopard-skin chaise longue, art deco mirrors mixed in with iconic black-and-white photos, white high-gloss floorboards, potted palms and a whole wall of recipe books. Hundreds.

Outside, through the wrought iron of the balcony railings, fat grey pigeons danced among the chimney pots and a hotchpotch of roofs led all the way to the Sacré Coeur. It was the classic Parisian view, a different story in each dormer window – who lay under the eaves, sleeping, dreaming, waking up, making love?

'You took control. Like they say, you owned it.' Nathalie's eyes narrowed. 'But you were too kind to him. You should have made him suffer a bit more.'

'There was no point. I had a moment of fun when he recognised me and wasn't too sure what was going to happen.' Juliet could laugh about it now.

'It wasn't supposed to be *fun*.' Nathalie scowled. 'I was there. I saw the damage he did. I lost a wonderful friend, and Olivier lost the love of his life . . .' She frowned. 'Have you heard from him yet?'

'No.' Juliet looked down at her phone. Every time she checked to see if she'd got a message from him, her disappointment grew less. Maybe she was getting used to the idea that she wouldn't have Olivier back in her life? At least she'd been able to let him know the truth. It had been a nice fantasy. But perhaps a little too optimistic. 'You know the best thing to come out of this?'

'No?'

'I've got my friendship with you back.'

She walked round the table to hug her friend, laughing as she felt her squirm.

'Are we going to do some work?' said Nathalie gruffly, wriggling out of Juliet's embrace. She was only good with physical interaction she had instigated.

'We are,' said Juliet, sitting back down. She picked up a pack of index cards. 'OK, so each of these index cards represents a different page of the book. Each recipe gets a card, and each anecdote, and each photo. And then we can shuffle them all around until the book gets a shape. Themes will emerge – maybe each section will be influenced by a particular person, or a food type, or a wine.

There has to be some logic underpinning it all. An order. Even if it feels delightfully random when you dip in.'

'Like the best meal – it looks effortless and spontaneous, but underneath is a great deal of thought and care.'

'You've got it.'

'I'm nervous,' said Nathalie. 'It's all here in my head, but I'm not sure how to get it out.'

'That's my job. And we can do it however you want. I can record you talking, or you can write it yourself, or a mixture. We'll soon find a rhythm.'

Nathalie nodded, chewing on a fingernail. 'I don't know where to start, though.'

'Go over to the bookcase. Find the books you admire, that speak to you.'

'I don't want to copy anyone.'

'Just for inspiration. We're not going to copy. This book will be one hundred per cent yours, I promise.'

'OK.' Nathalie walked over to the bookcase and ran her fingers along a row of brightly coloured spines.

Juliet could see she was daunted, but this was her forte: drawing people out and making sense of their story. She felt more excited than she had done for a long time. More excited than she was about her own book. She wondered if perhaps that had been more therapy than ambition: a way of her making sense of her past. Writing it all down had certainly given her the courage to set things right: rekindling her friendships and calling out the person who had betrayed her. And maybe things hadn't gone quite as she had secretly dreamed – for now she couldn't deny to herself how often she had fantasised about Olivier – but things were good. Life was exciting and rewarding.

She smiled as she breathed in the scent of the strong

coffee Nathalie had brewed, the spices from the candle flickering on the mirrored coffee table, the aromatic steam from the warm cake. She watched her friend pull out an armful of books and lug them over to the dining table, leafing through them, absorbed in her thoughts. Just Nathalie in her life was enough of a reward, she thought. To have Olivier as well would have been too good to be true.

'I'm thinking Julia Child meets Anthony Bourdain with a hint of Dorothy Parker.' Nathalie's voice broke into her thoughts. 'Smart with a really strong voice and a sense of . . . rebelliousness? Old-school with a rock-and-roll edge.'

'Ambitious,' said Juliet. 'Strong.'

'I don't really do wishy-washy.' Nathalie stood with her hands on her hips. She was in a black leather miniskirt and a Blondie T-shirt that Juliet was pretty sure she remembered from thirty years ago. Once seen, never forgotten.

'No,' agreed Juliet, smiling, and she vowed that every page would be soaked in her friend's spirit.

34

Juliet had been in Paris for over a week. She had crammed in so much already, made new friends, ticked so many things off her bucket list, had more feature ideas than she could possibly write. She was living the Parisian dream. Every morning she did her run around the Tuileries and had started to nod to the other people she recognised as she ran down the wide steps and headed through the trees. Then she took her laptop to her favourite café in the Place du Marché Saint-Honoré for coffee and croissants – they knew her by name now. She could weave her way through the traffic on her bicycle without her heart leaping into her mouth. People were starting to reply to her in French, not English. She'd been to the Picasso Museum, wandered the tranquil gardens of the Grand Mosque and sipped on sweet mint tea.

So why did she feel so flat?

Juliet lay staring up at the beams above her bed. She knew why, of course. Her hope had never faded. When her messages pinged, her heart leapt. But it was never him. It was Nathalie sending her ideas. It was Sarah and Lisa asking her to meet them for a farewell drink. It was Izzy, sending her a photo of her with a bunch of new friends, tongue out and peace sign, as was the modern way.

It was never Olivier.

Tonight, she had tickets to see the jazz singer, Melody Gardot. She knew deep down she had hoped to take him. For it was Olivier she thought of when she played Melody's music. It seemed to match the feelings he stirred in her – sleepy, dreamy, romantic. But that dream was not to be. The gig was eight hours away. Maybe she wouldn't go. But that would be a waste. Who else could she take?

Nathalie couldn't come because she was working. Sarah and Lisa were heading home. She could ask Melissa, but she wasn't sure it would be up her street.

Then she remembered the man she'd met on the train. The man who'd asked her for a drink. She still had his card in her handbag. Paul Masters. Would it be crazy to ask him? He'd been very attractive, very attentive. And he'd read *Le Grand Meaulnes* – surely there couldn't be a better indicator of someone's suitability?

Maybe somebody completely new would shake her out of her torpor? Arguably, Olivier wasn't the only man in the world who could make her happy, and maybe he had too much of his own baggage anyway? And she would only be asking him to accompany her to a gig, not walk her down the aisle.

Ignited by the prospect, she dug his card out of her handbag and quickly typed a text. She tried to keep it direct and non-flirty.

Hi Paul. It's Juliet from Eurostar. Bit short notice, but I have tickets to see Melody Gardot tonight if you are free. J

Was she being reckless? she wondered as she pressed send. It was no worse than swiping right on Tinder and meeting someone. And although you could never tell, he had seemed nice. His clothes had been impeccable, his card was very tasteful, in a stylish font. Superficial ways to judge, perhaps, but what else could you go on, in the modern dating scene? She could google him, she thought, and then decided not to. You could overdo the research, and it was no replacement for simply spending time with someone.

She didn't have to wait long for a reply.

How nice to hear from you. I'd love that. Thank you. P

Polite. Enthusiastic. To the point.

She felt a fizz in her stomach. A smile spread across her face. She was excited, she thought. There was something beguiling about unknown territory. Meeting up with a stranger she had met on a train. How romantic, she thought. She was proud of her boldness. It was very liberating, after many years of marriage, to have the courage to act on impulse.

This meant a mercy dash to Zara, she thought. There was a big one in the Fifth. If she hurried, she could pick up a new outfit without splashing out too much. The Zadig and Voltaire dress was a bit dressy for a gig with someone she didn't really know. She needed casual-but-sexy-but-not-too-sexy. It was quite the brief.

As she waited for Paul later that evening outside *L'Olympia*, Juliet felt skittish with nerves. She tried to shelter herself from the night breeze which was only adding to her

286

anxiety. This whole evening could be awkward. What if he was awful? At least they would have the performance to distract them, and she could make her escape. She worried that her outfit was a bit mutton. She'd bought some pewter-coloured leggings and a cream off-the-shoulder sweater that had seemed just right in the changing room, but now she veered between thinking the leggings were a bit over the top and the top showed too much clavicle.

She felt a touch on her elbow and turned around. He was there, smiling, looking as urbane and cool as she'd remembered.

'Hey,' he said. 'This was such a nice surprise. I didn't think I'd ever see you again.'

She shrugged sheepishly. 'I didn't want the ticket to go to waste. And I don't know many people in Paris.'

'Let's go in.' He put a hand on her elbow and guided her through the crowds. Chivalrous, she thought. Taking control, but not in a controlling way. Confident. Confident was good.

As they queued to get through the bag check, her phone beeped. It was a message from Stuart. A photo of him dressed in his new outfit, ready for his date. Her heart buckled at the sight of his sheepish smile, the blue shirt he'd chosen (on her advice) that was ever so slightly too big because he obviously wasn't used to his new size, and the freshly trimmed designer stubble he had started to sport. She gulped. She'd better be nice to him, whoever she was, the A and E consultant. She'd better be kind to her Stuart.

Marks out of ten? he asked.

It's a ten from me, she replied, wondering why she suddenly felt emotional. It was the same feeling you had when you sent your child off for their first overnight school trip. You knew they'd be fine, but you still worried yourself silly, because they were vulnerable.

'Everything OK?' asked Paul as he led her towards the bar.

'Fine. Yes. Just . . . home stuff.'

'Enough said.' He made a face, as if he sympathised.

She didn't know anything about him. There were a few key questions she should have asked, surely? Maybe it didn't matter. As he had said on the train, this is Paris.

And she felt a thrill among the crowd as they edged into the auditorium and made their way to their seats, everyone speaking in the language she was becoming accustomed to, now much more able to pick out what people were saying than she had been even a week ago, her ear attuned, her confidence growing.

The concert was spellbinding. The audience were totally in thrall of the woman who held them in the palm of her hand with her performance, her voice dancing around the instruments: the thrum of the double bass, the swish of a brush on the edge of a cymbal, the plink of a piano key. There was a melancholy to the songs that spoke to Juliet: a yearning, for times past and for things that might be. Memories, regrets, lost moments. The thrill of a lover's touch. Kisses. Tears. Farewells.

As the final song began, she felt overwhelmed with emotion. Suddenly, everything closed in on her. The end of her marriage. Her children leaving. The loss of her home. Coming back to Paris and finding Nathalie. And Olivier. And losing him again. Confronting Jean Louis and getting closure. Stuart with his silly grin in his new shirt . . . She felt as if she had lost everything and there was nothing left to build on. No one but herself to see the way forward. She was aware there were tears streaming down her face. The more she tried to stop them, the more fell.

Paul looked at her in concern.

'Come on,' he said, nodding his head towards the exit. She didn't argue. She couldn't stay here, sobbing her way through the finale. He took her arm as they left the building, and before she knew it, he had found them a taxi, asked for her address, and then they were gliding through the Paris night, the lights, the crowds, the traffic. She could see the Eiffel Tower lit up in the distance, sparkling, glittering, throwing its beam across the city. And she felt a sense of calm descend. Somehow, it gave her the resilience she needed. It was up to her to make the most of the time she had left in this wonderful city and not let what had happened diminish her.

Just before they turned into the street where her apartment was, they passed the bar she'd been to on her first night. She leaned forward to speak to the taxi driver.

'*Arrêtez ici, s'il vous plaît.*' Stop here. She turned to Paul. 'Let's have a drink.'

'Sure,' he said, getting out his wallet and paying the driver before she could protest.

The barman recognised her and showed them to a discreet corner. They ordered Boulevardiers.

'I'm so sorry,' she said to Paul. 'It all got a bit much, that's all. I've not long separated from my husband and I think it hit me. The future. It's scary.' She shrugged, not sure if she was articulating how she felt very well.

'It takes a long time, to unmesh,' he said. 'I still start to text my ex-wife sometimes, or see something I want to buy her. It's never the end, when you've been married.'

'So you're divorced?'

'Five years now.'

'And there's no one else?'

'Lots of nearlys. But somehow I don't have the heart for anything serious. And I relish my freedom. I live between Paris and London. Being unattached makes it easier.'

'Easier to chat up women on the train?' She was teasing.

'You looked interesting. I wanted to know what you were writing.'

'Ha!' She thought about the envelope with her story inside. 'I was trying to get something out of my system, that's all.'

'So did it work?'

She looked down at the amber depths of her drink. Was Olivier out of her system? She didn't know. She looked at Paul. He was very appealing, in a clean-cut, silver-fox kind of way. He had a good sense of humour and seemed refreshingly honest. And he'd been nothing but kind to her all evening.

'I guess so.'

Maybe Paul was the answer? Not long-term. He'd said himself he didn't want anything serious. She could tell he found her attractive, by the sparkle in his eyes, the teasing tone in his voice that had a certain warmth. What would Nathalie do? she wondered. Devour him, probably, she thought with a smile. Send him away with his head spinning.

'So what now?' He swirled the last drops of his drink, then threw it back and put the glass down on the table.

'*Now* now?'

'Yeah.' He held her gaze. 'Another drink. Or . . . ?' He

nodded towards the door. She felt a pulse inside her, thrumming like a bass note. The invitation was pretty clear. They were two hundred yards from her apartment. In ten minutes, she could be pulling her sweater over her head, letting him see her body, praying the light from the chandelier was kind to her, feeling the touch of unfamiliar fingers on her skin.

She swallowed. 'I'm sorry,' she said. 'But I don't think I'm ready.'

There was only a small pause.

'I totally understand,' he said. 'I just want to say, I've really enjoyed your company. But there's something you should know.' He leaned forward. 'Whoever he is ...' He paused for a moment, choosing his words. 'He's not out of your system.'

She looked at him, startled, as he put a fifty-euro note down on the table and stood up.

'Keep in touch, Juliet. You know where I am.' He kissed the first two fingers of his right hand and held them out to her. And then he walked away, out of the bar, and the door closed behind him.

The barman came over and discreetly took his glass away. '*Un autre?*'

She sat back in the comfort of the velvet chair. She knew happiness wasn't found at the bottom of a glass, but sometimes you needed something to blur the edges. And she thought she preferred the buzz in here to the emptiness of her apartment, just for now.

'*Pourquoi pas?*'

He winked at her. 'Why not?'

She watched as he walked back to the bar. She felt a text buzz through the leather of her bag. She felt the

Pavlovian leap of hope and hated herself for it. She wanted to sit on her hands to stop her from grabbing the phone. If she was going to enjoy her drink, she had to put herself out of her misery.

It was from Nathalie, asking how her evening had gone.

Very nice. Just on my way home. Alone!

She knew that was the detail her friend wanted.

Juliet sighed and dropped the phone back in her bag. Took the cool, frosted glass from the barman. Let the Campari-soaked whisky roll around on her tongue. Prayed she looked like a sophisticated woman of the world enjoying a nightcap and not a tragic figure drowning her sorrows in the corner. Remembered the lyrics of Melody Gardot, singing 'Baby I'm a Fool'. Resisted the urge to text Olivier, even though every atom in her body was urging her to.

35

Juliet ran twice around the Tuileries the next morning. She had to force herself to get out of bed. It would have been too easy to stay under the duvet and wallow. She felt brittle and fragile and vulnerable. Filled with unanswered questions and uncertainty. She had texted Paul first thing, to say thank you for a lovely evening and for being so kind and understanding. He hadn't replied yet and she wondered if she was being ghosted, if despite his apparent chivalry he hadn't taken kindly to her rejection. She wanted to text Stuart to see how his date had gone, but part of her didn't want to know. So a mood-boosting jog seemed the best way to shake herself out of her low mood.

She got back at eleven and sat down at her laptop to check her messages before she clambered into the bath. There was an email from Molly.

Hi Juliet, this sounds right up my rue! I'm looking for books with a strong, adventurous female at their heart, and Nathalie looks like a total inspiration. What I'd need from you is a fairly detailed proposal. Would you be able to have it for me before Christmas? I know that's tight, but I like to strike while the iron's hot when something grabs me. Let me know. Molly x

Juliet sat back in her chair with a whoop of delight. This was thrilling. Of course, it was a long way from a done deal, but she knew in her gut that Molly would be the perfect person to guide Nathalie's book to success if she got behind it. And she was certain they could come up with a cracking proposal.

Her phone beeped and she picked it up.

It was a wonderful evening. Thank you for introducing me to Melody Gardot. I'll always think of you when I listen. All my very best wishes to you, Juliet. Paul x

She felt relieved. It was a kind and gentlemanly response, perfectly pitched. It didn't make her feel bad for turning him down, which some men wouldn't have been able to resist.

She was just texting Nathalie – *Call me when you can* – when the doorbell rang. Melissa, maybe, or perhaps the landlord. She went to answer it.

There he was. In jeans, and a charcoal-grey pea jacket, his hair windswept. Holding the brown envelope. They looked at each other, almost as if for the first time. He looked exhausted, as if he hadn't slept.

'It was the postcard,' he said. 'That broke me.'

'Olivier . . .'

'Why didn't you tell me?' he said, looking anguished. 'Why didn't you call me when it happened?'

She nodded towards the inside of the apartment. 'You'd better come in.'

He followed her inside. He began to speak, not drawing breath, holding the manuscript to his chest.

'I am so angry. I could not speak for three days.'

'Oh.' She felt a little fearful. There was a tension in him she'd never seen. A nervous energy. 'I tried my best to explain. I know it seems awful, what I did—'

'I'm not angry with you. I am angry with that man, and that woman, for what they did to you. I'm angry that everything was taken away from us. I was so in love with you, Juliet, and I thought you hated me. That I'd done something to make you run away. I thought Nathalie knew the truth and was hiding it from me to save my feelings.'

'Nathalie didn't know. I've only just told her about what happened.' She looked at the envelope in his hand. 'I was so ashamed. I thought neither of you would want to see me again.'

'I did need some time. To think about it.' Olivier flopped down on the sofa and stared up at the ceiling. 'When I think about Jean Louis . . .' He bunched his fists up.

'I spoke to him.'

'You did? What did he say?'

She shook her head. 'There wasn't much *to* say. It was so long ago. And it's all too late now anyway . . .'

'No, it's not.'

'Isn't it?'

'Of course not.' He spoke with the fierce intensity she had loved in him when he was young. He jumped up and picked up her hand. This was not how she'd imagined it. Her standing there in her sweaty running kit, still red-faced, the sharp tug of lust, needling at her, sweet and urgent. 'You're here until the end of the month. We should make the most of it. You must do all the things you missed. All those things we planned. You didn't even begin to see Paris.'

'No . . .'

He was holding her hand as if he was never going to let it go. Staring at her. Was he going to kiss her? She braced herself, ready for the joy of it.

And then he dropped her hand with a sigh and looked at his watch. 'I'm really sorry. I have to go to work,' he said. 'I'm already very late.'

She nodded, embarrassed, thanking God she hadn't made the first move and made a fool of herself. Of course he didn't still fancy her. He was angry about the past, but it didn't mean she meant anything to him now. They were two different people entirely. He had moved on from their liaison. He hadn't spent the intervening years fantasising about her the way she had about him. Sometimes she had dreamed about him, waking up with her cheeks wet with tears, and she'd had to tell a concerned Stuart that she'd had a nightmare.

'Have dinner with me tonight,' he said.

'Of course.'

'Robert and Louise. Rue Vieille du Temple. Not Rue du Temple.' He grinned. 'You can remember that? You won't make a mistake?'

She rolled her eyes at his teasing. 'I can remember.'

'And this.' He held up the envelope. 'This is good. You must finish it. You must write more.'

And then he was gone.

She walked over to her bed and fell onto it, staring at the ceiling. How did life move so fast sometimes? She had no idea what to think, or what Olivier really felt. Anger at what had happened, yes, but what about now? She was very confused. What did she mean to him now? Something? Nothing? A little? A lot?

Her phone rang. She barely had the strength to pick it up. She looked at the screen. Nathalie.

'Hey. What's going on?'

She didn't have the energy to tell her friend about Olivier's visit. She couldn't find the words to explain her confusion. Besides, she didn't want it to overshadow the email from Molly. She didn't want to get Nathalie's hopes up too much, but at the same time she wanted to galvanise her.

'I have good news,' Juliet told her. 'Don't get too excited, because as you said to me the other night, the show's not over till the fat lady sings...'

Juliet wore her green dress for dinner with Olivier, knowing that deep down, when she had bought it, this was the occasion she'd had in mind.

The restaurant, Robert et Louise, was on the Rue Vieille du Temple, not so far away from the café where they had first met, and Juliet wondered if Olivier had chosen it on purpose because of that. Its front was painted burgundy, with red gingham curtains inside the windows, old-school Paris, cosy and welcoming. Inside, it felt like walking into someone's home, from the mosaics on the floor to the beams on the ceiling and the stone walls covered in pictures and photographs and ancient copper pots. On an open inglenook fire, slabs of steak were grilling, making her mouth water. Most of the tables were already full.

Juliet peered through the crowds as a smiling waiter approached her, and she pointed to Olivier, sitting towards the back. He led her to the table and pulled out her chair as Olivier stood up to greet her.

He was wearing a linen shirt the colour of the Provencal sky in summer. As their cheeks brushed, she felt a little shock. They drew apart and their eyes met. They had both felt it.

They perused the menu for a few minutes, relieved to have something to focus on as the waiter brought them *Kirs à la mûre*.

'We could share the *côte de boeuf*?' suggested Olivier.

Juliet could see one at the neighbouring table – a side of beef cooked on the open fire and served on a wooden board.

'Why not?' she said.

'And maybe the *assiette de crudités* to start?'

She was relieved to have the decision-making taken away, for she was finding it hard to concentrate. She was finding it hard to be interested in food at all. 'Yes.' She put her menu down.

'So, what happened,' asked Olivier, 'after you left?'

'I went home,' said Juliet. 'My father came to fetch me from the ferry. My parents couldn't have been kinder. They knew something was wrong, but I didn't tell them what happened. I just lay on my bed for two months. All through Christmas. I didn't even eat Christmas dinner.'

Olivier reached out his hand and took hers. 'Me neither.'

Juliet sat for a moment enjoying the warmth of his

fingers. Was he reaching out to comfort her, or something more? She looked up to meet his gaze. She couldn't tell what he was thinking.

'Eventually, my mum intervened. I think it took a lot of courage, but she took control of the situation.' Juliet remembered her mum coming into her room.

'You can't carry on like this forever,' she'd said. 'I'd have you here until the end of time quite happily, but you've got too much to offer the world. And you can't let whatever happened in Paris stop you. Your dad's going to get you a ticket to London. You're to go and find a job, and start living the life you always wanted. You need to get your spark back, my girl.'

Juliet's eyes welled up at the memory of her mum's kindness, and her bravery, for she knew she feared the streets of London almost as much as the streets of Paris.

'Hey.' Olivier put his hand up to wipe away the tear that had fallen onto her cheek.

She laughed, shakily. 'Sorry. I miss them, that's all. When you're twenty, you don't understand how much they love you and how much they fear for you. You just find them annoying, and that's so unfair.'

Olivier nodded. 'So you went to London?'

'Yes. And it was your notebook that got me my job. All the things I had scribbled down while I was there. I typed them up into an article. A kind of funny article about being an English au pair in Paris. It was terrible. A real jumble of ramblings about bookshops and cafés and the importance of red lipstick. But it got me through the door.'

'I am very proud of the little notebook.'

'I'm still using it,' she admitted. 'I brought it with me on this trip.'

'I like your writing,' he said. 'Very much.'

'That means a lot,' she said.

At that moment, the waiter arrived with their *côte*. It was on a chunky wooden board, and he sliced it carefully. For a moment, Juliet was taken back to that first lunch in Paris, when Jean Louis had taken them for *poulet rôti*. She batted away the thought. Jean Louis had no place in her memory anymore.

As they began to eat, Olivier poured them each a glass from a bottle of Gigondas. It was deep and rich, the perfect wine to melt away any lingering awkwardness between them. When they had finished, Olivier pushed his plate to one side, rested his head in one hand and gazed at her. He sighed.

'And now, I have to kill Jean Louis Beaubois. *C'est dommage*. But it's a question of honour.'

Juliet burst out laughing. She had forgotten how droll Olivier was. His dry, self-deprecating humour. And even if he was teasing, she loved the fact he was defending her.

'Not yet,' she said. 'Not yet. I don't want you to go to prison now I've found you.'

'There are conjugal visits.'

She blushed. 'He's not worth going to prison for. There must be a better revenge.'

'Yes. I know exactly what it could be.'

She looked at him, at the smile playing on his lips, his dancing eyes. She felt like the candle between them, as if she was melting into a pool of hot wax.

'Is that a good idea?' She spoke lightly, but she was very aware that they were both vulnerable, that they shouldn't be rushing into something just because they had history.

'You have what, three weeks left in Paris?'

'A bit less than that.' She felt panic. Time was going too fast.

'We might as well spend some time together. And it's not like we don't know each other.'

In some ways, the fact they were former lovers made it even worse. Would he compare her to her lithe, supple twenty-year-old self? Would he be shocked by the extra padding, the loss of tone?

'Hey. It's OK. I understand if you don't want to. But maybe we both need a little fun? We like the same things. We can go to the theatre, some jazz, a reading, maybe? And dinner. I miss going out to dinner with someone.'

Oh God. He was stroking the inside of her wrist. She could barely breathe. She didn't care about theatre or jazz or readings. She shut her eyes. She felt dizzy with lust and Gigondas and the drift of his cologne. He stopped stroking her and she opened her eyes, craving his touch. He was staring at her.

'*On y va?*' Shall we go?

Juliet leaned back and ran her hands through her hair. 'Where?'

'*Chez moi?*'

She swallowed her heart down. She could only manage a nod. She couldn't believe this was happening. She couldn't believe how she felt. The little diamond-tipped arrows of lust shooting through her, as piercingly sweet as when she was twenty.

Suddenly, the bill was paid, and she was on Olivier's arm, stumbling out into the street. She stepped forward to be nearer him, and then he did take her in his arms, for no one could see them here. And their kiss was a lifetime of longing and wondering; of daydreams and fantasies and tear-soaked pillows; of memories and hurt and reminiscence. She leaned against him and now his hand was on the back of her neck, massaging each vertebra until she nearly cried out with the pleasure of his fingers on her skin.

'Walk?' he asked. 'Or *Métro?*'

'How far?'

'*Quinze minutes.*'

She preferred to walk, although it was cold. She wanted the air, the moon, the smell of the streets, the sound of people and music. She wanted to be seen. She wanted, too, to know where she was going.

'My apartment is in Oberkampf,' he told her. 'It was not so cool when I bought it, but I wanted somewhere big enough for the kids. Now it is very... happening.'

Juliet guessed he had suffered the usual divorced dad compromise. It was usually the fathers who ended up in a too-small flat somewhere, squashed up and miserable, with the kids having to share a spare room. Emma had sounded like the kind of woman who would make sure she came out of any negotiations on top.

They walked their way out of the Marais east towards the 11th and onto the Rue Oberkampf. It was still buzzing at this time of night, filled with music and laughter and light spilling from a heady mix of basement dives, artisan restaurants and bijoux cocktail bars. It was party central, and the crowd were young and hip and full of energy. It should have made her feel old, but she felt like a goddess on Olivier's arm as they wove through the streets, lacing her fingers in his and holding them so tightly, desperate to communicate how she felt, how much this meant.

Eventually, they turned off into a quieter street, then

down a cobbled passageway between two tall, white buildings. It was lined with a jungle of plants: pots of olive trees and planters stuffed with ivy. Then Olivier came to a halt and opened a door, ushering her into a huge room arranged around a magnificent stone fireplace. The floor was hexagonal terracotta tiles worn smooth with age. The exterior walls were pale stone; the rest papered in a deep yellow *toile de Jouy*. At the far end was a kitchen area with a black range, an assortment of cupboards in dark wood and a long shelf with enough wine glasses to open a restaurant. Lamps and mirrors and three mismatched chandeliers spilled out a warm light. And there were bookcases, of course, with novels and atlases and dictionaries piled right up to the beamed ceiling.

'This is wonderful.' Juliet was wide-eyed. Everything felt just so, as if it had been there forever. But there was an underlying luxury. The linen on the sofas was thick and expensive, as were the kelim rugs scattered on the tiles. Olivier moved around the room as she drank everything in, lighting the fire, pulling two glasses off the shelf and opening a bottle of Cognac. He put a record on a turntable, and she recognised it immediately as a winsome saxophone filled the room.

'*Betty Blue!*' she said. It was the soundtrack of the film they'd been obsessed with and for a moment she was back on his bed in the Latin Quarter, under the purple bedcover, amidst the croissant crumbs and chocolate wrappers.

'*37°2 le matin*,' he corrected her, laughingly, using the French title. He was gazing at her. 'You have not changed.'

'Nor have you.'

It wasn't true, of course. They both had lines, a certain

softness here and there that lost the definition you need for true beauty, the glint of grey in an eyebrow, a thicker waistline. But they saw their old selves in each other. The faces they had spent hours gazing into. In that moment, they were twenty again.

Juliet stepped forward, leaning into him, breathing in his scent, not the Ralph Lauren she could still remember, but something more sophisticated: clean and modern with a hint of cedar. He reached out a finger and traced it over her collarbone, then down the edge of her neckline, pushing the green satin aside to reveal the pale skin of her breast. She tipped her head back and shut her eyes. She wanted him to go slowly. She wanted him to go fast. She wanted him.

And it didn't matter, those extra thirty years and the toll it had taken on her body as she peeled away her dress. He made her feel graceful and lithe, and she twisted and writhed above him and below him. She teased and laughed as she made him wait. She took control and held his gaze and when he came, she saw he had tears in his eyes.

'I didn't mean to make you cry,' she whispered.

'This is the first time,' he told her, and she understood that she was the first woman he had slept with since his wife left him. And she held him for a while, for he was trembling with emotion, and then he kissed her again, and the next time he didn't cry, she did, because they were as beautiful as they had been when they were twenty.

Their glasses lay untouched and the turntable played on and the candles shone bright long into the night, until they finally burnt themselves out.

36

Her phone alarm went off at four in the morning. She woke with a start in a tangle of linen sheets and Olivier. They had finally made their way into his bedroom, a vault of bare stone with nothing but a seven-foot bed and an oak wardrobe. She touched him on the shoulder.

'I have to go,' she whispered. She was meeting Nathalie at a quarter to five, to go to the market at Rungis. They were starting to put together the proposal, so Juliet was following Nathalie through a working day, making notes and taking rough photos of the shots they would need to brief the photographer.

To her surprise, he sat up and threw back the covers.

'I'll make you coffee. Go use the shower – there'll be a fresh towel in the cupboard.'

She watched as he strode across the room and pulled a blue paisley robe off the back of the door. She ran into the bathroom and had the quickest shower on record, using her finger to brush her teeth, then wrapped herself in a clean towel. She came back into the bedroom to find he'd brought her discarded clothes back upstairs and put them in a neatly folded pile on the bed. She laughed to herself as she pulled them back on. It was hardly the ideal outfit for going to a food market, but, she reminded herself, this was Paris.

Downstairs, Olivier handed her a tiny cup of espresso.

'Drink that while I get ready,' he said. 'I'll give you a lift.'

'You don't have to.'

'I know. But I want to.' He leaned forward to kiss her. A lingering kiss full of promise and longing, but eventually he pulled himself away. 'Two minutes,' he promised, and headed off to get dressed.

Juliet leaned back against the kitchen counter while she sipped her coffee. She hated having to leave, but she had promised Nathalie. Rushing meant there was no time to take stock of their situation or make plans. She thought they were both still reeling from the thrill of it all. Olivier was certainly looking at her with wonder, not doubt, and she thought his chivalry came from consideration, not a desire to see the back of her.

But she had no way of knowing if she was just a one-night stand. Lack of sleep and adrenaline and the sudden intake of intense caffeine made her feel jittery and uncertain. Her stomach looped the loop as he came back in, dressed in jeans and a utility jacket. He had a helmet in his hands which he thrust at her.

'You'll need this.'

'What?'

'No one sane has a car in Paris.' He grinned. '*Allons-y.*'

By four-thirty she was on the back of the Vespa he kept in the passageway outside. They rode through the grey pre-dawn of Paris, diving down a warren of backstreets, dodging the garbage trucks and the road sweepers as the cafés and *tabacs* began to unfurl their iron shutters. They pulled up outside She Cried Champagne just as Nathalie jumped out of her white Citroën van.

'*Salut, mec*,' she said to Olivier, as if she had only seen him the day before. They kissed each other on each cheek, and Nathalie punched his arm. 'It's good to see you.'

'*Oui*,' he said, smiling. There was no time for pleasantries, but it was obvious they were pleased to see each other. 'Look after her for me, please.' He put his hands on Juliet's shoulders.

'Sure thing,' said Nathalie, eyeing up Juliet's outfit with doubt. 'Could you not find a ball gown?'

Laughing, Juliet jumped into the front seat. Olivier raised his arm to wave them goodbye as Nathalie pulled away from the kerb. Juliet began to feel the tug of separation anxiety as he disappeared from view.

'It went OK, then?'

'Yeah, it was OK,' said Juliet with mock understatement.

'Good for you.' Nathalie grinned. 'You don't often see a woman of our age with a smile like that on her face.'

Juliet felt as if her head was still in the 11th. Her mouth was swollen from kissing. Her skin still tingled from the scrape of his six o'clock shadow. She couldn't remember the last time she'd only had two hours' sleep. Not because of a man, anyway. Chickenpox and teething, maybe.

'*Gueule de bois?*' asked Nathalie.

'No,' said Juliet. 'We didn't drink that much. A Kir and a bottle of wine.'

'Drunk on love, huh?'

'You could say that.' She was having flashbacks of the evening, and she felt her cheeks go pink. They'd always had chemistry, but they'd both learned a lot in the intervening years.

'So what happens now?'

'It's just a fling. While I'm here. Just a bit of fun.'

Nathalie looked sideways at her. 'Sure it is.'

'It has to be. I mean, I live in England and he lives in Paris.'

'Well, you'd better make the most of it. As long as it doesn't take your mind off the job in hand.'

'Of course not.' She stared out of the window. 'He cried, you know.'

'Oh, God. You must have been good.'

'His apartment is to die for.'

'Did you get pictures?'

'I didn't.' She smirked. 'There wasn't time.'

'That's an epic fail.'

'You can come for *apèro*,' said Juliet airily. 'We'll drink Campari soda and I'll make *gougères* and show you around.'

Nathalie shot her an amused glance. 'Maybe split the difference between insecure and overconfident?'

Juliet laughed. She felt slightly hysterical. Slightly hysterical and ridiculously happy.

Her phoned tinged and she nearly jumped out of her skin. She wasn't going to look at it straight away. She folded her arms and leaned back in her seat.

'For God's sake, see what it says!' said Nathalie. 'Who else is it going to be at this hour of the morning?'

Juliet leaned forward and grabbed the phone out of her bag.

'*Tu me manques*,' she read.

'I miss you,' sighed Nathalie. 'Oh. My. God. You're living the dream for all of us, baby.'

309

37

The food market at Rungis was on the outskirts of the south-east of the city, by Orly airport.

'They moved the market out there when they pulled down Les Halles. You won't believe it till you see it,' Nathalie said. 'The site's bigger than Monaco.'

'No way.'

'It's kind of scary and a bit weird. All very clinical and organised. A bit like something out of a Bond film.'

They were heading out of the city centre along the north bank of the Seine. It was thrilling, to be speeding along at such an early hour, with little traffic, the street lamps still alight as the dawn turned from slate to oyster then pearl as they passed bridge after bridge. Juliet saw the huge cranes looming over Notre-Dame: in an hour or so they would be hard at work on her restoration.

They crossed over the river, leaving the familiar landmarks behind and driving on a highway through suburbs that could have been anywhere: tower blocks and cemeteries and industrial parks and train lines. Eventually, they pulled into what felt almost like an airport: warehouse after warehouse, each the size of an aircraft hangar.

'We'll start with fish. Each warehouse is different: meat, cheese, vegetables.' Nathalie threw a white coat at her and a white cap to cover her hair. 'It's cold in there.'

Juliet felt a little self-conscious that she wasn't dressed for the occasion, but there was nothing she could do now. She shrugged on her protective clothing and followed Nathalie inside the first warehouse, where an elaborate ballet of forklift trucks, lorries and low-loaders brought in the day's catches. Wooden crates and boxes were piled up, filled with shards of snow-white ice to keep the contents fresh. Oysters, red mullet, lobster, salmon – everything was gleaming and bright-eyed, sparkling silver under the bright lights. The sellers stood proudly by their offerings, certain theirs were the best and ready to defend that opinion to the hilt and then negotiate the price they felt they deserved. It was a game of nerve and skill and bargaining power.

'Let's go,' said Nathalie, looking at the list on her phone.

For the next hour, Juliet stood by as Nathalie made her orders in each warehouse in rapid-fire French, examining the produce to make sure it was to her satisfaction, asking the seller searching questions. She bought plump *magrets de canard, poulets de Bresse*, shining lemons, glistening cherries, wedges of cheese in pale orange and chalk-white, glittering mackerel, tiny brown shrimp. Sometimes something wouldn't be up to scratch and she would walk away, to much protest. She knew exactly what she wanted and was never bamboozled into buying too much or too little. This was a tough business, thought Juliet. You needed vision, and clarity, and focus, and nerves of steel. She would, she thought, be absolutely hopeless, and it made her admiration for her friend grow even higher.

By half past seven, purchases complete, they were sitting in a café with a plate of sausage and *aligoté* – mashed potato beaten with copious amounts of cheese and butter – along with other customers and workers. There was an air of camaraderie as men in bloodstained tunics threw back glasses of beer or Ricard to wash down their hearty food.

'Most of these guys have been here since before midnight, so this is dinner for them,' said Nathalie, digging her fork into her food with relish.

'I love it,' said Juliet, swept up in the theatre of it all, taking notes.

By ten, they were back at the restaurant, and Juliet helped Nathalie unload everything into the refrigerators.

'You do this twice a week?' she said, admiring of her energy.

'Yes. I get deliveries too, but this way I know I get the best.' Nathalie was double-checking everything while she put it away. Her quality control was rigorous. Everything was kept at the optimum temperature, labelled, piled neatly and placed in the order in which it would be used. The week's menus were pinned to the wall, with all the ingredients listed and notes showing where they were stored. Nothing would be wasted or forgotten. The cheeses were lovingly catalogued: *Pont-l'Evêque, Crottin de Chavignol, bleu d'Auvergne, Saint-Nectaire.* Nathalie would serve them only when they had reached peak ripeness.

All this rigorous discipline and attention to detail was in marked contrast to the laid-back atmosphere in the bar. Every guest had the experience they wanted, whether it was the courage to try something new on a plate or in a glass, or the permission to linger as long as they wished. Juliet supposed that was how you made something a success: not leaving anything to chance.

'OK,' said Nathalie, clapping her hands. 'It's ten o'clock. We'll have a little *pause café* and then the day begins.'

'How do you do it?' asked Juliet. 'Where do you get your energy?'

'I was in bed by nine-thirty,' Nathalie reminded her with a wink. 'Not writhing around in the sheets until two a.m.'

They sat down at a table by the window, watching the street come to life with workers, shoppers, bicyclists, mopeds, delivery trucks. And despite her lack of sleep, Juliet marvelled at the change she had made to her life. A score settled, a new project to challenge her, an old love rekindled. She looked at the calendar on her phone. More than ten days had already passed. Time was flying by, and she didn't know what she could do to slow it down. She didn't want to waste a moment.

38

If falling in love at twenty was intense, the joy of recon-nection in later life when you'd always had a spark was absolute bliss, thought Juliet, especially when you had the benefit of a little more self-confidence and a willing-ness to be open and honest. To find that she and Olivier genuinely liked each other after so long was a delight: they made each other laugh, and think, and sometimes cry. And neither of them expected the physical intensity. It took their breath away.

'It's like film sex,' said Juliet to Nathalie. 'Honestly. I didn't think you could have that level of passion at our age. Sorry. I know I'm oversharing.'

'God, don't worry. It's great. It gives me hope. And you look like a total goddess. All glowy and bright-eyed.'

'Well, I've got you to thank. I wouldn't have had the nerve to go and find him if it wasn't for you.'

Olivier resolved for the first time since he had opened the bookshop to take some proper time off for the dura-tion of Juliet's stay.

'I've never bothered before, because there wasn't any point. The bookshop is my life and my escape. But now

I have a reason.' He'd smiled. 'And my staff will be so happy not to have me breathing down their necks. I will just check in every now and again.'

While Olivier was at the shop, Juliet worked on the book proposal with Nathalie. She became immersed in the rhythm of life at She Cried Champagne, getting to know its staff and its regulars. She watched Nathalie in the kitchen, devising recipes and experimenting with different flavours. She saw what an inspiration she was to the women who worked for her – for they were mostly women. Some of them came from troubled backgrounds, girls who'd had brushes with the law for one reason or another. Nathalie picked them up and dusted them off and gave them a purpose. She was tough on them, but they adored her.

'Watching these girls shine is more important to me than anything,' she told Juliet. 'Some of them were heading for the wrong side of the tracks and fast. I'm so proud of what they've become. They know they can get a job at any restaurant in this town if they've been trained by me.'

Juliet's awe of her friend was growing day by day as the proposal evolved. In the meantime, she had given more thought to her own book, *The Ingénue*, and she realised that was evolving too. It had started out as a coming-of-age book, but now she understood that it needed to be more important than that. It would be a coming-of-*middle*-age book, her own story, about how she had come to revisit her past and in doing so had found herself. She would have to change the names, and sprinkle in a little artistic licence, to protect the identity of the real people in it, but it was a book for women like her, women of a certain age who had lost their way and were unsure of the future. It was a book that would give them the courage to rebuild, to take risks with their minds and their hearts and their bodies. A book about friendships old and new; about holding on to the things they held dear, but having the courage to try new things. A book about making fantasy a reality – doing all those things they'd dreamed of.

And if, along the way, her heroine rekindled a lost love, recaptured the one who got away, then that, she thought, would be the perfect ending.

When they weren't working, Olivier and Juliet got under the skin of Paris. He devised funny little tours for her, with a theme. One day it was female authors, so they walked in the trail of Amantine Lucile Aurore Dupin, who spent her life disguised as George Sand, and Colette and Simone de Beauvoir, and more than anything, Juliet learned how lucky she was to have independence and a voice and an identity that didn't need to be hidden, or attached to a man.

Another day was music, so, of course, they had to go to the quaintly eccentric *Musée de Edith Piaf* – two rooms with a cardboard cut-out of the little sparrow, surrounded by her eclectic belongings, the walls crammed with letters and photos and fan mail and awards, the faint traces of 'La vie en rose' in the background. Then it was a candlelit concert of Chopin at Saint-Éphrem Church, so intense that it moved Juliet to tears. They finished in a scruffy club drinking rum and dancing salsa until the early hours.

'I can't take any more,' laughed Juliet, as they walked arm in arm back to Olivier's apartment. Olivier was quiet. 'What is it?' she asked.

'The time is going too quickly,' he said.

'I know,' she sighed. 'We just have to make the most of it.'

He pulled her into him a little tighter. They were both aware that the thirty days would soon be over, and she would be heading back to England.

'It's been fun, to be a tour guide,' he said. 'To get to know my city a little more.'

'I'll never forget it.' Juliet rested her head on his shoulder. Her throat ached when she thought about leaving him, but the pact had been to have the best time they could in the short time she was here. 'It's been perfect. I mean, neither of us are ready for something serious, are we? But it's been so great to have some fun. With no strings.'

She wasn't sure she believed the words coming out of her mouth, but all along she had sensed that Olivier was afraid of moving on and making a commitment, after what his wife had done. She certainly wasn't going to pressurise him into anything. And she wasn't sure she was ready either – it would be a mistake to jump in with both feet so soon after separating from Stuart. The last thing she wanted to do was jeopardise their relationship all over again by going too fast too soon. She valued their friendship too much. She felt sure Olivier would be a friend for life. Of course, the sex was mind-blowing, but she suspected that it was precisely because they were under no pressure that they were able to enjoy each other's bodies, care-free.

Some nights, they just stayed in, and she lay stretched on Olivier's sofa and he brought her wine and fat shiny dark olives and kissed her while they listened to the soundtrack of their youth in the candlelight. He still had the same LPs he'd had in his apartment. She remembered the exhilaration of staying up all night because there was too much to talk about and to listen to, the warm nest of his single bed, squashed up together until they only made the space of one person, his breath on her cheek, the scent of their mingled sweat.

She lay gazing up at the beamed ceiling feeling lighter of heart than she had done for a long time. She could breathe more easily. And her future felt as if it really was hers now. It was like when you went away on holiday, when you've recovered from the journey and got your bearings and the sun is out and you realise you have no work, nothing to do but enjoy yourself.

And this was a holiday fling, she reminded herself.

Suddenly, there was only a week left, and Juliet started to feel anxious about saying goodbye. She knew the deal. They had been clear with each other from the start. He was coming to her apartment tonight for dinner, so she headed for the *Marché des Enfants Rouges*, the oldest covered market in Paris. The entrance was so unassuming she almost missed it, but once she'd dived under the black metal arch in between two buildings, she found herself in a melting pot of cultures. It was scruffy and chaotic, lined with row after row of market stalls, zinc counters with high stools, refrigerated cabinets and clusters of tables and chairs where people gathered to eat the food on offer – Moroccan, Japanese, Lebanese, Italian; everything from tagines to *crêpes* to *moules* to sushi. It was loud and ebullient: friends met for lunch and families gathered as the stallholders outdid each other with their offerings. It was tempting to pick up something ready-made, but Juliet wanted to cook for Olivier in her tiny kitchen while he stood talking to her with a glass of wine – that, to her, was the ultimate in intimacy and companionship.

After a few contented minutes of browsing, she bought a selection of wild mushrooms. She'd cook them in butter and garlic and wine, maybe pile them onto a circle of puff pastry, with a little salad on the side. She was just queuing for a bunch of parsley when her phone rang. She pulled it out of her bag, not recognising the number.

She'd never been one to ignore a phone call. She just wasn't cool enough. Unknown numbers were usually offers of work, and she was keenly aware that she needed to get back on the treadmill before too long. She should be lining up projects already.

She stepped out of the queue to take the call.

'Is that Juliet Hiscox?' The man's voice sounded anxious. Not work, then, for that was not her working name.

'Yes.'

'Hi – I'm Matt. I'm a friend of Stuart's. Don't panic, everything's under control, but he's had a bit of an accident on his bike—'

'What?' Her stomach turned over and her throat went tight.

'I'm at the hospital with him. I found your number on his phone. They're ... um, they're just taking him in for a brain scan.'

'Oh my God.' Juliet felt the walls around her close in, the noise of the market recede. 'What happened?'

'We were heading back from our Sunday ride. Some bloody idiot pulled out right in front of him. His leg's pretty mashed, I'm afraid.'

'Which hospital?'

'Kingston.'

'I'll get there as soon as I can.'

'I'm so sorry. I know you're in Paris—'

'It's fine. It's not a problem. I'll throw my things in a case and get a train tonight. Is this the number I can get you on?'

'Yeah, yeah – any time.' Whoever he was, Matt sounded shaken but in control.

'Thank you. Has anyone told the kids?'

'You're the first person I phoned. Do you want me to?'

Izzy would completely freak if a total stranger phoned her with news like that.

'No. I'll do it. He's going to be OK, isn't he?'

There was a slight pause. 'He's in good hands.'

Her stomach turned to ice. That wasn't a definite yes.

'Can you tell him I'm on my way?'

Juliet had already left the market and had headed out onto the street, looking for the nearest taxi rank. Her hands were trembling and she felt sick, trying not to think about how easily Stuart could have been killed. This was everything she had ever feared when he took up cycling, but he had always batted her worries away, never seeing himself as vulnerable. She pictured his body on the road, splayed out, his bare white legs in those ridiculous shorts she teased him about. Had Matt said one was broken? She couldn't remember exactly. A brain scan didn't sound good, though maybe that was belt and braces. Maybe it was routine. He would have had his helmet on. They had a deal he would never go without. Ever.

She tried to keep a clear head, working out what she needed to do. Look up Eurostar times, get a ticket, get back to the apartment, pack, phone the kids... They might want to come home, so it was best not to panic them, she thought. Maybe she'd email, keep it light, until she knew a bit more.

Poor Stuart. He hated hospitals. He couldn't even watch the opening credits of *Casualty* without going green. She wondered if she should phone and try to speak to a doctor, but that would be difficult while travelling.

She found a taxi and jumped in, giving her address, then looked up the Eurostar on her browser. There was a train at seven. By the time the taxi arrived at her apartment, she'd got herself a ticket. She had about an hour spare to pack and get everything sorted. And Olivier – she must phone Olivier. He was due at her apartment at the same time the train was timetabled to leave. She dialled his number as she grabbed her suitcase and threw it on the bed. Her stomach churned as she thought about Stuart, presumably having his scan right now.

The phone went to voicemail.

'Olivier. It's me. Stuart's had a bike accident. He's having a brain scan right now. I've got to go back. I've booked the train. I'm really sorry.' Her voice wobbled. 'I'm really, really sorry...'

What if Stuart had suffered some terrible injuries that hadn't been obvious? What if he died on the operating table? She gave a half-sob as she packed up her laptop. They might be separated, but she still loved him, as the father of her children. And, let's be honest, the person she'd spent most of her life with. She couldn't imagine the world without him in it, and she couldn't bear the thought of Izzy and Nate being without their dad. She ought to email them before she got on the train. She looked at her watch. She had ten minutes.

Darling Nate and Izzy – silly old Dad's had a bit of a prang on his bike and is in hospital having his leg fixed. He's in good hands, but I'm heading back from Paris now to go and see if he's all right. You're not to worry, but I thought you ought to know. I'll ping you as soon as I know more. Lots of love, Mum xx

It was a fine line, making sure they knew what had happened so they wouldn't be furious with her for not telling them, but also not panicking them. She couldn't even get a clear enough head to remember what their time differences were. Her palms were sweating, making her fingers slippery as she ordered an Uber to get her to the station. There was one nine minutes away. She confirmed it. The apartment was more of a mess than she would normally leave a holiday let, but she couldn't worry about that now.

Don't go and die on me, Stuart Hiscox, she thought as she ran out of the door, slamming it shut behind her.

She was waiting on the pavement, staring at the little car on the Uber app, willing it to go faster. The time kept changing, from five minutes to six and then five again. And then she saw a Vespa at the end of the street. It drove straight towards her and stopped.

Olivier.

He jumped off, taking off his helmet, and rushed to hug her. She sobbed as he held her.

'It's OK,' he said. 'He will be OK.'

She was gulping in air, trying not to get hysterical. 'What if he's not?'

'He will be.' Olivier looked grim-faced.

'I'm so sorry. We had one more week.'

'I know. I know.' He held her tight, kissing the top of her head. She looked frantically up and down the street.

'Where's the cab? Where's the cab? I can't miss my train.'

'It'll be here. You have time.'

She started to shiver. She thought it was the shock. Olivier stroked her hair.

'You need anything, you call me, OK?'

She nodded. Rain was starting to fall. A car swooshed past, but it wasn't her Uber.

'Here.' Olivier was getting something out of his pocket. 'Take this.'

It was his copy of *Le Grand Meaulnes*. She stared down at it.

He hugged her again. 'It means you have to come back,' he whispered. 'One day.'

She was crying again. She put it in her bag. A white Mercedes came around the corner and glided towards them, slowing down. She put her arms around his neck.

'Thank you,' she said. 'For a wonderful time. For everything. I won't forget you.'

She breathed him in one last time. Felt his warm lips on her damp cheek. He picked up her case, opened the back door of the car so she could get in, then walked around the back while the driver opened the boot. Then he leaned in and squeezed her arm, shut the door and stood on the pavement as the car pulled away.

He stood in the pouring rain, watching them go, and she saw him getting smaller and smaller and then they turned the corner and he disappeared.

*

She was in good time for the train, but she almost wished she had only made it with moments to spare as now she had more than half an hour to kill. The waiting area was filled with people on their way back from a long weekend in the City of Lights – hen parties and loved-up couples and groups of friends without a care in the world.

Agitated, Juliet wandered around the shop at the top of the escalator that was by the departure gate. A selection of predictable paperbacks, some tacky souvenirs – you really would have failed in your duty if you left buying something this late – and refreshments. Should she stock up on something to eat now? It would be late by the time she got to the hospital. She had no appetite, so she just bought some bottled water. A stress headache had tied a tight band around her forehead and her stomach was churning. She clutched her phone in her hand, checking it every three seconds for a message. Thank God for Eurostar, she thought. She probably wouldn't have been able to get a plane until the next day, but she'd be able to get out to Richmond on the Tube and then take a cab to the hospital.

The departure gate opened. She headed towards it, not that getting through early would make any difference – the wait would be the same whichever side she was on – but at least it was positive action.

Just as the train was about to leave, her phone rang.

Matt.

She grabbed it, her heart in her mouth.

'Just to tell you that the scan was clear,' he said. 'There's no sign of any brain injury.'

'Oh, thank God.' She leaned her head back on the headrest, sweet relief flooding through her.

'He's still in intensive care, though. He's up to his eyeballs in painkillers. They're hoping to operate on his leg tomorrow. It'll probably need pinning.'

'Matt, I can't thank you enough for being there.'

'Of course I'm here. He's my mate.'

'Tell him I'm on the train. Two hours to St Pancras, then as long as it takes me to cross London.'

As soon as she hung up, she had a little weep, grateful there was no one in the seat next to her. She felt light-headed, almost as if her brain couldn't process reality but was instead filled with terrible possibilities and what-ifs, flitting from one catastrophe to the next. What if he died of complications on the operating table? What if they couldn't put his leg back together and had to amputate it? What if they had missed a bleed on his brain? She tried to tell herself she was overreacting. Once she could see him, it would be OK. She felt out of control, being so far away and not being able to ask the right questions.

She felt an overwhelming urge to protect Stuart; to get to his side as soon as possible and sort things out for him. It was more maternal than wifely, but it was powerful nevertheless, and it made her realise how very much she still cared for him. Admittedly, he hadn't been in her thoughts a great deal lately, but she would give anything for him to be all right.

A woman on the other side of the aisle reached over and touched her arm.

'Are you all right? Can I get you something?'

Juliet realised she was still crying. Not howling, just sniffing and wiping away tears with her sleeve.

'I'm fine, thank you,' she managed. 'My husband's had a cycling accident so I'm trying to get back.'

'Oh dear. Try not to worry. Easy to say, I know.' The woman made a face.

'I'll be fine once I'm there.' Juliet composed herself, not wanting to make a scene, not wanting this attention from a stranger. 'Thank you.'

'I'm sure he'll be all right.' The woman patted her arm.

It was a meaningless platitude, trotted out to make her feel better, Juliet knew, but for some reason it made her want to cry again. She smiled her thanks and turned away to hide her tears.

How on earth could she have let this happen? How on earth could she have agreed to this separation when they still cared for each other so much? It was naïve, to split when things were hunky-dory, because the whole point of marriage was to be there for one another when the going got tough. They needed each other. They had all that history. They knew each other's foibles and hang-ups and idiosyncrasies: she'd had more than twenty-five years to know Stuart gagged if a piece of cucumber came anywhere near him and wouldn't pull hair out of the plughole for love nor money, but was the best person to work out how to split the bill if a big group went out to a restaurant. And, in return, he knew she hated marzipan but could find the perfect pair of suede brogues in the right size at half price in the Christmas sales.

She remembered the first time she met him. She was in a pub garden near Hammersmith Bridge with friends on a May bank holiday. They were onto their fifth jug of Pimm's, getting sunburnt, ordering chips and smoking too much. Stuart was with his mates on a nearby table and came over to cadge a cigarette. He wasn't particularly good-looking, but he had a sunny swagger to him, and a very cool pair of aviator sunglasses. If Paris had taught Juliet anything, it was that smart accessorising went a long way, and she had approved.

'Oh my God,' he had said to her as she lit a Marlboro Light for him. 'You look just like Jane Birkin.'

And it was weird, because normally that would have set her off, but she didn't have some horrible flashback to what had happened in Paris and start having a panic attack. She had just laughed.

Stuart had dropped to his knees and begun to sing the organ introduction to *'Je T'aime'*, arms outstretched, then serenaded her with the Serge Gainsbourg section. He had a good voice and was hilariously funny, and she had joined in with the Jane Birkin bits, and although they were both pretty drunk, it had actually sounded good and everyone had watched with their mouths open as they reached the breathless climax, hamming it up and gazing at each other with fake wanton lust.

They'd finished to a round of ecstatic applause and wolf whistles, and Stuart had put his arm round her neck and pulled her to him, not in a smarmy way, in a blokey rugby-club sort of a way. More of a headlock than an embrace.

'I feel like we're going to be good mates,' he had said.

Theirs was the perfect friendship, forged on a hot summer's day in a haze of plastic glasses filled with booze-sodden strawberries, scorching pavements, blaring techno tunes and pink-faced people waving their arms in the air. Louche, unrestrained London at her rowdy bank-holiday best, the antithesis of cool, restrained Paris.

Stuart had jolted her out of her malaise. He made her do things. Life to him was a sweet shop of opportunity, and you had to grab it or lose it. They saw everything, from a shark submerged in a tank of formaldehyde to sweaty bands in a club in Camden to *Single White Female* and *Wayne's World* – after which everything became 'excellent'. They played Prince and Radiohead and *Automatic for the People* by R.E.M. over and over and over, and Juliet learned to listen to 'Everybody Hurts' without breaking down and remembering Olivier.

She never told Stuart what had happened in Paris. She didn't want it to define her. She told him she'd been an au pair there for a couple of months and it was cool but she was homesick, and he never asked any more except whether she'd been up the Eiffel Tower and she said no, but she wanted to. One day.

Gradually, Olivier faded in the brightness of Stuart's ebullience, though for a long time they were just friends. The benefits happened one night, after they each took a tab of ecstasy he'd been given: he wasn't a big drug user, but his philosophy was that you should try everything once. It was what they needed to move their relationship on, for they were both reticent about making the step from friendship to romance in case they spoiled something perfect. When they woke the next morning in his flat, he was in a daze.

'Well, that was something else,' he had said, and she didn't know if he meant her or the E.

She had murmured a sleepy agreement. 'Amazing.'

He had hooked his arms behind his head. 'Does this mean we're a thing, then, Dusty?'

He called her Dusty because her last name was Miller.

She'd had about five seconds to decide. Stuart was clever. Solvent. Generous. Kind. He made her laugh. He made her feel safe. He didn't instil in her any kind of fear that he would find someone more beguiling and ditch her. With him, she was living her best London life, and he pushed her, gave her confidence, never let her settle for second best. His room didn't have the bohemian glamour of Olivier's, but his sheets smelt nice – of lavender.

'Yes.' She had stroked his forehead with her hand. 'I guess we are a thing.'

39

As the train slid smoothly into St Pancras, Juliet felt a little calmer than she had done when she'd got on. There had been no more phone calls from Matt, so she took no news to be good news. Now she had the ordeal of carting everything across London: getting on the Northern line to Clapham, then taking the overground to Norbiton, where the hospital would only be a few minutes' walk. She thought about getting another Uber, but she could spend ages standing on the pavement outside the station waiting for someone to pick her up and take her that far.

She sighed as she shuffled onto the Tube platform, trying to keep all her things close to her. Her arms were already aching. She felt her phone go in her handbag as the next train arrived, but she was too laden with baggage to get at it. She hoped it wasn't bad news.

By the time she found a seat and was able to retrieve her phone, she saw it was Izzy who'd called. By now, there was no signal, so she had to wait until she got to Clapham Junction to call her back. Izzy answered on the first ring.

'Is Dad OK? Is he going to be OK?'

Juliet could hear the tightness of held-back tears in her daughter's voice.

'Darling, I'm sure he will be. I'm on my way to the hospital. I've just got off the Tube at Clapham.'

'Oh God.' Juliet could imagine her rubbing her face like she always did when agitated. 'Should I come home?'

'No!' Stuart would be furious if he ruined Izzy's adventure. 'I'll text you when I've seen him and give you an update.'

'Is Nate coming back?'

'I haven't spoken to him yet.'

'Only he should. He's near enough. I think I should too. I'm looking at flights.'

'Izzy, there's no point. It's really sweet of you, but you know Dad wouldn't expect you to.'

'But I'm so worried,' Izzy wailed.

'Sweetheart, I'm sure he'll be fine. As far as I know, it's just his leg.' Juliet was fibbing, for she had no idea what she was going to find, but she didn't want Izzy booking tickets back if it was nothing too serious. It would be such a waste. 'Hold fire until I report back in the morning.'

'OK.' Izzy didn't sound happy. 'Hug him from me, will you?'

'Of course, darling.' Juliet was raking the departure boards for the train to Norbiton. 'Look, I've got to go. I've got to find my train and I haven't got enough hands. I'll call you tomorrow.'

At last, she made it to the hospital and arrived on the ward flustered and exhausted just before midnight. It took her a while to persuade the ward sister to let her see Stuart, but eventually she was allowed five minutes.

She crept between the curtains and into his cubicle. He was wide awake, and his head turned sharply as he heard her come in. She was shocked by how drawn he looked. How old he looked. And his head gleamed naked in the half-light. She put a hand to her mouth.

'They've shaved your head.'

'No.' He gave a wry smile. 'That was me, last weekend. Blame Stanley Tucci.'

'Oh.' She managed a trembling laugh. She'd imagined some kind of *One Flew Over the Cuckoo's Nest* scenario, Stuart being pinned down by a burly nurse with a razor.

'Mistake?' he said, passing his hand over the pale, slightly shiny skin.

'It's hard to tell in here,' she said politely, not wanting to tell him it made him look like a tortoise, her heart aching for him. 'How do you feel?'

He indicated a green button at his bedside. 'Fine, as long as I keep pumping myself full of painkillers. What are you even doing here? I told them not to call you.'

'Matt phoned me. I'm still your emergency contact.'

'He shouldn't have.'

'He bloody should have.'

'I've buggered my leg, that's all. They're pinning it back together tomorrow.'

'You could have been killed.'

'But I wasn't.' He frowned. 'My bike's a write-off, I think.'

'Good.' Juliet couldn't help glaring at him.

He gave a sheepish smile. 'Are you going to stay at the flat?'

'I suppose so.' She hadn't thought about where to stay. It was weird not having Persimmon Road to go to. She felt light-headed, ungrounded, like a balloon someone had let go of.

'You'll have to have my bed. I haven't sorted the spare room yet. But, honestly, don't feel you have to stay. I'll be able to manage.'

Juliet just looked at him. 'You'll be out of action for a while.'

'You mustn't feel obliged. It's no longer your duty.'

'Don't be silly.'

He reached out a hand and she took it. They sat for a moment, a strange kind of love passing between them. The love of two people who still cared deeply for each other, despite going their separate ways. Fondness, respect, affection: even as a wordsmith, Juliet couldn't quite identify or name it. The Greeks probably had a word for it, she thought. The love of an ex-spouse of whom you were extremely fond; a love forged in family, in kinship, in familiarity. It was precious, she thought and felt proud that they still had such a strong bond. She lifted her other hand and wiped away a tear, relieved now she had seen him.

The ward sister came to hover at the crack in the curtain, making a face and pointing at her non-existent watch. Juliet nodded, realising she had to leave. She stood up, then bent down to kiss Stuart's cheek.

'I'll come in tomorrow.'

'I'm first on the list.' He crossed his fingers.

'See you, Stanley,' she teased, stroking his scalp.

His eyes flittered at her touch. 'See you, Dusty.'

He leaned back on the pillows and shut his eyes. She slipped back out between the curtains and crept out of the ward.

She lugged her case back through the ghostly hospital corridors, passing the occasional midnight wanderer heading outside for a cigarette, feeling certain that the distance was twice as long as it needed to be, trudging along the miles of shiny brown floor. The sliding doors at the entrance spat her out into a damp, self-pitying night, clumps of mist crowding round her for company.

Eventually, she managed to get a cab to take her back to Richmond. By the time it turned up, she was shivering, miserable with the cold and facing the reality of her situation. She should have been eating wild mushrooms with Olivier, should have seduced him on the floor of her apartment, smiling down at him as he gazed up at her in adoration. She'd fantasised about it all weekend, revelling in the anticipation and the sweet, sharp, exquisite drilling that started up inside her whenever she thought of him. It wasn't there now, though. It was as if a wet blanket had been thrown over her and put out her fire.

Stuart had given her the door codes for his apartment block. It was strange, letting herself into this place where she didn't belong. It took her a while to negotiate the locks and the lift and the light switches, but eventually she battled her way in through his front door, feeling like an intruder.

Even though he'd unpacked and settled in by now, the flat still felt stiff and unhomely. It looked as if he'd gone to John Lewis and got everything he needed without really thinking about it, safe in the knowledge that it would be decent quality and would all match if he kept within the same colour range. Teal and mustard, by the look of it. In the kitchen, there was a dirty coffee cup and a bowl with the remains of his morning granola and yoghurt. She opened the fridge. Chicken breasts, bags of salad, more yoghurt. All she wanted was a cup of tea and some digestive biscuits, but there was no sign of any kind of comfort food.

Was he enjoying his bachelor life? she wondered. It all felt in stark contrast to her slightly bohemian Paris existence. Very ordered and a bit dull, but she supposed that was how he wanted it.

She decided to go straight to sleep. She was exhausted from the stress and tension and the journey, and she wanted to feel fresh for tomorrow. She hesitated before climbing into his bed. She didn't know why she felt squeamish, for she'd slept with him for years and years, but it felt a little odd.

Even his sheets followed the teal and mustard theme. There was the slight odour of him on them, mixed with Lenor and Dior's Fahrenheit. It unsettled her. She felt a pang for Olivier's scent, for the warmth of him next to her. Was it too late to text him? She should. He'd been so kind.

She'd send him a short text.

Here! (She didn't specify where. She didn't want him to know she was sleeping in her ex's bed.) I think S is OK but they will operate tomorrow. Tired, so going to sleep. Speak tomorrow. Xx

She lay the phone down and waited for a reply. But there wasn't one. Was that it? Was everything over between them, now she had gone? Maybe that was his coping mechanism? To pretend it had never happened and move on. She sighed. At least this time they'd had a chance to say goodbye, and he knew how much he meant to her. She hadn't left him in any doubt.

Maybe this way was for the best. Cutting it short, rather than both of them living under the cloud of her departure. It would have spoiled those last few days, the dread.

She curled up on her side. Morning would be here before long. She'd have to sort out the flat for Stuart, making sure it was easy to navigate on crutches, filling the fridge so he didn't have to go out. She waited for sleep, hating herself for keeping half an ear cocked for another text, a sign that all was well between them.

When she woke in the morning, there was still nothing, and anxiety prickled at her, putting her on edge. Should she phone him? She was staring at the screen when a call came through and she jumped.

Nate.

'Darling.' She answered on the first ring.

'Mum.' It was lovely to hear his dear voice. 'I'm outside. Can you let me in?'

Dear, sweet, lovely, kind Nate. He'd jumped on the first flight from Copenhagen that morning, knowing that if he'd phoned her in advance she'd have told him to stay put. She put her arms around him, yet again marvelling how she didn't even reach his chin, rubbing her cheek against the roughness of his coat. He grinned down and ruffled her hair.

'I saw Dad,' she told him. 'I think he's OK. They're going to operate on his leg first thing this morning. You shouldn't have come.'

'I didn't want you to feel you had to look after him,' he told her. 'I mean, you guys aren't a thing anymore.'

'Oh sweetheart.' They hadn't talked about it much in depth, but she was touched by his perception. 'We still love each other, you know. We'd still do anything for each other.'

Nate's expression was gravely indignant. 'You're supposed to be in Paris, writing your book.' He was the only person she had told about her plan, because he was trustworthy and wouldn't tell anyone else or judge her if she didn't finish it. She hadn't told Izzy, because Izzy would want to read it, and she wasn't sure about that at all. Not yet.

'You're supposed to be in Denmark.'

Juliet fretted about him abandoning his studies, but he assured her that everything was under control.

'As long as I get my dissertation written by Christmas, no one minds where I am. It's nearly the holidays.'

'Really?' She supposed it was almost the end of November, and students seemed to come home about two weeks after they'd gone back these days. 'Well, your dad will appreciate it so much.'

'It's you I'm here for, Mum.' Nate looked at her. 'And Izzy. I knew if I didn't tell her I was coming she'd get on a plane, and that's not fair.'

'You've spoken to her, then?'

'Of course I have.'

Juliet hugged him, marvelling at how she had managed to produce such a splendid human being. He was very like his dad, she thought proudly. Solid. And she felt relief that he was here, because it was hard, managing a crisis, and it was nice having someone to discuss it with, and she realised, with a curious mixture of delight and regret, that he was now a grown-up and could be depended upon.

'We need to go to John Lewis on the way to the hospital,' she said. 'For more bedding. We can take Dad's car. I think I can drive it on his insurance.'

Her phone beeped. She wondered if it was Olivier. But it was Stuart.

> Bloody starving. Waiting for the porters to wheel me down to theatre. Curtain up at ten. You can phone at midday. Thanks again for coming. You're a leg-end. Geddit? (And I'm a bell-end.) S

She smiled, and texted back.

> I'd say break a leg but you already have. Nate's here.

It was only a moment before he replied.

> I don't deserve you guys.

Juliet knew that knowing Nate was here would have made Stuart well up. It didn't take much to make him cry where the kids were concerned.

> Yes, you do. Don't be daft. We'll be thinking of you while we splurge on your credit card.

It was in his bedside drawer. He'd told her to use it for whatever she needed to stock the flat.

'Let's go for breakfast,' she said to Nate. 'There's bugger all to eat here and I need carbs.'

At least if she was with Nate it would stop her checking

her phone every two minutes. She wasn't going to text Olivier again yet. She was confused not to have heard from him. She texted Nathalie instead, filling her in on what had happened and reassuring her that she'd be able to finalise the proposal as soon as Stuart was out. She pressed send, then scrolled back through all the recent messages from Olivier, reliving their time together. All the arrangements they'd made.

'Mum?' Nate was staring at her. 'You OK?'

'Yes. Fine. Just doing some work messages.'

'Mm hmm.' Nate looked at her knowingly. 'So why are you staring at the phone like that?'

'Am I?'

Nate put his arm around her and steered her towards the door. 'Come on. We need a carb dump and some caffeine.'

Oh God. She should be doing post-coital cuddling and croissants, picking up her abandoned clothing from the floor and putting their empty wine glasses in the sink.

Her phone beeped and she jumped out of her skin.

Nathan looked at her. 'Jesus, Mum. What are you like?'

'I'm worried,' she said. 'In case it's bad news about Dad.'

'Fairs.'

It was a message from Nathalie. Oh my God. Do NOT worry about the book. Just make sure Stuart is OK. I love you. Tell me what's going on. I'm keeping everything crossed.

All under control, Juliet texted back, but she'd never felt less in control in all her life.

40

The next twenty-four hours were a maelstrom of conflicting emotions. Anxiety about Stuart's operation. The agony of waiting for a message from Olivier. The joy of pottering about Richmond with Nate, getting breakfast in a cute café on Richmond Hill, whizzing around Waitrose doing a shop to fill the fridge and picking up bedding so they each had somewhere to crash once Stuart was home: there was a futon in the spare room and the sofa in the main room was big enough to sleep on.

Juliet found herself buying all the things they used to have as a family. Fresh pasta and arrabbiata sauce and Parmesan, big tubs of hummus and pitta bread, sausages and brioche hot-dog buns and hot sauce. She had a feeling most of this wouldn't fit into Stuart's new regime, but he could send out for whatever he needed once he was home. She and Nate needed comfort and familiarity. And she got plenty of salad and tomatoes. No cucumber, as that was Stuart's worst nightmare. She chucked in feta and olives – a big Greek salad was always good to have in the fridge. It was funny how easy it was to revert to her old role, navigating the supermarket shelves on autopilot.

Orange juice – no bits. Vintage Cheddar – extra mature. Bacon – streaky, unsmoked.

The minute she and Nate had finished unloading all the shopping in the kitchen, she got a call from Stuart.

'All done and dusted,' he said. He sounded tired, a little strained. He was probably in pain. 'They're pleased with how it went and with a fair wind I can come home tomorrow.'

'We'll come straight in to see you.' Juliet felt a flood of relief. It could so easily have gone wrong. There could have been complications.

She curled her arm around Nate's waist and leaned her head on his shoulder, filled with the pleasure of having him to herself, yet again relishing the pride she had in him: his solidity, his reliability, his practicality – he'd got the beds sorted in a trice with no fuss. He'd grown up so much since being away. It was strange, this new dynamic, for now they felt like equals.

'Let's go and see your old man,' she said.

Stuart's journey from the car to the flat when they brought him home the next day was slow and painful, and demonstrated to all of them how hard his life was going to be for the next few weeks. It dented the euphoria of his homecoming slightly, and Juliet found it agonising to watch his struggle. He was so obviously putting a brave face on it, but as he collapsed onto the sofa and lay his crutches next to him, he looked grey, his lips pinched and his eyes sunken.

'It's vegetable lasagne for supper,' said Juliet brightly. He needed feeding up. She wasn't going to take no for an answer. To her surprise, he smiled.

'Wonderful,' he said fervently.

The three of them sat round his small glass dining table. There was only just enough room for all their plates. Juliet poured herself a glass of Vinho Verde, so low in alcohol it almost didn't count, and Nate had a craft beer.

'I don't think I should drink on my medication,' said Stuart mournfully.

'I thought you were all about the clean living?' Juliet raised an arch eyebrow.

Stuart huffed. 'It's not all it's cracked up to be, you know.' He dug his fork into the lasagne with gusto, strings of mozzarella stretching from his fork as he lifted it to his mouth.

'I can't imagine it is.'

'Have I been really boring?'

'Pretty tedious.' Nate was happy to chip in where Juliet felt she should be tactful. 'I mean, it's one of life's joys, having a beer with your old man. I miss it.'

'Oh God.' Stuart looked down at his plate. 'I shouldn't have bought that rower.'

'You can still use it. It's a sexy bit of kit. Even I can see that,' said Juliet. 'But maybe dial down the fitness obsession?'

'Am I obsessive?'

'Yes!' chorused Nate and Juliet.

'All that *counting*,' Juliet went on. 'Calories and steps and measuring your blood pressure and your heart rate.'

'And that keto diet is rank.' Nate made a face.

Stuart looked down at his lasagne. 'This is the food of the gods,' he admitted. 'But I can't just stuff in the carbs suddenly, not if I'm on crutches. I'll blow up like a balloon.'

'It's about balance, isn't it? The French have got it nailed. They seem to be able to eat and drink what they want. But they don't binge like we do.'

'Don't they?' Stuart looked at her and she blushed. It was true though. Olivier was obviously more substantial than he had been as a twenty-year-old, but he was in pretty good shape. She felt a sudden longing to hear his voice. She poured another glass of wine. It dulled the ache.

Forty-eight hours and not a word. Did he feel as if she'd abandoned him again? Well, she had. Hadn't she?

She picked up her phone and her thumbs hovered over the keyboard, not sure what to say. Should she tell him Stuart was home safely? Or would that rub salt into the wound?

In the end, she decided it would be weird not to, so she sent a brief text.

Stuart is out of hospital but still in pretty bad shape.

Of course, sending him a second text meant the agony of waiting was doubled, for not replying to two texts in a row really was pointed.

After dinner, Nate went off to have a drink with an old mate. Stuart settled himself on the sofa. Juliet loaded the dishwasher, then came and sat in the old chair that had been his grandfather's. It was red tapestry and looked very out of place. It just needed re-covering, she thought. Should she organise that for him?

Of course not! He was a grown man with a life of his own. He didn't need her fussing over his interior design.

Old habits die hard, she reflected. She remembered Paul's words in the bar. You couldn't unmesh yourself overnight from someone you'd been with for years. You knew their strengths and weaknesses and vulnerabilities. Not that dodgy chair coverings were a vulnerability exactly, but—

'I can't thank you enough for being here.' Stuart's voice broke into her thoughts. 'You had no obligation to come. And I do really appreciate it.'

'You'd do the same for me,' said Juliet. 'Wouldn't you?'

'Of course. But I would have understood if you'd chosen not to.'

'I wasn't doing anything that important.'

'But I've ruined your stay. How many days have you got left?'

'Just a few.' She thought of the apartment she'd abandoned. She'd give anything to be back there now, tapping away at her laptop, the curtains open to the moon shining on the rooftops opposite. 'It doesn't matter.'

'You look different, you know.'

She touched her hair. 'I cut my hair.'

'You smell different, too.'

'That'll be the garlic.'

'No. Not garlic.'

She lifted her wrist to her nose. 'I've got a new perfume.'

She didn't tell him the name of it. French Lover. As she breathed it in, she imagined it mingled with Olivier's scent. Oh God.

'You haven't gone and fallen in love, have you?'

His tone wasn't accusatory. It was teasing. She looked over at him.

'I think I have. But not with a person. I'm in love with

Paris. It feels like home to me. I feel as if I belong. I love everything about it. From that first sip of coffee in the morning to the last digestif at night.'

Her eyes were shining as she spoke and Stuart was watching her.

'I haven't seen you look like that for a long time,' he said. 'You should go back.'

'How can I? I can't leave you like this.'

'Of course you can. I'll be fine here with Nate. He's going to stay on until Christmas.'

'He is?'

'Go and live your dream, Juliet. I don't want to hold you back.' He looked down at the coffee table. Their phones lay side by side on it. Identical methods of communication containing all their secrets.

She smiled. 'Are you waiting for a text?' she asked.

'Maybe.'

'The A and E consultant?'

'Looks like she's going to come in handy.' He grinned. 'She's already devising my rehabilitation programme.'

'Is that what she calls it?' She couldn't help teasing him back. 'Is she nice?'

'She is. She works way too hard. But I'm working on that.'

'I'm really glad.'

'Maybe I should have her as my emergency contact. I mean, it shouldn't be you anymore, really, should it?'

Juliet didn't reply for a moment. 'OK,' she said carefully. Somehow, that felt like the final unmeshing. 'But I would always be there if you needed me.'

'I know.'

They sat in companionable silence for a moment, contemplating this subtle shift.

'It's funny, though,' said Stuart. 'This second-time-around malarkey. You kind of think they know stuff about you, but, of course, they don't have a clue about all those little details that make you who you are.'

'I guess that's part of the fun. Discovering.'

'I suppose so.'

One of their phones beeped and they both jumped.

'That's mine,' said Stuart and picked his up. Juliet watched his face as he read his text, saw him smile and then answer. Her phone stayed balefully silent.

And then it beeped too.

She reached out a hand, casually, as if she didn't care. Even though whatever it said meant more than anything in the world.

I'm so glad he is OK. Missing you very much. O x

She put it back down on the table with a sigh. Stuart was looking over at her.

'For God's sake, just book yourself a ticket for to-morrow,' he said. 'You can be back in Paris by lunchtime.'

41

Just before midday the next day, Juliet headed straight from her train into the *Café Deux Gares*, a few minutes' walk from the Gare du Nord. She looked around at the tortoiseshell ceiling and the striking bold stripes on the banquette seating and breathed a sigh of relief. She was back, in Paris, where everything was just so and impossibly chic and everywhere you went there was something exciting to look at: a new idea, or a new take on an old idea. This was art deco a hundred years on, and she loved it.

She spotted Nathalie in the far corner and made her way over.

'I'm so glad you're back,' said Nathalie as Juliet sat down in the seat opposite. 'I had an awful feeling that was going to be it. That history was going to repeat itself.'

'Me too. But only for a while. I mean, if it had been more serious, I would have stayed longer. Though there was a moment I had a bit of a wobble and thought we were mad to be apart. I mean, twenty-five years is a long time. You don't just throw it away on a whim. But it's kind of confirmed we've done the right thing. We'll always be there for each other, but we have our own lives now.'

'Good.' Nathalie nodded. 'Because you can't put Olivier through that again. The disappearing act.'

'No.'

'Does he know you're back?'

'Not just yet.' Juliet signalled to the waiter. 'There's a couple of things I want to organise first.'

'Oh?' Nathalie looked at her friend over the top of the outsized glasses she'd put on to read the menu.

Juliet gave an enigmatic smile. 'You'll be the first to know.'

'What – even before him?'

'Maybe.'

'Anyway,' said Nathalie. 'Totally selfishly, I'm glad you're here, because I started writing the introduction. It all came tumbling out – how I passed that empty building and had my vision. And how I heard that song – "She Cried Champagne" – and it all fell into place. I hope you're going to be able to make sense of it.'

'That's literally my job.'

Nathalie pushed a piece of paper over to her.

'Be brutal. I can take it.'

Juliet began to read, and as she did, she felt excitement deep in her belly, the feeling she had when she knew something was going to strike a chord. Molly was going to love Nathalie's writing. It was bold and funny and passionate. The book was going to be the kind of empowering read that would inspire women everywhere.

'You're a natural,' she told Nathalie. 'This is so vivid. It's as if I'm with you when I'm reading it.'

Nathalie clapped her hands with joy. 'Do you think we're in with a chance? Do you think Molly will like it?'

'I can't say for sure,' said Juliet. 'But if she doesn't bite, there will be others. I'm going to start collating everything this week. We should have a proposal ready to send by the end of the month.'

'That's when you're due to leave,' said Nathalie. 'The end of your thirty days. I feel bad I've made you work.'

'It's not work,' said Juliet. 'Not really. I've loved it.'

'That's how I feel. About the bar. What do they say, do something you love and you'll never work a day in your life?'

'Exactly.'

They ordered coffee and pastries from the waiter.

Nathalie tapped her fingers on the table to get Juliet's attention.

'I think we should do something on your last night. Maybe I can throw a party at the bar, so you can say goodbye to everyone.'

Juliet folded up Nathalie's piece of paper and put it in her bag. She wouldn't look her friend in the eye.

'Maybe.'

'You're being a very dark horse.'

'Maybe.'

Nathalie threw a packet of sugar at her. 'Man, you're annoying.'

'Yep.' Juliet gave the waiter a dazzling smile as he put her coffee down. 'It's my prerogative, as your best friend.'

'It's OK,' said Nathalie. 'I know your secret. It's written all over your face, so it won't be any surprise.'

Juliet gave a little shrug and sipped the foam of her cappuccino. But the decision she'd made was probably the most thrilling thing she'd ever done in her life.

*

It wasn't revenge. She didn't need revenge, she realised, because as someone once told her, revenge was behaving better. But she couldn't pretend not to enjoy the look on Jean Louis' face when she went back into his office. She took a taxi, because she had a lot to do and the past few days had been wearing.

'I'd like to know,' she told him, 'if the apartment you showed me is still available. And if so, I'd like to buy it.'

He raised his eyebrows. She could tell he wasn't sure if she was winding him up.

'I have proof of funds,' she told him. 'And anything else you need.'

'Well,' he said. 'That's very exciting. Welcome back to Paris. I'm sure you will be very happy there.'

'I know I will,' she said. 'It's perfect for me. It's everything I've ever dreamed of.'

His face was impassive. He had aged very well, observed Juliet, still handsome and distinguished. And then he smiled, and she remembered the man she had liked so much, before it went wrong, the thoughtful husband and father and boss, and how kind he had been to her, and how he had taught her so much about wine and food and life. *Everyone makes mistakes,* she thought. *Everyone does something once in their life that fills them with regret.*

'I'm very pleased,' he told her. 'And, of course, if there is anything I can do to help, in your new life in Paris, just ask me.'

Afterwards, she walked down to the river. She felt elated, almost unable to believe what she had done. It felt concomitantly reckless and logical, and she veered between feeling a bubble of hysteria and telling herself all the reasons it was a good idea.

She stood on the bridge as a stiff breeze hurtled up the river, bringing with it the promise of icy rain, but she didn't care. She thought of all the times she had crossed over the Seine, from the Right Bank to Left and back again. That first Sunday, when Jean Louis had taken her for lunch. The day she had met Olivier for their first date, and he'd rollerbladed towards her. Cycling over it only a couple of weeks before, her heart filled with joy at being with him again.

She dug about in the inside pocket of her handbag. Her wedding ring was still there. It had been there all the time. For a moment, she was tempted to throw it into the air, watch as it spiralled downwards, spinning, spinning, until it fell into the murky green, almost the colour of water lilies. But something stopped her. She wasn't walking away from a marriage she wanted to forget. She didn't need to throw the ring away as a symbol of her freedom. Her time with Stuart was part of who she was, and she valued it. She would always remember it with fondness. So she tucked the ring back in her bag, thinking she could give it to Izzy, who might even use it for herself one day. Repurposing old jewellery was all the rage, and the ring would bring her luck. If Izzy had a marriage even half as good as theirs had been, she would be all right.

As Juliet turned to walk back up towards the Louvre, her phone rang. Jean Louis' office. Her stomach swooped. She prayed he wasn't going to tell her the purchase was off.

'Hello?'

'Juliet?'

It was a woman. A woman whose voice she recognised straight away. She would never forget.

'Corinne,' she said.

'*Oui.*' Corinne did not sound surprised. '*C'est moi.* Jean Louis has just told me about the apartment.'

'Oh.' Of course he had. They were business partners.

'I wonder if we could meet? I have . . . some things to say. I hope you will listen.' Corinne sounded softer than she expected. Almost deferential. Her English was much better too.

'I'm not sure,' said Juliet, wary.

'Just half an hour. Please.'

Juliet stared down the river. There were Christmas lights up on the plane trees on the pavements, she noticed. Thirty years ago, she'd been so excited about her first Christmas in Paris.

'OK,' she said.

'Meet me at the *Café de la Paix* at three o'clock. It's on the Place de l'Opéra.'

'I'll see you there.'

Juliet hung up, surprised at how calm she felt. She didn't feel afraid. She knew there was nothing more Corinne could do to hurt her. There was just time, to slip back to her apartment and put her things away.

Afterwards, she couldn't resist heading onto to the Rue Saint-Honoré and down to the boutique she had passed every day on her way to the mini market. In the window was a sleek black shirt dress with lace sleeves. She had eyed it up with longing every day since she had been here. It was the ideal dress for facing her nemesis. It would make her feel strong, powerful and in control.

She tried it on. It fitted perfectly.

'I would like to wear it now, please,' she told the assistant.

And she stepped out into the street to find a taxi, the picture of elegance, the kind of woman you turned your head to look at.

At three o'clock on the dot, Juliet glided into the *Café de la Paix*. This was a grander place than she was used to, with its old-school opulence, but she wasn't intimidated. Instead, she lapped up her surroundings: the belle époque décor in cream and pale green, with fluted columns and the ceiling painted with a celestial sky. Yet again, she felt as if she was in a film. She could almost hear the soundtrack, a percussive beat building in time with her heartbeat. The confrontation of two women linked by the same man.

Corinne was there, sitting at a table by the window, half hidden by a vase of lilies. Her hair was brushed back into a loose chignon. She had gold hoop earrings, carmine nails and lips. The epitome of Parisian chic, supremely confident and *bien dans sa peau*.

They brushed cheeks, barely making eye contact, and Corinne signalled to the waiter to pour Juliet a glass from the bottle of pink rosé in a bucket by the table. When they each had a glass, they looked at each other.

'I have had this conversation in my head so many times,' said Corinne. 'I never thought I would have the chance to speak to you. But when Jean Louis told me you were buying that apartment, I wanted to explain some things.'

'OK.'

'We were in a very bad place when you were with us. I was not well. Jean Louis did not know how to manage.'

She shrugged. 'That is how it was for men at that time. Now it is better, I think.'

'If you're lucky, yes.'

Corinne looked at her. 'You have been lucky?'

'I've been very lucky.'

Corinne was fiddling with a diamond on her ring finger. Whether it was subconscious or demonstrating to Juliet the strength of her marriage by the substantial number of carats in it, she couldn't be sure.

'I want to apologise to you,' she went on. 'And to thank you.'

'Thank me?'

'As I said, I was not well. You arrived, and you brought something into our lives. I think we all fell a little in love with you. All of us. You showed us how it could be: a happy family with happy children. But it was impossible.'

Her eyes filled with tears, and Juliet reached out a hand.

'I was so very ill. And you knew that. You were the only person who saw what I was going through. But I pretended to be OK, because that's what I thought I had to do. And I thought what was wrong was having you in the house. I thought the children loved you more than they loved me—'

'Of course they didn't!'

Corinne put up a hand to stop her speaking. 'I know now. But then, all I saw was a young girl who had everyone under her spell. Even me. I was so jealous of you. You were so young and so kind and so beautiful. I thought you and Jean Louis...' She stumbled on her words, her voice cracking. 'I thought I was going to lose everything to you.'

Juliet felt touched by her vulnerability. The memory clearly still pained her.

'Corinne, you must know. There was nothing between us. There was a moment one night, but we had too much wine, too much moonlight. It was nothing. I promise you.'

'I know now. Jean Louis told me the truth. After you had gone. That Christmas was terrible. I could not get out of bed. I went to a clinic in the end. I had very bad postnatal psychosis.' She met Juliet's gaze. 'You were the one who recognised how much I was suffering. And I punished you for it. I am so sorry.' Corinne was trembling with the emotion of the memories. 'I knew in my heart you had not stolen the jewels. But it was the perfect way to get rid of you. You were a threat to me, you see, and I did not want to confront the truth. Because it would have meant accepting I was a monster.'

'You weren't a monster. You were very ill.'

'It was all OK in the end. Jean Louis had the courage to tell me how he was feeling. How scared he was, and how he buried his feelings and saw you as an escape. From me.'

'Oh Corinne...' Suddenly, the complexities of the situation unravelled, and Juliet was able to see the nuances of everyone's mistakes, and their bad choices, and the consequences.

'I have always felt terrible that you paid the highest price. I was cruel. We were cruel. You were so young, and all you were guilty of was... being the person we all needed.'

'It was cruel,' Juliet agreed. 'But I was OK in the end. I married a very lovely man.'

Corinne surveyed her thoughtfully. 'But you are back here? On your own?'

Juliet gripped the stem of her glass. Corinne had been disarmingly frank, so perhaps she could share her own story. 'My husband and I have separated. It's very amicable. We just want different things.' She shrugged, with a rueful smile. 'I wanted to come back here. To see what my life could have been. I loved my time here, and I've never forgotten Paris. And now is my chance.'

'And maybe you will find love?'

Talking about love was a confidence too far. Juliet didn't want to jinx anything by telling Corinne about Olivier.

'Maybe,' she said.

'I think you will.' Corinne was definite. 'Paris is made for love. Never forget that.'

Corinne's eyes sparkled like the diamond on her finger. Juliet saw a glimpse of the woman she had become: strong, adventurous, stylish, passionate. She wondered if they could be friends. Maybe that was stretching it. But the final knot untied inside her and she felt her heart free itself from the memory of that long-ago betrayal and of her own guilt at her part in the drama.

It was time, she thought, to put the final piece of the puzzle into place. She had a blank canvas in the most beautiful city in the world, the best friend she could ask for, the opportunity to live an exciting new life. Love would be the icing on the cake – but a cake without icing could be just as delicious. She smiled to herself as she drained her glass of Whispering Angel.

Courage, she told herself, putting a French accent on the word. It sounded so much more galvanising.

42

Dusk was gathering as Juliet arrived outside the shop. En route in the taxi, Paris was looking her most ravishing, her lights shining silver and gold as people danced along the pavements, arms piled high with early Christmas shopping, heading to a rendezvous or an assignation. An early-evening *coupe de champagne*, perhaps, or just a *chocolat chaud* to warm the heart.

The *Librairie des Rêves* glowed her welcome. Juliet slipped inside, not wanting to be seen just yet. She saw Olivier at his desk, head bowed, frowning as he looked something up on the computer, then left to search the shelves. This was her moment. She crept up to the desk, hoping she had time, took something out of her bag and put it on his desk. Then she slid back into the shadows and waited.

It wasn't long before he came back carrying a book in his hand. She smiled as she saw him notice what was on his desk. He froze, stepped forward, put the book he was carrying down and lifted up the ancient copy of *Le Grand Meaulnes*. He opened it to check the front page. He smiled, but he looked puzzled, and then he looked around him.

He knew she had to be somewhere and she wasn't going to tease him a moment longer. She stepped out of her hiding place and walked towards him.

'You came back,' he said, staring at her.

'Of course,' she said, pointing at the book. 'I had to return this to you.'

Within two seconds, she was wrapped tightly in his arms.

'I thought I was going to lose you again,' he said. 'I thought I was going to lose you.' His voice was choked with tears.

'*Jamais*,' she told him.

Never.

The barman recognised her as they came into the bar that evening. She held up two fingers and did a raised glass motion with her hand to indicate champagne, as they took their seats in a discreet corner. She could see her reflection in the mirrored glass, and almost didn't recognise herself, her tousled bed-head hair, her red lipstick, the black dress that skimmed her knees, the extra button undone. And next to her, Olivier. They were so much more sophisticated than the young lovers they had been. Two debonair Parisians, she thought. People noticed them, she knew.

The barman was there in a trice, holding out two long-stemmed glasses on a silver tray.

'Thank you,' she said, and watched as he laid them on the table in front of her, together with a silver bowl of olives, almost holding her breath in anticipation of the celebratory bubbles.

'*De rien,*' said the barman, and she thought he gave her the faintest flicker of a wink.

They each picked up their glass and looked at one another.

'What shall we drink to?' asked Olivier.

She paused for a moment, looking around the bar, at the soft golden light and the faces of the other customers and the subtle glamour of it all, and thought she could only be in one place in the world, and this could only be happening in one place in the world.

'I think,' she said, 'we should drink to this city. To this city which brought us together.'

'Of course,' agreed Olivier, and they touched glasses with the gentlest of chinks and then drank. To love. To each other. To Paris.

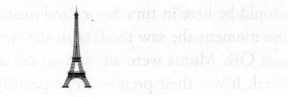

43

Epilogue

Fourteen months later

Juliet heaved the basket onto the kitchen table, though it could hardly be called a table – more of a butcher's block – for there was certainly no room for anything bigger in this eight-foot-by-nine-foot oblong she called her kitchen. But it was *her* kitchen – her kitchen in Paris! – and although she'd had to be ruthless about what she allowed herself to keep in it, she was loving her new streamlined life.

She had got used to only owning what she really needed: the most pared-back of wardrobes, a few possessions she really treasured from her past and a carefully chosen array of household items: one beautiful set of white linen sheets, six capacious wine glasses that would do for red or white (there was too much snobbery around glasses, she'd learned from Nathalie), one huge Le Creuset pot that she could cook just about anything she wanted in.

She started unpacking her shopping. Izzy and Nate were arriving this afternoon at the Gare du Nord and should be here in time for a late lunch. Juliet knew that the moment she saw them both she would cry, but that was OK. Mums were allowed to cry at whatever they liked. It was their prerogative, especially on their birthdays.

As she put her purchases away, she thought back to her first foray to the *Marché Bastille* and how far she had come since then. Now she could barter with the best of them, discuss the merits of different cheeses and judge the quality of tomatoes with a single glance. She'd bought butterflied lamb to cook in the oven with a dish of *pommes dauphinoises*, and a dark chocolate cake. She'd even stopped for a *fontaine à gâteau* – a cake fountain – to stick in the middle of the shiny icing. There was charcuterie and cornichons and a baguette to share while they waited for lunch, and cheese with a big box of cherries to finish.

She didn't think she had ever felt so content as she pottered about, putting a fresh white cloth on the table in the main room. Stuart had sent her a huge bouquet of pale pink tulips and she put the vase in the middle. They had spoken earlier, on FaceTime, and she hoped maybe he and Rachel, the A and E consultant he was still seeing, would come out and stay.

Nathalie was coming over, bringing some of her favourite wines for the celebration. In pride of place on Juliet's bookcase was a signed copy of Nathalie's book. It had been launched two weeks before, in the bar, with all the great and the good of the Paris food scene, and Juliet still felt filled with pride at how it had turned out. The words were as beautiful as the pictures. Nathalie had a talent for describing food and a strong instinct for story, which had made Juliet's job incredibly easy, and Molly had done them proud. It was in almost every bookshop in Paris, and Nathalie had done a sold-out talk at the *Librairie des Rêves*. She was on the verge of becoming a cult celebrity in this city that worshipped food and wine. She was, if not the queen, then certainly a princess of the gastroscene, and she wore her crown with pride. But she never underestimated Juliet's contribution.

'I would be nowhere without you,' she always said, although that wasn't true, for Nathalie had always had star quality. Juliet remembered her words at the introduction at the language school. '*Je veux être quelqu'un*,' Nathalie had said. I want to be someone.

Izzy had spent the summer before working at She Cried Champagne before she finally went off to uni, and completely worshipped Nathalie, who she viewed as a combination of godmother, crazy aunt and big sister. They never stopped talking when they were together. Izzy would be more excited about seeing Nathalie than Juliet, but Juliet didn't mind.

Olivier was coming later. She wanted to have some time with the kids before he arrived, but they had been super cool about meeting their mum's new French boyfriend the year before. She'd felt a little self-conscious, but he had understood the nuance of the situation and had, of course, completely charmed them. She'd met his kids too, last summer, and she and Olivier often took his son Charles out now he was studying in Paris.

Part Two of life was working. It could be complicated and messy, but also satisfying, and Juliet found it easier now to put herself centre stage, to do the things she wanted. Still there for everyone, of course, but only when they needed her, rather than at their disposal twenty-four seven. It was a much more relaxed way of living and took the sting out of the wiry grey hairs and the wrinkly knees and the endless need for reading glasses. She almost didn't care about any of that anymore. There was too much to distract her. Too much to achieve.

Her own book had taken a little longer than Nathalie's to complete. It was much harder, shaping her own thoughts and words than other people's, but at last she had reached the final chapter. Just one more paragraph to write. She might have time to finish before they all got here.

She walked across the room and flung open the balcony doors, stepping out and leaning on the railing, looking up and down the street. The scent of cherry blossom drifted in, for spring was on her way and Paris was dressing herself in baby pink. With the scent came the sound of accordion music. It was impossible to know if it came from a busker warming up for an afternoon in the city centre, or someone in an apartment like hers putting on a record and throwing open their windows. She listened and smiled as she recognised the tune. '*Je Ne Regrette Rien*'.

She walked over to the table and opened her laptop, finding her place in the document. Nearly a hundred thousand words, and just a few more to go. She began to type, putting herself in the shoes of her heroine.

She stood for a moment and sang along, for she identified with the words more than ever. She had no regrets. Your mistakes were what made you. And she couldn't be more pleased to be who she was – a mother, writer, friend, lover and honorary Parisienne – and couldn't wait to find out who she might become next.

And then she typed the words she had been longing to type:

THE END

Acknowledgements

First up is thank you to my mother for taking me to Paris for the first time when I was about 15. We stayed in a pretty grim hotel in the Place de Clichy, blinded by the flashing of the XXX signs, but it was a real coup de foudre and I fell in love! We soon found our way to more elegant surroundings and did what the French call lèche-vitrine – window licking! But that is Paris for you – peering with longing into shops and restaurants you can't afford and soaking up the glamour.

Second thank you is to my brother Paul, whose knowledge of Paris, gleaned from working at the legendary Juveniles in the late 80s, has enhanced my own. And in recent years, now he lives in Australia, we take the time to spend a few days there whenever he is in this hemisphere. The bottle count is shamefully high, and waking up with a gueule de bois inevitable, but the city suits our sybaritic tendencies. It feels like a home from home and we dream, one day, of perhaps sharing a little apartment in the Marais. It might never happen but it's dreams like this which fuel my writing.

My French is rusty A level spattered with colourful

argot cleaned from French exchange trips, holidays and endless episodes of Engrenages and Call My Agent. So merci beaucoup to Alison Arnold for painstakingly correcting any French grammar in the manuscript and making helpful suggestions.

Many thanks to Katie Espiner and Sarah Benton for encouraging me to embark on my dream to write a novel set in Paris. Thank you also to Charlotte Mursell for making sense of the dual timeline and helping the story be the best it could be. And Araminta Whitley always, for kindness and support when I lose the plot, literally and metaphorically.

And finally thank you to Paris, you beautiful, elegant, moody, sexy and endlessly surprising creature. I will never tire of you.

Discover your next uplifting read from
VERONICA HENRY

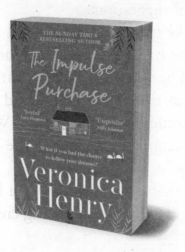

Sometimes you have to let your heart rule your head.

Cherry, Maggie and Rose are mother, daughter and grand-daughter, each with their own hopes, dreams and even sorrows. They have always been close, so when, in a moment of impulse, Cherry buys a gorgeous but run-down pub in the village she grew up in, it soon becomes a family affair.

All three women uproot themselves and move to Rushbrook, deep in the heart of Somerset, to take over The Swan and restore it to its former glory. Cherry is at the helm, Maggie is in charge of the kitchen, and Rose tends the picturesque garden that leads down to the river.

Before long, the locals are delighted to find the beating heart of the village is back, bringing all kinds of surprises through the door.

Could Cherry's impulse purchase change all their lives – and bring everyone the happiness they're searching for?

Escape to the glorious Somerset countryside with this joyful and uplifting story of family, love and hope.

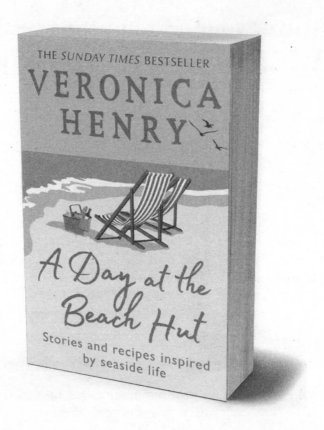

THE *SUNDAY TIMES* BESTSELLER

VERONICA HENRY

A Day at the Beach Hut

Stories and recipes inspired by seaside life

Escape to the coast with this delicious collection of short stories and beach-hut-inspired recipes.

On a shimmering summer's day, the waves are calling, the picnic basket is packed, and change is in the air.

It's just the start of an eventful day for a cast of holidaymakers: over one day, sparks will fly, the tide will bring in old faces and new temptations, a proposal is planned, and an unexpected romance simmers...

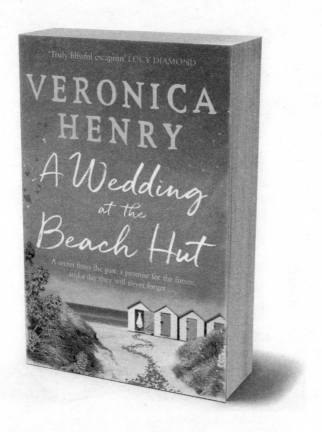

**Return to Everdene Sands, where the sun is
shining – but is the tide about to turn?**

Robyn and Jake are planning their dream wedding at the family
beach hut in Devon. A picnic by the turquoise waves, endless
sparkling rosé and dancing barefoot on the golden sand . . .

But Robyn is more unsettled than excited. She can't stop thinking
about the box she was given on her eighteenth birthday, and
the secrets it contains. Will opening it reveal the truth about her
history – and break the hearts of the people she loves most?

As the big day arrives, can everyone let go of the
past and step into a bright new future?

Sunshine, cider and family secrets...

Dragonfly Farm has been a home and a haven for generations
of Melchiors – archrivals to the Culbones, the wealthy family
who live on the other side of the river. Life there is dictated by
the seasons and cider-making, and everyone falls under its spell.

For cousins Tabitha and Georgia, it has always been a
home from home. When a tragedy befalls their beloved
Great-Uncle Matthew, it seems the place where they've
always belonged might now belong to them...

But the will reveals that a third of the farm has also been
left to a Culbone. As the first apples start to fall for the cider
harvest, will Dragonfly Farm begin to give up its secrets?

Credits

Veronica Henry and Orion Fiction would like to thank everyone at Orion who worked on the publication of *Thirty Days in Paris* in the UK.

Editorial
Charlotte Mursell
Sanah Ahmed

Copyeditor
Marian Reid

Proofreader
Jade Craddock

Contracts
Anne Goddard
Humayra Ahmed
Ellie Bowker

Design
Charlotte Abrams-Simpson
Joanna Ridley
Nick May

Audio
Paul Stark
Jake Alderson

Editorial Management
Charlie Panayiotou
Jane Hughes
Bartley Shaw
Tamara Morriss

Finance
Jasdip Nandra
Sue Baker

Marketing
Helena Fouracre
Lynsey Sutherland

Production
Ruth Sharvell

Sales
Jen Wilson
Esther Waters
Victoria Laws
Rachael Hum
Anna Egelstaff
Frances Doyle
Georgina Cutler

Publicity
Becca Bryant
Leanne Oliver

Operations
Jo Jacobs
Sharon Willis